Dedication

This book is dedicated to my beloved wife and children whose love, support and encouragement have enabled me in this effort. And to my precious grandchildren: May they and their children grow up in a world free from violence and bigotry.

The story is dedicated to my parents who made the long journey to these safe shores – and to my Uncle Jacob, my mother's brother, who remained behind and perished, one of six million Jewish victims of Nazi cruelty. He died on the last day of the war in the concentration camp at Terezin. I never met him but I felt his absence all of my life.

"Only guard yourself and guard your soul carefully, lest you forget the things your eyes saw, and lest these things depart your heart all the days of your life, ***and you shall make them known to your children and your children's children.*****"**

–Deuteronomy IV, 9

VIENNA
MARCH 1938

The city was dark beneath a moonless sky, lamplights, like store windows, shattered by stone-throwing mobs. Two decades of democracy were at an end. Vienna was in utter turmoil. Austrian Nazi sympathizers, daily more numerous, militantly demanded unification with Adolph Hitler's Third Reich. German troops, amassed on the border, awaited marching orders from their Führer.

Clutching a bundle in her arms, Fanny moved cautiously down Postgasse, working her way to the Danube canal through the inner city's narrow streets. In her haste, she had forgotten to take gloves. Her fingers felt numb. Still, she was thankful for the frigid weather.

It would keep the brownshirts in their beer-halls. For weeks, they had roamed the city unopposed, assaulting Jews and seeking confrontations with political opponents. The police chose to look the other way. The day was near when they would serve new masters.

The icy wind lashed at Fanny's face but was not the cause for her tears. She had been at home earlier in the day when the man appeared at her door. Pushing past her, he paraded through the apartment as if, in fact, he owned it. His threats left no doubt about the purpose of his visit. It was to intimidate. This man, who her father-in-law had once invited into their home, had turned on them like a rabid dog. Despite her fear, she blocked him at the entrance to her daughter's room, insisting that the girl was ill and must not be disturbed.

She begged him to leave. He issued an ultimatum and stormed out. When he was gone, her terror turned to fierce rage. She was determined to deny him what he wanted and set about doing what needed to be done in the short time remaining.

A few hours later, her husband and son returned from the factory and she told them what had transpired. Their fury matched her own. They wanted to find the man and confront him. She reminded him that as Jews they could no longer count on justice. The government was in shambles. They sat at the dining room table with the children, picked at their meal in mournful silence and listened to the news on the radio – all of which was bad. She waited until they were asleep and then slipped out of the house.

Picking up her pace, Fanny skirted the pool of light cast by a sole functioning street-lamp on the block. At that moment, she heard voices nearby. A spasm of fear drove her into the doorway of a store. She hid there, the bundle pressed tight against her breasts, knowing that if they found her, she would not escape without serious harm. As she turned, a stranger's face appeared in the glass of the window. She gasped, horrified, then recognized that it was her own image. She appeared to have aged twenty years in a single day.

Eyes shut tight, she composed herself; and then with an effort of will, she looked again. This time, she found a more familiar visage – her own steely gray-blue eyes and the thin line of her mouth, set in determination. As the voices gradually faded into the distance, she stepped out of the doorway and flew the remaining blocks to the river as if the wind was at her back instead of opposing her. Once there, without hesitation, she lay down on the damp grass. "*Yisgadal, v'yiskaddash, sh'mai rabor,*" she recited. "*B'orlmor devror che'rusei . . .*" Fanny sought to recall the remainder of the Mourner's Kaddish, but it eluded her. Overcome, she sobbed, the painful grief nearly paralyzing her. She fought it off, set the bundle into the swift-flowing current of the canal, and turned away, unwilling to witness the fate to which she had consigned this precious portion of her family's life.

Drained by the effort, Fanny lifted herself up and made her way back home. She would join the others and with the morning light, plan for their survival.

CHAPTER ONE

APRIL 1990

The traffic was backed up for a mile on the Belt Parkway. Ross Cortese inched the car forward. 1010 WINS announced a three-car accident, too late for him to catch the exit and use local streets. He hit the horn to let off steam and the driver up ahead gave him the finger. Ross returned the salute. Everyone suffers from the same condition in this town, he thought – impotent rage. Lifting his hand from the steering wheel, he rubbed his jaw and discovered a small patch of stubble he missed while shaving. It was typical of him these days. He tilted his head and examined his face in the rear-view mirror. His eyes were bloodshot, his cheeks sunken and his hair mussed. He looked like he felt, utterly worn out.

At last, Ross reached the bottleneck. EMS was working on a victim. Two cars had been cleared, and just ahead, the road opened up. With a glance at the dashboard clock, he accelerated. He was running late. He had called his folks telling them that he planned to stop by. "Something wrong, Rosso?" Pop had asked. Ross ducked the question.

As he picked up speed, the car began to vibrate. It needed a tune-up, just like he did. Switching lanes, he took the 4th Avenue exit and drove into Brooklyn's Little Italy, where his parents had moved four years ago from Corona as the ranks of their aging Italian neighbors were thinned by retirement or death.

Cutting across 85th Street, he turned left into their street and parked a few doors down from the house. For several minutes, he remained in the car, unable to move. He felt as if his ass was glued to the upholstery. Ross hated self-pity, but now it was rising up in him.

Six months ago, he'd lost Annie to cancer. The grief was immense, but work helped to keep the pain at bay. This morning the Borough Commander had informed him that he was suspended, pending an investigation of his shooting of a perpetrator.

"Sorry, Red," the Chief said, "There's pressure from the top."

Ross had been with the Department for nearly thirty years, his performance a source of pride until this recent incident. Now his job was threatened by racial politics. He had come to inform his parents before they heard the news from others. With a painful sigh, he forced himself out of the car.

As he mounted the steps to the brownstone, the front door opened. His father stood there, frowning. The old man looked younger then seventy-two. There wasn't a bit of gray in the full head of lustrous black hair. Though a little bent, Franco Cortese was in no way broken by the years he'd spent as a custom furniture finisher. Well-built, he stood three to four inches shorter than Ross's six feet.

"One day, you gonna eat potatoes off my head," his father used to tease him with each growth spurt, Pop's dark, expressive eyes sparkling with delight. Today, Ross felt uncomfortable beneath his gaze, like *he* was a piece of furniture being inspected for flaws in the finish.

"Me and your Momma . . . we seen you sitting there. You alright?" Momma, short and plump, stood behind Pop, as always, welcoming Ross with an adoring smile.

"I could be better," he said, not looking his father in the eye.

"There *is* something wrong. I told you, Gina," Franco said.

Momma's smile faded. As Ross came to offer a reassuring hug, she was shaken to see the suffering etched in his ruggedly handsome face, The green-flecked hazel eyes looked tired, as if in desperate need of sleep, and his red hair was more peppered with gray then she remembered. They embraced warmly, then trailed after Pop into the cozy living room. Ross could hear the radio playing in the kitchen, tuned as always, to the all-news station. Thankfully, the story hadn't made the wire yet.

"Let's sit down," Ross encouraged. He sat on the well-worn, recently slip-covered sofa, leaning forward tensely as Pop and Momma sat down in their club chairs. They were separated from him by a rectangular glass coffee table with a new silk flower arrangement on it that perfectly matched the colors in the slipcover. His parents amazed him sometimes.

"So what's happened, *figlio mio*?" his father asked anxiously.

What could he tell them that would soften the blow?

"When I reported to work this morning, the Commander notified me that I was suspended . . . until I.A.D. completes its investigation of the shooting."

"How can they do that to you?" Momma pleaded through her tears. "You was only doing your job. You've been a good policeman all these years. All those medals . . . the honors . . ."

"The PBA lawyer says not to worry. But the press and television is going to be all over the story."

"Lying bums looking for ways to sell newspapers," Pop snapped. "You got no hate in you like they make out."

"There'll probably be a Grand Jury. The lawyer says it's all politics. The DA has no case."

"Damn them to hell. All they care about is where the votes come from," Pop thundered fiercely.

"The kid was black, Pop. It's the times. It's gonna be tough on both of you these next few months," Ross said softly.

"On us?" Pop responded. "What about you? Your wife gone . . . now this? You worry about us? Listen to him, Gina. Always, he worries about us – since he was a boy."

Pop turned back to him, tears streaming down his cheeks. "Listen, Rosso. You worry about yourself – and your kids – not us. You need anything, you tell me, you hear?" he ordered. "It's gonna be okay, *figlio mio*. You trust your Poppa."

Ross forced a smile. "Your lips to God's ear, Pop."

"You look thin and tired, Rosso," Momma observed. "I'm gonna fix you a good lunch."

And a stiff drink, Ross wanted to call out, as she went into the kitchen.

THREE MONTHS LATER

His head listed forward, chin touching chest, then snapped back, as he was roused from a snoring sleep, mouth open, tongue cotton-dry from drink. His head throbbed. It was a long moment before Ross recognized that what he heard was a heavy fist rapping on the front door.

"Police! Open up!" a voice shouted. He looked at his watch. Ten P.M. Ross lifted himself from the sofa, against the gravity pulling him back down into sleep, and shuffled from the living room, a mass of aches.

Niall Kelsey and Dutch Steib stood beneath the amber porch light. Kelsey's cat's eyes gleamed with disapproval, belying the half-grin on his freckled face. "About time you showed your ugly face," he said. "You gonna stand there, or you gonna invite us in and pour two more?"

Ross looked at the glass in his hand, shaken to realize that lifting it from the coffee table had become such a reflex. He spotted a neighbor observing them through the open window of a darkened room. Shame covered him like a cold sweat.

He motioned them inside and they followed him into the living room. Framed museum reproductions and posters hung on the walls. The couch and leather chairs were comfortable and well used.

"Nice rug," Dutch commented, pointing to the oriental which Annie had bought in a thrift shop for seventy-five dollars. Ross remembered asking why she wanted something so old and worn. She encouraged him to see how time, light and wear had worked on the dyes, softening the colors and rendering them more beautiful.

God, how he missed her.

"We expected you down to Holy Name," said Dutch, a thick, burly man shaped like the beer can from which he was drinking. "The party's going full blast."

"What should I be celebrating?" Ross asked morosely.

"Lighten up, partner," Kelsey said. "You've been cleared, remember?"

"Yeah, I remember," Ross, frustrated, snapped. "I remember that fucking prosecutor indicting me on page one and the evening news. Two months later the Grand Jury drops the charge and where does that end up? Page thirty-five . . . buried with the classifieds. Now the Review Board does the same. Big deal."

"You're back on the job, Red. That's what counts," Dutch said.

A wave of pain caught Ross by surprise and he struggled to maintain his balance. The sorrow retreated before a swell of indignation. "Tell that to the Commissioner, why don't you? The brass called me in and gave me a so-called choice. Lay low in a desk job . . . or, if I don't like it, I can put in my papers."

"They said that? May those politicians rot in Potter's Field, their names forgotten by all but those who curse them," Kelsey swore.

"What about the PBA?" Dutch wanted to know. "What's Alonzo got to say?"

"He backed the wrong horse. He's got no clout in this City Hall."

"Ain't it grand we've got a union," Kelsey said sarcastically. "I always said a pol's a pol. The fucking world's upside down. But there's one thing I know besides my name. That animal you shot? He was a piece of shit."

"I just don't know anymore, Kelsey." Ross could not hide his despair. Silence filled the space between them as Ross lost himself to a blur of memories.

Kelsey broke into his ruminations. "Do us both a favor, Red. Save the sympathy for yourself." He hesitated, then said quietly, "You know what you need? Some pussy. It's been too long."

Ross glared at him. "When I want advice on my sex life, I'll ask Doctor Ruth." The coldness in his tone built a wall of ice.

Kelsey raised his hands, as if in surrender. He muttered a reluctant, "Sorry, Red." But Ross knew better. He waited, certain that his old friend would be unable to restrain himself from further comment. Sure enough, a moment later, Kelsey started up again. "So sue me. It's been nine months since you buried Annie. Nine months without a woman – that's against a man's nature."

What do you know? Ross wanted to cry, assailed once more by painful longing for the woman with whom he had shared his life for nearly thirty years. As much as he loved Kelsey, he felt the urge to hit him. Ross needed to inflict pain and to be hurt himself. Dutch, light on his feet for a big man, took a quick half-step into the space between Ross and Kelsey. "Go easy, Kels," he cautioned.

"Hell . . . everybody knows I talk too much. I'm *Irish*." Kelsey replied, grinning sheepishly. The tension evaporated like moisture on a slate blackboard and the icy wall melted. Dutch looked like Kissinger after a successful negotiation.

Ross poured drinks for them from the nearly empty bottle. "Guys. I appreciate your coming over – but after this drink, I'm going out."

"Sure," Kelsey said, pointing to the Scotch bottle, "you've got a date with your buddy, Johnny Walker."

Ross flinched.

"Look at yourself," Kelsey said, trying to sound tough but not unsympathetic. "You think this is what Annie would want for you? If it was the other way around and she put you in the ground . . . what? You'd have her wearing black like those Greek widows in Zorba? Okay, it's been rough. The department kicked you when you were down. We know that. But look at what you've got – two great kids, family, friends."

"Speaking of family, guess what, Red?" Dutch said. "I seen your Billy the other day, out on patrol. He looks good in blue."

Kelsey shook his head. "I used to think it was the greatest thing in the world when a kid followed his old man onto the force. These days, he'd have to have his head examined."

Ross disagreed. He'd been pleased when his son chose to follow in his footsteps and join the Department. "The job was always good to me . . . up until a few months ago," Ross insisted. "I wish I was back."

"Then go back." Kelsey urged. "Even if you sit on your duff 'til the smoke clears."

"I'm a detective, not a desk jockey," Ross said with indignation.

Dutch felt the tension build again and interrupted. "So, Red, how's the daughter?"

Ross instantly felt a lift of pride. "Amy made law school. Fordham. She starts this fall."

Kelsey poked a finger at him. "Make sure she finishes." He turned to Dutch. "You didn't know Red when he started at the fourteenth, a rookie doing a day beat and night law. The jerk quit to wash diapers."

"I hear it costs big bucks these days," Dutch said.

"Tell me about it." Amy's tuition was just another one of those things he'd rather not think about.

"There's the credit union," Dutch reminded.

"Used up my line for Annie's home care."

Dutch turned to Kelsey. "You good for a loan?"

"'Fraid not – I could *use* one. My brother-in-law put me in the crapper with stock tips you don't want to know about."

"You know a shylock?" Ross asked. "I could sell the family jewels."

"Save 'em. Never know. You may decide to use them again," Kelsey joked.

Ross shook his head. "You never quit, do you?"

"Not on you, partner."

Dutch looked around the living room. "Hey, Red, you got any pictures?" he asked. "You know, the hand-painted kind. Smitty, over at the twenty-second? His missus bought this picture at a flea market – paid bupkes for it. Damned if one day Smitty doesn't go up Madison Avenue and sees one just like it in the window of this picture gallery. He goes home, takes it down. She's yellin' up a storm. He turns his deaf ear on her, brings it in, gets twelve hundred, on the spot, just like that."

"Nope, no pictures, " Ross replied, "but there's an old malt I've been saving."

"*That* old malt?" Kelsey shook his head in wonder. "My old

partner Red here's teased me with that bottle for years."

They followed Ross into the dining room, staying close, as if having found their friend they were afraid to risk losing him again. A large buffet occupied the better part of the long wall. Ross bent down and turned the brass key in the ivory-framed lock. Kelsey let out a low whistle as he removed the unopened bottle of Glenkinchie. Ross was careful to match the rounded lip of one door into the groove of the other as he closed the buffet. The highly grained veneer caught the light and gleamed as though Annie had polished it just yesterday.

"Your old man make this?" Dutch asked, running his hand across the top. "And the one over there?" He pointed to the breakfront.

"Pop brought them from Italy. Gave them to us when we married."

Ross remembered his father's words. "I want you should have them, Rosso. You and Annie. They're for you."

"What about Terry and Joy?" Ross had asked, protective of his younger sisters.

"No! This belongs to you," his father said firmly. The more Ross resisted his birthright as the first born, the more Pop insisted.

"Still, Red, did he make them?" Dutch pressed.

Ross shrugged, the way Pop had when Annie asked him to tell her about the furniture. "There's nothing to tell," the old man had replied. "We brought the furniture with us."

"They're beautiful, Pop. Were they made in your shop in Udine?" she persisted.

"Somebody gave them to me."

"Who was that, Pop?" Ross inquired.

"What's the difference? You enjoy them, you and Annie. That's all." The subject was closed. Annie asked Ross, in an aside, "What's the mystery?"

"You got me," he replied.

She never pressed Pop again, nor had Ross.

Kelsey waved the bottle under Ross's nose, reminding him of the serious matter still at hand. Ross removed three brandy snifters from the breakfront and Kelsey did the honors. They raised their glasses in a silent toast and sipped the amber liquid. Kelsey, eyes closed, purred with pleasure.

Two hours passed quickly, conversation floating in a haze of smoky malt. Dutch was first to stand, excusing himself to take a piss, then returning with the sobering realization that it was two A.M. The warm ritual of departure was a stark contrast to their tense arrival.

Ross tidied up and washed the glasses. As he replaced the crystal, he paused to admire the exceptional workmanship on the furniture. The doors of both the buffet and the breakfront were inlaid with ivory, ebony and sycamore in a geometric design. The pieces were really too large for the room and dwarfed the simple, store-bought dining room table and chairs. Dutch's story about Smitty and his wife's painting came to mind. It gave him an idea. He had read in the Sunday *Newsday* that auction houses offered free appraisals to families who were considering selling their heirlooms. He doubted that these pieces qualified, but he'd see what they were worth.

He went out into the foyer. From the upper shelf of the hall closet, Ross retrieved the family Polaroid and an out-of-date package of film. He loaded the camera, shot the breakfront and repeated the procedure for the buffet. The pictures developed slowly, gradually adding line, definition and color. He finished off the package of film, photographing the furniture from different angles, then placed the prints on the dining room table to dry.

For the first time in months, Ross was overcome by weariness and a wish to sleep that boded well for a peaceful rest. Switching off the lights, he made his way upstairs. He looked at the bed and pictured Annie, curled there on her side, waiting for him. This time, the memory brought a smile. It had been good. They had been good.

In the morning, Ross checked through the Manhattan Yellow Pages, making a list of several well-known auction houses. He chose Archer's, on the East Side. He and Annie had visited there once, at her insistence, to view a collection of Impressionist paintings put up for sale by a Hollywood hotshot who had fallen on bad times. It had been like visiting a museum. He looked at the kitchen clock. He could catch Pop before he left for work.

"Hi, Pop," he said, when the old man replied.

"Rosso. How you feeling?"

"Getting there. Little by little. How's Momma?"

"She's good. You wanna say hello?"

"You give her my love. Listen, Pop, there's something I want to run by you. You know the furniture you gave me and Annie for our wedding?"

There was silence. He thought he heard his father breathing heavily. "You there, Pop?"

"Yeah," his father whispered.

"I thought I'd find out what, if anything, the pieces are worth. Maybe sell them – pick up some cash for Amy's tuition."

"No!" Pop said gruffly. "You need money, you come to me. That furniture you keep. You pass it to your kids when they get married. We see you here for Sunday dinner. You tell Amy and Billy to be sure they come. Take care, *figlio mio*."

What the hell was that all about? Ross wondered, taken aback by the intensity of his father's response.

Later, as he drove across the 59th Street bridge, he had second thoughts. Maybe Pop was right and he should save the pieces for the kids. Ah, what the hell. He could decide that later. It wouldn't hurt to find out if the furniture was worth something. For all Ross knew, he was on a fool's errand and they'd laugh him out of there when they saw the pictures. He patted his pocket for the tenth time to make sure that the Polaroids were there.

Ross fed the parking meter six quarters and walked over to the auction house. The mustached doorman allayed his anxieties somewhat, greeting him with a smile and a friendly "Good day, sir." Ross felt that he had passed the first hurdle as the man opened the door and stepped aside to let him in.

An attractive brunette looked up at him from behind a rosewood and granite reception counter. "Can I assist you?" she asked.

He hesitated, then took the Polaroids out of his pocket. "I'm interested in knowing what this furniture is worth," he said.

The receptionist's long, perfectly manicured fingertips brushed his hand as she took the prints. The contact sent an unexpected shiver through him. She studied the pictures intently. "Twentieth century. That would be Mr. Fredericks. Ordinarily you'd need an appointment," she said, looking him over.

Ross felt uncomfortable. This was definitely not his scene.

The receptionist glanced at the Polaroids once more. "If you fill out this form, I'll check to see if he's available."

Ross stood at the counter and filled in the brief questionnaire, providing his name, address, phone number and purpose of visit. When he had completed it, she said, "Please have a seat. I won't be long."

Ross sat on a plush gray leather sofa and selected an antiques magazine from the glass-topped coffee table. He flipped pages, not really looking, while she placed a call. After a brief conversation, she came from behind the counter, Polaroids and form in hand, and climbed the wide, sweeping marble staircase. Her skirt was stylishly short, giving him a generous view of her perfectly proportioned legs and lower thighs. The sight aroused him. Kelsey's right, he thought, nine months without a woman *is* against a man's nature. His eyes followed her shapely legs until she turned the corner.

For most of his life, Ross had been a one woman man – and Annie was that woman. There'd been no real fooling around, though the opportunities had been there – except once, when a young blonde's smile made him feel that life *did* begin at forty. Their affair had gone on for six weeks, the sex acting on him like a drug. The more he had, the more he wanted. With Trina, he was high. At home, he was depressed and withdrawn. Annie worried that he had a brain tumor. Mid-life crisis was more like it. Finally, he forced himself to confront the fact that his marriage wasn't the problem; he was. He said good-bye to Trina, confessed to Annie and faced her rage. Despite the pain he'd caused her, she hung in there and after several months, they became better friends and better lovers. They worked at it, right up to the end. It had been worth the effort.

Ross looked up from his reverie to find a tall, slim, dapper man with silver hair approaching him, hand outstretched. "Bill Fredericks, Director of Twentieth Century Decorative Arts."

Ross stood and took the extended hand. "Ross Cortese."

Ross was six feet, but Fredericks had a good two or three inches on him. He looked completely at ease in his neatly tailored suit.

"Cortese . . . Cortese . . . " He wrinkled his brow in thought. "Should I know the name? Are you a dealer in furniture?"

"A dealer? No." Surprise at the question was evident in Ross's tone.

"Then you've been here before . . . "

"Not to do business."

"Please join me, Mr. Cortese. My office is on the second floor."

His stomach rolled. The man's invitation meant that the furniture might be salable. Ross followed him up two flights of marble steps, into a spacious, well-appointed office, tasteful and smooth as the Scotch he and his friends had shared the night before.

Fredericks took his place behind the desk. From his vantage point, he regarded Ross skeptically. "If you're not a dealer, however did you come by these pieces?" He held the Polaroids close to his chest, fanning them like a poker hand.

"They've been in my family as long as I remember," Ross replied.

"You're of Austrian ancestry, then," he observed.

"Italian," Ross corrected. "Look, Mr. Fredericks, what are you getting at?"

"Please understand, Mr. Cortese. When exceptional pieces

appear on the market after many years, we must make every effort to determine their provenance."

Ross wasn't sure about that provenance word, but still he felt his chest tighten. "You say these are exceptional pieces?"

"More than exceptional. They are museum quality." He paused. "Now suppose you tell me what business you're in, Mr. Cortese, and whether these pieces are yours or are you representing the seller?"

I'll be damned, Ross thought. The man acted as if he believed the furniture was hot. "They're not stolen, Mr. Fredericks, if that's what you mean. Like I said, they've been in the family."

Fredericks could not resist a smirk. Ross felt the urge to deck the asshole. Instead, he blurted out, "If you need further assurance, I'm a sergeant – in the New York Police Department."

Once the words were uttered, he immediately wanted to send out a recall and bring them in for repair. A guy like Fredericks would say to himself, what does that prove? How does a cop come by these pieces? Half the cops in town are dirty.

"Then you, of all people, should understand our concern when rare, long-lost objects suddenly surface," Fredericks said in a patronizing tone.

"What are they worth?" Ross asked, wanting to get it over with and leave.

"You're telling me you have no idea what you have here, Cortese? That's difficult to fathom."

"Look," Ross said hotly, starting to rise, "I don't like your tone. I better be going before this gets nasty."

The threat was enough to change Fredericks' demeanor. "I'm sorry if I've offended you, Mr. Cortese. Please believe me. I'm here to facilitate business, not drive away clients."

Ross sat down again, albeit reluctantly, and began to explain. "Pop brought me and my mother over from Italy in nineteen-forty, just before the war. The furniture came with us. He gave these pieces to me when I married. That's it. End of story."

Fredericks rubbed his cheek with his index finger. Ross could almost hear the mental gears working. "Let me tell you about these pieces, Mr. Cortese. They were designed and crafted by Kirmen Mosel." He watched for a response but Ross's expression didn't change. "I see the name means nothing to you. Mosel was one of the greats of the Viennese Secession movement. It presaged the Bauhaus movement. This furniture was made around nineteen-twenty. If memory serves, they are illustrated." He rose with an athlete's grace, went to the mahogany bookcase and removed a large book from the shelf. Turning to the index, he ran a polished finger down the page, checked the reference and turned to the proper place. Ross saw Fredericks' eyes brighten with excitement.

"Here they are," he announced smugly. "Just as I thought. They were, at one time, in Mosel's own home. Like so many beautiful objects, they disappeared during the Second World War." He glanced up at Ross, held his gaze and pointedly remarked, "If you put them up at auction, there will surely be questions of title. How your father obtained the furniture . . . "

"My father's an honest, hardworking man. He always has been. I'm sure there's a simple explanation for how he came by the furniture. Here. Let me see that picture," Ross insisted, standing up and reaching for the book. Fredericks crossed the room and handed it to him. Ross stared in amazement at a photograph of his buffet and breakfront, or their exact duplicates, in an elegant, high-ceilinged dining room. The dining table and chairs were inlaid with squares of ivory alternating with dark and pale woods, set in geometric designs, just as his pieces were. The walls were stenciled. A portrait of a beautiful bejeweled woman hung over the buffet.

"Who's to say my pieces aren't copies?" Ross challenged. "My father's always worked in a custom cabinet-shop.

"That's extremely unlikely, Mr. Cortese. The selection of rare woods, the patina, the detail. Even from your Polaroids, the pieces have a glow of authenticity."

Ross studied the illustration again and broke into a cold sweat. From Vienna, of all places. The old man had never been out of Udine. He felt a weight on his chest. All at once, it felt as though the furniture Pop had given to him and Annie belonged to someone else. How the hell had Pop gotten hold of it?

Hoping that Fredericks had not noticed his discomfort, Ross turned the page. An unusual apartment house was pictured, its simple, modern white facade set between two ornate nineteenth century buildings.

"This looks like it could have been built yesterday," Ross observed, concentrating on the illustration in order to get control of himself.

"That's the beauty of Modernism. The building is one of the purest examples of Secession architectural design. Absolutely inspired. One of a kind. Mosel himself lived there."

Ross closed the book and looked Fredericks in the eye. "You haven't told me what the furniture is worth."

"That depends upon the condition. Has there been restoration?"

"I don't know. Like I said, the pieces have been in my family's possession for years, and in my home ever since I was married."

"Are they signed?"

His first impulse was to say no, but a vague recollection surfaced. "Come to think of it, they could be. When we moved the pieces from our old apartment to the house I noticed that there was something scratched into the back of the buffet. I meant to ask my father, but didn't get around to it. I never gave it a thought 'til now. I'll check it out. In the meantime, give me a ballpark figure."

Fredericks rubbed the tip of his nose, choosing his words with care and observing Ross for his reaction. "On the basis of recent sales, even allowing for the softened market in twentieth century decorative arts, I estimate that the pieces would fetch anywhere from forty-five to fifty-five each."

"You're telling me I can clear ten for the two of them?"

"Ten," Fredericks mumbled, momentarily confused.

"Ten . . . ten thousand."

Fredericks smiled patronizingly. "Dear, dear, Mr. Cortese. Forty-five to fifty-five *thousand* each! In round numbers . . . " He held up the Polaroids. "You're looking at one hundred thousand dollars."

Ross sat there, stunned. His mind whirled, a tumble of confusing thoughts. He had read about people finding masterpieces in dusty attics. So what was Pop's real story?

"Ordinarily," Fredericks observed, "We'd offer your pieces in the next suitable auction – that would be "Important Twentieth Century Decorative Arts"– in September of this year. However, there is that potential problem with provenance and title. I don't know if there are any Mosel family members who might lay claim to the furniture. In those circumstances, it's bad for both the seller and for the auction house. The publicity could be dreadful."

That's all I need now, thought Ross, *another can of worms*. "Maybe we better forget the whole thing. Thanks for your time, Mr. Fredericks." Ross started for the door.

Perturbed, Fredericks followed him. He placed a heavy hand on Ross's shoulder, as if to deter the departure. Ross glared at him and he removed it immediately. Fredericks spoke in a confidential tone, just above a whisper. "It occurs to me that given the circumstances to which I've alluded, you would do better selling privately – to a collector. It's discreet and eliminates the possibility of embarrassing third-party claims."

Fredericks took his silence as assent and warmed to the selling task. "I know just the man. He is a Viennese businessman and *the* major collector of Mosel furniture and decorative objects. We've worked together on side deals in the past. I can let him know about the furniture and have him contact you directly."

"What's in it for you?"

"A client's gratitude is always a valuable asset."

That and the fat commission you pocket for yourself, Ross thought. "I'll think about it," Ross said.

"Please do, Mr. Cortese. The cat's out of the bag now. I'm aware of the existence of the furniture – and as an antiquarian specializing in the Modernist Period, I have . . . a responsibility."

"Are you threatening me?" Ross seethed.

"In no way," he replied smoothly. "Merely apprising you of the realities. By the way, Mr. Cortese, is your father living?"

"Yes. Why?"

"Ask him how he obtained the furniture. I'm sure it's an interesting story. And that portrait you saw in the illustration of the dining room? It's a Klimt. Extremely valuable. Missing as well, unfortunately. Perhaps he might have some idea of its whereabouts. I'd be most interested. In the meantime, I'll notify my client."

"You do that," Ross snapped. A tumble of conflicting emotions assaulted him as he left the office and started down the hall.

"I have your address and phone number, Mr. Cortese," Fredericks called after him. "I trust that you can find your way out."

Ross fled the auction house, as if to put distance between himself and his feelings. Two blocks later, he slowed his pace, still agitated. Pop had not wanted him to make this visit. Was he hiding something?

Ross recognized how little he knew about his father's life prior to 1940. At that time, Pop, Momma and two-year-old Ross emigrated to New York. His father's family, and Momma's too, for that matter, remained behind. Now they were all gone. Unlike other Italians, his parents showed little desire to visit their native land, having returned only once, in the mid-seventies. Pop hadn't said much about the trip, except to remark that it made him sad, what with all the friends and family he had lost. When Joy and Terry urged that they go back again, Pop insisted, almost defiantly, "America is my country. You are my family . . . the only family I need."

Standing on Third Avenue, crowded with traffic and pedestrians, Ross flashed on a disturbing memory. He had come home from fourth grade class with an autobiographical composition assignment. As he pressed his father to tell him more about the first two years of his life in the old country, Pop's eyes glazed over and became frighteningly vacant. Anxious, Ross had asked, "What's the matter, Pop?"

Momma was there, quick to assure him, "Your father's tired, that's all. He works too hard."

Questions Ross had long submerged suddenly felt urgent. Like a match to a fuse, Fredericks' suspicions had lit his own. Ross made a career of investigating people, working them for the facts. Never his own family. Could he do it now?

CHAPTER TWO

Afternoon traffic flowed smoothly on the Ring, the wide boulevard that circled Vienna's old city. Willi Hanfnagel tapped her fingers impatiently on the armrest of the cab door.

Her father had insisted that she be at his apartment within the hour. She'd canceled her last appointments and was halfway out the door when an important call came in from Philadelphia. As a result, she was twenty minutes late. Her father prized punctuality and Willi knew that lateness, no matter what the reason, was inexcusable.

She looked to her right. The Stadtpark was crowded with tourists, visiting the gardens and paying homage at the statues of Strauss, Schubert and Bruckner, three of Vienna's numerous favorite sons.

"Let me off here," she said to the driver as he stopped for a light. She paid the toll, added a generous tip and started to exit the cab. A young businessman, waiting for a taxi, graciously held open the door. She murmured thanks and hurried off.

The man could not take his eyes off her. Tall, beautiful and elegantly dressed, she looked as if she had stepped off the cover of a fashion magazine. He watched as she crossed the Ring and turned into Himmelpfortgasse, entering the old city. For a moment, he was tempted to forget his meeting, go after her and introduce himself, but instead, he simply sighed for the lost opportunity, got into the cab and gave the driver instructions.

Willi used her key to let herself into her father's turn-of the-century building. She rang for the elevator, smoothed back her long blonde hair, and paced while waiting for the birdcage to arrive. Father would not mention her lateness, of course, but the anticipation of his reproachful stare made her feel awful.

Otto, her father's butler, chauffeur and general factotum, greeted her with a curt bow of his head. "Wilkommen, Fraulein

Hanfnagel," he said. She brushed past him without a word and swept into the magnificently appointed salon. Erich Hanfnagel was standing at the window, adjusting the rich magenta velvet drapes. His back was to her, but when he heard her footsteps, he turned and glanced at the Hoffman clock on the mantle. There it is, she thought. Perform well, he adores you, disappoint him and it's as if you've affronted him. She was surprised, however, when she saw a smile instead of the frown she expected.

"You look *ravissant*, liebchen," he said in his most charming voice.

Willi knew at once, from the extravagant compliment, that he wanted something from her. She could feel his excitement as she went to him and offered her hand in their established ritual of greeting. He brushed the back of it with his lips, then said, "I've received wonderful news."

"What is it, Father?"

"Fredericks called from New York. Two Mosel pieces – a buffet and a cabinet – have mysteriously surfaced." He paused for maximum effect. "They appear to be my missing pieces."

"After all these years? That's incredible," she exclaimed. "Did he provide details?"

"The seller claims to be a police officer. The man's story is that the furniture has been in his family since before the war."

"He's Austrian?"

"Italian. Fredericks is suspicious that the man may be fronting for someone else. Who knows how many hands the pieces have passed through since they were stolen fifty years ago? When Fredericks pressed the question of title and provenance, the man became resistant to the idea of selling and bolted. I've asked Vicky Neurath to use the Police Department's resources to do a background check on him. Frankly, I don't care what it reveals. I want those pieces. Only one thing matters to me. Bringing the furniture back home."

Arm-in-arm he led her into the spacious, high-ceilinged dining room. Otto stood at the ready to help her to her seat, but Hanfnagel waved him away and pulled out her chair himself. As he strolled to the other end of the magnificent table, he spread his arms and gestured around the room.

"I had long since given them up for lost. Imagine. The room whole again – but for the painting. Who knows? Perhaps the man possesses knowledge of that, too."

"What will you do?"

"If it were up to me, I'd be on the next plane to New York. And if, as Fredericks suggests, the pieces are authentic, I'd negotiate their purchase. But the good Herr Doktor insists that I not fly for another month."

"Sound advice, Father. A long flight caused the blood clot in the first case."

"Damned phlebitis," he grumbled.

"Your condition is curable. Not everyone is so fortunate at your age."

She saw him flinch and immediately regretted the reference to his age.

"The doctors assure me that I possess the body and constitution of a man fifteen years younger," he said proudly.

"You see?" she agreed. "Then it's only a matter of time before you enjoy full activity once more."

"You're right, of course." He picked up his wineglass and saluted her. "You, my dear, must go to New York on my behalf."

"Oh, Father," she sighed, "can't Dolph go? I've been back for only a week." She saw his pale blue eyes grow dark and she thought of a sky suddenly filled with threatening clouds.

"Willi," he said sharply. "I would not entrust such a sensitive task to your brother. It's not what he does best." Then, softening his tone, he added, "You know what this means to me, liebchen. It would break my heart if, having finally found the furniture, it was denied to me. Go there. Do what you must. Offer what you must. But get it for me."

"Yes, Father." In the end she always submitted to his wishes. Not once in her life had she been able to sustain a disagreement with him.

His eyes glowed with approval. "That's my liebchen."

Secure in his approbation, she responded, "I'll arrange to leave tomorrow. You'll have your furniture. After all, I was taught the art of negotiation by a master."

He was pleased with the compliment and beamed at the thought of his acquisition. His good spirits prevailed throughout their dinner, beautifully prepared and served by the loyal Otto. Nothing more was said about the Mosel pieces, but they were never far from Hanfnagel's thoughts.

As Willi prepared to leave after dessert and cognac, her father kissed her cheek and said, "Have a good flight, my dear. And call me as soon as you've met with the seller and seen the pieces. You know I'll be waiting . . . ."

CHAPTER THREE

Amy and Billy were coming to dinner, so Ross went out and picked up salad, pasta and the ingredients for their favorite sauce. He continued to turn over the meeting with Fredericks in his mind, incredulous at the thought that the furniture was worth a small fortune. He felt sick over his suspicions about Pop, though he was fearful that behind the smoke Fredericks blew his way, there was an actual fire. He decided to tell Amy and Billy only the bare bones about his visit to the auction house and not burden them with his doubts.

Ross spent the afternoon straightening up the house and cooking the meat sauce, stepping out only to buy a bottle of wine at the local liquor store. Twice, he tried calling Pop to question him, but each time hung up before completing the call. He couldn't treat his father like a suspect. He'd wait for Sunday and find a way to bring up the subject then.

His kids arrived together. Billy had a bottle of champagne under his arm, to toast the end of Ross's ordeal.

"When are you coming back on the job, Dad?" he asked.

"In a while," Ross replied noncommittally. He didn't have the heart to tell them he'd been consigned to a desk. There'd be time for that. Right now he was just happy to have them home with him, happy to see them looking so good. He was struck by Amy's prettiness. She had inherited her mother's creamy complexion and dark hair, accented by Ross's green eyes. Billy was tall, with a darker complexion than his sister's, and ruggedly handsome. Right now, however, he looked like he could use a good night's sleep.

During dinner Ross drew them out about their lives. Billy talked about his latest girlfriend, Amy about her excitement at the prospect of law school. Then over dessert, he gave them the edited version of the story of his visit to the auction house. They gasped when he dropped the number.

"It's like you won the lottery," Billy said.

"You don't have to sell on my account," Amy insisted. "I can take out loans – work summers in a law firm. It pays pretty well. Really, Dad." Ross gave her an appreciative hug.

"What did the folks say?" Billy asked. "Bet it blew them away."

"I haven't said anything to them yet. I figure I'll surprise them on Sunday – at dinner. You guys gotta come, too.

"Hey, I almost forgot, the guy at Archer's wanted to know if the pieces were signed. Give me a hand so we can check it out."

Together, they removed the dishes and glasses and set them carefully on the dining room table. Then, they lifted each piece of furniture, in turn, away from the wall. Billy found an inscription in German on the back of the buffet. Amy copied it and said that she'd get it translated.

"Mom really loved this furniture." Amy lovingly moved her hand over the grain pattern on the buffet. "When I was little, she'd let me help to polish them." She chuckled and added, "When I was older, she *made* me polish them."

Some great kids, Ross thought, looking at them and remembering Annie.

CHAPTER FOUR

Ross came out from under the hood of the car and tossed the oil can off the wall and into the garbage can. *Good shot.* He hadn't lost his touch. Resuming his position, he removed the distributor cap, worked the sparkplugs loose from their connections and dropped them into the tool kit. Suddenly, he sensed another presence in the garage. Straightening in one swift move, he banged his temple hard against the edge of the hood.

"Oh, shit," he muttered, rubbing his forehead as he turned and faced the figure framed in the doorway. The instant she came into focus, he regretted the expletive.

"I'm sorry if I startled you. Are you hurt?" the woman asked.

They took a moment to size one another up.

He's very good looking, she noted, his hair a wonderful red, features clean and rugged. The day's growth of beard and oil stained T-shirt only made him look sexier to her.

She's quite a looker, Ross thought, everything about her spells quality. He figured her to be in her mid to late thirties, and even though the afternoon sun haloed her, glowing through her blonde, coiffed hair, she appeared cool and very elegant. Beautifully dressed in an expensive beige linen suit that outlined a stunning figure.

Then it dawned on him. "You're the woman from Vienna."

"When you didn't return my call, I thought I'd take a chance on finding you here."

"You found me alright," he said ruefully, touching his temple where a lump was forming. She laughed and reached into her pocket-book. He figured it for crocodile. She pulled out a quarter and offered it to him. "If there's no ice, press with this," she suggested.

"My mother used to do that. It was a nickel then. She'd let me keep it."

She grinned and her ocean blue eyes sparkled at him. "Please. Keep it. For luck."

"Thanks." He hesitated before saying, "Didn't Fredericks explain that I wasn't interested in selling?"

"He did say that you were reluctant."

"Unwilling would be more accurate. I'm sorry. Looks like you came a long way for no reason."

She looked crestfallen. "Do you think I might just see the furniture, having come this far?"

What the hell, he thought. "I guess the least I can do in exchange for your quarter is to show it to you."

"I'd like that, Mr. Cortese," she responded, making no effort to hide her eagerness.

"My friends call me Red."

"Mine call me Willi. I hope we can be friends."

Fat chance, he thought. "I put a Willy away once. Ten to twenty. Armed robbery," he joked.

"Is that a warning?" The ocean blue of her eyes seemed to turn a shade deeper.

"To myself," he muttered, "just to myself."

Ross led her out of the garage and into the house. She hurried into the dining room ahead of him and gasped, her eyes flitting back and forth between the pieces of furniture. As she moved closer and considered each in turn, Ross saw her frown.

"No good, huh? I asked Fredericks if he thought they might be copies."

Willi shook her head, continued studying the pieces, then finally turned to him. "They're superb," she announced. "Father would kill to own them." Though stated matter-of-factly, it seemed as if an unwelcome presence had come between them. She read the change in Ross's expression and quickly explained, "A cliché common among collectors. I don't know anyone who's done so." Turning on the charm, she smiled again and the beautiful ocean blue appeared again.

"I wish I could say the same – but I've been a cop too long."

Her smile faded. Ross was pleased that he had gained a measure of parity in the situation.

"It's strange," he said, "all these years, the furniture was there. . . just something we lived with. Now . . . "

"Mr. Fredericks told my father that you were unaware of the furniture's value," Willi interrupted.

"That's right."

"Well, if there's anyone who can tell you about the furniture, it is my father. He's an expert on the period. Recently he was asked to do a book."

"You're very proud of him, aren't you?"

"Of course." Her look said, how could I be otherwise?

"I'd be very interested in finding out what he knows about these particular pieces," Ross said.

Good, she thought. If we can continue the dialogue, perhaps he'll have a change of heart. "I'll mention that to Father and report that I have no doubt as to the authenticity of this furniture. Why – if I may ask – are you reluctant . . . " She caught herself, "or I should say . . . unwilling to sell?"

"It's complicated. Let's just say they're not for sale at this time." He crossed his arms on his chest as if to say that's all for now on that subject.

He's opened the door a crack, Willi realized. She remembered her father's first rule of business – don't underestimate your adversary. This could be Cortese's negotiating strategy. "You should know, Mr. Cor . . . . *Red*, there will be an offer made. What did the godfather say? An offer that you can't refuse?"

"Whoa. No dead horses in my bed, please," Ross joked. She laughed and he enjoyed the sound of it.

"Father can be very persuasive when he wants something for his collection."

"I'll bet he can."

Willi sensed that he was warming up to her. Time for her exit. She checked the gold Cartier on her wrist. "I seem to have lost track of time. I'm running late for an appointment."

Ross noticed that she wasn't wearing a wedding band. "What do you do when you're not checking out furniture for your father?"

She pointed to her earrings, small, elegant spiral coils. "Gold earrings. I design and manufacture them. It brings me to New York often. I love the city."

"Good to have a booster. Say . . . . can I offer you a cup of coffee?"

Willi wondered if there was a Mrs. Cortese. "I'm afraid I must go. Business appointments." She looked around the room once more. "Your home feels well lived in. A woman's touch . . . Your wife?"

"I lost her. Nine months ago. Cancer."

She noticed his crossed arms tensed, holding in his emotions. "I'm so sorry."

He thought that he heard something in her voice beyond the

polite consideration of a stranger. They moved slowly to the front door and Ross opened it for her. As Willi was about to step outside Ross said, "Wait a minute, where are you staying?"

"At the Carlyle Hotel."

"We'll talk further."

"I hope so. Good-bye, Red. It was a pleasure."

"How will you get back? I'd take you, but you saw my car."

"I asked the driver to wait for me."

Ross pushed open the door. There was a pewter gray Lincoln Town car parked at the curb. He watched her move down the path. Her hair was caught in a slight swirl of breeze and looked like spun gold, two shades lighter then her eighteen-karat watchband. Her legs were shapely and athletic, her stride graceful and confident. The driver straightened with respect and Ross felt a surge of jealousy as the man helped her into the car. The lucky stiff would be with her in the closed compartment of the vehicle, his eyes taking her in through the rearview mirror. Sure enough, Ross watched the son-of-a-bitch adjust the mirror, not for traffic but for a better look at Willi. The motor came on so quietly that Ross was unprepared when the car pulled out. He stood there as the silver car carried the golden lady from view.

Alone in the house, he felt oppressed by the silence. He needed a drink but decided that he would settle for a cup of coffee. As he passed through the dining room, Ross paused for another glimpse of the furniture. There was no longer any doubt. Willi had confirmed that the pieces were the Real McCoy.

Sunday he would be at the folks for the weekly family dinner. Sunday he would confront Pop. He was not looking forward to that prospect.

Ross made fresh coffee – the steaming, bitter espresso a match for his mood. Annie had said to him during those lost dark days, "We had a good life, Red. Great kids. You're still a young man. Please don't dry up."

He buried his face in his hands at the memory.

CHAPTER FIVE

Willi found herself distracted throughout the presentation to the jewelry buyer at Saks. Nonetheless, her pitch succeeded and she closed the sale, a substantial one at that. In the taxi back to the Carlyle, she settled back and replayed the scene with Ross Cortese. It was obvious that he was attracted to her, as she was to him. She liked his look, the day's growth of beard, even the slight bump in his nose, evidence of an old break. Athletic injury or a fight? she wondered. The man seemed sad. The combination of his vulnerability and intense virility appealed to her. She decided to wait a day or two before any further attempt to contact him. Her father would be frustrated by the delay, but she'd assure him that things were under control.

It was four-thirty when she arrived back at her suite and found her father's message on the voice mail. She dialed direct and Otto answered the phone.

"Let me speak to my father, please."

"Gruss Gott, Fraulein Willi. He left an hour ago. I believe he's attending a meeting at your brother's office."

Willi found the information disquieting. "At this hour?" It was ten-thirty at night in Vienna. "What kind of meeting is this?"

"It's not for me to say."

"I'll ring my brother's office. Thank you, Otto."

She found Dolph's number in her Wizard and punched it in. The phone rang a dozen or so times and she was about to hang up when Dolph's familiar voice came on the line.

"Ja . . . "

"It's Willi . . . "

"Ach. Dear Sister, calling from Niggertown," he said in a snide tone.

"Let me speak to Father," she demanded brusquely, ignoring his remark.

"He's gone. The meeting is still going on, so give me your message and I'll relay it to him in the morning."

"What meeting is this?"

"Mind your jewelry – leave politics to the men."

"*Politics*? You're joking. Father has had nothing to do with politics for years. He abhors it."

"Austria is in crisis, Sister. Open your eyes. The time has come for each of us to take a stand. Even you will have to choose – between those like your baby brother, the faggot, Jew-loving Rudy, and the Hanfnagel family."

"Save the speech for your drinking buddies, Dolph. Rudy *is* family – though you choose to deny it."

"You'll learn. But until you do, it would be best if you confined yourself to playing hostess for father's dinner parties and accompanying him to the opera. That way we'll all be happy."

"Dolph, the only time you're happy is when you make someone else miserable. Give Father this message. Tell him that I've seen the furniture. It is authentic – and I'm dealing with Herr Cortese. I'll call him as soon as I have further information. He's not to worry."

"I'm sure you'll do whatever you must to convince the spaghetti-eater to sell. If your business acumen fails you, there's always your body."

Willi hung up furious, grabbed the remote and turned on the television. She channel-surfed and settled on Oprah Winfrey. It would be a relief to hear about other people's problems for a while.

Dolph Hanfnagel chuckled and re-lit his cigar. His little sister was not entirely wrong, he thought. He very much enjoyed taunting her. He was ten years old at the time of her birth – twelve when the little faggot came along. He could have gotten along just fine without either of them. She was a royal pain in the ass and Rudy, a major embarrassment among Dolph's comrades and business associates.

He returned to the conference room and the sweet aroma of Cuban cigars. Settling back in his chair at the far end of the table, he listened with pleasure as Victor Neurath outlined in detail the first phase of their operation. Dolph owed his father's friend a great deal. Years ago, Victor had taken him under his wing and acted as his mentor while Erich Hanfnagel played the role of cultural philanthropist, garnering plaudits from all sectors of Austrian society.

Dolph studied Victor as the old man stood before the Board, concluding his report. Militarily erect, he slashed the air with his hand to punctuate his remarks. "Our letter devices will deliver a telling blow. With the public crying out for order, the weak coalition formed by so-called centrists and their socialist bedfellows will come apart. In a special election, the Freedom Party will gain a majority – and we will control the levers of power."

The six men at the table applauded as Neurath sat down. Strasser, their liaison to Germany, said, "A superb presentation, Victor. I would like the Board to consider extending the project to Bonn as well. The time is ripe."

"No!" Dolph exclaimed, rising from his chair. "That is out of the question." He tempered his tone. "We must remain mindful of our purpose. The majority of Austrian voters are disgusted with the government. As a result, we're close to obtaining power by legitimate political means. Establish a successful base here and that will encourage our friends in Europe and elsewhere."

They listened with respect. He wished that his father were here to see him perform. "The eyes of the world always watch Germany," he continued. "German leaders, however sympathetic they may be to our cause, are forced to take action against extreme political protest from the right or left. We must not give them cause to do so." He smiled with self-satisfaction, aware of their nods of approval.

"No one fears Austria – this time!" He pounded the table for emphasis. "Much to everyone's surprise, the march to a greater Germany will begin here. Remember, we are not terrorist rabble. We are a political force."

They stood as one and applauded him. Brenner, an industrialist and major financial supporter of the Board's activities, piped up, "Do we have sufficient separation from the action arm of the Party? You've used cut-outs, I trust?" he added pompously.

Victor laughed. "Where would we be, gentlemen, without the writings of Ludlum and LeCarre? Don't worry, Bruno . . . " He pointed to Oskar Fertig, an official in the Interior Ministry. "Our colleague has seen to it. We will never be linked to the action."

Dolph recalled his brief conversation with his sister. Willi had no idea of the central role he played in recasting Austrian politics. Few did, outside of this room. The Board was the brain and spine of the Party. Hidden from view, it controlled the speech and movements of puppets assigned to perform in public. Those that they had elevated to elective office served them, controlled by financial arrangements and incriminating dossiers. They were to be found not only within the Freedom Party, but elsewhere as well. As for the next Chancellor – Dolph smiled – the members of this Board had ratified his choice.

Following Santayana's injunction, they had learned the lessons of history. The wheels were set in motion and the time frame was short. Dolph glanced at the clock. Victor had arranged a secure rendezvous with Doschenko, the organizer of their action arm. He would give the ex-KGB freelancer the final list of recipients of the letter devices, approved tonight by the Board.

Dolph would wait 'til after the mail had been delivered before informing his associates that he and Victor had set in motion a second act of violence to be carried out by Doschenko and his operatives within one week. It would shake Austrian society to its core, as the Reichstag fire had done in Germany sixty years earlier.

Dolph stood. "Gentlemen. If there are no further questions, I move that we adjourn." The motion was carried unanimously.

CHAPTER SIX

Sunday dinner with the folks was a long-standing tradition. In recent months, Ross had missed more than he had made. His brother-in-law, Ralph greeted him at the door. "Good to see you, Red. Amy just got here. Where's Billy the kid? Pop said he was coming with you."

"He pulled a last minute double tour."

"Too bad, " Ralph said, genuinely disappointed, "I haven't seen him in months."

He's been ducking the family like I have, Ross thought. Too much a reminder of Annie's absence.

"It's great news about Amy and law school. She was just telling us . . . "

Joy pushed past her husband. "You deserve some good news, big brother." She planted a wet kiss on his cheek, then rushed off to help Momma in the kitchen.

Ross felt a tug on his trousers, looked down and saw his four year old grand-niece, Carol. "Unca Ross . . . you bring me a present?"

Damn. He had forgotten that it was her birthday. Before he could apologize, Amy came to the rescue. "Uncle Ross has a special present for his birthday girl – and so have I. It's for later, when we sing you happy birthday."

Delighted, the child went off in pursuit of Grandma Joy. Ross hugged his daughter. "Thanks, sweetheart."

"What're you drinking, Red?" Ralph asked.

"Black Label, if Pop has some."

"Pop's got a regular saloon with all the booze he gets from those decorators at Christmas. Gotta give 'em credit. Fags buy the best."

Terry, sister number two, heard the remark and stepped in front of Ralph, holding her hand up like a cop directing traffic. "What's with the gay bashing, Ralphie?"

"Who's bashing?"

"That's how you hope to teach your kids?"

"I didn't do nothin'," he protested.

"Everybody hates everybody. You call that nothing?"

Mamma come in from the kitchen and sized up the situation. "Come, children . . . dinner's ready," she announced.

"I'll get you that drink, Red," Ralph promised.

"He don't need whiskey," Pop intruded. "I got plenty of wine."

Ross ignored his father. "It's okay, Ralphie. I'll fix it myself."

He poured a generous helping of Black Label over two ice cubes all the while feeling Pop's eyes on his back. The old man's disapproval lodged between his shoulder blades. Ross carried his drink into the dining room and took his customary seat alongside his father's chair at the large walnut table. He looked around the room, studying his parents' furniture for the first time, rather than taking it for granted. These pieces were heavily carved, the designs sinuous and leafy. In no way did they resemble the pieces designed by Mosel. Ross knew that this furniture had been built in Biaggone's cabinet shop. He had seen Pop working on the pieces. The client had changed his mind and lost the deposit. Pop then bought them cheap.

Terry broke into his thoughts as she offered the antipasto. He looked up at her with a smile, then helped himself to a portion of peppers. Still beautiful at forty-four, a brunette like Momma, she had been called a Sophia Loren lookalike. Joy served the seafood salad. She was a good thirty pounds overweight but her face, within its pudgy borders, was the image of Momma's when she was younger. He saw little Carol pointing to him, as if she had made a discovery. "Unca Ross has red hair."

"That's why we call him Red, sweetie," Terry responded.

"Why can't I have red hair?" Carol pouted.

Joy and Terry looked at one another and giggled. Joy explained. "The girls in school was always saying, how come you don't have red hair like your gorgeous brother. We told them to ask the iceman."

"You girls should show a little respect," Pop said irritably.

Momma came in from the kitchen with the breadbasket. "Stop teasing your brother."

Pop went around the table pouring white wine. "Best white in Italy comes from my region," he announced, as he did at every dinner. Ross tasted the wine and complimented Pop on the choice, observing the ritual. It made Pop feel good.

Amy, seated next to him, leaned over and whispered, "Tell Poppa about the furniture."

"Not now," he replied, equally softly.

"Now's as good a time as any."

"Later," Ross said tightly. "After dinner."

Amy, puzzled, shrugged. Ross drank up his wine and helped himself to a refill. He needed to dissolve his reluctance. He saw Pop's frown. The old man was worried about his drinking.

They finished the antipasto and a few minutes later, a primo piatti of penne with eggplant and tomato was served. Murmurs of pleasure and compliments to Momma followed. Ross picked at his pasta. Amy tried again. "Come on, Dad. Tell them, why don't you?"

"What, sweetheart'?" Pop inquired, hearing her question.

Ross took the plunge. "That furniture you gave to me and Annie. Where did you get it?" he asked bluntly.

One look at his father made him instantly regretful. Pop's mouth gaped like an open wound and his color drained until his complexion matched that of the wine. He seemed to have aged ten years in a minute. He looked at Momma anxiously, and when his eyes moved back to his son, Ross saw fear in them and he felt awful.

"Why you wanna know, Rosso? What's happened?"

"Tell them," Amy said, with an impish grin, apparently oblivious to her grandfather's reactions.

"Yeah, Red. What's the story?" Ralph demanded.

"I took some Polaroids of the furniture into the city to an expert. It looks like they're worth a lot of money."

"How much, Red?" Joy wanted to know.

Ross observed his father as he replied, "As much as a hundred thousand dollars for the two." There were gasps and whistles. Someone murmured, "You're putting us on." Everyone looked absolutely incredulous.

"Who made 'em? Michelangelo?" joked Phil.

"The cabinet-maker's name was Mosel. Viennese. The expert told me his furniture's in museums."

"Pop? You know any of this?" Terry asked.

Franco stuttered, "I don't know."

"Where'd you find them, Poppa?" Amy questioned.

Ross saw pain working new lines into his father's face. Pop suddenly slumped and Ross was afraid that he might have a heart attack.

"Yeah, Pop," Ralph pressed, "where *did* you find them?"

When Pop spoke, it was with great effort, his voice thin. "I get them in Vienna."

Now there was a shocked silence at the table. "But, Poppa. You never told us you lived anywhere but Udine," Terry reminded him.

When Pop continued, it was as if he were talking to himself. They strained to hear him. "I'm working for Pazetti in Udine. Nineteen and thirty-seven. He says, 'I'm gonna send you to Vienna. You learn from this Mr. Mosel. A great one.' Pazetti says, 'You come back. You be the best in Udine.'" Pop shrugged. "I'm young. He pays for the train fare. So I go."

Exhausted by the effort, Pop stared straight ahead. Ross saw that vacant look appear again in his father's eyes, the one that he had recalled so vividly outside of Fredericks' office.

"Your Poppa never wants to remember those times," Momma intervened. "Me. I'll never forget. In Italy – in Udine there were Fascistis. Mussolini's blackshirts who make our lives miserable." A shiver caused her to pause. "And those poor people – refugees from that Hitler."

"What's a Hitler, Grandma Gina?" Carol asked innocently.

"A very bad man," Joy whispered to her granddaughter.

"I pray to the Virgin every day that God never lets you know, my little one. It felt like the end of the world. Your Poppa and me, we save every lire with one idea. Get to America with our bambino . . . our Rosso, just a baby." She stared at Ross.

"But the furniture, Momma. What about the furniture?" Joy urged.

Gina looked sadly at Franco. Ross felt that he was witnessing a moment, so painfully intimate, that to observe made him a voyeur. He averted his gaze and turned to Amy, but she too was transfixed by the drama. He was drawn back to his father's face. The man's suffering was immense.

Pop groped for words. "The Germans – they were coming to Austria. Mr. Mosel – he was trying to get papers to take the family out. Selling – he was selling things."

Joy finished the thought. "So you bought the furniture from him."

With what, thought Ross. You didn't have two nickels to rub together. Pop stared down at the table.

"That's so sad," Amy murmured.

Terry climbed on the bandwagon. "People do what they have to in bad times – to survive." It was clear. No one wanted to press Pop any further.

"What happened to the family in Austria, Grandpa?" Amy asked.

His father seemed not to hear the question. Pop shook his head back and forth, "I don't know . . . I don't know." He repeated it like a mantra.

Amy broke through the chant. "We found some writing . . . in back of the buffet."

"Cool," shot Gino. "What did it say?"

"It was in German." She hesitated, embarrassed to pronounce the foreign tongue. "*Fur meine liebe Ariella.* I asked Margie Steib. It means, for my beloved Ariella."

"Can Ariella come to my party?" Carol wanted to know.

A steady stream of tears rolled down Pop's cheeks.

"Look." Carol pointed and said, "Poppop's crying. . . Please don't cry, Poppop," she pleaded.

Momma, tears in her eyes, went over and comforted the little girl. Pop dried his eyes with the linen napkin, rubbed his cheeks with the back of his hand, then gulped down the wine remaining in the glass. Ross reached for the bottle and refilled his glass. Pop nodded. "What you gonna do with the furniture, Rosso?" he asked, his voice still choked.

"I'm thinking of selling it. Amy doesn't want me to."

"She's right," Pop said, his voice a little stronger. "It's in the family. You keep it. Someday you give it to Amy, like I gave it to you."

Sure, Ross thought. Forget about selling it. Don't ask where it came from. How it got here. Forget the lies, the words not said. For the first time in his life, he felt as if his father were a stranger.

"Hey, Pop," Ralph joked. "A hundred thousand clams makes a lot of sauce. You got any more of that furniture socked away for the girls?"

"Ralphie!" Joy cried out. "Mind your business."

"What did I say?"

"Too much . . . like usual."

"Ah, forget about it . . . " Ralph muttered.

"This Fredericks at the auction house," Ross said. "He tells me some wealthy collector in Vienna might be interested in a private deal. His daughter came by today to check out the furniture. She said there's sure to be an offer."

Suddenly Pop erupted. "You stay away from that place, you hear me?" He gained control of himself quickly. "You need money for Amy, you come to me. I got some put away."

"That money's for your old age, Poppa," Amy interjected.

"I'm never gonna be old! You ask Momma. Ha, Gina?"

Pop's innuendo cracked them up. For the family, life was restored to the present.

Basta! He, too, would put on a party mask. They would eat, drink, tell stories and celebrate little Carol's birthday. But for Ross, the respite was temporary. His parents were both hiding something. He felt it.

CHAPTER SEVEN

The following morning, Ross was clearing the breakfast dishes when the doorbell rang. It was Joy, on one of her stop-bys, a frequent occurrence since Annie's death. This morning, he was not happy to see her. She came inside, carrying her obligatory box of Dunkin' Donuts like a votive offering.

"You look terrible," she observed.

"That's what everyone says."

"You been drinking?"

"Try not sleeping."

"Try not drinking."

"I've cut down," he said.

"Cut *out.* Come into the kitchen."

He followed Momma's clone into the kitchen and watched as she made a fresh pot of coffee. "You talk to the folks this morning?" she asked, over her shoulder.

"No.

"Call, why don't you? Pop's not feeling good. That old country talk last night didn't go down good with Momma's polenta."

"It's not what he said that upset him, but what he didn't say."

She turned, frowning, and brought their coffees to the table. "Come again?"

"He's hiding something."

Her mouth opened in astonishment. "Pop? You gotta be kiddin' me. The man wears his insides outside. He cries like the Leaning Tower leans. I think you're a cop looking for a case. Look some place else." She sipped her coffee. "Damn. Too hot." Then she muttered, "Pop hiding something . . . sweet Jesus. The sooner you get back to work, the better."

"All these years he never mentioned he was in Vienna. And the furniture's worth a fortune. You don't find that strange?"

"You heard what Momma said."

"Yeah, I heard it. I also heard all of you rush in to make it right. Pop never said he bought the furniture from this Mosel. You guys said it for him."

"Cut it out! Don't go making Pop out to be . . . to be something that he's not."

"You think I like feeling suspicious of my own father. He's been there for me whenever I've needed him. Whatever it is, I could accept it – but I've got to know. What's wrong with that?"

"It's wrong if it makes him sick. He wants to forget. So leave it that way." Changing the subject, she began, "You ask me . . . "

"I didn't," he warned lightly, hoping to head her off at the pass before she really got wound up.

"I'll tell you anyway," she insisted. "This woman . . . the one from Vienna?"

"What about her?"

"You had a look when you mentioned her. A woman knows. I bet she's a knockout."

"Yeah. So what?" he growled.

"Why don't you ask her out?"

"Why don't *you* mind your business?" The joshing was familiar now – friendly.

"Family is my business," she growled back at him. "I'm a born matchmaker. You know that."

"Not this time. She's class, money. I'm Queens, over the hill and out of work. Besides which, I'm fifty-two."

"Ah, so you are interested. Good. It's time, Red."

"You sound like Kelsey."

"I always liked him. Listen up . . . "

"You've been watching too many cop shows."

"Look at Elizabeth Taylor and that truck driver hunk she married. My girlfriends – most of them in their thirties – keep calling, asking if I can give them your number. So before I do, call up this what's-her-name. . . "

"Willi," he said and instantly saw her, remembered her eyes.

"Go out with her. Have some fun. Practice safe sex. If you're embarrassed, I'll go in the drugstore and buy you rubbers. She's probably got her own these days."

"I can't believe this. You've already got me in bed with her."

"It's time, Red." She picked herself up. "It's also time for me to baby-sit Carol." Reaching the kitchen door, she turned and pointed at him. "You call!"

The front door slammed, punctuating the command. Call. Call the folks. Call Willi. He went to the phone, dialed information and obtained the Carlyle's number. After three rings, her voice mail kicked in.

"It's Red Cortese," he said. "If you get this message in time and you're free for dinner tonight, call and leave a message. I'll pick you up in front of the hotel at eight. There's a little Italian place in East Harlem. Nothing fancy – but great home cooking. You've got my number. Hope you can make it."

Ross puttered around the house for an hour or so, an ear peeled for the telephone. At one o'clock, he drove to Borough Headquarters and picked up Kelsey. They grabbed a quick sandwich at the Diner on Queens Boulevard.

"Got news for you, pal," Kelsey reported. "Got drunk with the Chief. I'm working on him. Hang in."

Ross told him about the furniture. Kelsey insisted that he'd be nuts not to take the money and run. When he described Willi, Kelsey licked his lips. "Take a package deal – with her as the ribbon."

Ross returned home from lunch at three and found her callback on the machine. "I'd love to join you tonight. I'm in Philadelphia but I'll be back in time for dinner at eight. Ciao."

She'd love to, he thought. Be still my heart.

He vacuumed, washed and polished the car, did the same to himself and was ready to go by seven.

CHAPTER EIGHT

Evening traffic into Manhattan was extremely heavy. Ross arrived at the Carlyle fifteen minutes late to find Willi waiting for him in the lobby. She welcomed him European style, a kiss on each cheek. Her perfume filled his nostrils, heady, rich and sensual. An expensive black silk suit clung to the outlines of her lithe body and didn't hide a thing. Ross wore a navy blue blazer and gray slacks, but felt shabby by comparison.

They made small talk on the ride uptown. The car radio was tuned to WBGO and the station was celebrating Billie Holiday with two hours of uninterrupted recordings. They listened as Billie sang, "The night is cold, I'm all alone. I'd give my soul, just to call you my own." Her boozy voice was filled with longing. The weight of the lyrics caught Ross like a short jab, setting him up for a k.o. "Got a moon above me, but no one to love me . . . Lover man, where can you be?"

"So, what did your father have to say about the furniture?" Ross asked. He figured that sooner or later one of them would have to bring it up.

"I wasn't able to reach him," she replied, staring ahead.

They drove through East Harlem, Willi observing the street life and tenements. "This is not your typical neighborhood for a New York restaurant visit," she noted.

"It's not your typical restaurant either," Ross responded with a grin. He turned off East 116th onto Pleasant Avenue. It was deserted, except for parked cars.

"We're here?" she asked nervously.

He parked on the diagonal, between a Jaguar and a Lincoln. He pointed out of the back window and there, on the corner, several steps below street level and behind a cast iron railing, was Rao's. "How can they park those fancy cars in this neighborhood?" she asked, as they crossed toward the storefront.

"They used to have a big dog sitting on the steps . . . Jocko. He kept an eye on the cars. He could tell the good guys from the bad."

Willi arched an eyebrow. "Tell me about your Rao's."

"New Yorkers follow the food. The word got out that Rao's serves the best Neapolitan this side of Napoli. Politicians, entertainers, garmentos, celebrities, you name it. They all want to eat here. Now it's impossible to get a reservation." Ross realized that he was showing off for her.

The bartender spotted them as they entered. "Hey, Red," he called out. "Good to see you back."

"Nickie," Ross waved.

"He knows you," she remarked.

"I came before it was fashionable," Ross explained. "Frank's loyal to his old customers."

The attractive couples at the bar looked their way, then leaned together, whispering.

"They're trying to figure out where they've seen your picture – if you're a model or a movie star."

She looked at him with disbelief. Like many beautiful women, she denied her own effect.

From the bar, they surveyed the small restaurant. The open kitchen was to their right. The main dining area held four booths and three tables. Autographed photos of celebrities covered the walls.

Frank came out of the kitchen and saw Ross. He came over with a warm, welcoming embrace. "I'm glad you called, buddy. It's good to see you."

Ross nodded. "Frank. Meet Willi Hanfnagel . . . here from Vienna."

"My pleasure." Frank took her hand and smiled warmly. He led them to the booth, positioning Willi so that she could observe the scene. Nick was at their table without a signal. Ross ordered a bottle of wine.

"I'll bring the Riserva Ducale. Some Pellegrino?" Nick asked.

"No, thank you. I like New York water," Willi said, "If you don't mind."

"Mind? It's the best . . . and it comes from the tap. I know a guy who bottled it and labeled it New York water. They bought it in Canada like it was champagne."

He left them laughing. "I like your choice of a restaurant. It's charming and homey."

"Annie used to say that. My late wife. She'd bake cookies every year at Christmas for Frankie, Nick and the gang in the kitchen . . . "

"She sounds like a wonderful woman."

Suddenly Annie had joined them at the table – a presence neither of them knew how to deal with – and there was a brief lull in their conversation until Nick returned and poured the wine. Frank dragged a chair over to their table and sat down. "So. What would you like? Everything is good . . . "

"I can attest to that," Ross said with a smile. The discussion was brief. Willi asked Frank for his suggestions. He recommended seafood salad, peppers, baked clams, pasta with cabbage and the veal parmigiano. "Leave room for the cheesecake," he added. They laughed, as Frank urged them to enjoy dinner and left to place the order.

"It's comforting to have a place like Rao's," Willi said. "Were you born in this neighborhood?"

"Uh, uh. I'm like you. I can never be President."

The reference puzzled her. He went on to clarify the remark. "European by birth. American by choice. Pop and Momma's choice. I was born in the north of Italy in thirty-eight. Not the best of times. The folks got us out in forty. They say it was the last ship. I was too young to remember. My sisters were born here – after the war."

"You were fortunate to have emigrated."

"Did your people have a hard time of it?"

"The war is never talked about. By the time I was born, in nineteen-fifty, Vienna was a divided city. Those in the Russian zone did not fare so well. We lived in the American zone, great good luck."

"Who's the we?" he asked.

"Father, mother and two brothers. Do you have children, Red?"

"Yeah, two great kids. A boy and a girl. Billy followed in his dad's footsteps into the NYPD. Amy starts law school in the Fall. That's what led me to Fredericks and you to me."

"I'm glad that you called," she said simply.

"I almost didn't. I haven't asked anyone for a date in a lot of years."

"Is that what this is?" she asked, too coyly by half, he thought.

Ross shrugged.

"Fredericks told my father that you knew nothing about the provenance of the pieces."

"I know more now," he said defensively. "My father got them directly from Mosel." He watched as her face registered surprise.

"In Vienna?" she inquired.

So it's back to business, he thought, disappointed. "It turns out that Pop worked with him for awhile. I never knew until yesterday, when I asked him. He bought the furniture, brought it to Italy, then over here."

"It's true then. The furniture has been in your family all these years."

"You had reason to doubt it?" he challenged.

The confrontation was unexpected and she flustered. "Fredericks implied . . . "

"Say it, Willi. That I was a thief." She flinched. "That's why I told the son-of-a-bitch to forget it. Look. I told you the furniture wasn't for sale. If that's why we're here, we should settle for a drink and call it an early evening."

"That's not why we're here," she insisted. "Well – it's part of why we're here, of course. Without the furniture, we would never have met. I'm really sorry if Fredericks treated you badly. But all these years, Father lived with the assumption that the furniture was stolen."

Ross decided to keep his own doubts to himself, but his tone was somewhat abrupt. "He assumed wrong." There was a brief pause. "What does your father do?" he asked.

"What doesn't he do?" She laughed. "He made his first fortune in real estate, then dealt privately – and I might add, successfully in the art market. Recently, he and my older brother started a video and software distributing company. They have outlets in a number of Austrian and German cities."

"Are you two close?"

She nodded. "Father raised us. My mother died young."

They might not have much else in common, Ross thought, but they did share loss. "That's tough on a kid," he said.

As the waiter arrived, placing their clams, peppers and seafood salad on the table, Willi leaned forward and suddenly asked, "Do you ever blame yourself for Annie's death?"

"Where the hell did that come from?" Ross demanded, taken aback by the question. Before she could reply, he bitterly counter-punched, "Is this a Viennese parlor game? Playing Doctor Freud?"

He looked away from her, gazing at the other diners, listening to their lively chatter and remembering such nights with Annie.

Willi put her fork down and flushed. "I'm so sorry, Red," she apologized, wanting to bring him back. "That was rude. I was thinking about myself. I was eight when my mother died. For a long time I felt that I was somehow to blame."

"Kids feel that way," he offered, touching her hand lightly in a gesture of understanding. Her openness had enabled him to speak of certain feelings for the first time. "There are times I wish I gave her less aggravation and more of what she needed . . . I lived my life like I had all the time in the world, like nothing ever would change. Like death is something that happens in someone else's family. I took her to Italy for our twentieth wedding anniversary. Rome and Florence. She read up on the history, the art, churches – planned the whole itinerary down to the smallest detail. She loved every minute. I promised that we'd go back. We never did. One day, you wake up and realize you've got a short lease on life and you're out of tomorrows." He stopped suddenly. "Enough of me. Tell me more about you. Have you ever been married?"

"Yes," she said sadly. "I was twenty-five. I should have known better. He was weak, threatened by my career. He wanted me to stay at home. Six awful years. Long enough to come to hate one another."

They continued the first course in silent communion, eating and sipping wine until a voice boomed, "Red, you son of a gun . . . " and a large, bearded, heavy-set man stood next to the table.

"Donny," Ross said. "Son of a gun. It's been a while. How are you doing? Willi, this is Don Cabell. Ex-cop. Old friend. Now a big-shot television producer. Donny, Willi Hanfnagel."

"Any friend of Red's is a friend of mine." He shook her hand with a strong grip.

"I heard the great news," Donny said. "Bullshit charges. About time those bums cleared you. You should never have been suspended in the first place. You back on job?"

"Not yet," Ross tried to sidestep. "Working out some details."

"You decide to chuck it and take early retirement, see me. I got a few gigs going. TV series. A new security firm."

"I might do that. Thanks."

"I'll leave you to your dinner. Nice meeting you Willi. Willi . . . ," he said as he turned. "Didn't you once put away a Willy, Red?" he asked with a grin. Ross groaned.

"What did he mean about suspension – and you being cleared?" Willi asked, concerned.

"It's yesterday's news, Willi. Not dinner conversation. So, where's our pasta?" He looked around for the kid who was waiting on their table. "Excuse me for a minute, will you?"

Ross went to the small bathroom. I should have known better then to bring her to a place where I'm known, he thought, embarrassed by Donny's revelation. He washed his face with cold water, then returned to their table. The pasta had been served. "You get results, I see," he tried to joke.

"It's delicious," she acknowledged. "Now will you tell me what your bearded friend was referring to?"

"I don't want to talk about it, okay?"

"I want to know, Red. Don't hide from me, if we're to be," she paused, "friends."

"And what if you don't like what you hear?"

"That's a chance that we both take." She leveled her gaze at him and the deep blue washed over him.

Ross shook his head reluctantly, refilled both of their wine glasses. "It was a little over three months ago. I was off-duty, driving through Astoria. That's a neighborhood in Queens, where I live. I passed by as a Korean shopkeeper staggered out of his store. He'd been robbed and beaten. He was a bloody pulp. The perpetrator was fleeing down the block. A teen-age kid. The shopkeeper pointed after him before collapsing. I shouted a warning. The kid kept going, then turned suddenly. It looked to me like he had a weapon. I fired. I didn't kill him, but I crippled him for life."

"Was he guilty of the crime?"

"Unquestionably." Ross nodded emphatically.

"Then you were only doing your job."

"You have to know the political terrain. Black kid. White cop. He had no gun – just the metal pipe he used to beat up on the storekeeper. And I sentenced him to life – in a wheel chair."

"What did they accuse you of?"

"Excessive force."

"But he committed the crime, not you," she insisted.

"That's what the Review Board and the Grand Jury finally decided. A lot of people still don't agree."

"That's nonsense. You're innocent . . . " Now she sounded indignant.

"Thanks. Only one more person to convince."

"Who is that?" she asked, confused.

"Me . . . "

"I've never met a man like you, Red Cortese."

He wanted to believe her, but a small voice warned, maybe she never met a man with two pieces of furniture her father would kill to own.

Fortuitously, at that moment, their main course arrived. They ate and drank, and, protected by the food and wine, slowly revealed more about themselves. Willi's business had grown rapidly and she was experiencing problems managing its success. "I like to be in control of design and production and it's gotten out of hand. I'm told that I have a problem delegating authority. I'm like Father in that regard."

"Who sells your line in New York?"

"Are you planning to buy something?"

"You never know."

"Macy's. Saks. I'm angling for Bloomingdales."

"Bloomies. Then you'll know you've arrived." He toasted her with his glass.

She laughed, and the sound of it delighted him. Ross was so engrossed in their conversation that he hadn't seen the waiter clear their plates and deposit their dessert. He took a forkful of cheesecake and fed it to her. She said, "Mmm." A distant look came into her eyes.

"Where did you go?" he asked.

"Nowhere." She stroked his hand. "I find I'm very drawn to you, Red."

"It's more than mutual," he said and signaled for the check.

In the car, she moved close to him. He felt the heat of her thigh. He felt doubly intoxicated by her body. She was more dangerous to his driving than drink. He drove cautiously through Harlem, down Fifth Avenue and over to Madison and Seventy-sixth where they double-parked outside the Carlyle. She took the initiative and leaned toward him. They exchanged passionate, open-mouthed kisses.

"How long are you going to be in New York?" he asked, as they paused to catch a breath. He had just found her and was already afraid of losing her.

She answered with another kiss, her tongue thrust deep in his mouth. He moaned and there was no mistaking his excitement. As he began to heat up further, Willi called a halt, pleading an early appointment at Macy's.

"When will I see you again?" he asked, feeling disappointed.

"Is tomorrow soon enough? . . . I'll call when my meeting is over."

"You've got my number." Does she ever, he thought.

She kissed him once more. He watched as she went into the Carlyle, then drove off to Queens and his lonely bed.

Willi went up to her room. Still aroused from the contact with Ross, she was wide-awake and restless. She wondered what it would be like to make love to him. It was one-thirty when she got into bed – early morning in Vienna – a perfect time to call her father. He'd be on his treadmill, exercising and watching the news.

Hanfnagel answered on the speakerphone, puffing a bit. "Liebchen. You're up quite late."

"I just returned from dinner with Herr Cortese."

"Good. Good. How are the negotiations proceeding?"

"Dolph gave you my message?"

"He mentioned that you called."

"There's something of a problem."

"What was that you said?" Part of their conversation had broken up.

"I said there's something of a problem."

"What is it?"

"He's reluctant to part with the furniture. It really has been in his family for more than fifty years. He was extremely offended by Fredericks' suspicions."

"In the family, you say?"

"His father was apprenticed to Mosel as a young man. He purchased the pieces from him."

"I don't believe it. Not for a minute," Hanfnagel scoffed.

"I do, father. Cortese seems a decent and honorable man."

"You always were naive, liebchen. Nonetheless, ask Fredericks to call Cortese with an apology . . . if you think that will help."

"It won't hurt."

"Have you made an offer?"

"The timing didn't seem right."

"Do so, liebchen. Money talks. Offer one hundred thousand dollars. Tell Herr Cortese that I'll cover Fredericks' commission on the sale at both ends. He need not have any further dealings with him."

"That's wise, Father."

"Close the deal, Willi. If you must, offer him tickets to Vienna. A stay at the finest hotel. I want the furniture here by next week. So . . . go to sleep now, liebchen, and dream sweet dreams."

CHAPTER NINE

The Prater, Vienna's enormous natural park, often served Victor Neureth as a rendezvous site. Today was no exception. At lunch hour, the park was crowded and lively, good cover for a meeting. Sniffing the fragrant early summer bloom, Victor enjoyed his stroll across the park. He paused now and then to scatter birdseed. A bluejay landed boldly on his outstretched hand and fed from his palm. "Eat your breakfast, my noisy one," he said softly. Looking up, he saw Dolph approaching from the opposite direction.

"If it isn't St. Francis," the younger man said with a smile.

Victor shooed the bird off and shook his friend's hand. Then, he led him in the direction of the Punch and Judy show, where their discussion would be screened by the shouts and laughter of children.

"You seem in exceptional spirits." he said.

"I spent the evening with Hugo Vilmers," Dolph replied.

"Should I know him?"

"He's an old friend, dating back to university. I'm bringing him onto the board."

"We usually discuss such matters and make decisions jointly," Victor said, making no effort to disguise the annoyance in his tone.

"I assure you, there's no such need. Hugo is a genius. A computer programmer. He informed me that within the next year or two, there will be an explosive growth in what he calls the information superhighway. People the world over will be connected through their computers, in an electronic web. Through Vilmers, we will have access to them – and them to us. Think of it, tens of millions of individuals. We won't need tanks to conquer this highway."

Dolph grew more impassioned as he spoke. "We will make known the truth about the international conspiracy of Jewish bankers, Wall Street financiers, Marxists and America's foreign policy establishment – and the truth will swell our ranks with like-minded men and women. Aryan patriots in Europe and America."

"I've never seen you so excited," Victor remarked.

"You've never seen me on the verge of acquiring a weapon of such immense power."

The man looks like a clod, Victor thought, but he brings his father's brains and a ferocious will to the bargain. "This Vilmers shares our beliefs?"

"He's not political. A technician. A genius, to be sure, but still a technician. All that interests him is the tool – and the finances to support his research."

"That's readily provided." Victor nodded. "There's news for you as well. The mail will be ready for delivery in forty-eight hours – and my planning with Doschenko for the follow-up operation is nearly completed."

"Excellent. When does it take place?"

"Within ten days. Will you call a meeting of the Board?"

"We are the Board, dear Victor." They shared a laugh, bid each other good-bye and went off to their respective offices.

When the phone rang around noon, Ross rushed to it. He was disappointed to find a contrite Fredericks on the other end. Fredericks did not want his unintended offense to interfere with Mr. Hanfnegel's sincere interest in acquiring the furniture. Ross cut through the profuse apologies. "In other words," Ross rubbed it in, "you're afraid you queered the deal." Fredericks ate his words again. Ross let the dealer twist in the wind, in no mood to give him satisfaction.

By twelve-thirty, there was still no word from Willi. Fuck it, he thought. He threw on a worn department T-shirt and running shorts, dug out his Nikes and prepared to go jogging, for the first time in many months. Her call came just as he was going out the door.

"I thought I'd be finished earlier," she said, "but the buyer here at Macy's insisted on lunch. I'm stuck."

"I heard from Fredericks," he informed her.

"Good."

"I liked him better when he was being a snot."

"You're wicked," she teased. "Meet me at the Carlyle at four. I'm sure we'll find something to do," she added seductively.

"I'll be there."

At three thirty, he drove into Manhattan. He found a space reserved for diplomats and slipped his police identification onto the visor. With the shit the department had given him, the least they could do was let him park illegally. He gave the desk clerk his name, his mouth suddenly dry with anticipation. "Ms. Hanfnagel is expecting you, sir. Room 1412."

Willi greeted him with a friendly kiss and offered him a choice of drinks from the minibar. "Or we can have champagne . . . "

"Champagne's fine," he responded. She popped the cork on a half-bottle and poured a glass for him. They clicked glasses. "Do you feel better about Fredericks now?" she asked.

"He'll never make my A-list. Who put him up to the call?"

"I called Father. He agreed to set Fredericks straight."

You didn't waste any time reporting in, Ross thought to himself.

"What else did your father say?"

She studied him. Perhaps her father had been right and Ross was like any businessman with a valuable asset, playing the game. He was difficult to figure out. "Father asked me to make an offer on the furniture. He believes that you'll be in a better position to make your decision with a proposal in hand."

Money talks, Ross thought. Before he had a chance to reply, she said, "Our offer is one hundred thousand dollars net. No commissions to be paid by you."

There it was. Cold cash. More money than he ever dreamed of having. Enough for Amy's tuition – and some left over. He decided to give her an inch and see if she went for a yard.

"Tell him that I'll think it over."

He didn't need a magnifying glass to read her expression of pleasure. She moved up to him, offering champagne from her glass, the signal clear. He sipped the drink, then kissed her on the lips, lightly at first. She responded passionately and he abandoned himself to it, his heart pounding. Willi guided him to the sofa. They sat very close and drank champagne. He kissed her again, then traced the line of her face with his finger. "You're beautiful, you know . . . absolutely beautiful," he whispered thickly.

"Thank you," she said, looking down with a hint of shyness.

She was a piece of work, Ross thought, coming on with him one minute, responding to a compliment like a schoolgirl the next. He let his desire lead him, kissing her eyelids, lips and neck. He caressed her breasts through the light cotton blouse she wore and felt her nipples stiffen. She drew him close and returned his kisses, her lips hot and moist. Ross licked them, sending a shiver of excitement through her. She was aware of the wetness between her thighs and a sensation of great urgency.

"I want you, Red. Do you want me?"

Wasn't the answer obvious, he asked himself. "More than anything."

His words removed the last barrier of her reserve. "It's been so long since I felt this way," she said. She kissed him ardently one more time, then stood and began to undress. Her body was magnificent. Completely naked, she raced for the bathroom, smiling back at him over her shoulder, tempting him to follow. He stripped off his clothes and pursued her, fully erect. Willi opened the door to the spacious stall shower, stepped in and turned on the water, hot and forceful. He followed her into the steamy cabinet, her firm, white flesh already pink from the heat. She was a mouth-watering fruit, waiting to be eaten by a starved man. Ross reached out for her, not knowing where to plant his mouth first – on her lips, her full breasts, her neck. He ran his hands over her, marveling at the texture of her skin.

She reached down and played her fingers on the crown of his cock, then knelt to take him in her mouth. He lifted her away from him, wanting to prolong the pleasure, afraid that he'd come instantly, "Slow," he said. "Let's go slow." She nodded. But there was no way that they could go slow enough. When she soaped his cock, stroking it several times, he came so explosively, his knees buckled. He tried to apologize but she put her finger over his mouth, shushing him. They playfully washed the soap off each other and stepped out of the shower. By that time, his erection was starting to build again. As they dried each other with the large bath towels, the phone rang. Willi reached over and picked up the bathroom extension. Her father was on the line, his first word, "Liebchen?"

She felt embarrassed. She saw Ross looking at her and, composing herself, switched into German.

"*Ein moment, bitte*," she said to him. She covered the mouthpiece with her hand and said "Excuse me, Red, I'll take this in the other room." She took a terry-cloth robe from the hook, threw it over her shoulders and went into the living room, leaving the bathroom door ajar. Ross heard her whispering in German.

A glass of champagne and a roll in the hay, he thought angrily. When you've got me by the balls, spring the contract and close the deal. Ross grabbed his clothes and went back into the bathroom. Willi was still talking to her father when he came out.

She looked over at him and was surprised to find that he had dressed. Panicked, she ended the phone conversation abruptly, rose and made a move toward him. Ross raised his hand like a traffic cop. She stopped. Her robe was open, revealing her beautiful breasts, flat belly and exquisite thighs. He wanted to make love to her, but not this way. He thought of the line, a stiff prick has no conscience.

"What's wrong? Why are you dressed?" she asked.

"Your father speaks English, doesn't he?"

"Yes . . . but . . . "

"But nothing. He wants the furniture. You want to deliver it."

"Don't you see that my feelings for you have nothing to do with the furniture?"

"No, I don't. Maybe you can keep the two separate, but obviously I can't. I'll make my decision and we'll see where that leaves us."

He recognized her disappointment but said nothing to ameliorate it.

"I'll be in New York for a few more days," she said.

"I have a few things to check out. I'll call you," he replied.

She became alarmed. Would he use her father's offer to secure a better price? She could not chance that happening.

"What sort of things?" she asked.

"Things," he said.

"If it's the price, my father . . . "

Ross cut her short. "It's *not* the price. Let's just leave it at that, Willi." He picked up his bag and went to the door. She followed him.

"I'll speak to you." he said.

She closed the door, her eyes welling up, feeling as if she had failed on every front.

CHAPTER TEN

Ross turned onto his side. The illuminated clock face read five A.M. He shut his eyes, trying to sleep. After tossing and turning for two more hours, he forced himself out of bed. His whole body ached. A hot bath might help. While the tub was filling, he stood at the sink, staring at himself in the mirror, trying to sort out last night's fiasco. He could have had her, but he blew it. Why had he made such an issue over the phone call when they were a moment away from her bed?

He climbed into the bath. The hot water eased the aches in his muscles, but did nothing to lessen his mental pain. He was shaving when the phone rang.

"Red?" Willi's voice was distant and thin. There was static on the line.

"I'm glad you called," he said. "I was going to call you. To apologize for last night . . . Willi? You there?"

"Yes."

"Are you on a cellular?"

"Yes. I received a message this morning from Vienna. There's a serious problem in the production of my new line. I'm on my way to JFK. I take a morning flight to London and connect from there to Vienna . . . "

"You said you'd be here for three or four days. Is it really an emergency . . . or did I blow it permanently last night?"

"Believe me, Red. I have no choice. My foreman can't handle the problem."

Good-bye and have a good life, he thought morosely.

"Red? Are you there?"

"I'm here – but you're not."

"It doesn't have to be that way. Come to Vienna."

"Just like that? You know my circumstances."

"Father had a splendid idea. He'll provide you with a prepaid ticket – and arrange hotel accommodations. It won't cost you a cent. He's convinced that when you visit his home, see his collection and learn of his plans for the furniture, you'll be persuaded to sell. He also said that he's prepared to negotiate further on the price," she added.

"I don't think so," Ross said wearily.

"It's an opportunity, Red. For us to be together for a week." She hesitated. "I was hoping that last night would turn out differently," She added softly.

"So was I," he sighed.

"Then come. We'll have a wonderful time . . . I'm at the terminal now, Red. I must go in. Say you'll come. . . " she pleaded.

The connection was broken before he could reply. One way or another, he thought wryly, they couldn't seem to finish things off.

As he shaved, he thought about the offer. A visit to Vienna wasn't such a bad idea. He needed a change of scenery . . . and he had time to kill. And it could provide him with an opportunity to find out more about Pop's connection to Mosel.

Ross dressed quickly and called his folks.

"Rosso!" Momma answered, surprised and pleased to hear his voice. "How are you?"

"I'm okay. I want to come over, Momma . . . if it's a good time for you and Pop."

"It's always good when you come."

"I should be there in an hour. No fussing, please."

He made it to Brooklyn and the Cortese house in near record time. After the obligatory hugs, Ross settled into a well-worn easy chair in the living room.

"Joy tells me you're not feeling good, Pop. Something about chest pain."

"Your sister, God bless her." Pop shook his head. "Indigestion is all."

Momma intervened. "Your Poppa goes to the doctor with me yesterday. The doctor . . . he says to take it easy. Take time from work."

"Gina, I take it easy when I'm in the ground. What does this doctor know anyway? This new one, Rosso? He's not much older than your Billy. I already outlived Doc Lorenzo."

"That wasn't hard, Pop. Doc smoked three packs a day and drank like a fish."

"Your Poppa had this heart test."

"A cardiogram, Momma?" Ross asked anxiously.

"A piece of paper," Pop insisted. "I know how I feel."

"Talking to you, Pop, is like talking to a brick wall."

"And you, Rosso. You're a chip off the same brick."

"Sure, Pop." Ross drew back from any confrontation.

Pop appeared to grow more confident. "What's new with you, Rosso? Any word on the job?" his father asked.

"Not much doing, Pop. I'm still trying to get things worked out. You know . . . " He felt uneasy. "I'm going away for a week."

"That's good, Rosso. You need a vacation. Where you going? Florida? Maybe I take a week off . . . you and me . . . we'll go together. Fishing. Like when you was a kid. Remember?"

Ross could never forget. It had been the high point of his young life. What was he then, thirteen? He and Pop had gone down to the Keys and deep-sea fished in the Gulf. He had felt very close to his father then.

"I'm going to Vienna, Pop," Ross said.

There was dead silence. It felt as if all the air had been sucked out of the room and in the vacuum, each held onto what he had, afraid to inhale or exhale, as if the move could be fatal. Pop's facial muscles twitched and when he spoke, it was with effort, in a voice made distant by anger.

"If you gotta sell the furniture, you sell it here. They got plenty of places."

"I'll go upstairs," Momma said, standing abruptly. Ross saw that she wanted to flee from the dreadful tension in the room.

"Sit, Gina!" Pop thundered. Neither she nor Ross had ever heard him speak to her that way. She remained, but did not sit. What was happening to his family? Ross thought guiltily.

"Look, Pop. This collector has offered to pay for me to go to Vienna, meet with him and see his collection. It's free – why not go?" His tone was pacifying.

"You stay away from there." Pop shook his finger at him. "You don't know what a rotten place it is."

"That was a long time ago, Pop. Things have changed. I'm not looking to fight a war."

"We'll go to Florida, you and me," Pop beseeched. "We go out, deep-sea fishing. Salt air. It's what the doctor ordered. For both of us. We make your Momma happy."

Pop was playing all of the guilt cards: his health, Momma's happiness. "I'd like that, Pop. But not now . . . another time, okay?"

Before the words were out, Pop leaped to his feet. "It's not okay. You always was a stubborn kid." Suddenly livid, he shouted, "You listen to me, Rosso. You don't go! You hear me? Your father's telling you, you don't go!"

"This is crazy!" It was Ross's turn to explode. "You talk to me like I'm a kid. Tell me the truth, is the furniture mine?" he demanded.

Pop nodded weakly.

"Then if I want to sell it, it's mine to sell. I don't know what the hell is going on with you, but I don't like it. If you've got something to tell, now's the time."

"Nothing to tell," Pop whispered, his voice cracking.

Momma rushed to intervene. "Stop this, Rosso. You're upsetting your Poppa too much."

For the first time in memory, his anger was directed at her. "How many times have I heard that, Momma? My whole life, every time I try to get something straight with this guy, you always say, be careful, you're upsetting Poppa. The hell with it. I'm going. I'm a grown man. I don't need your approval."

With that, Ross stormed from the house, hearing Pop's voice, even after he had closed the door, this time beseeching, "Trust your Poppa, Rosso. Don't go back there. Please, *figlio mio.*"

Gina Cortese held Franco in her arms, rocking him like a child. He looked at her through his tears and said, "What's going to happen, Gina?" She said nothing, just tightened her hold on him. The moment she had feared for what seemed like a lifetime had arrived – and she felt helpless to cope with it.

CHAPTER ELEVEN

The next morning, a messenger arrived at Ross's door with a packet from a Manhattan travel agent. It contained an open, first-class ticket to Vienna on Austrian Airlines. He hadn't even called to tell Willi that he'd come. *They want my furniture real bad.* No matter. The decision was made. Ross called the airline and arranged a reservation for the following evening. Willi's office and home numbers had been enclosed with the tickets. He left a message on her voice mail announcing the time of his arrival.

He spoke to his kids and his sisters, but by the time he reached Kelsey, he was having second thoughts. It took his partner only a minute to pick up on them.

"Free tickets? All expenses paid? Sounds good to me."

"They want to put the arm on me for the furniture. You know these collector types."

"Tell me about it. We spent two years nailing Teedmen. Wasn't enough to leave his Mrs. for his bimbo secretary. That would've cost him part of his art collection. Miserable bastard had to hire a hit. I hope he's collecting body lice and hemorrhoids in Attica. But this deal? What've you got to lose? The lady's willing . . . "

"I said I'm going."

"I'd like to hear a little enthusiasm."

"Ah . . . it's Pop. He busted a gut when I told him I was going."

"What's the old man got against a free ticket and a shot at a hundred thousand bucks?"

"Damned if I know."

"In the old days, you caught a whiff of marrow, you were a hungry mutt, looking for a bone."

"They paid me to do that. This is my old man's dirty laundry."

"Come on, Red. Pop's the best. I've known Franco what? Twenty-five years?"

"It feels bad, Kels. He's closed up like a clam."

"Everybody's got secrets. Anyway, I'm your car service to JFK. What time's the pickup?"

It was late evening in Vienna when Willi picked up Ross's message accepting her offer. She informed her father immediately. Hanfnagel was gratified. "You've done well, liebchen. We must plan a reception for Herr Cortese. Do you think he would enjoy the opera?"

"I know for a fact that he does."

"Good. Confirm our box for his first evening and I'll invite Dolph's family and a few friends. The usual . . . "

"I'll arrange it with the caterer."

"What would I do without you, liebchen?"

First thing in the morning, Hanfnagel placed a call to Victor Neurath at home. "Good morning, Vicky. Are you free for breakfast?"

"I'm meeting Dolph at Demel's. Nine-thirty . . . why not join us?"

"I've got a meeting at ten. Can you meet me earlier?"

"Of course. Will nine do?"

"Yes. Nine – at Demel's."

A proud Erich Hanfnagel strode briskly down Himmelpfortgasse, paused to examine a Jugendstil vase in the window of an antique shop and quickly dismissed it as second-rate. He arrived at the illustrious café on Kohlmarkt at two minutes before the hour, where he was greeted with a bow by a formally attired headwaiter. "Gruss Gott, Herr Doktor Hanfnagel," the man said, accompanying him across the marble floor of the gilded, rococo dining room to a private table in the rear.

Hanfnagel was pleased to find that Victor Neurath had arrived early. Though the custom in the two-hundred-year-old café was for clients to make their selections from a huge buffet, take a number and be seated, Hanfnagel and Neurath were treated as exceptions. A waitress in a modest black dress approached and asked for their order. Hanfnagel requested black coffee and handsemmeln, while Neurath chose a torte with his juice and coffee.

"Tell me, Erich . . . to what do I owe the pleasure of this meeting?" Neurath inquired.

"The man I asked you to inquire about . . . what have you turned up on him?" Hanfnagel's tone left no doubt – this was a business meeting, pure and simple.

"His dossier was placed on my desk last night. A decorated police officer, he holds the rank of sergeant, serving in the Major Crimes

Division in the borough of Queens. Not very ambitious, but highly regarded."

"No dirt?"

"He was recently reinstated after suspension – the initial charge, use of excessive force."

"See what else you can find, should I need leverage."

"My men are combing the old files to see if there is anything on Cortese's father. It will take a while."

"I can't tell you how excited I am at the prospect of obtaining the furniture."

"No need to, Erich. I was there at the start, remember?"

"How can I forget?" They sipped their coffee, lost in memories of the past. Then, business completed, Hanfnagel became almost friendly. "Vicky, are you free to join us tomorrow evening for a late supper?"

"Indeed I am. What is the occasion?"

"I've invited Cortese to Vienna. A small party in his honor."

Neurath smiled knowingly. "I look forward to meeting this Herr Cortese."

They made small talk while finishing breakfast. Hanfnagel checked his watch, stood abruptly and said, "You'll excuse me. 'Til tomorrow. Auf wiedersehn."

He stopped at the cashier and settled the bill. When he stepped outside, he nearly bumped into his son.

"Good morning, Father," a flustered Dolph said weakly.

"Good morning, Dolph. Forgive me, but I must run. I will see you later – at the office"

"What was that about?" Dolph inquired when he joined Victor at the table.

"Your father's obsession with furniture. It appears . . . "

"Yes, I know," Dolph said impatiently. "Two pieces turned up in New York and father sent his fair-haired girl to get them."

"There's more. Your father invited this Cortese to Vienna."

"Anything I should know?"

"The cop crippled some scum, then was accused of brutality."

"I don't think much of spaghetti-eaters. Mussolini was the best of them, I suppose – and still a clown. But we could use more friends in New York. Perhaps we'll get value for Father's money beyond a few sticks of wood."

"Don't let Erich hear you say that about his collection," Victor cautioned.

"I'll decide what I say to my father," Dolph snapped. "Save the advice." He paused, recovered his demeanor and asked softly, "Are we on schedule?"

"Doschenko assures me that the letters are prepared and will be delivered tomorrow morning."

"You're sure?" Dolph asked, still tightly wound.

"I'm certain."

Now Dolph smiled broadly. "Excellent, Victor. In celebration . . . " He reached into his breast pocket and removed a large cigar case. "Join me in a Cohiba. Castro is a swine, but he does smoke only the very best."

Sitting in the first class lounge of Austrian Airlines, nursing a large Scotch, Ross made the call that he had put off until the last possible minute.

"I'm calling from the airport, Momma."

"Si," she sighed. "Your sister told us you're going."

"Where's Pop?"

"He's sleeping now." As if reading his mind, she continued. "You don't need to worry. Your father's strong."

"Look, Momma. I know there's something that Pop's not telling me. I love the two of you. You tell me, Momma. Tell me before I go."

She was crying, softly.

"It's not for me to say, Rosso. It's between you and your Poppa. You do what you got to do. You go well and come back well. That's all we ever want."

Just then a voice over the loudspeaker announced that first and business class passengers were being boarded. "Sorry, Momma, I gotta go," Ross said. "I'll call as soon as I'm back." He picked up his carry-on and followed the flight attendant through final check-in and onto the aircraft. It turned out that he was the only passenger flying in first class. An attractive stewardess plied him with Dom Perignon, caviar and pleasant chatter. When Ross revealed that he was a cop, she inquired if he was traveling on official business.

"Why?" he joked, already high on champagne. "Someone there you want me to bust?"

"There are a few . . . "

They shared a laugh. After dinner, he settled back and was soon asleep.

CHAPTER TWELVE

The offices of Rights for Refugees was located on a quiet, tidy residential street not far from the Palais Liechtenstein. Frank Kreisler, an energetic man of twenty-eight, recently reappointed to a second two-year term as Executive Director, was deeply committed to his work as a human rights advocate. An early riser, he arrived to work promptly at eight A.M. He liked to look through his mail before his secretary arrived at nine. Today, he planned to rewrite the speech he was to deliver at a major fund-raiser. He had reviewed the previous draft with his wife over dinner and, as usual, benefited from her cogent arguments. Magda insisted that he make more emphatic the parallel between the horrific consequences of the scapegoating of Jews in nineteenth and twentieth century Austria, and the present attitudes and actions against immigrants from the East.

He unlocked the door, picked up his mail and carried it inside. The aroma of freshly brewed coffee greeted him as usual. God bless the automatic coffeemaker, he thought, pouring himself the first of many cups to come. It makes life easier for us addicts.

Seated at his desk he sorted the mail, setting aside the second class and selecting those items which might need his immediate attention. He found a bulky envelope mailed from Hungary, the return address unknown to him. As he slit it open, there was a flash, then a loud bang and the envelope exploded in his face. He screamed in pain. He tried to lift the telephone, but it dropped from his hand as everything went black.

Within an hour, Ernest Mahler, director of Doctors for Humanity, Maxine Trieb, a secretary to Councilwoman Gertrude Lange, President of the City Council and Arthur Mannes, Deputy Commissioner for Social Services, were all victims of similar letter bombs. Doctor Mahler, critically injured, was rushed to a surgical trauma unit where a team of eight physicians fought to keep him alive. Word of the events spread throughout Vienna like an out-of-control fire. Sirens and alarms could be heard throughout the city as anxious recipients of the morning mail, alerted by warnings issued by local authorities on radio and television, swamped the communications center of police headquarters with hundreds of calls. While the vast majority of the calls proved to be false alarms, six unexploded letter bombs were discovered and removed for examination by the Bomb Squad.

Scores of protesters from the left and right of the political spectrum materialized in front of City Hall, shouting blame at one another for the current state of affairs in Austria. Serious altercations broke out, with two beatings and a knifing taking place before the riot squad could intervene.

Those with long memories shuddered, painfully reminded of Vienna's deadly violence in the thirties. Many tried to reassure themselves that it could never happen again. A significant minority wished that it would – while a powerful cabal worked to ensure that it did.

CHAPTER THIRTEEN

The line for Customs and Immigration at Schwechat airport moved very slowly. Ross noticed the unusually extensive deployment of both police and plainclothes officers. Those in uniform were heavily armed. He wondered if there was a terrorist threat against the airport or an airline. When his turn came, he presented his passport and landing card which requested visitor's name, occupation and purpose of visit. Ross had filled in Law Enforcement as his occupation. The officer typed his name into the computer and compared person to passport picture.

"You are police?" he asked Ross.

"Yes."

"Official business?"

"Vacation."

"Are you carrying a weapon, Meinherr?"

"No. What's going on here?"

"Welcome to Austria, Herr Cortese. I hope your stay is pleasant." So much for professional courtesy, thought Ross.

Retrieving his baggage from the carousel, he walked briskly through the "Nothing to Declare" line into a spacious, spotlessly clean terminal. A large, noisy multi-ethnic crowd waited to greet relatives and friends, much like at JFK. He scanned the terminal, but saw no sign of Willi. Great, he thought. I traveled three thousand miles to get stood up. A group of drivers stood off to the left holding up cards bearing names. A woman rushed up and joined them, waving her placard. Scribbled on it in large letters was HERR CORTESE.

"I'm Ross Cortese," he shouted, trying to get her attention amidst the hustle bustle.

She spotted him and hurried over. "Meinherr," she said politely, "I apologize for my lateness. Fraulein Hanfnagel had planned to meet you herself but for an unexpected complication."

"Is she alright?" Ross asked, concerned.

Ignoring his question, she continued, "She will join you at the hotel. Bitte . . . " she said, reaching for his luggage.

"It's okay. I'll carry it." Ross picked up the suitcase and carry-on.

She shrugged. "Follow me, bitte."

She led him out of the terminal and into the parking lot. A military truck pulled in, disgorging a dozen or so troops in combat gear. Ross commented on the security at the airport. "It is not usually like this," she replied, offering no further explanation. Moving past four lines of perfectly parked cars, she stopped next to a large Mercedes sedan and opened the rear door for him. Ross said, "I'll sit up front, if you don't mind."

"Not at all."

Ross let himself in on the passenger side, settled into the plush leather seat and adjusted his safety belt.

"How far into Vienna?" he asked, as she started up the engine.

"Fifteen kilometers, Meinherr."

She pulled out smoothly, the motor almost silent. Nearing the approach to the autoroute, traffic slowed to a crawl.

Ross leaned forward. "What's causing the jam?" he asked. Before she could reply, he caught sight of a police roadblock up ahead. Officers were stopping cars and questioning the occupants. Their turn soon came.

His driver said, "Er ist ein American," and the officer waved them on. She drove up the ramp and quickly merged with the traffic on the expressway. "I regret that this is your introduction to Vienna, Herr Cortese."

"What's with all the police activity?" he asked.

She picked up speed and changed lanes before replying, "Until recently, Vienna has been a wonderful city in which to live. Now . . . " she shrugged.

"Now *what*?"

"This morning, a number of letter bombs exploded in Vienna. There were serious injuries."

"My God," Ross said, initially shocked, then concerned. "Are Willi and her family alright?"

"Of course, Meinherr. The bombs were directed at certain officials."

"What's going on? Who's responsible?"

"Who? No one has claimed responsibility. But I will tell you who is truly responsible," she exclaimed, her voice rising with indignation. "It is those vagrants from the East. They bring crime and drugs, take away jobs from our citizens – are given handouts from socialists in the government – housing, welfare . . . all paid for with our tax money."

She paused, out of steam, then resumed more soberly. "I worry for my city. We are in recession. I myself lost a job after ten years. Now, only my cousin's kindness – he owns the car service – provides me with an income." She stopped, afraid that she had overstepped her boundaries. "I talk too much – I'm sorry, Meinherr."

"That's alright," he reassured. "I'm interested."

"Would you like some music, Herr Cortese?" she asked, turning on the radio.

So much for the news of the day, Ross thought.

The outskirts of the city were nondescript: light manufacturing, warehouses and a few farms, residual evidence of an agricultural past. A few miles down the road, the driver pointed left and exclaimed, "Look there. You can see St. Stephan's!"

Ross turned and caught his first glimpse of the city. The spire of the Cathedral rose majestically, silhouetted against the sky above Vienna, a mix of morning sun and threatening clouds. "It is our pride and joy," she said. "For eight centuries there has been a St. Stephan's."

"I see you double as a tour guide," Ross said, encouragingly.

"True Viennese know and love the history of their city," she responded, pleased by the acknowledgment.

Soon, the route edged along a canal. "This waterway," she explained, "feeds into the Danube." Across the canal, Ross saw an enormous stretch of parkland. "The Prater," she announced. "Ten kilometers, end to end. On the other side is the Danube. You must take a stroll in the Prater. It is a Viennese tradition."

Over the treetops, Ross saw a giant ferris wheel slowly turning. Suddenly remembering, he blurted, "Orson Welles . . . THE THIRD MAN." She nodded confirmation.

They exited the expressway and in a few minutes were driving through twentieth century Vienna. Approaching the city's center, the buildings became more ornate and very impressive. The driver clicked off the names of palaces and ministries as they drove by. Traffic flowed onto the Ringstrasse, a wide, planted boulevard which, she explained, had been built by Emperor Franz Joseph in the nineteenth century to circle the heart of old Vienna.

"We're not far from the hotel," she announced. "The Royale is one of the grandest in Europe. You will like it. Heads of state stay there when they come to visit Vienna."

A few minutes later, she pulled up in front of a palatial nineteenth-century building. A liveried doorman greeted Ross with deference, removed his bag from the trunk and handed it to a porter. Ross reached for his wallet to settle with the driver, but she said, "That will not be necessary, Meinherr. Fraulein Hanfnagel has an account with us."

Ross thanked her and followed the porter into the beautifully appointed lobby. The formally attired head clerk greeted him warmly and announced that his suite was ready. "We hope that you will enjoy your stay in Vienna. Please, Herr Cortese, let us know if there is anything that we can do to make your visit more enjoyable. I will require your passport – just a mere formality. It will be returned to you within the hour."

The assistant manager accompanied him to his room. After checking that the room was satisfactory, he left and a moment later, a porter arrived with Ross's luggage, followed immediately by a bellman who presented him with a bottle of champagne and a bucket of ice, compliments of the hotel. *What's with the royal treatment,* he wondered. The suite faced out onto the wide avenue. The rain, which had threatened since the plane landed, finally came, a heavy, summer downpour, sweeping the streets clean of all but the hardiest pedestrians.

Ross went into the elegant marble bathroom and washed up, then turned on the television and settled back in a comfortable chair to wait for Willi. He found the channel for local news and though he didn't understand the language, the hellish pictures told the story – bombing victims carried on stretchers from blasted offices, violent clashes on the streets of the city. Except for the Middle-European architecture, the scenes could have been Belfast in Northern Ireland.

Victor and Doschenko shared a bench in the Volksgarten Park near the Theseus Temple. The Russian was a man in his forties, of average height and compact build. Both men wore dark business suits and ties. Doschenko's looks, while Slavic, were undistinguished, an appearance he cultivated. Each man read his newspaper and looked up from time to time as police, fire engine and ambulance sirens shattered the morning calm.

"Well done, Doschenko," Victor complimented.

"My pleasure, Comrade."

Victor winced at the former Soviet *apparatchik* referring to him as comrade. Politics did indeed make for strange bedfellows. "I want to review the next operation."

"The target's movements are established. He visits his mother at the nursing home Tuesday and Thursday afternoons at four. He remains for exactly one hour. The man is utterly predictable. There is a hole-in-the-wall tailor shop across from the nursing home, its proprietors an elderly man and his wife. Proper middle-class Viennese.

"We will take over the shop at three forty. My men will be masked, speak in a Slavic tongue and appear to be drug addicts. They will assault the owners and any customers who have the misfortune to be present. They will then tie up the victims and wreck the shop." He barely paused for a breath in his monotone recital of the upcoming action.

"At precisely four o'clock, the men will burst out of the shop, shooting down the Minister and his driver. It will appear as though the Minister and driver were in the wrong place at the wrong time."

"Superb," Victor responded enthusiastically. "The public will be terrified. No one will feel safe with a gang of murderous immigrants roaming the streets of Vienna."

"The Slav we've chosen as a set-up is a loner," Doschenko continued, "with a long history of drug abuse. We have him under twenty-four-hour surveillance. We'll pick him up the night before the action, hold him captive and pump him full of PCP. The murder weapon will be found in his hand when he is shot to death by an off-duty officer – one of your group within the department, arriving on the scene."

Victor nodded approvingly. "I've chosen the man, utterly reliable and committed to our cause. The headlines will read, '*Minister of Justice gunned down by immigrant addicts fleeing from robbery scene.*' The Minister is well liked. Public opinion will drown this government and its policy of open borders."

"The idea was yours, Comrade. Brilliant, if I may say so."

Victor nodded, folded his newspaper and left it on the bench before he stood and walked away. Doschenko picked it up. Inside was an envelope containing the equivalent in Austrian schillings of fifty-thousand dollars. He smiled to himself. The Soviet Union had fallen, but he was thriving. A man with his skills would always find a place in the scheme of things.

Abe Feder came around Borseplatz, nearly knocking down an old woman in his haste to reach the Center for Holocaust Research.

He ran past the startled guard and up the stairs, shouting as he fumbled with his key in the lock, "Avia! Don't touch the mail." Before he could turn the key, she opened the door. The sight of her quelled his adrenaline surge, but he was left thoroughly drained. "I need to sit down," he sighed.

"You look terrible."

"You heard the news?" he asked. She nodded, pointing to the radio.

"What did you do with the morning mail?" He felt his anxiety mount again.

"It's there," she said calmly.

He looked over at the desk. The mail had been opened.

"My God . . . You could've been . . . "

"I examined each piece with great care," she interrupted.

"Still . . . it was foolish to take such a risk."

"Call me a shlemazel," she shrugged, "but I don't think it was a risk. This operation was directed at key supporters of open immigration – not Jews. Not this time."

"Don't be so sure. The morning isn't over – and there are afternoon deliveries as well."

"Alright, Abe, alright. I get the message. It's to be especially careful, right?" She was very fond of her associate, but at times he was a 'nudnik.'

Abe sat down, lit a cigarette and inhaled deeply.

"You worry about me?" Avia mocked gently. "Look at you, smoking those coffin nails."

He raised his hands in surrender, but continued to puff away.

"*The Free Press* called for an interview on the bombings," she went on. "I referred them to you. I don't want my picture in the paper. Not now."

"You're determined to go ahead with the meeting?" he asked.

"What choice do I have?" Avia responded. "If this kid is prepared to play turncoat, who knows? He could lead us to those who are pulling the strings."

"We already have a notion of who that is."

"A notion is one thing, Abe. We need proof."

"They may have gone too far this time."

"For someone trained in science, you can still be a wishful thinker. This will surely gain them recruits."

She was one tough-minded girl, Abe realized. "You're right, Avia," he acknowledged sadly. "And as for the authorities, we know what to expect. Nothing!" He was resigned to the fact that she knew the risk of trying to recruit a neo-Nazi defector. Whatever he said, she would do what she wanted. Maybe, just maybe she could nail the bastards. Or was that more wishful thinking?

CHAPTER FOURTEEN

Ross had been waiting for nearly two hours. He was amusing himself, watching an old Lucy and Desi sitcom dubbed in German, when he heard a knock at the door. He opened it and there stood Willi with a big smile on her face. Her glorious blue eyes sparkled as she came into his arms. They kissed like long-lost lovers, the passionate undercurrent surprising both of them. He drew her inside and closed the door.

"I'm so happy that you're here," she said, her voice husky with emotion.

"So am I," he said.

"Are you comfortable? Do you like the room?"

"Now that you're here, I love everything."

"And the hotel?" she smiled.

"Very ritzy – but a bit overdone. That chandelier in the lobby looks like it belongs in an Opera House. I hope the hotel doesn't have a phantom."

She laughed with delight and walked around the room, appraising it with a smile and slight nod of approval.

"I missed you at the airport," he said. "I thought for a minute that you had stood me up."

"No," she replied, a grimace replacing her smile. "I went with my father to the hospital."

"What happened?"

"Something absolutely dreadful. A colleague of Father's was injured by a letter bomb."

"The driver told me about that. Was it someone close to you?"

"Yes. I know Dr. Mahler and his family very well. Father serves with him on the Board of the Opera."

"How badly was he injured?"

"Quite badly. The bomb tore out his throat. Blinded him in one eye. He's still in surgery."

"Do they know who's behind it?"

"The lunatic fringe. I suppose every society has them."

"If they need an out-of-work detective who doesn't speak the language, I'm available."

"Don't even think it. You're here for play, not for work. Remember that!" she scolded.

"Yes, ma'am." He mock-saluted her.

Willi looked at him intently. "It's said that those who've loved well, seek love soon again," she said softly.

"I've heard that." He paused before asking pointedly, "What about those who've been disappointed?"

"We avoid involvement for a long time." She moved closer. "It's been a long time . . . . 'til now . . . "

She reached out and fiercely embraced him. The touch of her body triggered a hungry arousal deep within him. He felt himself growing rock hard. They kissed, licked, bit and tongued one another as his fingers fanned across her breasts, teasing her. Ross moved his lips down her neck and grazed the satin covering her taut nipples before kneeling and burying his face in her belly. Willi gasped and pushed his head down into the cleft of her thighs. His cock was pulsing so hard now that he wanted to tear off the skirt and penetrate her on the spot.

"Undress me," she demanded urgently, stroking him through his pants. He wanted to say "don't," fearing a repetition of their first encounter, but he stood and unbuttoned her blouse. God, how he wanted to be inside her – her mouth, her cunt – joined somewhere was all that mattered.

Willi slid her blouse off, revealing a flesh-tone bra that only accented her lovely nipples. Removing her bra, she stood for a moment cupping her breasts, offering them to Ross. He devoured them with his mouth and hands.

"Yes, yes my darling, oh, yes, liebchen." She arched her back with pleasure.

Ross couldn't wait any longer. He unzipped her skirt and it fell to the floor. Willi removed her panties and dropped to her knees as he began to undo his trousers. She kissed him on the crown of his cock, sucked him into her mouth and teased him with her tongue, lips and teeth. This was more than he thought he could bear. He had to have her before he exploded. Lifting her up, he carried her to the bed and took off the rest of his clothes.

"Come to me," she cried. "Please, Red, now . . . inside. . . Fuck me."

The words were fuel on the fire and he lifted himself over her, found her with the head of his cock and plunged into her heat. He closed his eyes and let the sheer pleasure of their union wash over him. She broke the stillness with a throaty moan of pleasure which drove him to a frenzy. He came into her and she came around him, spasming, taking him under her control, drawing him out of himself so that it felt as if his spirit had joined her on the wave of her orgasm. Emptied, throbbing, gasping for breath, they wrapped their arms around each other, needing the cocoon of their embrace to spin a tender web within which their needs could rise again.

When at last they lay silent, her hand across his groin, he dozed, aware of her endearments, whispered in German. Then she was there again, down on him. He felt her hair caress his thigh and lower abdomen. He took a pillow and moved it under his head, encouraging her to straddle him. She was an incredible lover. He told her so. She laughed, leaned over and kissed him with a full-lipped softness. He pulled her down and entered her.

They lay there, savoring the sensations. After awhile she stirred, then whispered, "Liebchen. It's getting late. We've got to get going."

"If you say so," he responded reluctantly.

She kissed him, got up and headed for the bathroom.

"I'm going to shower," she tossed back. "Join me?"

"I thought you didn't have the time."

Apparently she found it.

An hour later, they were getting dressed. Ross looked around the room and grinned at the disarray. Pillows tossed about, coverlet on the floor, tangled bed sheets. No wonder I'm so hungry, he thought. "Where are we going?" he called out.

"To my father."

"Do we have time for lunch?"

She came out and looked at her watch. "A quick bite in the hotel café. Will that do?"

Willi had a salad and Ross a sandwich and a beer. They said little, basking in the warm afterglow of sex. Twenty minutes later, they went outside and the doorman brought her car around. A shiny, pearl white BMW 733i. It cost more then he made in a year, he guessed, letting out a low whistle.

"For me or the car?" she asked.

"What do you think?"

"You men and your cars," she teased.

"You women and your insecurities," he teased back.

She pulled out of the driveway and around the block onto the Karntner Ring. As she drove, she pointed out the sights.

"On your right, the State Opera. We'll be going there tonight. Father's arranged a small party in your honor. There . . . " she continued, "the Hofburg Palace . . . and on your left, the Kunsthistorische Museum . . . Beyond it, the Natural History Museum, which contains one of my favorites. You must see The Venus of Willendorf . . . "

"I've already seen the Venus of Vienna . . . in all her glory."

She blushed. "The Venus of Willendorf dates from the Stone Age, proof that Austria was an important settlement – as far back as twenty thousand years ago."

"Not to change the subject, but I've been meaning to ask you. How did you get the name Willi? I thought it was Dutch."

"Father named me after a woman he believed had posed for a painting by Klimt. He saw it once, when he was very young. I think he fell in love with it."

"With it – or with *her*?"

Willi shrugged. "He wasn't sure of her identity but imagined that it might be a portrait of a Dutch artist who lived in Vienna at the turn of the century – Wilhelmina van Brugen. The woman in the portrait had long red hair and marvelous blue-green eyes. Later, when he had money, he apparently tried to buy it, but it had disappeared."

"Like the furniture," Ross murmured. Two concrete structures caught his eye. "What are those monstrosities, water towers?"

Her face tightened. "Flakturme. Flak towers. Built by the Nazis in an attempt to make Vienna a fortress . . . secure against the Russians who were attacking from the East."

"Why weren't they torn down after the war?"

"They are concrete walls, ten feet thick. It was decided that the dynamite needed to blast them apart would take surrounding buildings down . . . and so they stand, monuments to a world gone mad. The one to the left is used today as an aquarium."

"Where does your father live?"

"In the old city. Himmelpfortgasse. It's off Schubert Park Ring, near Beethovenplatz."

"Schubert and Beethoven. Strike up the band."

She turned off the Ring, down a side street and pulled into a parking space. Willi pointed to the building opposite them. Ross, following her direction, recognized it at once as the simple but elegant white modernist apartment house he had seen pictured in the book in Fredericks' office.

Mosel's building contrasted sharply with the others on the street, all of which were heavily ornamented with lions, cupids or floral motifs.

"Unusual, isn't it?" Willi observed.

"One of a kind," Ross agreed.

A bronze plaque was set into the wall alongside the elegant wrought iron gate. Inscribed on it was *1912*.

"You can't imagine the scandal buildings like this created in those days," Willi asserted. "Two years earlier, the architect Loos designed a building for a Jewish tailoring firm opposite the main entrance to the Imperial Palace. From that day forward, the emperor refused to leave by the front door."

"You Viennese take your architecture seriously, don't you?"

"Especially my father," she agreed, opening the gate and unlocking the heavy interior door.

"Are the lobby furnishings original?" Ross asked, studying the simple seating arrangement against the wall.

"Wiener Werkstatte. Hofmann and his associates."

Ross placed his hand on her arm, restraining her lightly. "Before we go upstairs . . . does your father know that there's something between us."

"It's not his affair."

They laughed at her double entendre and entered the birdcage. It came to a jarring halt on the fourth floor. Hanfnagel's was the only apartment on the landing. Stepping out of the elevator, they entered a spacious foyer. A gold mirror hung above a wide console topped with a black marble shelf. The forged iron base of the console was an unusual design. A matching umbrella stand and small chair completed the decor. Willi rang the bell. The door opened and Otto greeted them. "Wilkommen, Fraulein Willi und Meinherr."

"Guten tag, Otto," Willi replied.

The man struck Ross as an ugly piece of work – well over six feet, close to three hundred pounds. Ross's cop's nose told him that the guy had served time. What's someone like him doing working here, he wondered.

Otto led them through a grand foyer, lit by two magnificent ceiling fixtures. As they passed an exquisite commode, Ross slowed to stare at it. The piece reminded him of his furniture and made his brain snap back to the business at hand. Otto opened the double doors to the living room and announced them. Hanfnagel stood and waited for them to come to him. Here was a man accustomed to being courted, was Ross's first impression.

"My dear, Willi," he said in thickly-accented English. She approached him and he kissed her on each cheek. Only then did he turn and acknowledge Ross. "I'm pleased that you accepted my invitation, Herr Cortese. I regret that I could not meet you this morning. May I offer some coffee – or tea? Perhaps a sherry?

"Thanks. Coffee would be fine."

Hanfnagel signaled to Otto who was standing at attention just beyond the doorway. Otto nodded and left for the kitchen.

Ross studied his host. Hanfnagel was an inch or two taller than he was. Straight-backed, sharp-nosed and lean, Hanfnagel had an aristocratic air about him. He had to be over seventy but didn't look it. The manicured nails and full head of close-cropped silver hair revealed his precise attention to personal detail. His eyes were cool, clear and blue, without the clouding of cataracts, but his complexion was sallow, that of a man who passed his life under artificial light. Elegant in a maroon satin smoking jacket, Hanfnagel wore his white shirt open at the collar, presenting the knot of a blue silk paisley scarf, tied perfectly. No doubt about it, the man was impressive.

Ross took in the living room with a sweeping gaze. A large painting attracted and held his eye, a portrait of a young, blonde woman. It gripped him with its opulent sensuality, as if the painter had clothed her in threads of gold and bedecked her with real jewels.

"I see that you admire my Klimt, Herr Cortese. It is surely one of his finest. You're familiar with his work?"

"Can't say that I am."

"A pity. I had hoped that you might be." A look passed between Hanfnagel and his daughter. Ross saw it and felt uncomfortable. "Please sit down. We'll have coffee and then I'll tell you about my collection."

Willi and Ross sat on the sofa and Hanfnagel settled into a chair facing them. Otto poured them coffee from a silver pot inlaid with ivory bands, then set a matching tray with finger sandwiches and petit-fours on the cocktail table.

"Everything in my home, Herr Cortese – silver, china, lamps, rugs, lighting, paintings and sculpture – and, of course, the furniture – was designed and created during the Secession. With the exception of a few Biedermeier pieces which belonged to my family, it is all . . . how do you say it? . . . *of a piece.*"

"You'll have to explain that, Herr Hanfnagel. The only Secession I know of was the Confederacy from the Union. It led to the Civil War."

Hanfnagel chuckled. "Our Secession was quite different. Ridicule, mockery and heated debates, yes – bloodshed, never. The movement was a break away from academic tradition. For the first time since the Renaissance, artists and craftsmen worked side by side.

"Each object in my home expresses the true German character. Gone are the wretched imitations of the French. In their place, simple beauty, expressive of the strength of the Volk – the German people. The high point of Austrian culture, save for our music."

"Where did Mosel fit into it?"

"A good question," Hanfnagel approved. "Mosel was a qualified cabinetmaker before he joined the Wiener Werkstatte, then in its infancy."

He pointed to the chair in which he was seated. "Early Mosel. 1906. Note the reference to Biedermeier in the *fauteuils*. Yet the statement is totally modern – never before seen in the decorative arts."

"Strange to think that my father worked with him." Ross wondered if Pop even knew what those *foe*-something-or-others were. *He* certainly didn't know what Hanfnagel was talking about.

Hanfnagel looked askance at Ross. "Most unlikely, Herr Cortese. By the nineteen thirties, Mosel had retired and his son was in charge of the factory. The son was competent, but uninspired."

"What happened to the elder Mosel?"

"What happens to all old men, Herr Cortese. He passed on."

"And the rest of the family?"

"My interest is purely esthetic. Now, if you please, follow me." He rose and led them into the dining room. "Do you recognize something, Herr Cortese?" Hanfnagel asked slyly.

Ross paused on the threshold. The sight was astonishing. The picture he had seen in the book came to life. Ross scrutinized each piece – buffet, console, china cabinet, dining room table and twelve chairs – then went wide-angle again and took in the room as a whole. Hanfnagel waited like an impatient professor with a slow student. It soon became evident. The table, chairs and console matched his pieces. The buffet and cabinet, while similar in style, were not a match. Hanfnagel read the look on Ross's face and nodded, needing no formal confirmation.

"You see before you my life's passion." The man's intensity was so formidable Ross could feel it reaching out to him across the room. "I was born in nineteen-twelve, Herr Cortese – in the same year as this building. Stone and flesh, born under the same sign. A mystical connection? Perhaps. The quest for beauty, harmony and perfection of form has sustained me through difficult times. I've waited for many years for the return of the pieces in your possession. Have you known serious collectors, Herr Cortese?"

"Only one. He had a Colt that was said to belong to Wyatt Earp. The man loved his guns . . . I put him away for twenty years."

"What on earth happened?" Willi demanded.

"He used one . . . on his business partner."

"I trust decorative arts is a safer passion, Herr Cortese," Hanfnagel observed dryly.

"Careful, Father," Willi chided, "I told Red you'd kill to own his pieces."

Hanfnagel smiled broadly. "My daughter makes a joke. I don't even own a gun."

"Mr. Hanfnagel, there's an inscription on the back of my buffet . . . from Mosel to an Ariella. Can you tell me who she was?"

For a moment, Hanfnagel seemed taken aback. Ross thought he detected a hint of fear in the man's eyes, but Hanfnagel quickly recovered, shrugging off the question. "I hope, now that you have visited my home and seen my collection, you will reflect on my offer with the utmost seriousness. These pieces should never have been separated. They were designed to live in the same space, as an ensemble. They belong *here.*"

Neither Willi nor Ross dared say a word, as Hanfnagel walked the length of the table, stroking the tabletop with his fingertips in one long caress. The gesture reminded Ross of his own touches an hour ago and he lost himself in thoughts of Willi . . . until Hanfnagel's voice brought him back to reality.

"I look forward to making your stay in Vienna a memorable one. I've planned an evening at the Opera and a small supper party in your honor." He walked to the door. "I fear that I've kept you too long. I'm sure you want to go to your hotel and rest before the evening's entertainment. And I must prepare for a foundation meeting."

"Father," Willi said, "have you any further word on Doctor Mahler's condition?"

"Unchanged, liebchen. Please. You must excuse me." With that, he quickly left the room. Again, no handshake, Ross observed. Strange.

Willi came closer to Ross. "What do you think?"

"I've never met anyone like him. But tell me, what's a guy like your old man doing with an Otto in the house?"

"He's been with father for many years. He's very loyal."

"I bet he is," Ross murmured.

They returned to the living room. Ross noticed an Iron Cross, prominently framed and sitting on a shelf of a wood and glass vitrine.

"Who won the medal?" he asked.

"My grandfather . . . in the Argonne Forest. Father's very proud of it."

"Tell me something – did you grow up in this museum?"

"Yes. And Father was very strict that we show great care and respect for the furniture and objects."

"My Aunt Josephine covered everything in plastic . . . even the kitchen chairs. I hated going to her house . . . except she made great lasagna." Willi laughed and kissed his cheek.

Becoming serious, Ross said. "You know, it's strange – your father didn't say a word about Mosel once living in this building."

"You knew that?"

"I recognized it from a picture I saw in a book. It's hard to mistake it for something else."

"Well, what difference does it make?"

As Willi led him out of the apartment, Ross realized that Otto was nowhere in sight. He was definitely bothered by the man's presence.

The birdcage elevator deposited them on the first floor. Ross opened the door and a frail, elderly woman, unaware of their presence, tried to step in. She bumped into him and lost her balance. Ross caught her, preventing a fall, then held her until he was certain that she was solidly on her feet. She looked up at him and murmured, "Danke," then did a double take, stepping back, her eyes riveted on his face. Only Willi's greeting broke the spell.

"Annalee!" she exclaimed. The old woman broke into a big smile and the two of them hugged and kissed with great affection. As they did, her eyes darted back to Ross, searching his face.

"Annalee, I went you to meet my American friend, Ross."

"Please forgive my bad manners," Annalee said in perfect English. "My eyes are poor. They play tricks. Please, Willi, you and your friend must join me for tea. I've baked butter cookies, your favorite."

"We can't now, Annalee. I've got to get to the office." Annalee sighed, clearly disappointed. She kissed Willi and shook hands with Ross. He could feel the brittleness of her bones through her translucent skin. As he assisted her into the elevator, she said, "It's been so long since I have spoken English. Please come and visit, Herr . . ."

"Cortese . . . Ross Cortese."

He could see her through the grid of the elevator cage, even as it began to rise. Her lips moved. He tried in vain to read them. "What was that about?" he asked Willi.

"What do you mean?" Willi apparently hadn't noticed anything strange.

"Did you see the way she looked at me? As if she'd seen a ghost. Who is she?" he asked.

"You could say she's my fairy godmother. She taught me to sew and to bake. She was my first teacher of English. Her door was always open." Her voice dropped. "I could bring my joy . . . my sorrow to Annalee and count on her for wisdom. You heard her just now. The dear women still bakes me cookies."

"She lived here all the while you were growing up?"

"She's always lived here, from the time she herself was a little girl. She became a surrogate mother to me – after my mother died." They got to Willi's car and she asked, "Where can I drop you off? Back at the hotel?"

"Is there a museum that exhibits Mosel's work?" Why not get right to it? Ross figured he had a lot to learn and he better start learning it quickly or Herr Hanfnagel would eat him for breakfast.

"Of course. The Museum for Angewunde Kunst. We call it the MAK. But it's in the process of renovation. One day, Father plans to donate his collection there. It will be exhibited in an Erich Hanfnagel wing."

Yes, indeed, Ross thought, I've got homework to do.

Willi drove across town and in ten minutes deposited him in front of a nondescript 1950s building. "For now, Secession furniture is housed here, until the renovation of the MAK is complete."

Ross's eye was drawn to a huge church standing a short distance away on the right. "Karlskirche," Willi explained. "Early eighteenth century, when Vienna was part of the Holy Roman Empire." She did not explain that Karlskirche was also the center for Opus Dei, a right-wing Catholic faction. The less Ross knows of the ugly nature of Viennese politics, the better, she thought.

Willi gave him strict orders to appear in the hotel lobby, ready for the Opera, at seven-fifteen, not a minute later. "I'll see you then. Enjoy your afternoon." She waved good-bye and drove off without a kiss. *Like father, like daughter*, Ross mused.

Abe and Avia chose a beerstube in the old city six blocks from the Center for their meeting. The current political situation required particular precaution. Their office had been subjected to electronic surveillance at least once in the past. A noisy jukebox and a table at the rear of the tavern afforded them a reasonable guarantee of privacy. They made small talk until the waiter brought their beers. Only after he left did Avia speak.

"What did your contact have to say?"

"The Attorney General is apoplectic. He has quietly made a request for a Task Force. The government, as usual, is divided. Oh, there'll be condemnations from every level – but as for concerted action? Unlikely."

"So what's new?"

Abe quaffed his beer and wiped his mouth with the back of his hand. "One detail. Our friend tells me that the signature of the letter bomb, its ingredients and method of construction, are telltale Soviet . . . "

"Are you thinking what I'm thinking, Abe?"

He nodded. "Our worst fears. They're beginning to link with extremists in the former Soviet Union."

"Anti-Semitic, authoritarian, goose-stepping right-wingers. Zhirinovsky supporters. A nightmare scenario – Stalin and Hitler rise again."

"Our friend said one thing more. He's convinced that the Federal Prosecutor is ready to move against the leaders of the Bavarian Underground . . . but he must have proof. Conjecture will not do."

"I meet with Brecker tonight."

"Where?"

"In church."

"What?"

"St. Stephan's. There's a special midnight mass. I thought it would be a safe rendezvous."

"A good choice. But listen to me, Avia. If he suggests going anywhere else, the answer is no! Is that clear?"

"Why is it that you sound so much like my father, even though you're just a few years older than I am?"

Abe laughed and raised his beer glass. "Because your willfulness reminds me of my seven year old."

Once inside the museum, Ross obtained directions at the reception desk from a uniformed functionary who spoke English. Ross climbed the stairs to the second floor and found late nineteenth- and early twentieth-century furniture and objects on display. There were reconstructions of the architect Loos's apartment, Otto Wagner designs and Wiener Werkstatte furnishings, but only a few examples of Mosel's work.

Ross returned to the main floor and spoke to the clerk once more. "Do you think the curator would talk to me about Kirmen Mosel?"

The man was resistant at first, but Ross pushed on. "I'd appreciate your cooperation," he said firmly.

"Do you have some identification, sir?" he asked.

Ross showed his badge and I.D. The tone of the conversation changed to instant obsequiousness. The man picked up the phone and placed a call. When he hung up, he directed Ross to a corridor across the hall.

"Herr Visser is the museum director. He invites you to meet with him." Ross suddenly remembered Dutch once quoting a German saying, "Bow down to those above, step on those below." It looked as if Vienna was one place where authority still meant something.

The director's secretary was waiting for him. She knocked and then admitted Ross to a simply furnished office. "I am Doctor Visser, Director of the Museum. Please be seated, Inspector Cortese." Ross stifled a laugh at his sudden promotion.

Visser was short, no more then five-five, paunchy and gray. His distinctive feature was a fish-like mouth. His lips twitched slightly, as if from the strain of the pucker. He seemed uneasy, staring out at Ross from behind thick glasses. Sputtering, he said, "I'm happy to be of service to you, Inspector. The deskman tells me that you are here on official business. How may I assist?"

"Actually, that's a misunderstanding."

Visser frowned. "I beg your pardon."

"I am a police officer but the matter is personal. I own two pieces of Mosel furniture. I'm investigating their history." Ross offered him the Polaroids.

Visser studied them. "They are handsome," he murmured, the look on his face one of immediate recognition. Visser leaned forward, his tone confidential. "The museum is always interested in the possibility of such acquisitions."

"I'm in Vienna as a guest of Erich Hanfnagel. He's made me an offer to purchase the furniture. I've come to the museum for information."

Visser stiffened. "Herr Doktor Hanfnagel is a most important patron of the arts. In no way would I interfere with his dealings. It would be inappropriate, I daresay unethical."

"I'm not looking for a deal or checking out prices. I'd just like you to tell me what you know about Kirmen Mosel. My father worked for him at one time."

Visser, looking like a man who'd swallowed a bad oyster, found no relief in Ross's assurances. "That's most interesting, but you must excuse me, Herr Cortese. I'm due at a staff meeting." He came out from behind the desk, signaling that the interview was over.

I've been demoted, Ross thought.

It turned out that the hotel was not far from the museum. Ross walked there slowly, wondering how he could find out more about his father's connection to Vienna. Hanfnagel said it was impossible for Pop to have worked for Mosel, then had stonewalled him when he'd probed about Ariella. Willi's old man had one thing on his mind – and one thing only.

When he entered his room, he found that the suite had been straightened up and the bed made. There was no sign of the passion he and Willi had shared a few hours earlier. Ross suddenly felt exhausted – the jetlag was bearing down on him full force. He was running on fumes. If he was to remain awake through the opera he needed to grab some serious Z's. He stripped down to his shorts, slipped between the crisp linen sheets and was out as soon as his head hit the pillow.

CHAPTER FIFTEEN

The noise grew louder. Ross struggled with great difficulty to trace the source. He was on the street, hiding in shadow – waiting. The man stood halfway down the block. He was arguing with a young woman. His hair gleamed silver in the moonlight. Ross could see that the man was sweating. Why? he wondered. It's cold here. Ross pressed deeper into shadow to avoid being seen just as the man looked his way. He needed to make his escape. The ringing persisted. He feared that it would call attention to him.

With that, he awoke, shaking himself like a wet dog emerging from a pond. He was in the hotel and the phone was ringing.

Bad news about Pop, he thought guiltily. Fumbling for the phone, his body tensed against a blow. It came, but from an unexpected source. It was Willi, and she was extremely angry.

"Where are you?" she demanded. "It's seven-fifteen."

He opened his eyes, separating from the dream and the shock of waking. "Oh, my God. I fell sound asleep and didn't leave a call. You're in the lobby?"

"Of course. Where you're supposed to be."

"Give me fifteen minutes."

"Hurry. I'll keep the car in front. Father *detests* lateness."

He threw water on his face, fumbled in his suitcase for a clean shirt, dressed and made it downstairs in twelve, knotting his tie as Willi skidded out of the hotel driveway, heading recklessly across the Ring toward the Opera.

"Take it easy," he said. "They never start on time."

"This is Vienna, liebchen. They *always* start on time."

"So, tell me, Pretty Lady, how did your afternoon go?"

"Not bad . . . and you?"

"I saw some furniture . . . and a few pretty museum-goers," he kidded.

"Should I be jealous?"

"Nothing to worry about."

"Will you prove it?"

"Scrub the opera. Let's go back to the hotel and I'll show you."

"You can't be serious. Father would never forgive us. It's part of his campaign to woo you and win the furniture."

Ross was startled by the statement. "Are you part of the same campaign?"

"How can you say that?" She seemed hurt by the implication.

"Sorry. It's the cop in me talking."

"Leave him home next time!" she insisted.

"I apologize," he said, instantly improving the emotional climate. Willi smiled and nodded her acceptance.

"Who else is coming?" he asked.

"Father. My brother, Dolph, and his family . . . " She bit her lip. "My younger brother, Rudy – he won't be there. He and father don't get along."

Ross read the dashboard clock. It was 7:40. "Looks like we'll be on time," he reassured her.

She parked illegally opposite the main entrance to the Opera, locked up and led him hastily across the street. The domed building did not look particularly impressive from the exterior, except for five tall bronze statues which gazed out on the Ring from pedestals set high above the entrance.

Ross scanned the crowd. Women were in evening dress and many of the men wore tuxedos. "If I had known – and if I owned one – I'd have brought a tux," Ross commented.

"It's a bit stuffy, but it's tradition."

"Well, my dear, *you* look anything but traditional," he said, turning to look at her. She wore a strapless cocktail dress, the same shade of crimson as her lipstick. The dress showed a lot of cleavage and, ending well above the knee, a lot of leg.

They merged with the high-spirited crowd and slowly climbed the grand staircase. When they reached the grand parterre, the crowd thinned. Willi drew him past marble sculptures and gilded fretwork down a long corridor. Its walls were covered in velvet. A formally dressed usher come forward, bowed, clicked his heels and greeted her by name. Ross suppressed a grin. He could feel Willi's nervousness as the man led them down a long corridor to the front box. He pulled the curtain aside and announced them, "Fraulein Hanfnagel und begleiter." Willi anticipated his question and whispered, "Escort."

Ross noticed Hanfnagel check his watch. They had arrived with five minutes to spare. For certain men of power, like Hanfnagel, punctuality and respect were a weave, lateness an insult to the fabric.

He rose from his seat to make the introductions. "Herr Cortese. My son, Dolph."

Ross offered his hand. Dolph made contact reluctantly.

Father and son had the same features, but the resemblance ended there. Where Hanfnagel at seventy-eight was fit, the son's face was spidered by heavy drinking. His expression was fixed in a permanent sneer. Dolph's wife, a skinny blonde, was standing next to him. Her long dress was as colorless as she was and her translucent skin and pathetically skinny figure reminded him of anorexics he had met. Hanfnagel introduced him to the last occupant of the box, his grandson, Reinhold. The kid looked like he knew his way to the gym, Ross observed. He was bulked up to the ears. Reinhold took his hand and tried to crush it. Ross was prepared for the show of strength. He used a counter-grip which foiled the display and provoked a scowl from the teenager.

"Nice to meet you," Ross smiled. "You've got quite a grip there."

With pride, Hanfnagel announced, "The boy is captain of his football team."

The houselights dimmed and they hastened to take their seats. Ross was relieved to find himself seated next to Willi in the rear of the box.

The conductor entered from the wings to a huge ovation. Ross joined in the applause, taking the opportunity to study the hall. The simple facade had deceptively understated the interior scale of the Opera House. It reminded him of the old Met. His father had taken him there several times. They always sat in the Family Circle, opera's equivalent to bleacher seats and high enough for a nosebleed. For Pop, it was heaven on 39th and Broadway. In later years, his father followed the Metropolitan Opera to Lincoln Center, bemoaning the loss of the old beauty downtown.

The conductor struck up the overture to "Don Giovanni," its initial somber chords and cautionary notes soon giving way to Mozart's lively music. Ross settled in, allowing himself to be transported. The Vienna Philharmonic was in the pit and he appreciated that he was hearing extraordinary ensemble playing.

The first act ended to thunderous applause. Hanfnagel turned to him, all smiles. "Our Mozart, Herr Cortese. His opera . . . where it was born."

Ross regarded him quizzically. "I understood he composed

Giovanni in Prague." Hanfnagel, taken aback, nonetheless looked impressed.

Karin, the mousy wife, could not resist. "Oh, very good, Herr Cortese – rarely does someone best Father."

Ross caught the dirty look Dolph threw at her. He watched her wither beneath her husband's disapproving stare.

At the intermission, Hanfnagel led them to the Opera Café where a table was reserved for them. Formally outfitted waiters served caviar and champagne, while Ross hopped up and down from his seat for half an hour as Willi's father introduced him to a succession of acquaintances who stopped by to say hello. He was relieved when the lights dimmed, signaling the third act.

Don Giovanni's musical descent into Hell provided ample opportunity for the baritone and orchestra to exhibit their wares. If Ross thought the earlier applause thunderous, he had never witnessed a storm like this one. One curtain call followed another. Reinhold was restless. He showed off his English, blurting out, "Grandfather, I'm starved. Can't we go to supper?"

Dolph, purple with rage, snapped at his son in German. Ross didn't understand the words, but got the message. The boy was being told to shut his trap. Hanfnagel, on the other hand, did not seem at all disquieted by his grandson's request. "You're right, my boy. We must go feed you – and our guest – at once."

In the car, Willi explained that her father had invited a few of his closest friends to a late supper at his home. "In your honor, of course." She tensed up when they turned into a sidestreet and found traffic at a standstill. "We'll be last to arrive," she said grimly.

"Relax, my dear, we'll get there," he offered reassuringly.

"Yes – but when?" she replied, tapping nervously with her fingers on the steering wheel.

Stephansplatz is at the center of the inner city and a crossroads for tourists. Even after midnight, the square in front of the Cathedral bustles with pedestrian activity. Mingling with a group of Scandinavians in the shadow of the tall spire, Abe watched Avia join a stream of worshippers and enter through the Singer Gate.

The service was in progress as she entered the church and tiptoed to the rear of the center nave. The voices of the choir and the accompanying organ music soared in the magnificent Gothic space. Hans Brecker was seated in the last row, on the aisle, as arranged. He was difficult to miss, with his shaved head and metal-studded black leather jacket.

Avia found a point of view from which to study him. He was medium height, slender, almost pretty. She moved to stand directly behind him and tapped once, lightly on his shoulder. Brecker jerked away at the contact. The man's nerves were shot.

Recovering from his momentary panic, Brecker turned and glowered at her. He was embarrassed that he had revealed his nervousness and was furious at her for provoking it. The urge to smash her smug Jewish face was strong, but he forced himself to suppress it. He motioned with a tilt of his head to the far rear of the church and waited a minute before joining her there.

They stood in a dark corner, beneath the organ gallery. Their conversation was all but drowned out by the music; however, no one paid them any attention.

"I'm here at *your* request," she stated matter-of-factly, "So what do you have for me?"

"You make it sound like you're doing *me* a favor," he retorted.

"I am. I know your record. You're nineteen. You served eleven months in jail for assault. From what I hear about life in prison, it could not have been pleasant."

She saw him flinch.

"I had time to think things over," he responded. "What I was doing made no sense. That's why I'm here. That – and for money to get a new start."

He sounded flat, unconvincing. Money, maybe, she thought, but he certainly wasn't changing stripes. Not this cat.

"You know something, Brecker? If you're serious about wanting to get out, I can be a big help."

"I wouldn't be here otherwise. If they knew I was talking to you, I'd be a dead man. I'm risking my life. You better understand that. So what are you paying?"

"That depends on what you give us."

"What have you paid the others?"

"What others?"

This bitch is tough, Brecker realized. He would love to get her alone and work her over. The thought of it aroused him. "Come on. You want me to work for you, you got to give a little trust."

Avia smiled. "Earn it." You little shit, she left unsaid.

"What do you want?"

"Names. The brains and money men backing the Underground. *Proof.* For that I'll pay you well."

"That's a tough assignment. We're organized in cells. The big guys keep away from the street soldiers."

"Bring me the information and you can name your price."

Name your price.

The organization owed him for his loyalty. They gave him shit instead. He knew things that he might have traded for a shorter sentence, but had kept his mouth shut for eleven long, miserable months. He shuddered at that recollection. He didn't know what he feared more, the thought of going back to prison or the idea of being found dealing with the Jews.

"How about something up front?" he cajoled.

"You give, you get."

"Do you play video games?"

Avia had a pretty good idea of where he was headed, but decided to play dumb. "No," she replied. "What's that got to do with anything?"

"I've got one that will interest you. It's called Concentration Camp. The object of the game is to kill Jews. It's being marketed secretly. I can get you a copy."

Avia already had copies of the hate games, not only the version Brecker referred to, but those that had appeared in Germany and were directed at Turks.

"I need more than the game. I need to know who's producing it . . . how it's distributed."

"Tell you what. Come with me to my place. I'll show you how the game works. You can have my copy. To show good faith, it's free of charge." Except maybe for a piece of your ass, he thought. "Tomorrow, I'll start nosing around for the names you're after. I think I know where to look. When I find them, we're talking big money, understand?"

"You produce – we'll pay. As far as your place is concerned, forget it. All we need is for one of your pals to see us and start asking questions. Mail the video game to me in a plain brown wrapper – to this address."

She slipped him a piece of paper. "It's not mine. Nor can it be linked in any way to the Center. Memorize it. Then get rid of the paper. There's a phone number, too . . . with an answering machine on the line. That's how you contact me to set up the next meeting. Leave the number of a public phone and a time to call. I'll reach you there."

"I'll do it," he spit out. "But when we talk money, remember what you promised – don't try *jewing* me on the price."

Avia looked at him with contempt, then turned and walked away. She spent twenty minutes strolling leisurely through the streets of the old city, checking at various intervals to see if she was being followed. Only when she was convinced that she was not under surveillance did Avia reverse direction and rush to catch the bus. She needed a bath to wash away the stench of Hans Brecker.

CHAPTER SIXTEEN

Willi's apprehensions proved correct. Stuck in traffic, they were delayed by twenty minutes. The guests were all there in the apartment when they entered.

"What happened to you?" Dolph asked his sister coldly.

"Same the world over, Dolph," Ross intervened. "Garbage trucks and double parked cars."

The elder Hanfnagel proceeded with formalities: "Herr Cortese, may I introduce some of my dearest friends and associates. Frau Ilse Sturmer and Herr Doktor Friedrich Sturmer, Herr Victor Neurath, Herr Doktor Franz Vyneker."

Ross looked around the table. Hanfnagel had seated him beside Frau Sturmer with Karin on his left. Willi sat opposite him, between Neurath and one of the Herr Doktors. Dolph and Reinhold took up places on either side of Hanfnagel. He liked his boys close, Ross thought.

Two waiters served a supper of foie gras and cold lobster. He noted that the white wine poured was Austrian.

"The wine is very good." he complimented Hanfnagel.

"You know our Austrian wines, Herr Cortese?" Vyneker inquired.

"No. But I know good when I taste it."

"And speaking of good, Herr Cortese," Frau Sturmer said, "our Giovanni was in excellent voice, nein?"

"He was, Frau Sturmer. Very good."

"Please. Call me Ilse."

"Then please me call me Red."

"An unfortunate choice of names in Austria, Herr Cortese," Dolph interjected, with a twisted smile. "We don't like Reds. We lived under Soviet occupation for too many years."

There were a few uncomfortable chuckles at the table. Willi broke in and brought them back to the discussion of the tenor. "Ross is being polite, Ilse. Brandt was a less than adequate Giovanni."

Hanfnafgel, bemused, chided his daughter gently. "Must you, Willi?"

Turning to Ilse, he explained, tongue-in-cheek, "You must excuse my daughter. She should have been a critic."

Dolph, well into a bottle of pepper vodka, reinforced the reproach with a vigorous nod of his head.

Friedrich Sturmer piped up. "New Yorkers are spoiled by this Pavarotti."

"Domingo gets my vote," said Ross.

"Does your African mayor get your vote too, Herr Cortese?" Dolph asked snidely.

"No. Fact is, I voted for the other guy," Ross countered.

Dolph would not let it go. "Of course. Mr. Guiliani. Italian. Your countryman . . . "

Ross shrugged. The guy's a first-class prick, he thought, refusing to let Dolph get under his skin . . . .

Johann spoke. "I visited New York in 1960. Then it was a vibrant, beautiful city."

"It's still a great town. All big cities have *big* problems," Ross explained.

"*Tzu fil mit schwarze und Juden,*" Dolph muttered under his breath.

Ross picked up the slur and its meaning.

Sturmer was quick to agree with Dolph, pausing only to pick a piece of lobster from his teeth. "Soon, it will be as bad here. Vienna teems with trash from across the borders. Magyars. Slovaks. Gypsies. Ex-Soviets of every stripe . . . freeloaders and peddlers. It is a disgrace that our country does not recognise the menace and close the borders."

Hanfnagel broke in. "Just as baseball is your national past-time, Herr Cortese, so is politics ours. We are weaned on it."

By now, Ross was working on his third glass of wine.

"By the way, Herr Cortese," Hanfnagel continued. "Did you enjoy your visit to the Historisches Museum?"

Ross was shocked out of his torpor. How does the son of a bitch know what I did today?

"You look surprised . . . Herr Visser phoned me."

Neurath, silent until now, spoke softly. "Vienna is really a small village, Herr Cortese. It's difficult to keep secrets here. I understand from Erich that your father acquired Mosel's furniture while in Vienna."

"Be careful how you answer, Herr Cortese," Johann smiled.

"Doktor Neurath is a colleague of yours. Deputy Commissioner of Polizei. After many years of notable service, officially retired. Unofficially, still quite active."

The others laughed.

"I found out that Mosel once lived in this building, Herr Hanfnagel," Ross said, ignoring his remarks. "You didn't mention that this morning."

"To be sure, Herr Cortese – not only is the address the same, this was Mosel's apartment. The apartment became available just as I was in need of more spacious quarters. A most fortunate serendipity."

"Like your father, Herr Cortese," Neurath interjected, "it appears that Herr Doktor Hanfnagel was in the right place at the right time."

Hanfnagel leaned over the table, his face flushed with wine, his lips reddened by reflected candlelight. "You see Mr. Cortese, with the addition of these pieces, a major gap in my collection is filled – and the dining room returned to its original glory."

"I will have the agreement completed by tomorrow," Sturmer declared. "Shall I come to your hotel in the morning with the papers, Herr Cortese? Or would you prefer to sign in my office?"

Ross felt the squeeze. He tried to suppress his annoyance, reminding himself that this was, after all, why they had brought him here. "To tell you the truth, I haven't made up my mind to sell. I'm still thinking about it."

"Of course, Herr Cortese," Hanfnagel graciously assured. "You've only just arrived."

Through clenched teeth, Dolph hissed, "*Er schwindled vie un Jude.*"

Ross only heard the last word but caught the drift of Dolph's drunken comment.

Hanfnagfel rebuked his son sharply. "Dolph! That's no way to speak of our guest. I want you to apologize to Herr Cortese . . . at once!"

The son submitted instantly. "My apology, Herr Cortese."

Looking at Dolph's expression, Ross realized the truth behind the words was evident. Sell – or I'll beat the living shit out of you. How had Hanfnagel, who sired the lovely Willi, produced this piece of work, Ross wondered.

Willi, embarrassed by the exchange, suddenly announced, "It's been a long day, Father. Red just arrived this morning. He can barely keep his head up and I'm exhausted, too. Please excuse us."

Hanfnagel nodded. Willi kissed her father, then came over and took Ross's hand in a signal of solidarity. The others rose to bid them good-bye.

Neurath had the last word. "You must visit me tomorrow, Herr Cortese. I maintain an office at Central Police Headquarters." He offered his card. "I'd like to discuss a matter of mutual professional interest. I'm sure you'll find the visit . . . useful."

"One day here and already in trouble with the law," Ross wisecracked.

No one laughed, not even Willi as she pulled him from the room.

After Willi and Ross were gone, Victor asked Dolph to join him for a cigar. The men excused themselves and went into the library. There, they helped themselves to Erich Hanfnagel's finest aged Cuban selections.

"What's your impression of Herr Cortese?" Victor asked.

"Not much," Dolph grunted.

"I believe your sister is sweet on him."

"Willi is known for her bad taste in men," he said, annoyed. "Just see to it that Father's lust for his precious furniture is satisfied or I'll never hear the end of it."

Neurath nodded.

"So . . . the official response to the mailings?" Dolph asked.

"Talk of a Task Force. It will amount to nothing," Victor replied.

"You're satisfied with Doschenko's performance?"

"Immensely so. Thoroughly professional. The KGB trained their operatives well," he added grudgingly.

"Nothing must interfere."

"Nothing will."

Dolph signified approval, then said, "Let's join the others for a nightcap."

"And give up this magnificent cigar? I think not." Neurath plunked himself in an easy chair and puffed his Havana. Dolph reluctantly rejoined the supper party.

The street was deserted at one A.M., the air mild and fragrant with late spring blossoms. Ross pointed up at the nearly full moon hung three dimensionally against the velvety black sky. "Looks like it followed us from New York."

When Willi didn't respond he stopped walking and looked at her face. She appeared distressed. "What's wrong, Willi? Is it something I said upstairs?"

"You? No. You've done nothing. It's I who feel ashamed."

He put a consoling arm around her. "You mean Dolph? What exactly did he say? That I . . .swindle like a Jew?"

She looked surprised. "You understood."

"I caught the drift. I've heard worse . . ."

"You don't have to defend my brother. "

"I'm not defending him when I say I've said a few things like that in my time."

"If you did, you didn't mean it."

"Hey, I'm not Saint Rosso," he responded. "Well . . . maybe Saint Dolorosa," he added, beating his breast lightly before getting into the car.

His attempt at irony drew a zero. Willi concentrated on making every green light on the brief route back to the hotel. The lobby was deserted except for the night clerk. Willi walked directly to the elevator. Ross picked up the key and joined her.

Despite the troubling finale to the supper party and Ross's fatigue, they could not resist the opportunity to explore the newness of each other. They lingered, took their time, and built slowly to long-lasting climaxes. Ross finally fell into a deep sleep.

When he awoke at nine, she was gone. He suddenly felt terribly alone, as he had in the long weeks after Annie's death. Only when Willi called from work to apologize for her hasty departure, did his mood lift.

"What are you going to do today?" she asked.

"Have you forgotten? I've been called in to police headquarters. Where can I reach you if I need to make bail?"

She didn't appreciate his humor.

"I'd like to meet you for lunch. I thought perhaps we might . . . actually, my brother Rudy owns a café . . . "

Something's bothering her, Ross thought, picking up on her tentativeness. "What is it, Willi? Is there a problem?"

There was silence on her end, then, as if she was afraid to be overheard, she whispered, "Rudy's gay."

"That's it?" he asked. "It's not a crime where I come from."

"Viennese police sometimes act as if it is. Rudy and his lover own the Café Freiheit . . . "

"So?"

"It's frequented by homosexuals . . . as well as artists and writers," she added.

"I can handle that," he reassured her.

Her relief was palpable across the phone line. "You'll find it on Naglergasse. In the old city. Don't forget . . . Café Freiheit." She even spelled it for him to be sure. "I'll see you there at noon."

"I'll find my way."

Ross opened the window to the white light of a sun-drenched day, then dialed the switchboard and gave them his home number. The machine picked up. He left a message that all was well and asked Amy to pass it on to the family. He ordered coffee from room service and by the time it arrived, he was dressed and ready to leave.

In the lobby, Ross ran a gauntlet of "grosse Gott, Herr Cortese," from concierge to doorman. It was supposed to make him feel welcome but had the opposite effect. There was little that escaped hotel staff. He was sure they were especially curious about him because Hanfnagel was picking up the tab. By now, they had catalogued his luggage and wardrobe down to the underwear, as well as classifying his social and economic status.

It was a few minutes past ten when he hit the street.

CHAPTER SEVENTEEN

There wasn't a cloud in the sky as Ross strolled toward the center of the city. His mood, however, did not match the weather. He found himself strangely uneasy and dyspeptic as well. His stomach growled. He needed some breakfast. Distracted, Ross started across the Ring as the light was changing. He was buzzed by three skinhead bikers. They passed within inches of him, shouted and gave him the finger. "Fuck you," he shouted after them, only to feel embarrassed by the attention he attracted from pedestrians.

Stopping a passerby, he inquired for directions to Central Police headquarters. He was offered a long route around the Ring or the short cut through the quaint, narrow lanes of the old city. Ross opted for the latter and made his way, with the help of two further inquiries, to Schottengasse. There, he paused at what turned out to be a venerable coffehouse, the Haag. Customers enjoyed coffee and pastry as they read newspapers and a variety of international periodicals offered by the management. A friendly waiter recommended the rhum baba and a Kapuziner, a small bowl of delicious black coffee with a drop of whipped cream and a sprinkling of cocoa. Ross polished both off in short order.

Fifteen minutes later, his mood improved, Ross found the nondescript headquarters on Deutschmeisterplatz. He was surprised by the low level of police activity. The atmosphere was a stark contrast to the hubbub of New York. Within minutes, the desk sergeant assigned a young woman in uniform to show him to the Deputy Commissioner's office.

Neurath greeted him but did not rise. He motioned Ross to a chair, immediately establishing his authority. "I'm pleased that you decided to stop by."

"Thanks for the invitation."

"You're enjoying your stay in Vienna?"

"I am."

"What do you think of our headquarters?"

"It's quiet, compared with what I'm used to."

"Perhaps we do a better job of crime prevention."

Ross caught the barb and gave it back. "How are you doing on yesterday's bombings?"

"The investigation is, as you say, under wraps." Neurath smiled knowingly.

"Okay. No shop talk. Let's get right to the point."

"I like that. I'll be equally blunt. When my dear friend Erich informed me that important Mosel pieces had surfaced in New York, I felt it my duty to make certain that you are who you say you are – and not, shall we say, a scam artist."

Ross made no effort to hide his irritation.

"I'm informed that you're highly regarded by your department, despite your recent difficulties – and I am especially pleased to hear from Chief Francis that you've been cleared of all charges. It's a dreadful day when police are persecuted and the criminal element is free to have its way. I assure you – that will never happen here."

"Lucky you," said Ross.

"It's not a matter of luck, but of determination. There are those of us in law enforcement committed to strictly maintaining order now – rather than managing anarchy later. Are you sympathetic to that approach, Sergeant?"

"No cop would argue with the principal. It's the practice that's the problem. We've got a system of law that frowns on vigilante justice, if that's what you mean – even when practiced by the police."

"So much the worse for you, Sergeant."

"What's the point, Commissioner Neurath?"

"Just my way of getting acquainted. With regard to the purpose of your visit to Vienna, I ordered a search of our records. We're rather proud of how well they've been maintained – back to the first decade of this century. I turned up a file from 1938."

Ross regarded him quizzically.

Neurath paused to light a small cigar. "Your father's name – is it Franco Cortese?"

"Yes."

"It's my unpleasant duty to inform you that he was named a prime suspect in the theft of furniture and a painting belonging to the Mosel family."

Angry, Ross started to rise but forced himself back with an effort of will. He spoke quietly, but sternly. "My father is *not* a thief."

"Please, Herr Cortese. I said suspect. Those were chaotic days. Will we ever know the truth? Witnesses reported that one Franco Cortese, employed by the Mosel firm, was observed loading furniture and packages onto a Mosel company truck. Truck, furniture and your father were never seen again."

"He bought those pieces," Ross said heatedly, his jaw set.

"On an apprentice salary? Come, come, Herr Cortese. You're an investigator. That's most unlikely."

"What's the date this supposedly took place?"

"Early March of nineteen-thirty-eight."

"Then it's pure, unadulterated horseshit. I was born in February of thirty-eight. Pop was in Udine with my mother. There's no way he could have been here."

"All I know is what the record shows. I'm sorry to be the bearer of such tidings. Believe me, Herr Cortese, I have no wish to interfere with your business. Quite the contrary . . .

"I did not tell Erich Hanfnagel my reason for asking you to visit. I wish to spare him the painful thought that these pieces, which mean so much to him, might be stained by the nature of their acquisition."

Neurath paused then smoothly urged, "Sell the furniture to Herr Doktor Hanfnagel, Cortese. Go back to New York richer for your visit. The Mosel furniture will be returned to its rightful place – and your father's file will be buried deep. I promise you that."

Ross's thoughts raced. "I'll think about it. I'd appreciate a copy of that file – including those statements."

"I'm sorry. I can't permit that – without an official request through the proper channels."

The Commissioner looked at his watch then beckoned his secretary over the intercom. "My assistant will show you out, Herr Cortese. Enjoy your visit – and if there's any way in which I can make it more pleasant, don't hesitate to let me know." His voice was clipped, dismissive, beneath the superficial politeness of his words.

After Ross left, Neurath locked his door, set the scrambler on the telephone and placed a call.

Ross found a tavern in the vicinity of Headquarters. He ordered a beer, then asked directions to the men's room. It stank as bad as his meeting with the Commissioner. Ross felt certain that his father was hiding something, but equally certain that Pop was no thief. The time frame Neurath referred to supported his disbelief. Besides, Neurath's offer to deep-six the file proved that he was capable of lying to advance Hanfnagel's interests.

You get a whiff of marrow, you're like a hungry dog looking for a bone, Kelsey had said. Neurath, instead of scaring him off, had given him the scent. He was determined to find the truth. Where to begin? Right now, he had a date with Willi. He would not tell her about the meeting. Her deep attachment to her father was evident – that would be where her loyalty lay.

Walking back slowly through the old city, Ross reached Naglergasse, a medieval lane. A Renaissance stone relief above the portal to Number Thirteen depicted an expressionist Holy Trinity. Lucky thirteen, he thought glumly. He spotted Willi down the block, seated alone at a table in front of the café. Greeting him with a warm kiss, she led him inside. The spacious room was decorated with turn of the century style furnishings and poster art from the same period. Willi pointed to a table near the bar where two well-dressed men in their thirties stood to welcome them.

One, dark-complexioned, wore small gold-framed glasses and was conservatively, though stylishly dressed in a three-piece suit. The second shared Willi's coloring and appeared more boyish. He wore an expensive long-sleeved black silk shirt over gray flannel slacks. An elegant, silver-buckled black belt and highly polished, expensive shoes completed the impression of a man who enjoyed fine clothes. That's her brother, Ross thought. He reached out to shake the suit's hand first. He was closest. But the younger, more flamboyant man moved quickly to embrace Ross and kiss him on the cheeks.

"I'm Rudy. I've heard so much about you from Willi. You're everything she described – and more. *That hair.* I'd die to have it." He turned. "Meet my mate, Jacky Gold."

"Welcome to Freiheit," Jacky said signaling to the waitress. The tall, dark haired woman in a short skirt came to the table. When she handed out the menus, Ross recognized with a start that *she* was a he. This place is a scene, he thought. He opened the menu and found that it was printed in German and English.

"You get a lot of Americans?" he inquired.

"Brits more than Americans. Gays seek out gays when they visit foreign cities. Freiheit is well known," Rudy stated proudly.

Ross set down his menu. "A club sandwich sounds great."

"And to drink?" the waitress asked.

"What are you drinking?" he asked Jacky.

"Don't go by us. We're health nuts."

Willi picked up the slack. "A glass of white wine and a salad, please, Heidi," she said, addressing the waitress.

"Make mine Scotch – on the rocks," Ross added.

Rudy raised his eyebrows. "Are you preparing to meet my father?" he joked.

"What will he drink when he meets Dolph," Jacky joked.

"I met both of them yesterday. Let me in on the joke?"

"My apologies, Red," said Rudy. "I'm a recovering alcoholic. Sober for three years. When I meet Father, which is almost never, I double up on AA meetings – two each day, to prevent a relapse."

Willi straightened. "I didn't bring Red here to listen to you attack Father."

"My sister Willi is the proverbial applesauce of Father's eye, while I am the rotten apple in the barrel. Dolph is the frog who father has turned with his power and wealth into the Hanfnagel prince."

"You're outrageous, Rudy," Willi protested.

"But incredibly accurate, eh, my darling?"

Jacky stepped in. "Red must be warned: when one comes to Freiheit, one hears fairy tales."

Everyone laughed and that broke the ice.

"What does *Freiheit* mean?" Ross inquired.

"It means freedom," Rudy replied. "We've tried to re-create the café tradition which existed in Vienna in the years before the so-called Great War of nineteen-fourteen. Great, indeed," he scoffed. "The cafés were places where artists and intellectuals could exchange ideas – where people of differing life styles felt accepted. It is an anachronism, I fear. All you have to do is listen to the news."

"Apart from the mayhem which greeted you yesterday, how do you find Vienna?" Jacky asked sardonically.

Ross thought about his meeting with Neurath, but set it aside. He glanced at Willi. "Beautiful . . . and most welcoming."

Rudy observed the interaction and smiled with approval. But a moment later, his mood changed and he said darkly, "If you look below the schlag . . . our whipped cream . . . you'll find another Vienna. A Vienna which is less than hospitable to strangers. The Viennese are experts in what locals call 'schmah.' You can never be sure that what they say is what they mean. On the contrary, what they mean is rarely what they say. It's an accepted way of life."

"Rudy! You're at it again," Willi snapped.

Rudy shrugged. "She hates it when I trash Vienna . . . or . . . "

Or your father, Ross thought.

Heidi arrived, balancing a large tray expertly. She served their sandwiches and salads and set drinks around the table. As they ate and drank, the small talk continued.

"You're the first American detective we've met," Jacky remarked.

"Oh, I've known a few American dicks in my time," Rudy quipped. Willi warned him with a sharp look.

"Are you acquainted with anyone in Vienna?" Jacky asked.

"Present company excluded, no. My father recently told me that he lived here before the war – working for Kirmen Mosel. He'd never mentioned it before."

"In Vienna it's a given that fathers don't speak to their children of those days," Rudy said sadly.

"Why the silence?"

The partners passed knowing glances between them.

"A four-letter word causes people to lose their voices," Jacky explained elliptically. Ross had no inkling of what he meant.

"What word?" he asked.

"J-u-d-e . . . " Jacky spelled out. "Jew."

"My father said Mosel was trying to get his family out of Austria. He didn't say he was Jewish."

"I know for a fact that he was," Jacky responded unequivocally. "Let me tell you something about Vienna, Red.

"Many do not know and others prefer to forget that a young Adolph Hitler learned his political lessons in the use of anti-Semitism in this city – from then mayor, Karl Lueger. Lueger was a hero to workers who saw their jobs threatened by Jewish immigrants. Sound familiar? He was elected and reelected on a frankly anti-Semitic platform."

"Later, a section of the Ring was named in his honor," Rudy added bitterly. "The same forces are again at work. Witness yesterday's bombing."

"I was told no one had claimed responsibility."

"They have now. The Bavarian Underground, or put less euphemistically, the new Austrian Nazis."

Willi stood abruptly. "I've got to get back to the office for a meeting."

"What about coffee?" Rudy asked.

"Can't stay . . . Red? I'll meet you at Schwedenbrucke landing tonight at eight for dinner and dancing. My treat."

She kissed him, did the same with her brother and Jacky, then quickly departed.

"What's this Schwedenbrucke landing?" he asked the men.

"The departure point for the Danube steamers. I hope you like to waltz," Rudy answered.

"I'm not exactly twinkletoes, but it sounds like fun."

"The way my sister looks at you warms my heart," Rudy added.

"She's a very special woman."

Both men smiled and nodded in agreement. Ross found himself freer in Willi's absence to raise the question that had gnawed at him since the meeting with Neurath. "Suppose I want to find out everything there is to know about Mosel and his family," and my father's involvement with him, he thought to himself. "How would I go about doing it?"

"Be very careful," Jacky said. "In this city, you show an interest in a Jew, you risk becoming a Jew yourself – in the eyes of others."

"I'll take that chance."

"Your host in Vienna might not like it."

"Rudy's father seems an okay guy. When Dolph made a nasty crack last night, the old man put him down fast."

"There's only so much an American can understand of the Austrian mentality," Jacky said resignedly.

Rudy took Ross's measure, then spoke. "Why do you think my father cuts me out of his life, Red? Because I'm gay? He's lived with that unhappily since I was a child. No, it's because my lover is a Jew."

"For Viennese fathers, gays and Jews fall into the same class – despised outsiders, beyond the Pale," Jacky declared.

"Look. I really don't want to get in the middle of family problems. I've got enough of my own. How do I find out about Mosel?"

Jacky cleared his throat. Ross and Rudy turned to him.

"Among Jews," he began, "there is a special prayer for those who are buried nameless in unmarked graves. There are centers in Vienna which seek to give them back their identities – and track down those who put them in those graves. I know of one. You could begin there."

"They'd have records?"

"They're young admirers of Simon Wiesenthal, the Nazi hunter responsible for bringing Adolph Eichmann, himself an Austrian, to justice. If they don't have records, they have access to them."

"I want to go there," Ross announced decisively.

"Now?" Rudy asked, a bit nervously.

He nodded. "Just point me in the right direction."

"I can't take you. The accountant is coming," Rudy replied. "Jacky? What about you?"

Ross noted their discomfort. "No, that's not necessary. If you give me the address, I'll go there on my own."

"Willi asked me to look after you," Rudy insisted.

"We can both be away for an hour," Jacky reassured his mate.

"The accountant will be occupied with the books."

"You take him, Jacky. They'll recognize you as a supporter. It's better if I stay," Rudy replied stiffly.

Was he concerned about going against his father? Ross wondered. Jacky was right. The Viennese mentality was hard to comprehend.

Jacky stood and motioned to Ross. "We'll leave through the kitchen. It's a shortcut."

The rear exit led into an alley which wound behind medieval buildings. "What's with Rudy?" Ross asked. "He seemed uptight."

"Whenever we talk about his father, it's painful."

They cut through the Am Hof. A right turn brought them into Judenplatz. The lovely square reminded Ross of an Italian piazza. "This area was the Jewish ghetto until fourteen-twenty-one," Jacky lectured. "There at Number Two was the Schulhof, one of the major schools of the German-speaking world. You see the relief on the facade?"

They were close to the building now. The scene depicted the baptism of Christ. Beneath it was a plaque with bas-relief lettering.

"It describes the terrible events associated with the expulsion of the Jews from Vienna at that time. More than two hundred people were burned to death."

"How come you stay here?"

"Oh, Rudy and I often discuss living in New York, London or Paris. But – we have a good business, friends – and, of course, there's Willi. So we stay – and I, as a Jew, do what little I can to support the forces of reason against those who hate and would again destroy."

"Pop always talked about how lucky we were to grow up in the States."

"Believe me, you were."

When they arrived at their destination, they saw a policeman stationed in front of the building.

"Why the guard?" Ross asked.

"In Vienna, police protection is provided for all places where Jews congregate. It would be an embarrassment to the government if there was a terrorist attack."

They went inside the old building and climbed a steep set of stairs. At the top, they found a reinforced steel door with a peephole. Ross rang the bell. He heard footsteps and felt eyes on him. A woman's voice asked them their business.

"Do you speak English, miss . . . fraulein?" Ross called out.

"Yes. Who are you and what is your business with us?"

"Ross Cortese. From New York."

"An American Jew?"

"No," he stammered, taken aback by the question. "Italian-American. I'm a cop."

Feeling foolish, he pulled out his I.D. and held it up to the peephole.

"You should have called for an appointment. Are you alone?"

"I'm with a friend."

"Please ask him to step in front of the door where I can see him."

Jacky complied. A moment later the door opened to reveal a pretty brunette in her mid to late twenties and a minimally furnished office crammed with file cabinets and cartons.

"Sorry for the third degree. I'm Avia Hirsch, Mr. Cortese," she said, extending her hand. He took it and returned her firm grip with his own. She was dressed casually in black jeans and a black sweatshirt which didn't quite hide an ample figure.

Jacky took his turn. "Jacky Gold, Fraulein Hirsch."

"I recognize you from Freiheit," she said with a nod, then introduced the man seated at a desk. "My colleague, Abe Feder."

Feder looked up from his file and removed his metal-framed glasses. He reminded Ross of a Viking sea captain. His Ahab beard was blonde and trimmed short. He looked at them with penetrating blue eyes. "What do you want, gentlemen?"

His tone was neither friendly nor unfriendly.

"I'm looking for information," Ross explained. "About a man named Kirmen Mosel. My father worked for him at one time. That's Kirmen Mosel, the cabinetmaker."

"I know who he is," Abe snapped. "Calling him a cabinetmaker is like calling Liszt a piano player."

Ross disregarded the sarcasm. He wanted cooperation, not conflict. "I own two pieces of Mosel's furniture. I found out recently that they're quite valuable. Before I decide what to do with them, I want to find out if there are any members of the family still living . . . children, grandchildren . . . "

Abe stared at him. Ross felt like a specimen under a microscope. "If I look at you with disbelief, Cortese, it's because in six years at the Center, I've never heard such a story. Have you Avia?"

The young woman shook her head. Abe returned his gaze to Ross. "Why don't you go ahead and just sell it?" he challenged.

"I didn't come here for business advice. Can you give me a lead?"

"Listen, Cortese. Hundreds of thousands, perhaps millions of Gentiles live comfortably with the spoils of the war. From what we know, most paid nothing, but simply looted. When you exterminate six million and more, there is much to profit from."

"My father tried to help. Would it have been better if some Nazi got the furniture?"

Ross saw Abe glance in Jacky's direction, his eyes burning. Avia spoke, in an effort to ease the tension. "Please try to understand our position, Mr. Cortese. The subject of your unusual visit is a painful reminder of a heritage that is gone and will never be returned. Property, precious mementos, objects which in the ordinary course of events parents pass down to their children and their children's children – the vessels of memory by which the generations are linked across time are lost forever. What was not stolen was destroyed, depriving the survivors of the Holocaust from a connection to their lost loved ones."

Ross felt the power of that simple, profound truth. He realized, then, his own strong attachment to the furniture. "They've been in the family," Pop had said. "They belong to us."

Abe stood abruptly. "We'll consider your request and get back to you."

"I'm only in Vienna for a few days – I'm a guest of Erich Hanfnagel."

Ross caught Avia's involuntary grimace, but poker-faced Abe revealed nothing except an extra blink of the eyes. "He wants my furniture for his collection."

"We're well aware of Herr Hanfnagel's collecting. And you, Herr Gold? Are you the agent in this transaction?"

"I'm here to help Mr. Cortese. The furniture is no business of mine."

"Hanfnagel supports this search?" Abe probed.

"Hanfnagel doesn't know," Ross declared.

"He'll know soon enough. Vienna is a small city."

"I keep hearing that," Ross stated. "Do you know a Victor Neurath?" Ross asked Abe.

"Everyone in Vienna knows of him. Why do you ask?"

"I met him last night – at Erich Hanfnagel's home. Next thing I know, he's inviting me into his office for a chat and putting the arm on me to sell the furniture to Hanfnagel."

"That doesn't surprise me," Abe responded. "From what I know the two are very close. I'll tell you this about Victor Neurath. He's not a man to be crossed. He's been a police official all of his life and was active in the Party."

"A Communist?" Ross asked, shocked.

Abe looked at him as if he was speaking to a child. "No, Cortese. The National Socialist Party. We know them as Nazis. As a young man Neurath was an officer in the Gestapo. After the war, supposedly de-Nazified, he continued to serve the postwar government. He rose over the years to assume the number three position in the Police Department."

Ross turned to Jacky. "Did you know this?"

"No. Rudy never said a word."

"That would be Rudy Hanfnagel," Avia observed. "Your – ah – business partner?"

"You want to know more, Cortese?" Abe challenged. Ross shot him a look. "Neurath and Erich Hanfnagel served the same master. Hanfnagel was a gauleiter – a district leader. An important official. One of the many Austrians who welcomed Anschluss and Adolph Hitler with open arms. Like our Chancellor, Herr Waldheim, Hanfnagel served the Third Reich with distinction. As for your request, Cortese, we'll make contact if we have something for you."

"I've got the feeling you've got plenty you could tell me right now. One cop to another, Feder . . . how about it?"

"I'm not a cop. Don't *schmeichel* me. I have work to do."

"I thought this is your work. What are all these files doing here?"

Avia stepped in between him and Abe. "You walk in off the street and demand information from us. What do we know about you?" she said pointedly. "You're supposedly a pure-hearted Gentile seeking to make some form of restitution to a Jewish family. We have enemies, Herr Cortese," Avia continued, softer now. "They are constantly seeking to discredit our work. Are we wrong to be cautious?"

"If you think I'm your enemy, you're wrong."

"You come here with the partner of Hanfnagel's son . . . "

She talked about Jacky as if he wasn't there.

"Jacky's a Jew, for crissake. A supporter of your Center. You know he's alright."

"I can represent myself, Red," Jacky said. Then he spoke to Avia sternly. "Rudy's father won't even speak to him . . . he's written him out of his life. Still, you blame the son for the father's sins?"

"I'm sorry if I've offended you, Herr Gold. We know the history of Freiheit. We also know Vienna. Rudy Hanfnagel is a Hanfnagel. Blood is thicker than water."

"God help us," Jacky said, shaking his head.

"We have to help ourselves," she replied firmly.

"I'm asking you to be straight with me," Ross declared. "This morning Neurath accused my father of stealing furniture from Mosel in thirty-eight. It's horseshit – a tactic to intimidate me into selling – and then getting the hell out of here. So I've got a personal stake in this. Is that enough to convince you?"

Abe sighed, then nodded. "I'll tell you what I can."

Ross sat down on a battered wooden folding chair. Jacky followed suit. Abe went to the cabinet and in a few minutes pulled out a slender file. He turned pages, reading them silently, then looked over at Ross and said, "Lucy Mosel – a granddaughter of Kirmen Mosel."

Ross held his breath while Abe lit a cigarette, inhaled deeply and blew out a cloud of smoke. "Lucy Mosel had been hidden on a farm throughout the war. After the war, she remained there for seven more years, surfacing in Vienna in nineteen-fifty-two."

"Is she still alive?" Ross asked, his urgency apparent.

Abe held up a hand. "Let me tell the story my way. When she finally came out of hiding, she went to a Jewish agency. With their assistance, she made a claim for reparations – the Mosel cabinet shop, the family apartment and its extremely valuable contents."

"Did she get them back?"

"No. The original law which had been established under Allied occupation required the return of assets stolen or seized by Austrians from Jews and other 'undesirables'. But in the early fifties, the law was rewritten by the Austrian Parliament. The revised law favored those who had taken over property and assets between nineteen-thirty-eight and nineteen-forty-five."

"How could they get away with that?"

Avia answered. "Austria succeeded in being named an occupied nation, in spite of the fact that Hitler was welcomed and Austrians served willingly and eagerly in every branch of Nazi Germany's military and civilian operation. Austrians were top SS leaders – Ernst Kaltenbrunner, Arthur Seyss-Inquart – and also Gestapo like Victor Neurath. Austrians ran concentration camps and were leading architects of the Final Solution.

"The Cold War came and led to unholy alliances – often between ex-Nazis and your intelligence people in the U.S. And so Communism was now the enemy and Vienna a frontier in that war. The Allies decided to look the other way."

"What happened to Lucy?"

"Lucy received a token settlement for the Mosel business, a pittance compared to its true worth."

"And the apartment?"

"Hanfnagel was a member of Parliament – a Senator – elected by the Freedom Party."

"I thought he was a businessman."

"What better way to do business than through politics? His party's platform was neo-Nazi and anti-Semitic. They represented powerful business interests. The outcome on the apartment was never in doubt. The commission ruled in Hanfnagel's favor. Lucy Mosel never had a chance."

"I don't believe this shit," Ross said through gritted teeth.

"You'd better believe it," Abe shouted, losing patience. "These are documented facts, not opinions."

Avia gave him a look and he calmed down quickly. "After the Nuremberg Trials, laws were passed in Germany outlawing the Nazi party and anti-Semitic activities. Some effort was made to face up to the enormity of their crimes."

He ground out his cigarette butt in an overflowing ash tray before continuing, "Not so in Austria – not until last year, when the revelations of Chancellor Waldheim's wartime role in the Wehrmacht confronted Austria with its past. Waldheim went on television, acknowledged that many of the worst deputies of National Socialism had been Austrians. He apologized for the crimes committed by Austrians. Then he added a big *but*: "'But as a nation,' he said, 'Austria was Hitler's first victim.' Abe shook his head and snorted dismissively. "Thus, he reduced the Austrian role to a handful of horrible men who had committed evil deeds. The complicity of the majority was denied. He failed to mention that Hitler entered Vienna, not like a conqueror, but like a conquering hero – the leader who would rescue Austria from its true persecutors – the Jews, the Reds and the Pinks."

He paused to light another cigarette.

Ross looked at Jacky. Jacky was holding his breath, waiting for Abe to continue. He was pale and sweaty. Leaning closer to him, Ross put a hand on his shoulder. "Are you okay?"

Jacky nodded, but said nothing.

Ross turned back to Abe. "What else have you got for me?"

"The Freedom Party still exists today. It made such a strong showing in the 1987 elections that the Socialists were forced into a coalition with the Conservatives to defend the state from the threat of the fascist right. They continue to pose a major threat."

"And Hanfnagel?"

Abe shrugged. He would say no more right now. "I've told you what I can about Hanfnagel and his cronies. I will add this. His son, Dolph, follows in his footsteps."

This is Willi's father, Ross thought. A smooth, lying bastard, if ever there was one. Pop was right. Ross was sorry that he ever set foot in Vienna. He needed to find Lucy Mosel, if she still was alive. He had to talk to her. "You'll see if you can get a lead to this woman – or her survivors?" he asked.

Avia nodded. "I'll cross-check our files and contact other centers for information on her whereabouts. I'll be in touch. Where are you staying?"

"At the Royale."

"Police are paid well in New York," Abe mused.

"Hanfnagel's picking up the ticket." Ross felt defensive. "He really wants the furniture."

"So I see," Abe said quietly.

"I will speak to you soon," Avia reassured him, showing them to the door.

"Thanks," Ross replied.

As the door closed behind them, Ross heard the locks click into place. He looked Jacky over and was glad to see his color had improved. "You sure you'll be alright?"

"Yes. I was shocked for a moment . . . but after all is said and done, not surprised. I'm not looking forward to telling Rudy."

"Are you positive he *doesn't* know?"

"If he does, that would surprise me. Will you come back to Freiheit with me?"

"Uh, uh. I have to sort things out."

Ross took a long look at Jacky as they shook hands. Despite his reassurances, the man appeared daunted by the prospect of facing his mate with the facts that they had uncovered. Rudy might be estranged from his father, but the guy was still his old man. How much did Willi know about Hanfnagel's role during the war – and how would *she* feel about Ross stirring up the mud?

Pop's admonitions about Vienna rang more and more true. A dark current ran through this city, a stream separate from the Danube, polluted by a history which he did not comprehend and which left hatred as a sediment upon its shore.

When the footsteps had faded down the stairs, Avia turned to Abe. "What do you think of the American?"

"An innocent, I suspect. I'll check him out."

"Can we use him?"

"We can try. What do you have in mind?"

"Let me make some calls."

She sat down and started to explore several possibilities.

CHAPTER EIGHTEEN

Ross entered the Royale hotel and headed straight for the bar.

"What would you like?" the bartender asked.

"Malt Scotch. Make it a double."

"Please. Take a table."

As he found a quiet corner, he suddenly thought – Imagine, I could be sitting where Adolph fucking Hitler sat.

The waiter brought his drink. "Is there anything else I can get for you, Meinherr?"

Yeah, he thought, a ticket out on the next flight. He shook his head and sipped his drink, trying to distance himself from what had taken place at the Center. The whiskey made him feel light-headed, a not unpleasant sensation. Within minutes it seemed that he had emptied his glass. He caught the waiter's eye and motioned for a refill, then thought better of it and cancelled the request.

He wasn't going to wait around for Avia's call. Ross remembered the brief encounter with the old woman, Annalee Speitz. Willi said that her "fairy godmother" had lived in the building forever. Annalee must have known the Mosels. She had invited him to stop by for a chat, hadn't she? That's where he'd begin! The certainty that Willi wouldn't like it caused him to hesitate, but only for a minute. He signed the bar tab, picked himself up and made his way to the building on Himmelpfortgasse.

This time, Ross tried to look past the seductive charm of cafés, taverns, palaces and concert halls, red-tiled roofs and streets laid out for horse-drawn carriages. But he soon realized that like most people, his ignorance of history left him without the means to explain how terrible evil could grow out of the same soil as magnificent cultural achievement.

Ross found her name on the directory and rang the intercom. There was no response. He gave it a minute and tried again.

A woman's voice questioned, "Wer ist da?"

"Ross Cortese, Frau Speitz . . . Willi's friend. We met the other day. I should have called first, but I was in the neighborhood and thought I'd take you up on your offer to chat. If it's not a good time I can come back."

"It's all right, Herr Cortese. I'll ring you in. Apartment four. Third floor."

Ross stepped off the elevator. The door to Annalee's apartment was slightly ajar and she stood just inside, examining him closely, as if to be sure that he was the man she met with Willi. For a moment, a startled expression appeared on her face and he was afraid that she was going to shut the door. Instead, she said, "Please . . . won't you come in."

He entered and followed her through the large foyer into her living room. "Would you prefer tea or coffee?"

"Please don't fuss. Whatever you're having will be just fine."

"I'll be only a few minutes. Make yourself at home."

Alone, Ross took in the space. The room was cluttered with sofas, loveseats, armchairs and two pieces of furniture that appeared to be by Mosel – a refectory table and bookcase. The paintings on the wall were pretty and decorative, still lifes and landscapes, easy to live with. He was drawn to the magnificent grand piano, draped with a lace throw. On it sat a dozen framed photographs, most of them vintage. Ross picked up one of a boy and a girl, close in age, maybe nine or ten. They looked oddly familiar. Annalee returned shortly, carrying a silver tray.

"Here. Let me help you," he said, replacing the photo and taking the tray from her.

"Thank you. Put it on the table please, Herr Cortese."

He set it down and said, "You have a lovely home." Pointing to the photo, he asked, "Your children?"

She smiled wistfully. "No, that's Willi and Rudy. My late husband and I were unable to have children of our own. When Frau Hanfnagel died, the children visited very often. They brightened our lives."

"You mean a lot to them. Willi talks about you like family."

"You're very kind. Please, sit and have coffee. Cream?" He nodded. She spooned on the whipped cream. "We call it *schlag* and use it too freely for our own good."

He sipped the rich, bittersweet coffee through the layer of cream.

"Try a cookie. I bake them myself." The thin, crispy browned butter cookies were delicious and he told her so.

"So . . . tell me about your family, Herr Cortese."

He winced at the formal manner of address.

"Do me a favor. Everyone's called me Red since I was a kid."

"Red . . . of course." She felt pressure on her chest and took a deep breath.

Ross saw her pained look and bent toward her, concerned.

"It's alright," she assured him. "It comes and goes. I'm fine, Herr . . . I mean Red. You'll forgive me if I don't use the familiar easily. In my generation that was not the custom. Are you married?"

"My wife died nine months ago."

"Forgive an old woman's intrusion. Your sorrow is still fresh." He squirmed as she continued, "It never goes away . . . but with time, it is easier to bear. You have children?"

"Two great kids," he beamed.

"You're fortunate to have someone with whom to share your grief. Your father still lives? . . . and your mother?"

"Both in good health, thank God. Two sisters. We're a big family – and close."

Her eyes welled with tears. "You're fortunate indeed. Do you carry photos of your children?"

"I used to – when they were little. I don't now. I should. Amy's twenty-two. She starts law school in September. Billy, he's three years older, a cop like me."

Wariness rushed in to replace welcome. He knew the signs. "You're polizei?" she asked.

"Twenty-five years plus. New York Police Department."

"But your visit to Vienna . . . it's not official."

"No. Certainly not. I own two pieces of Kirmen Mosel's furniture and Herr Hanfnagel wants to purchase them."

"You'll sell to him?" she asked cautiously.

"I was leaning that way. Now I'm not so sure. I need some information that I thought you might be able to provide – to clear up some things. The pieces I own were inscribed by Mosel – For my beloved Ariella."

She stood, then turned away from him and went to the piano.

"Can you tell me who she was?" Ross asked.

Her shoulders and upper back convulsed, in an effort to hold back sobs. Ross watched, not knowing what to say or do.

"I'm sorry to have upset you," he murmured.

She turned again and her tears flowed without restraint. Instinctively, he moved to help her back into her chair. Her voice broke as she explained, "Kirmen made them for Ariella when she was little more than an infant. She was his first grandchild. They were to be for her home when she married." Now she made no effort to hide her anguish.

"You obviously knew them well. Please. What happened to the family?" Ross pleaded.

She put her hands over her face and shook her head from side to side, a witness seeking to rid herself of traumatic memories. Telling him the story was more painful than she could bear, but Annalee forced herself to go on.

"Destroyed," she said, in a haunted whisper. "Along with so many other innocent people."

"I've been told that a Lucy Mosel survived the war. Do you know if she's still living?"

She slid her hands down her cheeks until they came together in a pose of prayer beneath her chin. "Why do you want to know?" she asked, her attitude more searching than belligerent.

"I'd want her to have a say in what happens to the furniture – or to share in . . . in the . . . "

He couldn't say the word. Her pain was contagious and he felt sick inside.

"Perhaps we'd all be better off if you let the past remain where time has buried it." Her voice was flat but still friendly.

"To listen to you speak, it never has been buried. I know it's difficult for you, but I've got nowhere else to turn. My father, Franco Cortese, worked for Mr. Mosel before the war. Did you by any chance ever meet him?"

Annalee went blank. Her eyes squeezed shut. He watched as she withdrew. He'd gone as far as he could with her and would push no further. When she opened her eyes, she continued as if she had never heard him. She spoke hoarsely. "Lucy was Ariella's younger sister. She was not home when the Storm Troopers came to take them."

"I know that she returned to Vienna in nineteen fifty-two. Have you seen or heard from her since? I must know, Frau Speitz."

She clutched her chest and he felt terribly guilty. "My heart. I tire easily. The doctor insists that I rest. What else does an old woman do?"

"Will you be alright? Can I get something for you before I leave?"

She lifted her hand and stroked his cheek. Then she rose and slowly led him to the door. "Take care," she urged, closing the door behind him.

Ross left the building, heading toward Kartnerstrasse. He was a jumble of emotions. He'd gone less than half a block when he heard his name called. Looking back, he saw Erich Hanfnagel striding briskly toward him from the other end of the street.

"Herr Cortese," he called out. "An unexpected pleasure. Were you looking for me?" he asked eagerly.

Ross stared at him and said nothing. You're the last guy I want to see right now, he thought, reining in words of accusation. He would not confront Hanfnagel about his meeting with Neurath or the visit to the Center until he had a chance to speak to Willi.

"Perhaps we were fated to meet," Hanfnagel smiled, disregarding Ross's rudeness. "Are you prepared to move forward with our transaction? Come. We needn't stand around like street vendors."

He moved toward the house, expecting Ross to follow. Instead, Ross edged away from him.

"Sir, I haven't made my decision about the furniture."

"Then what are you doing here?" Hanfnagel asked, nonplussed.

"I paid a call on Annalee Speitz."

"Annalee Speitz?" Hanfnagel asked, his bewilderment increasing.

"Willi and I ran into her yesterday. She asked me to stop by."

"What does a visit to Annalee have to do with our business?"

"I asked you about that inscription on the furniture. It turns out that Ariella was Mosel's granddaughter. He made the furniture for her."

"Yes?"

"Her sister Lucy survived the war. That name mean anything to you?"

"No. Why should it?"

The man was out-and-out lying. Lucy Mosel had made a claim against him. "I'd like to give her or her family a say in what happens to the furniture."

Hanfnagel turned livid. The tension rose in his voice like steam from a kettle. Ross expected to hear a shrill whistle.

"Herr Cortese, we sing a song in Vienna. The opening verse begins – happy is he who forgets what can't be changed. We Austrians were the first victims of a war which we did not seek. It is forty-five years since the war ended. Don't you think that if there were survivors they would have come forth by now and made their claims? Besides," Hanfnagel continued, "one day my collection, including your pieces, will be in a museum. Could Mosel and his family be other than happy with such an outcome?"

Hanfnagel assumed that Ross's silence meant that he was

wavering. "So, Herr Cortese, do we have a deal?" He stretched out his hand, convinced of his own rationale and supreme right to the furniture.

The lies and manipulations stuck in Ross's craw. "No deal," was all that he could utter, afraid of what he'd say if he took out the stopper.

Hanfnagel forced a smile, but it read as a rictus of painful disappointment. "Then good day to you, Herr Cortese." He clicked his heels and made an about-face with military precision. Throwing his shoulders back, he marched into the apartment house.

Ross hailed a cab. As he gave the driver instructions, he noticed a brown Mercedes pulling out behind him. It followed at a distance, then passed and pulled into a no-parking zone near the hotel. Was he paranoid, or was he being followed? He paid the driver and went into the hotel.

CHAPTER NINETEEN

Ross was running late. It was getting to be a habit. He told the cabbie to make time to the ferry landing at Schwedenbrucke. There'd be an extra tip. "Meinherr is going dancing on the Danube, eh?" the driver asked in perfect English.

"If you get me there in time," Ross replied.

The man nodded and the cab flew around the Ring, across a bridge over the Donaukanal and through the heart of the Prater. Ross looked at his watch instead of the scenery. They arrived at the boat landing on the tree-lined bank of the Danube with a minute to spare. Ross heard the last call for boarding and saw Willi pacing the dock.

"I was afraid you'd miss the boat," she said as they dashed up the gangplank of the Danube Queen.

Once on deck, she kissed him passionately. "Now have a look at our river," she urged proudly.

Ross looked out and saw sunset reflected on the dark wavy surface, in shades of crimson and gold. The river was about the width of New York's East River. A beautiful sight, but not enough to make him forget what he had learned about this city today.

Willi took his hand and led him into the ballroom and up to the bar. "When the boat turns into the Danube," she continued, "the band plays the Blue Danube waltz. Then your welcome to Vienna is official. It sounds corny but it's tradition. Come. Let's celebrate with champagne."

She ordered and the bartender poured. Looking at her in such a romantic setting, Ross felt like he should pinch himself to make sure it all was real. They lifted the tulip-shaped glasses, clinked and drank. "How did the rest of your day go?" Ross asked, needing to make small talk.

"Uneventfully. And yours?"

The music started before he could speak. Willi put down her glass and dragged him onto the dance floor. Unfortunately, his body couldn't lie.

"Why the resistance?" she asked.

"Ask my two left feet," he covered.

She laughed, holding his gaze with her beautiful eyes. "Come on, you can do it."

And so he forced himself into the spirited whirl.

"See that . . . you're not half-bad," she said, once they really got going.

Finally, the waltz ended. They applauded lightly. Willi could feel him tighten up again. "Something's wrong. What is it, Red?"

"Nothing."

"There's a change in you. Is it me?"

"You. No. No way."

"It's Annie then."

"No, it's not her either."

"Please. Don't brush me off. I know how much you loved her – but I believe there's room inside of you to love me, too."

Her sentiments overwhelmed him. He took her hand. "Let's go out on deck."

They stood at the railing, looking out on the Danube, listening to the faint strains of the music. He felt the slight roll of the boat as it moved upriver, against the current. "How would you feel if I didn't sell the furniture to your father?"

"Why wouldn't you?" She sounded hurt.

"Does there have to be a reason? Let's say I chose not to."

"I'd need to give him an explanation," she insisted.

He let go of her hand. "Why?" he asked reproachfully.

"I introduced you to him . . . made the arrangements."

"Come on, Willi. Fredericks made the contact. You're not responsible." He looked at her closely. "Did you guarantee that when I came over here I'd sell," he pressured.

"Not in so many words. Something's going on, Red. One minute we're lovers with a future . . . the next, you're creating a problem."

"Why does it have to be a problem?"

"Well, it is. The furniture means a great deal to him. You know that."

"That's for sure," he grumbled.

"What's that supposed to mean?" she demanded.

"It's been a rough day, Willi."

"What? The visit to Victor?"

He looked at her sharply. “What do you know about that?”

“Nothing.”

“Well, it wasn't exactly a tour of police headquarters. The son of a bitch brought me there to tell me that the Mosel furniture was stolen . . . and that my father was a suspect in the theft.”

“Oh, liebchen. How awful. I'm sorry.”

“You saying you think it's true?” he snapped indignantly.

“Why would Victor lie?”

“To make sure that your father gets what he wants.” He couldn't quite buy her naiveté. It put him off.

“Victor would never do such a thing. He's a man of integrity.”

“You know him that well, do you?”

“Since childhood. He's Father's closest friend . . . ”

“That's what I mean.”

“Stop it, Red. Victor's like an uncle to me.”

“Maybe you should stick to fairy godmothers. Did you know that your ‘uncle’ was a Nazi official?”

She shook her head in a fury of disbelief. “I won't listen to you slander Victor Neurath.”

“But it's alright for him to accuse my father. Listen, Willi. After meeting with your ‘uncle’ Victor. I visited the Center for Holocaust Research. Jacky Gold came with me. They told us about the Mosel family – and what happened to them.”

“Why are you doing this?” she asked angrily.

Ross seemed not to hear her. “They all died in the war. All but one. There was one survivor – Ariella's sister, Lucy. I asked if they would help find Lucy Mosel or her heirs. They gave me information about Neurath . . . ”

He took a deep breath before diving in. “And about your father . . . ”

She looked like a trapped animal as she twisted away from his reach.

“Whatever it is, it's in the distant past,” she cried, shaking her head wildly in denial.

He stepped forward, took her by the shoulders and forced her to face him. “You can't keep hiding!” he insisted.

“I'm not hiding. There's nothing to hide from.” Her chin was defiant, but trembling.

“Your father was a Nazi official. A Party leader,” he hurled, wanting to penetrate her shield. “After the war he continued to serve their interests.”

“You're lying! I won't hear it.” Her face was contorted with rage, her beauty ravaged by pain. “You remember what happened in New

York? How the truth about you was distorted. Can't you see? These people do the same to my father. They lie," she accused, "and you believe them . . . "

"Try and hear me, Willi. My father was accused of committing a crime. I didn't come here to go after yours."

He held her very tight. She rested her head on his shoulder, her rage spent. He felt a slight easing in her body.

She spoke, but still did not look at him. "Sell Father the furniture," she cajoled. "Then you and I can leave here. We'll go to Paris – or Venice. You've never been there."

"I can't do it. Ariella's sister may still be alive. I feel like the furniture's not mine to sell."

She pushed him away. "You say you care for me . . . you don't. You couldn't treat me so cruelly if you did. Go after your father, if you must. Leave mine alone, do you hear?"

She backed off two steps, then ran inside.

Ross didn't follow. He leaned his elbows on the railing and gazed at the moon's reflection in the Danube. She didn't return to his side for the rest of the voyage.

CHAPTER TWENTY

Doschenko paced the alley across from the ferry terminal. He was furious. His small favor to Neurath was costing him. He had picked up a dazzling young Hungarian woman at a bar. She was leaving Vienna in the morning and had agreed to spend the night with him. As they were leaving the bar, his beeper signalled. It was Herdlo, the man he had assigned to follow the American. The fool had eaten some junk food at a sidewalk stand and was ill with vomiting and diarrhea. Unable to come up with a last-minute substitute, here he was, a KGB master reduced to this role. He soothed himself with the thought that in a few short days, the assassination that he had planned could conceivably change the face of European politics.

When the gangplank went down two hours later, Willi was the first one off the boat. She ran as if she was being chased, found her car, jumped in and sped off. Her only thought was to put distance between herself and Red. Her hopes for a relationship with him were dashed. How could he treat her so cruelly? It was *his* father who had to account for himself, not hers. Her father was a man of character, a respected citizen and philanthropist. He had loved and cared for her all of her life. The idea that he had been involved with the Nazi party was absurd.

Ross saw the white BMW pull out of the car-park. He shook his head sadly and made his way to join the long line at the cabstand. Weariness overtook him and he waited listlessly. When his turn came, however, he asked the cab driver to take him to Café Freiheit. The driver regarded him through the mirror with a look of contempt.

As they approached the inner city, traffic was backed up. Ross spotted a brown Mercedes two cars back. He asked the driver to take the next left. The Mercedes followed. This time, he asked for a right turn. Again, the car followed, trying to remain at a distance. Ross told the driver to stop at the next corner, paid the fare and got out. He strolled for a block then stopped suddenly, pretending to study the interior of an antique shop. The Mercedes slowly passed him, pulling in fifty feet up the block alongside a hydrant. There was no longer a doubt in Ross's mind. He was under surveillance. It had to be Neurath's doing. Ross tried acting casual as he walked past the Mercedes. In fact, he was resisting a strong impulse to yank open the door and drag the guy out. He continued down the block, feeling the man's eyes on his back. As he turned the corner into Naglergasse, he heard a car door shut. He was now being followed on foot.

It was nearly midnight, but a small crowd was gathered just beyond the entrance to the café. Ross moved to the edge of the crowd.

A young, casually dressed black man was backed up against the building wall by two tattooed skinheads in leather and heavy metal. They were poking and taunting him. A few bystanders yelled to leave him alone; others egged them on.

Jacky came out of the café and shouted at the skinheads. Two cops stood across the street, utterly indifferent.

Ross pushed his way through the crowd and went up to them. The skinheads laughed, then leveled curses at the "old man" as he placed a protective arm around their scapegoat and took a step toward the café. The 'heads moved to block him.

"Get the hell out of my way!" Ross growled, glaring at them. Something in his fierce demeanor and confident stance drove one of them back a step. As the skinhead moved away, he snarled, "*Der schweinhund ist Americanische.*"

The other man, bolder, gestured contemptuously at Ross. He spoke in English, his tone menacing. "We send a message to Jew-lovers and *schwarzes* that Austria is for Austrians."

He reached down into his boot to draw a knife. There was a gasp from the crowd. Before the skinhead straightened up, Ross moved in swiftly, seized his arm and forced it away in a wide arc. As he did so, he kneed the man in the crotch, then finished him off with a short hard blow to the solar plexus. The man toppled to the ground, offering no resistance as Ross relieved him of his weapon.

His blood still pumping madly, Ross went after the other skinhead. The man looked as if he had met the Terminator and he hastily retreated out of range, leaving his companion retching on the sidewalk. Only then did the police start to cross the street.

Ross and Jacky led the shaken man into Freiheit.

Once inside, Jacky introduced them. "Archie Tonamburo of South Africa. Ross Cortese of New York. Archie is a pianist, on scholarship at the conservatory."

"I'm grateful for your intervention, my friend," the young man said in beautifully accented English, gripping Ross's hand firmly. "Please excuse me now. I see my girlfriend – she looks worried." He left them to join her at a nearby table.

Jacky moved behind the bar and poured Ross a double Scotch.

"Is this a frequent occurrence?" Ross inquired.

Jacky shrugged. "In Vienna, yes. In this district, no. The police are usually quick to step in here – otherwise, it's bad for tourism. By the way, what happened to waltzing on the Danube?"

"My first was my last. I told Willi that her father was a Nazi. She went ballistic."

"No one can accuse you of discretion."

"How did Rudy take the news?"

"Calmly. He said he should have suspected it. His father keeps his hands clean, but seems quite comfortable with Dolph's politics. Drink up, Red. You look like you need it. Willi called a while ago. She sounded very agitated and asked Rudy to come to her apartment. He ran right over to her place."

Jacky sighed. "Did you know that their mother was a suicide?"

"God, no," Ross cried out. "She told me that her mother died when she was a kid – but she never mentioned suicide. Jesus. You think she'll be alright?"

"You mean am I afraid this news will kill her? Not at all. Willi's a survivor."

"What do you know about the circumstances of their mother's death?"

"Only that Frau Hanfnagel was deeply depressed for months. I think their father blamed Rudy, the little 'faggot', for his wife's death – though never overtly."

"What about Willi?"

"He adored her. And why not? Dolph's a clod. Rudy a sissy. Willi is beautiful, intelligent and artistic."

"How could she not know about his past?"

Jacky shrugged. "The silence of the fathers. Denial by the children. I never heard of his tenure in the Parliament until our visit to the Center. Insofar as I can tell, he's kept out of overt involvement in politics for decades. It's true, he supported Waldheim when Waldheim's military service in the Wehrmacht was exposed – but so did many people."

"It's no wonder then. If she believes me, her world collapses. She's buried in the rubble. Better she kills off the messenger."

"You're not dead yet. Sleep it off. Tomorrow will be better."

"Don't bet on it," Ross said gloomily as he turned and left the café.

Ross hailed a cab and asked for the Royale. He checked through the rearview mirror as the driver turned into a darkened street. The Mercedes had reappeared and remained several car lengths back. *Not this again.* What the hell, he muttered. Enough of this crap. "Drop me on the next corner," he declared to the driver.

"But you asked for the Royale, Meinherr," the driver insisted.

"Never mind that. Just drop me there," Ross snapped.

The puzzled cabbie pulled into a bus stop. Ross paid him and headed quickly down the nearest sidestreet.

He could taste the anticipation, convinced that his tail would have no choice but to ditch the Mercedes and follow on foot. Pausing halfway down the block in front of a store window, Ross made his tail. Forty something, fit looking, drably dressed and trying his damndest to look inconspicuous as he sauntered down the street. This guy was assuming that the surveillance had gone unnoticed, or maybe he just didn't give a damn, Ross thought. Resuming his walk and picking up the pace, Ross turned the corner and ducked into a narrow alley.

Doschenko fell for the feint and was shocked when Ross grabbed him and pulled him into the shadows. Ross shoved him up against the brick wall, and dug his forearm into the man's larynx. Ross saw his eyes bug out with fear. He's not used to being on the other end, he thought.

"Who do you work for?" Ross snarled, easing the pressure slightly so that the man could speak.

"*Nicht verstehen,*" Doschenko croaked.

"Go on. Play dumb . . . but make a move and you're dead meat."

Ross squeezed hard to reinforce the warning. With his free hand, he patted Doschenko down and found the telltale bulge of a small automatic in a shoulder holster. He took the weapon and, removing his forearm from the man's throat, pointed the gun at his gut.

"Let me have your I.D.," Ross growled.

Doschenko complied, slowly removing his wallet from his breast pocket, cursing himself for carrying his real documents. Ross flipped it open. There was no police I.D. He read the driver's license. Vladimir Doschenko. Other permits, including a visa, were printed in Cyrillic. Was the guy Russian? What the hell was going on?

"Who are you working for?"

Doschenko remained silent. He was angry with himself. He was dealing with a professional. He should have insisted that Neurath provide him with more information about this man. Was it possible that Cortese was working for an intelligence agency? It was more than a little alarming that he knew Doschenko's name. Terminating an American agent was a complication he did not need at this time.

Ross also knew a pro when he met one. He would learn nothing from Doschenko without hurting him and that was out of the question. He took a shot.

"Tell Commissioner Neurath that he'll be hearing from me soon."

The gleam faded from Doschenko's eyes and a faint twitch of the man's eyelid assured Ross that he had nailed it. By morning, the Commissioner would know that the surveillance had been blown. Ross was prepared to eject the clip and shove the gun back into Doschenko's holster when he caught a look in the man's eyes that made him think again.

He had been the object of looks like that before – looks that threatened violence. He decided to keep the gun and pushed Doschenko out onto the street.

The man hesitated, then wheeled and walked away. "I'm going back to my hotel," Ross called out after him. "You're finished for the night."

Doschenko kept walking. Perhaps circumstances would, after all, require that Cortese be eliminated. That prospect eased the sting of humiliation.

Ross moved quickly in the opposite direction and hailed a cab. The driver understood English, especially when accompanied by a fistful of bills. "A brown Mercedes is going to come out of that street, any second now," Ross said, pointing. "I want you to follow it at a distance. Keep cars between you. There's a bonus if we're not spotted."

It never occurred to Doschenko, despite his extensive field experience, that Ross would attempt to follow him. He drove fast, wanting to get back to his apartment and assign another operative to the American. He'd speak to Neurath first thing in the morning and then select an appropriate course of action.

Ross's driver enjoyed the game – and they were lucky. Doschenko's route took him up Linke Wienzeile, a two lane street, past the Naschmarkt. The Mercedes swung right into Morizgasse.

"Don't follow him down that street," Ross warned. "Wait here on the avenue." He got out and closed the cab door quietly. Hugging the edge of the building, he turned the corner and watched Doschenko's car come to an abrupt halt a third of the way down the block.

Ross would soon know whether this was a tactic chosen by the Russian to determine whether he was being followed. He remained in the shadows as Doschenko parked. Only when the Russian locked up and was half a block away did Ross move out after him.

He followed at a distance for two blocks, occasionally slipping into a doorway for cover. Doschenko went into a modest apartment building on Gumpendorfer Strasse. From where Ross was observing, he saw a light come on in a second floor window. After waiting five minutes, and with no sign that Doschenko was studying the street, he casually walked past the building, noting the number.

Once around the block, Ross made his way back to the cab on Linke Wienzelle. The driver grinned. "Successful, Meinherr?"

Ross shrugged. "Royale Hotel, please," he said, settling back into the seat, exhausted.

Fifteen minutes later, he paid the driver, using almost all of his remaining schillings, then went directly to his room. He fell into bed exhausted but passed the night in an uneasy sleep.

The next morning he awoke with a splitting headache. Bright light streamed in the window. He checked the clock – seven thirty. Ross called valet service and asked them to press a jacket and slacks. "Immediately, Meinherr."

He then dialed Willi's home number. She picked up after two rings. "Willi? Please listen to me. We need to talk." She hung up.

At nine, he entered the hotel dining room and ordered breakfast.

At precisely that moment, Vladimir Doschenko, in a foul mood, intercepted Victor Neurath as he was leaving home to go to his office. As they passed each other on the sidewalk, Doschenko spoke in a whisper: "Ten-thirty, Fleischmarkt." Neurath nodded and they proceeded on their separate ways.

Neurath waved to the owner of Griechenbeisl, a five-hundred-year-old ivy-hung tavern on a cobbled lane, turned the corner and chose a table at Café Fleishmarkt. From this vantage point, he enjoyed a sweeping view of the shopping street and could detect any sign of surveillance. Not that he had anything to worry about – it was merely the habit of a lifetime. Meetings with Doschenko were rarely arranged more than a few hours in advance, a piece of tradecraft which each had learned in their separate schools.

Doschenko eased himself into a chair at the next table and

ordered coffee and rolls. Neurath sensed the man's tension. The waiter returned with the order, then quickly disappeared inside the café.

"I was forced to substitute for my watcher last night and had an unfortunate occurrence with the man I was following," the Russian whispered through his bruised larynx.

Neurath looked over at him sharply. "I told you he was to be kept under surveillance – that was all."

Doschenko smiled bitterly, revealing stainless steel caps. "I bear the marks of the encounter, not he. He's skilled. Next time, don't send a man on an assignment without providing what he needs to know about his subject!" the Russian snapped.

Neurath let the reproach pass without comment. He did not need a pissing contest over tradecraft. "It serves my purpose for him to know that he is being followed."

Doschenko bristled. "It may serve *your* purpose, but not mine. He knows my name." He was not looking at Neurath but felt him stiffen.

"What else did he learn from you?" the Commissioner demanded.

"Absolutely nothing. Who is he?"

"He has nothing to do with us. He's a New York police officer, here on personal business with Erich Hanfnagel. His time in Vienna is short . . . "

"It will be shorter if he gets in my way – I promise you that."

"No cause for alarm."

"You are certain that he's not seconded to an agency?"

"Impossible!"

"If he should mention me to someone?"

"He knows no one here other than the Hanfnagels."

Neurath paid his check and departed without another word, leaving Doschenko to deal with his disappointment. He had hoped that the Commissioner would sanction the American's termination. *That* he would have enjoyed.

CHAPTER TWENTY-ONE

At breakfast, Ross mapped a plan of action from among his limited options. Leaving the café, he covered seven blocks in seven minutes. He reached the building on Himmelpfortgasse and rang Hanfnagel's bell. Otto answered and Ross announced curtly, "Cortese here to see Mr. Hanfnagel."

He was buzzed in at once.

Upstairs, Hanfnagel came to the door. "Herr Cortese. An unexpected pleasure. Please, come inside."

Hanfnagel led him into the salon. "I hope that the early morning visit means that you're prepared to conclude our arrangements. There's no problem which men of good will cannot solve."

"And, of course, you're a man of good will . . . "

Hanfnagel appeared genuinely baffled by Ross's unveiled sarcasm. He drew back his head haughtily and said, "You doubt that?"

"I've got reason to."

"Then let's talk like civilized men and clear up any misunderstanding. Please, sit down. Can I offer you a coffee?"

"No, I'll stand. And no coffee."

"Have it your way."

"Your good friend Neurath accused my father of stealing Mosel's furniture," Ross declared indignantly.

Hanfnagel was quick to interrupt. "I don't know what Victor said to you, Cortese . . . "

Sure Ross thought. Play it dumb.

"But quite frankly," Hanfnagel continued, "I don't care how your father came by the furniture as long as . . . "

"As long as you complete your collection. That I can believe. You may not care, Hanfnagel, but I do. Very much. I think your pal fabricated a file to coerce me into selling to you. It won't work. I know my father. Like everyone, he's got secrets." I sound like Kelsey, Ross thought. "But I know in my heart, he's not capable of stealing."

"Your loyalty is admirable. I would hope for the same from my own children. Victor Neurath said nothing to me of this. But even if it was true, those were difficult times. One survived as best as one could."

"So I'm finding out," Ross said grimly. Hanfnagel did not overlook the tone.

"Is there something else that concerns you?"

"I see that you haven't spoken to Willi this morning. She won't have anything more to do with me. I hurt her very badly."

Hanfnagel frowned. "Perhaps she hasn't said anything to me because it's not my business."

"It is your business. Neurath's accusation led me to ask questions. I went to this place . . . a Center for Holocaust Research. They told me about you – and I told her."

Hanfnagel lost his composure for the briefest instant, a hairline crack in his smooth facial expression and the merest twitch at the corner of his mouth.

"What did you find out that could possibly have disturbed my daughter?"

"That you were a Nazi official," Ross shot back without hesitation. "That you welcomed Hitler's annexation of Austria."

"And, of course, you accepted *their* story without question, swallowing it whole," Hanfnagel replied calmly. "I'm surprised at you, Herr Cortese. You're a police officer, a trained investigator. You know there are two sides to every story. So this is the problem that's come between you and my daughter?"

"She didn't want to hear it."

"What is there to hear?"

"You live here – in this apartment – Mosel's apartment – with furnishings and art that belonged to an innocent family, which your kind hated and destroyed."

"My kind?" Hanfnagel said haughtily. "I served Austria. I hated no one – and obtained everything I own through legal means."

"Sure . . . tell me about it," Ross said icily. "What's your story?"

Ross heard the outer door close loudly and Willi call out, "Father?" Then she was there, standing in the entrance to the living room, horrified to discover Ross's presence. "He has no right to be here," she insisted to her father.

To Ross, she said coldly, "I want you to leave."

Hanfnagel chided her gently. "Liebchen. Herr Cortese is my guest.

He came here troubled that he had upset you. Don't compound a misunderstanding with rudeness. Your friend was informing me of his findings when you arrived."

"Then I'll leave!" she declared.

"No, Willi," Hanfnagel said firmly. "You'll stay and listen to what I have to say."

He turned to Ross. "If you listen with an open mind, Herr Cortese, you'll find that the truth is never simple. Please be seated, as a courtesy to me."

Ross and Willi sat on the sofa, keeping an ocean's distance between them.

Hanfnagel paced as he lectured. His eyes moved between them, pausing to hold each in turn with his gaze.

"When the Great War broke out," he began, "Austria was second only to England in the size of her empire. The loss of that war resulted in the loss of the empire. The victorious Allies extracted a terrible price. The Treaty of Versailles was cruel, lacking generosity.

"From fifty-four million under one ruler, we became six million. A squabbling republic, a nightmare of inflation and speculation in which hunger and poverty became the norm. Very much like Russia today, I might add.

"My family had been well-to-do landowners for several generations. When I was six, we lost everything. My father had served the Kaiser as an officer and been awarded the Iron Cross for bravery. He could not cope and died five years later, a victim of the *peace*. I was eleven. I and my older brother became the breadwinners in the family."

"That's a sad story," Ross said impatiently.

Before he had the opportunity to say another word, Willi cried out, "Give my father a chance to speak, why don't you? You listened to those others . . . "

Hanfnagel thanked her for her support with a nod and a smile, then continued. "Yes, and so the rise of National Socialism appealed to us. Hitler promised to restore to Germany, and through a greater Reich, restore to Austria as well, the dignity that Versailles had stolen from us. Who could have foreseen the devastating consequences? Communism under Stalin threatened from the East. I loved my country. Is that a crime?

"By the time of the Anschluss I was serving as an administrator – seeing to it that people were clothed, fed and housed through the difficult war years. I harmed no one. When peace came, I worked hard and cared for my family. I was fortunate to achieve success during the postwar rebuilding of Austria."

Willi went to her father and kissed his cheek.

"You see, Red. You should have come to Father first, not to those who'd make us all out to be criminals."

Hanfnagel patted her hand.

Ross suspected that Hanfnagel's story left out much more than it told. It was too pat, almost rehearsed. The man had to be pushed.

"And the Jews? The camps?" Ross demanded.

"I had nothing to do with that. Believe me. In every war the people know only a fraction of the truth. We were told that the Jewish population was being relocated – to work for the betterment of the Reich. They had emigrated from the East to Vienna in large numbers in the previous century. And for the most part, had never integrated into Austrian society. They are, after all, a clannish people."

Ross saw Willi flinch.

Hanfnagel barely missed a beat. "After a war, the victors rewrite history."

"What's that supposed to mean?" Ross growled.

"In the realm of politics, money is king. Before the war, your political leaders, Roosevelt included, refused the offers of the Reich to relocate the Jews. There was a Depression. Your government did not want large numbers of immigrants competing with Americans for jobs.

"After the war, to deflect their guilt and to maintain the financial support of their wealthiest backers, Western leaders emphasized the cruelty of Germany toward the Jews and denied their own role in the abandonment of these same people."

He took a breath before boldly asserting, "Furthermore, Truman had the blood of Hiroshima and Nagasaki on his hands. What better way to wash those hands than with exaggerated stories of millions killed in concentration camps by barbaric Germans."

Ross glanced over at Willi. She appeared totally engrossed in her father's story, like a child listening to a parent read a fairy tale.

"Just wait a minute!" Ross demanded, outraged by the lies. "I've seen pictures and film footage of the concentration camps being liberated by our G.I.'s. The dead piled high. Old and young, women and children . . . babies. The survivors barely skeletons. How were they a threat to your Reich."

"Did you know that those women and children were there because of a policy which emphasized keeping families together?"

"You mean *dying* together, don't you?"

"There was concern that Jews, with their roots in Poland and

Russia, were subversives, potential spies and saboteurs. You did the same to your Japanese during the war."

"Not the same! We didn't starve, beat or experiment on them. We didn't gas them and send them to crematoriums."

"Those who were cremated died of typhus and threatened the population with contagion. Are you aware, Herr Cortese, that there is a new generation of scholars in the United States and Europe who have grave doubts about the exaggerated numbers claimed as Jewish victims?"

"Yeah . . . and there are those who believe that Elvis is still alive."

Hanfnagel shrugged. "You accept what your leaders and the media tell you. Often, that's propaganda to serve their political ends."

Ross saw the look of smugness on Hanfnagel's face.

"You have an answer for everything, don't you?" Ross snapped, in disgust.

He looked at Willi. Her expression was blank. "If you can buy this Willi, I'll sell you the Brooklyn Bridge real cheap."

Her face flushed and when she spoke it was with hysterical intensity. "My father hides nothing. He speaks the truth. You won't be satisfied until you destroy everything I hold dear. Get out now! Out of this apartment. Out of Vienna. I never want to see you again."

"Don't you see it, Willi? He takes no responsibility. He explains everything away. It's all someone else's fault."

"It's you!" she shouted. "You're doing this because you refuse to face the facts about your own father – a thief!"

She ran from the room.

Let her go, he said to himself. There's no way to reach her. He walked to the door, Hanfnagel stalking him.

Ross turned and said, "You're lucky to have her for a daughter."

Hanfnagel seized on that acknowledgment as an opportunity for a final effort at persuasion.

"Please, Herr Cortese. Reflect on what I've said. I know it's a departure from what you were brought up to believe." And with that he smiled the smile of a winner. Ross let him have the last word. Go on and smile, he thought. You'll never have my furniture in your house.

Ross stepped into the elevator. As it began its descent, he thought about Willi. She had awakened him when he was convinced that it could never happen again. Now he was left to face a turmoil of emotions – and sleepless nights again. Hanfnagel would comfort her, sealing over the cracks in her faith with the Crazy Glue of his slick salesman's speech. Ross felt she was truly lost to him.

Erich Hanfnagel went into the library and called Dolph. Although Dolph acted sympathetic when his father described the turn of events with Cortese, privately he was delighted. The situation had forced his father to seek his counsel. Dolph urged him to turn the matter over to him.

"You can rely on me to take care of this, Father." Not like my bitch of a sister, he added under his breath.

When Hanfnagel returned to the salon, he found Willi collapsed on the sofa in tears. "Liebchen . . . what is it?" He came up behind her and put his hands on her shoulders, kneading the tense muscles.

"It's Red. Oh Father, those terrible things he said . . . "

"Willi, my dear child. I'm truly sorry. Herr Cortese is a naif, incapable of understanding the complexities of life as Europeans have experienced it."

She turned to face him, her face grim and haggard. "Why have you never spoken to me about those years?"

"To what end? They were miserable, painful, filled with hardship and privation. I saw no need to burden you with the tragedy of those times."

"What Red says about the apartment, the furniture – this Lucy Mosel?"

"A combination of half-truths and lies, fed to him by vengeful people. The poor fellow will believe anything so long as it supports his denial of his father's crime."

"You're certain then, that Red's father stole the furniture?"

"The police records are clear. Victor was scrupulous in his search. There are depositions by witnesses to Franco Cortese's departure with a Mosel firm truck and furniture. How else to explain it?"

Willi dried her tears with a handkerchief offered by her father. "I felt something for him, Father. For the first time in many, many years, I thought I might have found someone I could love."

And leave Vienna? Hanfnagel thought. I would never allow it. Never! But to her he said, "He's an attractive man, liebchen. But you're from different worlds. I doubt that it could ever work."

"I'll never know now, will I?" she said weakly.

"You'll be alright?" He took her hand.

"I'll be fine, Father. Right now I think I'll just go to the office. Would you like to meet for tea at the museum – say four o'clock."

"I'd like that very much, liebchen," Hanfnagel responded with a satisfied smile.

CHAPTER TWENTY-TWO

When Ross arrived back at the Royale, the concierge gave him a message from Avia Hirsch. She requested that they meet at the hotel at two thirty and that he call to confirm. He asked the operator to connect him to the Center and left word on her answering machine that they were on for two-thirty. Since there were still several hours 'til the meeting with Avia, Ross decided to put the time to good use.

He took a cab to the American Embassy, located in Ottakring, the densely populated Sixteenth district. The quarter, not far from the fabled Vienna Woods, was undergoing extensive rebuilding. Ross's badge gained him entrance to the Embassy and access to Walter Thomas, the Chief of Security. The man himself – late fifties, paunchy and balding – came out to reception and greeted him warmly.

"It isn't often that we get a visit from stateside cops."

He led Ross into a small office on the main floor. The room reeked of stale smoke. "Always happy to see a fellow American. What can I do for you?"

"I'm looking for information."

"NYPD didn't let us know that you were coming. What's the deal?"

"It's not NYPD business. It's personal."

"Oh . . . " he said, appearing disappointed.

"Things quiet here?" Ross inquired.

"This place is a morgue for spooks since the Wall came down. OPEC's wasted. An occasional rumble from the Arab world, terrorist squeak. Not much comes of it. Eyes and ears stuff is all. What have you got going?"

"Call it Missing Persons. I'm looking for a woman who survived the war."

"This isn't Jewish stuff, is it? I took you for Italian."

"I am Italian. And she's Jewish. Does that matter?"

"Does it matter? You've got to be joking. Where were you born, on the moon? This is Vienna, old buddy. Where it all began. Talk Jews and it's Clam City – and you're looking at number one clam. I've got three months left on this tour of duty. Then a soft deuce in Washington. After that, pension time. A condo in Scottsdale and hi diddly dee, a golfer's life for me."

"Sounds like you've got it all worked out."

"Damn straight I have – and nothin's gonna interfere." He suddenly softened. "Okay, who's the mystery lady . . . and what's your connection?"

"I've got a couple of pieces of furniture made by her grandfather. If she's alive I'd like her input on what to do with it."

"What a heart. Why the fuck should you care? You play golf?"

"Why?"

"I've got an option on a second condo. You can buy it at a good price."

Ross smiled in spite of himself. "You really are out of here."

Thomas pointed to his desk calendar. "Counting the days."

"So how about it? A tip where to look?"

"Gimme a break, Cortese. I get a speck of Jew shit on my hands, the Department'll send me to Kazakhstan to serve out my time. You don't know those white shoes upstairs."

"Are you acquainted with a Victor Neurath?"

"Vicky? Sure. We work with him. Good team player. Why?"

"I heard he was a Nazi. Gestapo."

Thomas grinned mirthfully and shook his head. "Ooh. Big fucking surprise. Scratch the epidermis of most guys over sixty-five in this town, you'll find a swastika. For crissake, the Chancellor of Austria's an ex-Nazi."

"What are you doing about it?"

"You kidding? We thanked God when he decided not to run again. Now we can get back to normal business."

"Are you saying it's okay with you?"

"It's what it is. For the past forty-five years, we've been fighting World War Three. Don't you read the papers? We just won. The Austrians called themselves neutral but they knew on what side the bagel was buttered. We needed the fuckers. We'd've done deals with the devil to stop the Commies. Don't quote me."

"These guys were mass murderers."

"Don't wave a Boy Scout badge at me. This is Europe. The game's played by different rules.

Thomas added pointedly, "I'm counting down, mister. Two

minutes left and playing defense. I don't want trouble."

"I hear you. But tell me this. Why would Neurath have a Russian working for him?"

"Huh?"

"He's had a tail on me for two days. Guy's name is Vladimir Doschenko."

"How do you know?"

"I asked to see his I.D. last night."

Thomas frowned. "It's a familiar name. Hang on."

He went outside and came back a few minutes later with a file folder. "This the guy?" He showed Ross a fuzzy black and white photo taken with a long lens.

"He's older – and stockier . . . but that's him."

"Last we heard, this guy was KGB. The truth now – who're you working for and what are you holding back on me?"

"I'm working for myself. Trying to find this Lucy Mosel. Nothing more."

"You're lucky to be sitting here. Your tail is a heavyweight in operations. He gets things done. Mostly to people."

"Where does Neurath fit in?"

Thomas shook his head. "It's a new world since the curtain came down. I don't know."

"A friend of Neurath's – an Erich Hanfnagel brought me to Vienna."

"I've heard of him."

"He wants to buy my furniture for his collection. I figured Neurath was doing Hanfnagel a favor and keeping an eye on me. Making sure I don't double deal."

Thomas sighed. "I'll nose around. You keep yours clean, get me? If I hear you're stepping out of line, I'll call your department and get you yanked back so fast, it'll make you feel like you flew the Concorde."

He got up and shook Ross's hand. "Remember my offer on the condo."

"I don't play golf."

"You can always learn."

Thomas escorted Ross to the door of the Embassy, waved him off and returned to his office. There, he picked up Doschenko's file, opened it and stared at the picture.

For a brief moment, he felt the stirring of the cold warrior, then it faded. "Fuck it," he said out loud, returning the file to the cabinet.

CHAPTER TWENTY-THREE

Ross left the embassy and tried to relieve his frustration with a long walk. He felt as if he had hit a wall. He rued the day he had come to this city. His relationship with Willi was finished. His own father was accused of being a thief. Chasing tail had led him to chase his own. He could expect squat from Thomas.

If Avia had no information for him on Lucy Mosel, he'd pack his bags and get the hell out of Vienna. He hailed a cab, returned to the hotel, went to his room and cleaned up. On an impulse, he decided to call Neurath. He was connected without delay.

"Herr Cortese. What a pleasure to hear from you."

"Save the schmah, Neurath."

"So you are learning German."

"More than the language."

"So I'm informed."

"I'm sure you are. What's the matter, Commissioner? Can't get good local help?" he said scornfully.

Neurath was silent, then spoke coldly. "You'd be well advised to conclude your sale with Herr Hanfnagel before you bring trouble on yourself. You are not in your own country."

"I'll tell you what, Neurath. Let's do a deal. Help me find Lucy Mosel . . . "

Silence. Ross couldn't even hear breathing. "You still there, Neurath?"

"I'm here, Sergeant."

"If she's alive and agrees to sell the furniture to Hanfnagel, I won't stand in the way."

"And if she's deceased?"

"Then the furniture stays in New York. Count on that!"

"I'll consider the matter," Neurath replied curtly and hung up.

It was two o'clock. Ross went down to the bar, where he hungrily consumed a sandwich and a beer while waiting for Avia. She arrived promptly, half an hour later, carrying a large backpack on one shoulder. It appeared to be quite heavy as she set it on the floor.

"What have you got for me that's so important?" he asked, skipping the niceties.

A small bluish vein pulsed at her temple. She was very nervous. "We made inquiries with other agencies."

She reminded him of a cop delivering bad news to a victim's family.

"What did you find?"

"The Mosels were killed, shortly after the Anschluss. The information I was able to obtain, based on official records from that period, says they were resisting removal to the ghetto."

Ross was aghast. "Ariella?"

"Kirmen Mosel, his son Joshua, Ariella and her mother. All of them."

Ross felt a heavy weight on his chest as he saw tears come into her eyes. Look at her, he thought. She's grieving for four strangers who've been dead for more than fifty years. He felt rage. That bastard Hanfnagel, the great survivor, lives in a house of death and collects the belongings of a man who was murdered for refusing to leave his own home.

"Was there independent corroboration at the time?"

"How could there be?"

"Witnesses?"

"None on record."

"And Lucy Mosel?"

Ross saw her look over his shoulder. Her lips thinned. He turned and found Dolph Hanfnagel standing behind him. Ross smelled liquor on his breath and saw contempt in his eyes. Just how long had he been standing there, Ross wondered.

"Excuse the interruption, Herr Cortese," Dolph uttered mechanically. "I stopped by to see you and the concierge informed me that I'd find you in the bar."

Avia stood abruptly. Ross stood too. "I'll wait outside," she announced, and stepped into the lobby.

Dolph watched her retreat out of earshot. "I'm here on business. My father authorizes an additional twenty-five thousand dollar payment."

He smiled through swollen lids. A dangerous Porky Pig, Ross thought.

"That's a lot of money for a dead Jew's furniture. Must eat you up."

"The offer stands at one hundred twenty five thousand dollars American, Herr Cortese."

"I can count."

"That's a considerable sum for a man in your position."

"I'll tell you what I told Victor Neurath – and you can tell it to your father. When I find Lucy Mosel, and she says, sell to Hanfnagel, I'll do it. Otherwise, forget it. And I'll make damn sure that anyone I sell to isn't shilling for you. Now get lost . . . " Ross turned his back on Dolph and sat down.

"You sit with a Jewish whore and dare to speak to me in that tone of voice?" Dolph exclaimed, seizing Ross's shoulder and squeezing it.

Big mistake, mister, Ross thought. Pushing up from the chair, he twisted free of the grip, then grabbed Dolph's arm and twisted it, swung it into his back until he screamed.

"I should break it and give you something to remember this Jew-lover by. Stay away from me or next time I'll finish the job."

Ross released his hold and shoved Dolph across the room, where he stumbled and fell to one knee. The bartender rushed to assist him, but Dolph shook him off. He glared at Ross with hatred in his eyes, then limped out of the bar.

Avia saw Dolph leave and hurried to the table. "He looked furious. You've made a dangerous enemy."

"I'm really scared, don't you see?" he said, trying to make light of it.

She didn't find it funny in the least. "I'm serious. He's well-connected to the extreme right movement."

"That figures. Most of them are clowns."

She frowned. "Letter bombs are hardly the work of clowns. If times get worse . . . " She didn't have to finish the thought.

"Time's running out. I can't afford to stay in Vienna on my own. And after this, forget about Hanfnagel footing the bill."

"Let's go to your room," she suddenly urged.

"Don't you think I'm a little old for you."

"When you see what I have to show you, you won't make jokes."

The bartender eyed him warily as he picked up Avia's pack and left.

As soon as they entered his room, she asked him to put out the Do Not Disturb sign and lock the door. He complied.

She removed a portable VCR from her backpack and connected

it to the television set.

"Sit down, please."

She inserted a cassette into the VCR and, using the remote, operated the recorder. "The film quality is not first-rate. This is a tape we made of a videogame as it was being played by a fourteen year old boy, I'm sad to say."

The blood-red letters of the title flashed on the screen: KONZENTRATIONLAGER. Although Ross could not translate the instructions, the format became clear as the game progressed.

The player assumed the role of Commandant of a Concentration Camp, his goal to move Jews by train or forced march as rapidly as possible to the Camp. There, they were executed by means of poison gas or bullet and delivered to the crematorium. The player received points for number of exterminations and bonuses for speed in reloading firearms, accuracy of fire and replacement of cannisters of Zyklon-B gas. If a Jew successfully defended himself by killing a camp guard or staff member, heavy penalty points were deducted from the player's score, on the principle that one Aryan life was worth five hundred Jews. The special effects were vivid with Jews depicted as subhuman, grotesquely ugly cartoon characters while the Commandant and his soldiers were tall, handsome, brave Aryans.

The game ended suddenly. The score flashed on the screen over and over again. 23,357. Meisterschaft Niveau.

"What does that mean?" Ross asked, half-suspecting the answer.

"The boy who played this game achieved Championship level."

The tape was over, scattered lines and blips all that remained on the screen, like the molecules and atoms of the 23,357 Jews that had gone up the chimneys of the crematoria, ghosts on the screen.

"This shit is being distributed to kids?" Ross shouted. "These people are nuts."

"Hitler began with a handful of what you call nuts."

"Go public with the tape," Ross urged. "Show it to the press, the media . . . "

"There have been a few stories in the papers – here and in Germany – but no one has taken the matter seriously. I have copies of other games which target Turks and gypsies. Government officials mouth the proper platitudes, but are reluctant to take on the extremists. There are many – and they vote!

"The authorities fear, too, that there are highly placed, *respectable* citizens behind this. We need hard evidence to present to the Federal Prosecutor, irrefutable evidence. Help us, Cortese," she pleaded desperately.

"What can I do?"

"We have reason to believe – a rumor here, a whisper there – that the manufacture and distribution of these games is a Hanfnagel enterprise."

"Son of a bitch," he muttered.

"We located their production facility and contacted the authorities. There must have been a leak. They moved before action could be taken. Where to, God knows? We're trying to track down the new location. The man who just paid you a visit runs the family business on a day to day basis."

"Jesus . . . Willi said they were in video distributing."

"Use your relationship with that woman."

"No," Ross said vehemently. "Leave my relationship with her out of this."

"They've tried to manipulate *you.* Do it to them."

"Even if I was willing to make this my quarrel, you saw what happened downstairs. I'm on the Hanfnagel Shit List. Victor Neurath's even gone so far as to have me followed. Now *there's* a story. The guy who's following me is a Russian. Doschenko. Ex-KGB."

Her breath quickened. "How do you know that?"

"I turned the tables on him late last night and followed him home. I mentioned his name to the Chief of Security at the American Embassy. He says Doschenko was in operations."

"You have his address?"

"It's yours if you want it."

She nodded eagerly. Ross dug the slip of paper out of his wallet and gave it to her. She committed the address to memory and tore it up. Damn it, she thought, of all times for Abe to be out of town. Neurath, Hanfnagel, and an ex-KGB officer. Letter bombs of Russian design. Perhaps Cortese had helped them more than he would ever know.

She went to the VCR, ejected the tape and set it on the table. Returning the recorder to her backpack, she said, "Work with us, Cortese."

"Sorry . . . " Ross mumbled.

"I'm sure you are." Her voice was tinged with bitterness. "Like many decent, well-intentioned people, you'll send a small contribution to clear your conscience – and leave it to us to end this plague."

"It's not that way," he responded.

"Whatever . . . Safe trip home, Cortese." She looked at the clock on the bureau. "I have an appointment to meet an animal at the zoo," she said sardonically.

"What?"

"A skinhead claims that he's prepared to turn over evidence for a fat fee. Who knows?"

"Be sure it's not a set-up, Avia."

Ross watched from his window as she walked away from the hotel. Her back was held straight against the weight of the pack. He admired her spunk. Then he turned and noticed the videotape she'd left on the table for him. My souvenir of Vienna, he thought grimly. Ross picked it up, hefted it in his hand, then tossed it into the open suitcase. Teddy Banion at *Newsday* was an old friend. Maybe he'd be interested in the story.

Ross thought back to Avia's description of the destruction of the Mosel family. Goading Neurath now looked like a dumb thing to do. If Lucy Mosel was alive, the last thing he wanted was the Commissioner finding her. Maybe it was time to have another go at Annalee Speitz. He had no doubt that she knew more than she let on. She had lived in the building all of her life. That included the period in question, when murder took place within those walls. It was not difficult, in the light of what he now knew, to understand her reticence. He was a stranger – a guest of Eric Hanfnagel. What reason was there for her to trust him? Still, he was hopeful that she might hold the key. That is, if Willi hadn't gotten to her first. He rang the switchboard, gave the operator Annalee's name and address and asked her to place the call.

"Ja?" Annalee's tremulous voice questioned.

"It's Red Cortese, Frau Speitz. I've got to speak to you."

"Mr. Cortese, if you did not call, I would have called you. I must see you. Can you come now?"

"I'm on my way."

CHAPTER TWENTY-FOUR

Neurath wiped dry the thin line of perspiration that had formed above his brow. The calls to police headquarters had come in within minutes of one another.

First, Doschenko, who challenged Victor's earlier assertion that Cortese knew no one in Vienna.

"The American visited his Embassy. If he's an agent, they know of my presence in Vienna by now."

"Your concern is misplaced. Cortese called a short while ago to gloat. You were mentioned only in passing. In my judgment, he's driven, not by politics or professional mission, but by personal obsession."

"There's a great deal riding on your judgment, including my ass. I think we'd be better off if this Cortese was cut out of the picture – an accident, a disappearance."

"No! If either of those were to occur, it could come right back to our door. Hardly something we need – especially at this juncture. But you are right about one thing – the sooner he's out of Vienna and on his way home, the better for all concerned. I'll see to it."

"I have more experience in these matters than you, comrade. But I'll defer to your judgment, for now," Doschenko replied grudgingly and hung up.

Before Neurath could sort through his options, the second call came. He listened patiently as Dolph ranted on about Cortese and the Jewish whore. Erich had given his son the Führer's name at birth, dropping the first letter after the war. But whether Dolph or Adolph, the young Hanfnagel had proven himself to be a true believer with strong leadership qualities. Neurath was his mentor and had been for many years.

"I remind you, Dolph, that you must separate personal feelings about Cortese from your principal objective," he insisted. "Of course, you're right to be concerned with the Jewess Hirsch."

He did not tell Dolph about Doschenko's concerns. He'd handle this his own way. "I'll put her and her colleague under immediate surveillance."

Dolph acquiesced. "Good. But keep me informed."

"I certainly will."

Now Victor drummed his fingers on the desk. He took a cigar from the humidor, rolled it between his fingers, clipped it and lit up with a wooden match. Smoking a cigar served to free his thinking from the shackles of conventionality. He closed his eyes and puffed away.

Five minutes later, a plan in mind, he was on the line with Erich Hanfnagel.

Ross knew the route very well by now. He reached the house quickly and rang Annalee's bell. She ushered him in and locked the door behind her.

This woman is very frightened, Ross thought, seeing the look in her eyes.

"You wouldn't happen to have something to drink, Frau Speitz?" he asked, hoping to distract her.

"Where are my manners? Please . . . a moment."

She went to the cabinet, took out two amber-colored, gold-rimmed cordial glasses and placed them on the table. After wiping them with a linen napkin, she reached back into the same cabinet and brought out a bottle of slivovitz. It was nearly full.

"My doctor tells me it's good for the heart to have one each day. Will you pour?"

Ross detected a tremble in both her voice and her hands. He poured a finger of schnapps for each of them, and then they settled down, he on the sofa and she in an armchair a few feet away.

She took a tiny sip and studied his face, as if examining each feature in turn. Ross realized she would only move forward at her own pace. Finally she spoke. "Rudy tells me you visited the Holocaust Center."

So Rudy had paid Annalee a visit. No big surprise, he thought, as he nodded his assent.

"What did you learn there?" she asked.

"Rudy only knows about my first visit. I had a second meeting. That's when I learned how the family died. It's a terrible story. Hard to believe."

She nodded, the lines in her face deepening.

"You know, my father warned me not to come here," Ross said. "I guess he knew."

The reference to his father seemed to startle her. Her hand trembled and a few drops spilled on her lap. Ross offered her a napkin and she dabbed at the stain.

Then, she stood with great effort, tottering a moment before finding her equilibrium. She slowly moved to the piano and picked up an old framed photograph. It was a family portrait, apparently three generations.

"The Mosel family. Taken in nineteen-thirty-five. That's Ariella, with Lucy beside her. Ariella was then sixteen, Lucy fourteen. And the older man is Kirmen Mosel himself."

Ross remarked that the girls were very pretty. Kirmen, looking very patriarchal, wore a large Habsburg-style mustache that took up most of his face. Joshua, clean-shaven and smiling, had an affectionate hand on each daughter's shoulder.

"Rosa, Kirmen's wife, was ill at the time that the picture was taken, but you would not know it. For her, the family was a source of the greatest joy. She died the following year. Perhaps she was the fortunate one, to be taken by illness, rather than the violence which followed."

"And Ariella's mother?"

Annalee touched the picture, as if seeking to re-establish contact. "This is Fanny, here. She was my good friend . . . "

She looked up at Ross. "I'm old and tired. I was frightened then. I'm still frightened. With you here, I feel a little braver. What I am about to tell you, I only told to my husband – and one other – with tragic consequences."

She began to cry. "I begged Lucy when she returned and made her claim . . . never to speak of that day."

"What day, Frau Speitz?"

"The day that her family was . . . the day that they all died." She walked to the window and parted the drapes slightly. "Lucy was at a friend's house, saying good-bye. The Mosels had papers and were planning to leave Austria within a few days. As she was returning home, she saw the Storm Troopers coming into our building. She hid in a doorway . . . *that* doorway . . . "

She pointed to a building across the street.

"Within minutes, we could hear the screams from her family's apartment. Blood-curdling screams. I saw her . . . I was afraid that she would come inside, so I grabbed my coat and ran down to her."

She shivered. Ross held her firmly, trying to infuse her with the strength of his rage. "She saw them . . . "

She closed her eyes, seemed to be shrinking pitifully with the exhaustion of remembering. "She saw them die."

"What?" he blurted. "How?"

"I can't . . . I can't," she moaned, burying her face in her hands, seeking darkness in which to hide, in which to obliterate the images. He eased her back into the armchair and held her hand. She looked at him gratefully.

Continuing, she said, "I took the child to a friend's apartment. She was in shock and offered no resistance. By nightfall, I had hidden her on my cousin's farm. She remained there throughout the war. I visited when I could. We tried to mend her spirit, but there is only so much the human heart can bear.

"After the war ended, it took seven years before she dared to come out of hiding and return to Vienna."

"Didn't she tell this to the authorities when she made her claim?"

She shook her head, as shame was added to her burden of grief. "I asked her not to tell. I was afraid."

Her eyes darted to a locked cabinet, then back to him. "You don't know Vienna. From a few, there would have been acceptance, perhaps even praise. But others – neighbors, those my husband worked with in the bank – I feared that they would consider us traitors."

"Why, for God's sake?" he asked her, unable to comprehend.

"I lacked courage."

"That's not true. You showed more than most."

Annalee smiled for the first time, reassured by his support. "Lucy wants to meet you," she said softly.

"She is alive!" Ross exclaimed. "Thank God."

It was a break, an opportunity to cut through the lies and deceit and settle his doubts about his father. There was more. He remembered what Avia had said – 'precious mementos, the vessels of memory by which the generations are linked, lost forever.' He had the chance to offer Lucy, the sole Mosel survivor, a connection to her family.

"When can I meet her?" he asked eagerly.

"She's away for several days. She'll come to your hotel on Tuesday at one o'clock. You'll be there?"

He nodded.

Annalee placed her hand on his arm. Using it as a lever, she lifted herself. She embraced him, resting her head against his chest. Looking up at Ross, she forced a smile through her tears. When she released her hold, she accompanied him to the door. Before saying good-bye she looked back into the room and Ross felt that she was about to say something else. Instead, she thanked him and closed the door. He heard the locks click into place.

Annalee waited until she heard the elevator door close and then walked slowly to the desk. She took a small key from a hidden drawer and used it to unlock the Biedermeier cabinet. She removed the white sheet which wrapped a large framed painting and stared at the vibrant portrait.

The subject was a beautiful woman of great dignity. The canvas was signed Gustav Klimt. It was the equal, she thought, of any of Klimt's paintings in the museum of the Belvedere.

Startled by what she believed to be footsteps in the hall, Annalee hurriedly removed a fresh sheet from the linen closet, carefully rewrapped the painting and locked the doors to the cabinet. For more than fifty years, she had repeated this ritual. For more than fifty years, no one but she and her late husband had seen the painting.

Ross crossed the street to stand in the doorway in which Lucy had hidden. He imagined that he heard the curses of the Storm Troopers and Kirmen and Joshua Mosel's cries. Batons and pistols smashing into flesh and bone; cracking, tearing.

Remaining in this city was a grim prospect. It was all over with Willi. She had made that clear. Between him and her old man, it was her old man, hands down. No surprise there, he thought. But Ross still had strong feelings for her – and that would make it a long few days until Tuesday.

Brecker had insisted that Avia meet him in the Tiergarten, Europe's oldest zoo, located on the grounds of Schonbrunn Palace, well away from the environs frequented by his buddies. "Wait for me at the lion's den," he growled, then laughed as he hung up.

She caught the 15A bus to Hietzing. It was crowded with local families and tourists, bubbling with excitement over their visit to the Baroque eighteenth-century palace and park. Edgy, she exited the bus on Schlossstrasse and followed the crowd in through the main gate.

Making her way through the courtyard of the palace into the park, she continued on past Neptune's fountain up the hill to the Gloriette. This handsome arcade commemorated the victory of Maria Theresa's troops over the Prussians in 1757. A left turn took her past the Tyrolean garden to the zoo. She found the lion's den and paced impatiently waiting for Brecker to arrive.

An hour passed. He was nowhere in sight. She looked for a public phone and called in to her drop. There was a message on her answering machine. She recognized Brecker's whiny voice. He indicated that he was onto something big and that he would call with further instructions. He added a warning that she had better be prepared to pay as promised. Frustrated and angry, Avia returned by bus to the Center. Seated at her desk, she scribbled the name Doschenko – and the address given to her by Cortese – on a small pad. Staring at it, she thought about Hanfnagel's money, Neurath's official connections and Doschenko. A powerful, unholy triangle.

What about Brecker? she wondered. Was he really onto something, or just jerking her around? There was nothing she could do but wait for his next contact.

She felt tense and wished that Abe was there. What would he say in this situation? "Let's get a beer and talk it over." She couldn't talk it over with him, but she could use a beer. Avia set the alarms and locked the office. On the street, she paused and carefully checked the vicinity for watchers.

But she was no match for the professionals Doschenko had imported from Budapest.

"I want the Hirsch girl followed," Neurath had ordered. "No locals," he added.

The couple, free-lancers, had worked for the Rumanian secret service until Ceausescu's downfall and were eager for the assignment. The woman signaled to the man that the situation was under control and he dropped off. She waited as Avia selected an outdoor table, then entered the café through a side door. An expert in quick-changes in appearance, she made for the lavatory where she artfully used comb, lipstick and silk scarf before returning outdoors and choosing a table near Avia.

She ordered a black coffee and watched as the young woman ordered a beer. They would follow her every move and the poor twit would never know.

CHAPTER TWENTY-FIVE

As Ross reached his hotel room, he paused before entering. The door was slightly ajar. He automatically reached for his weapon and came away empty. He was sorry that he had tossed Doschenko's gun into a garbage can.

Knocking softly, he stepped aside and waited, heard the familiar voice inquire, "Yes?"

Ross pushed the door open. Willi was seated on the sofa. Her long legs were crossed, hiking her short black skirt up and showing lots of thigh. The intense longing triggered by the sight of her was almost enough to make him forget their scene at Hanfnagel's apartment. Almost, but not quite. How could he trust her? She was her father's daughter.

"First Neurath does his number, then Dolph comes by with a basketful of money. Now it's you – dressed to kill. Daddy's pulling out all the stops . . . or is it the strings?"

"That's not why I'm here," she responded, her eyes flashing with anger.

"I'm listening."

"I came to tell you that I care about you. As for your business with my father . . . that's between the two of you."

"Thanks," he muttered. "That's big of you."

Avia's words came back to him. Play them like they've played you. We need your help.

"You look awful," she said, "and I'm to blame."

"You said you never wanted to see me again. What's changed?" he demanded.

"Those things you said . . . I became hysterical. Try to understand and to forgive me. I don't want to think about my father. I want to get out of Vienna. With you. Let's go somewhere – anywhere, just the two of us. You've never been to Venice. We can be there in two hours. Please, please say yes."

She came up close and then was all over him, covering his face and lips with frantic kisses.

He eased her away, watching closely for her response to his news. "Can't go. I'm meeting Lucy Mosel on Tuesday."

"You found her?" She was surprised but not upset, and that reassured him a little.

"Yes. I found her."

"We can visit Venice and be back in Vienna in time for your meeting. If we hurry we can catch the night flight. I checked the schedule."

Was she that confident, he wondered, or merely efficient? "I don't know if that's such a good idea, Willi."

She caught his equivocation and sought to resolve it in her favor. This time her kiss was long and lingering, deep and soulful. It raised goosebumps on him. Ross was amazed to find that in spite of everything, he remained alive to her in the right places.

"My bag is downstairs," Willi said. "I was hoping you'd agree to come. Say yes, Red," she pleaded.

"Why not?" he replied, his tone flippant. "I've always wanted to ride in a gondola."

He added silently, and I'll have one Hanfnagel in my sights at all times.

"Wonderful!" she exclaimed. "You pack. I'll go down and make arrangements with the concierge."

"That was Willi on the phone," Dolph announced as he came into his father's dressing room. "They're as good as on their way to the airport."

Erich Hanfnagel smiled as he straightened the knot in his tie. "Willi did well," he said approvingly.

"You did well to convince her."

"Give credit where credit is due. It was Vicky's idea. The man has lost none of his cunning."

Dolph nodded. "He'll be rewarded for his service. I think the portfolio of Minister of the Interior would be appropriate."

"How many times have I told you not to count your chickens?" Hanfnagel warned loudly. "That is a weakness which you must overcome!"

The air went out of Dolph. He felt resentment rising from his chest, a thick phlegm which he wanted to spit out at his father. But he managed to control himself. "Yes, Father. Of course, you're right.

It's so close, just within our grasp."

Hanfnagel softened. "It is within our reach, not within our grasp. You must appreciate the difference, Dolph. All your thoughts and efforts must be directed toward seeing to it that each element of the plan is carried out. To believe that has been accomplished before the fact is to expose yourself to error. I will not have it! Do I make myself clear?"

"Clear as fine crystal, Father."

"Good. You can drop me off. I'm due at an emergency meeting of the Opera Board. We must plan a fitting memorial for Dr. Mahler – and then select his successor."

"Yes, I heard that he succumbed to his wounds. Ironic that a bleeding heart liberal should die of a bleeding heart, don't you think?"

Dolph waited for a response from his father. When none was forthcoming, he changed his tune. "A great loss to the Opera, of course, and to his family."

"Yes. Be sure to place that call to Fredericks for me."

"Immediately, Father. But one question, if I may?"

Hanfnagel nodded. "What do we do when Cortese returns to Vienna?"

"He won't be returning, Dolph," Hanfnagel promised coldly. "Victor is seeing to that."

CHAPTER TWENTY-SIX

Venice was little more than a puddle-jump away – barely time for the cabin crew to offer a drink. Ross made an effort to put the situation in Vienna behind him, to treat Willi separate from her father and Dolph, at least in his mind. It wasn't easy. He knew that if a crunch came, her loyalty would always be to her old man. So why did I come, he asked himself.

His silent reply said it all. Because I can't resist her.

Meanwhile, Willi was handling her discomfort with a smooth stream of talk, trying to involve Ross in plans for sightseeing Venice and its environs.

With each passing mile, the tension eased a bit. By the time they landed, they were holding hands. A few minutes later, they were dealing with Italian passport control. The officer glued his eyes to Willi's cleavage and hardly glanced at her passport.

He asked Ross, "Affari o turismo, signore?"

"Vacanza."

"Buona vacanza." He leered, but so innocently that Ross and Willi had to restrain themselves from laughing.

"The big bad wolf. If looks could eat," Ross said as they left the counter.

This time, they cracked up.

During the short run from the airport to Piazzale Roma, across a bridge which connected the mainland to the city, the driver extolled the romance of Venice and recommended a charming small hotel managed by his cousin.

"It is sometimes difficult to find a room in this season," the cabbie warned. "I will call him . . . if you wish me to."

Ross looked at Willi who nodded approval. They waited in the taxi while he ran to a pay phone and made a quick call. Grinning, he returned with a thumb up. "Buono vacanza, signor e signora."

"He thinks we're married," Willi whispered.

They purchased tickets for the vaporetto and went aboard one of the small steamers that serve as the public transport system for Venice. By now it was nine-thirty. A vaporous fog surrounded the lighted lanterns lining the Grand Canal. They could hear the cries of the gondoliers as they floated through the night on the gently lapping current of the Grand Canal.

The conductor announced "Rialto," the vaporetto stop where the driver had told them to disembark. Ross grabbed their luggage and they hopped off the ferry. With the directions that their cabbie had provided, they found their way to the hotel through the narrow, twisting streets of Venice.

The desk clerk was expecting them and showed them to their room which was clean, if a bit shabby. Ross asked him to recommend a neighborhood restaurant for dinner. They followed his directions and found it a few blocks away.

There, they drank a lot of wine, ate salad and pasta, didn't say much, but reminisced about their evening at Rao's and smiled. Back at the hotel, they showered and watched a few minutes of a Clint Eastwood movie dubbed in Italian. They had a big laugh when Clint said, "Bongiorno, Tex."

Turning off the TV, they kissed tenderly and mutually agreed to postpone sex in favor of a good night's sleep.

"Tomorrow will be most wonderful," Willi promised, snuggling up next to him.

"Mmm," he said, retreating into sleep.

CHAPTER TWENTY-SEVEN

Avia entered her apartment on Landstrasse, taking care to double-lock the door behind her. She threw her bag on the bed, undressed and showered. She had checked her machine from the café, then again from the restaurant where she met a girlfriend for an early dinner. There had been no messages. She decided to try one more time before settling into bed with a book. She dialed the drop number and tapped in her code.

Brecker's voice came across the line, out of breath – excited or nervous, she could not tell which. "I found what you're looking for. Bring the money. Lots of it. Tonight. Turkenschanzpark. Eleven o'clock. I'll wait there for you until midnight."

Oh, Abe. Where are you now that I need you? She was truly frightened. The park would be deserted this time of night. What if this was nothing but a scheme to rob her? She suddenly thought of the American. Maybe he'd back her up. She looked up the listing for the Royale and placed the call.

"Herr Cortese, bitte."

"He checked out this evening."

Avia hung up. She was on her own.

Don't panic, she told herself. Meet with Brecker at the park. Make it clear from the start that you've come without money – but that the cash is in the office safe. If she was convinced that he was on the up and up, she'd meet him for the final exchange in a busy downtown location.

Avia threw on jeans and a sweater, reassured that her plan provided reasonable protection against a set-up. She placed a can of Mace in her bag just to be sure and departed.

It was ten forty-five when she left the building and walked two blocks to a taxi stand. She gave the driver her destination, unaware that she was being followed by two cars.

The Rumanian sent a signal to Doschenko's beeper and the Russian called back a few minutes later. "She's in a taxi, heading away from the center of the city. Either she has a late date or an urgent meeting," the operative said.

"Stay with her. Keep me informed," Doschenko responded brusquely.

Twenty minutes later, the Rumanian called back to inform him that Avia Hirsh had alighted from the cab on Hasenauerstrasse and entered Turkenschanzpark. The taxi-driver appeared to be awaiting her return.

"Follow on foot," Doschenko ordered. "I'll remain on the line."

The Rumanian contacted his partner by micro-radio. "Get as close to the girl as you can without being observed."

"Roger that," she replied, bringing a thin smile to his lips. His wife loved American slang.

After a long silence, he heard her whisper. "She's met up with a skinhead."

He relayed the report to Doschenko.

"So . . . we have a traitor in our midst," Doschenko mused. "As soon as she leaves, pick him up. Bring him to the farmhouse in Grinzing."

"If he resists?"

"Bloody him if you must, but I want him alive."

"Why not take both of them?"

"This is not the time to spill Jewish blood in Vienna, unless security absolutely demands it."

"Whatever you say."

After carefully surveying the area, Brecker stepped out from behind a giant oak tree and greeted Avia with a phoney smile. He soured quickly when she informed him of her terms.

"I have ten thousand in my office safe if you can deliver what you promised. It's yours within the hour – if I'm convinced that you're information is genuine."

"How do I do that?" he asked suspiciously.

"Tell me your source."

"A buddy of mine. He plays soccer with Reinhold Hanfnagel."

"The son . . . of Dolph?"

"Yes. Reinhold hired him to make deliveries while he went off to soccer practice. The deliveries went to video stores. They were unlabeled – to be delivered only into the hands of the manager."

"So?"

"My friend was curious. He loosened a flap on a carton and had a look inside. KONZENTRATIONLAGER."

Brecker grinned, waving a small envelope. "A few more beers – and I had the address of the production facility. Now, I want my money."

She was prepared to gamble that he was telling the truth. If the address was correct and if they could convince Federal authorities to follow up on the lead without leaking the raid, the payoff would be enormous. The exposure of the Hanfnagels as purveyors of this filth would shake Austrian society to the core.

Avia was excited, but played it cool. "I'm not sure that's worth ten thousand. What else do you have for me?"

His face twisted into an ugly grimace. "Bitch. Are you jewing me?"

She hid her fear behind a steely gaze. "What do you know of Doschenko?"

Brecker's expression changed to one of terror. She had him. The shoe was on the other foot. "The Russian . . . " he mumbled.

"You know him," she pressed.

"I've heard of him."

"What does he do?"

"You wouldn't want to be on the receiving end . . . "

"Then he is connected to the Bavarian Underground," she stated flatly.

Brecker nodded, more frightened. "I want my money. I'm out of Vienna on the next train. Do we have a deal?"

"Yes." She looked at her watch. "We'll meet in two hours. That's at one-thirty – at Central Station. Near the ticket booth. Play it straight with me and I'll do my best to hide your tracks."

She paused. "If you cross me," she warned, "I'll see to it that they know you betrayed them."

"Alright," he grunted. "One-thirty. Central Station. You leave first."

Avia felt the urge to run to the cab. Instead, she forced herself to walk from the park as if out for a late night stroll. She breathed an immense sigh of relief only when she had slammed the cab door shut, locked it and given the driver the address of the Center. She pressed back into the seat of the small Mercedes, not knowing whether to laugh or cry. She had done it, on her own. The pieces were coming together. Now there was a chance they could break the back of the neo-Nazi movement.

Brecker was equally pleased. Ten thousand would get him to Bangkok – or maybe Tahiti. He had his passport. Wherever he chose, it would be far from Vienna, out of their reach.

He glimpsed a shadow, but before he could turn to face the

figure, the woman administered a carefully controlled chop to the back of his neck and he collapsed unconscious to the damp grass. Her husband responded to a signal and helped her to place him, bound and gagged, in the trunk of the car.

Doschenko met them at the safe house outside of the quaint village of Grinzing, with its old houses, lanes and Heurige, inns serving wine from recently harvested grapes. A most unlikely setting for an operations center, the farm was isolated amidst sixty acres of vineyards.

The Russian wasted no time in getting to work. He tore the gag out of Brecker's mouth and slapped him around. The boy opened his eyes, looked around and pissed his pants.

"Do you know who I am?" Doschenko growled.

"No," Brecker lied. Reading the truth in his eyes, the Russian administered a swift, vicious blow to the boy's ear. He howled in pain.

"Don't lie to me again," he warned.

"She knows about you," Brecker whimpered defensively, as if that would somehow serve to protect him.

"What makes you believe that?" Doschenko demanded.

"She asked me if I knew about you. I tried to cover up, but she saw my reaction."

"What else did you tell her?"

"Nothing. That's the truth. I'm supposed to meet her at one-thirty, Central Station. Trade information – for money."

"What information?"

"Where they produce KONZENTRATIONLAGER . . . "

"You know that?"

Brecker was prison smart. He knew that he had to focus all of his energy on denying his knowledge. If he admitted to it, he was dead. If Doschenko knew he was lying, he was dead.

"I know squat. I tried to con her out of the money. I was going to beat the shit out of her, take it and run. She was Jew shrewd. She left it in the office safe."

"But you managed to convince her," Doschenko said, toying with him.

"I lied to her. Told her I got a buddy drunk and he spilled it. Believe me, I'd never help the Jews. I can bring her to you. I'll kill her for you, if you want me to."

Sure you would, you lying piece of shit, Doschenko thought. You'd do anything to save your ass.

Somehow this scum had found the location of the warehouse. Hirsch didn't have that information yet – but she did know

Doschenko's name – and had connected him to the Underground. Her fate was sealed. But how many others knew?

Doschenko decided there and then to move the action up from Thursday to Tuesday. That had always been a possibility. The Minister was punctilious about visiting his mother at the nursing home on either day. The old lady would outlive her son, he thought. And the assignment completed, he, Doschenko would collect the two hundred fifty thousand in German marks promised to him.

He drew his gun and screwed on a silencer as a horrified Brecker thrashed in his chair, pleading for his life. Doschenko stood behind the skinhead, held the gun to the base of his skull and executed him, KGB style. Brecker slumped in his chair. "Clean up. And bury this piece of shit deep – where he'll never be found."

Then Doschenko placed a call.

The Commissioner immediately conferenced it with Dolph.

"I'm moving up the schedule," Doschenko announced.

"That's your decision," said Neurath. "I'm sure you have sufficient reason to do so."

"I do."

Dolph was excited by the news. The sooner the better. Doschenko felt the younger man's lust for power. It surged across the phone line. One day it will destroy you, the Russian thought. 'Til then, it will make me rich.

"There is one small problem. I've got to do something about that girl . . . " He didn't mention her name, but they knew who he meant.

"If it's a problem, solve it. Use any means you deem necessary," Dolph said. "And I mean anything."

"Commissioner?" Doschenko said.

"You heard Herr Hanfnagel. Get on with it."

After waiting for more than an hour at the Central Station, a disconsolate Avia headed back to her apartment. She felt alternately furious, then let-down, convinced at one moment that Brecker had tried to play her for a fool, and the next that he had a case of acute cold feet. Had he been engaged, from the start, in a ploy to get money from her? Or did he really have the information – and had her threat to expose him to his comrades scared him off?

Avia worried that she had screwed up a good opportunity. As she put the key in her lock, she realized that though she had not obtained the location of the video production facility, Brecker had confirmed her theory about Doschenko. That could prove important.

Cortese had helped, more than he knew. She wished that she

could tell him so. Her words to him had been harsh. Abe would be back from his out-of-town visit in the morning. She'd discuss the situation with him then. Right now what she needed most was a night's sleep.

As soon as Avia stepped into her dark apartment she sensed an intruder in the room. Dodging, she avoided the blow aimed at her head. Avia kicked out hard and made contact with a leg or thigh. She could tell that the man was very large as he came at her. Raking his face with her nails, she drew blood, enraging him. His hot breath stank as he worked his hands around her neck.

God help me, she thought. He wants to kill me. Had Brecker set her up?

Desperately, she tore at the man's hands, and when that did not succeed, kneed him in the groin. He yelped with pain and loosened his grip. Elated, she turned to make a run for the door.

Before she could take a step, someone else seized her from behind. Avia opened her mouth to scream but was stilled by the large fist that smashed into her face, broke her nose and drove sharp chips of bone into the base of her brain.

She was mercifully unconscious when the man, whose face she had lacerated, lifted a lamp and crushed her skull. Her body slumped, dead weight in the second intruder's arms. Together, the two of them lifted her and threw her onto the bed.

Then, methodically, they emptied the drawers and searched the entire apartment for documents. There were none. They ransacked the rooms, wrapping whatever valuables they found in a sheet before exiting the way they had come in, through the window.

CHAPTER TWENTY-EIGHT

During the night, Willi brushed up against him, clung to him when Ross reached out to her. They made love as they had that first morning in Vienna, then drifted into a contented sleep.

He was the first to awaken. He drew the curtains and opened the window, inviting morning in, then stared out at the teeming life on the Grand Canal. Cargo steamers, water taxis, gondolas and vaporettos were plying their trade in both directions. A funeral procession moved slowly by beneath their window, gondolas draped in black.

Willi came up behind him and kissed his neck. "Buongiorno," she said softly.

He turned and embraced her. "Let's have breakfast in San Marco," she insisted. Her enthusiasm was contagious.

They were out of the hotel in twenty minutes. It was market day around the Rialto Bridge. Abundant fresh fish, vegetables, olives, bread and cheeses were beautifully arranged on long tables. They climbed onto the humpbacked, yet graceful bridge and made their way past the shops that lined its center. Ross leaned out over the side of the bridge, entranced by the view down the Canal. The river was alive with traffic. Once across, they traversed narrow streets, passing beneath flower-bedecked balconies and across tributary canals.

They meandered through pretty squares and suddenly emerged from the shadows into a sun-drenched Piazza San Marco. Ross was stunned by the spectacle. None of the pictures he had seen did justice to the sight.

He stepped back and stood beneath the arch of the covered gallery, staring at the Byzantine basilica, its facade adorned with marble sculpture, colorful mosaics and the famous bronze horses. Pigeons swoooped in flocks, eating from the outstretched hands of tourists. Willi led him across the piazza to the terrace of the Quadri café. They ordered breakfast and listened to the band playing love songs. Vienna seemed a million miles away. Over café latte and rolls, they opened up in a way that they hadn't since the night at Rao's.

Ross told her about his life with Annie and the toll her loss had taken – then talked about his work on the force. He had her laughing with tales of Kelsey.

"I'd like to meet him," she said.

"He can't wait," Ross told her.

Willi asked him about his parents. He related what little he knew of their life in Udine – that they had returned to Italy once, in 1964, but now the family was so dispersed there weren't any relatives left in the old home town.

"I gotta tell you, Pop has always been a wonderful father and far as I can tell a pretty terrific husband. I can't believe Neurath's accusations," he added.

"It must be a mistake," she replied, "whatever the records show."

She sounds as if she means it, he thought.

"I spoke to my father after you left," she said softly. "You were wrong about him, Red. If anyone should understand how damaging false accusations can be, it's you."

He heard the plea in her voice and saw the fear in her eyes. Ross knew that if he told her what Annalee had told him, it could destroy her. He just nodded. They sat quietly, sipping coffee, not knowing where to take the conversation next.

Willi finally broke the ice. She spoke of her devotion to Rudy, how they had been one another's best friends. "It's been difficult dealing with the estrangement between him and Father," she observed sadly.

Ross heard the bells of the tower. Nearly two hours had passed.

"We have today to make Venice ours," Willi announced, changing the subject. "Tomorrow, let's rent a car and drive to Udine. It's little more than an hour away. Would you like that?"

"It's a great idea," he replied.

Ross reached across the table and took her hand in his, thinking to himself, I'm going to find someone there who knew Pop. I'll prove once and for all, that Franco Cortese was in Udine in March 1938 – and I'll shove that fact down Neurath's throat.

"Yeah, let's do it!" No sooner were the words out when he remembered. "Uh, oh. Scrub that. I've got the meeting with Lucy on Tuesday."

"Not a problem. I've got to be in Vienna Monday afternoon. We can fly back from Trieste. It won't take long to get there by car from Udine."

"Then we're on. Right now, let's see Venice."

And so they did. They visited the Basilica and the Doge's Palace, then found a wonderful restaurant on a tiny canal where Willi got her wish – spider crabs and linguini with a good bottle of red wine. By mid-afternoon, they were holding hands, by late afternoon stopping to kiss on the streets. They returned to the hotel when the heat rose in them, made love for a long time and then napped.

CHAPTER TWENTY-NINE

Abe stared down at the plain wood coffin in which Avia's body lay wrapped in a simple shroud. The rabbi and mourners spoke the prayer for the dead at her graveside in the Jewish Cemetery. Then, according to tradition, he took part in the burial, joining friends and family in filling the grave with shovelfuls of earth. After that was completed, he went over to her weeping parents and embraced them, breaking into sobs himself.

"Will you come to the house?" her father asked weakly.

"Later in the week," he promised.

Abe went straight from the cemetery to the office. Once there, he looked around the room, felt her absence acutely and pounded his fist against the nearest wall. He welcomed the pain which came jolting up his forearm. Stop it now, he told himself. Save your anger for those who did this to her. Still, he blamed himself for her death.

He slumped in the chair behind his desk and a great shuddering sob escaped him. How he had loved that bright spirited girl. Abe shook his head in despair as he thought of her parents and their grief. They had gone to her apartment and discovered her body when she failed to appear at the family Sabbath lunch.

Picturing the scene, rage replaced his grief. He recalled his meeting with the detective in charge of the case.

"All of the evidence points to a burglary," the cop insisted. "She walked in on it. A pity. Fucking drug addicts. We even found a syringe in the apartment."

"Fingerprints?"

"Unfortunately, no . . . "

"You don't find that odd?" Abe asked.

The detective shrugged. "Not especially . . . "

Abe urged him to consider the possibility that the killing was related to her meetings with a potential informer. He gave him

Brecker's name.

"We'll check this guy out, but I doubt if we'll turn up anything worthwhile. Why would an informer, looking for serious money, settle for a little cash, jewelry, credit cards and a small television set? No – it was a bungled burglary." These people, the detective thought. Every crime involving a Jew becomes a national case.

Abe chain-smoked, deep in thought. He could read the writing on the wall. The police would make a token effort, then close the case. After his third cigarette, it occurred to him to press the speaker button on the phone and punch in Avia's drop number. He listened as several old messages replayed. Suddenly, he heard Brecker speak, inviting Avia to meet him with the money at Turkenschanzpark. Abe hurried to the safe and opened it. The money was still there. He went to the cabinet and pulled her current files, spreading them across her desk.

After poring over them for an hour, he quit in disgust, finding nothing. Abe returned the papers to the cabinet and slammed it shut. If the Nazis had found out that Brecker was about to betray them, why not take Brecker out? Why risk killing Avia? What had she learned? He would follow up himself.

He sat down at her desk again, and with a sigh, began shuffling through some loose notes and stick'ems left there. He spotted a slip of paper with an unfamiliar name and address written in her hand. Who is this Doschenko, he asked out loud, as if she was there to answer. But there was no answer and Abe buried his head in his hands and wept.

CHAPTER THIRTY

The manager of the hotel arranged for tickets to the evening performance of "La Traviata" at the Teatro Fenice, on a beautiful square. Willi and Ross walked the few blocks to the Theatre. The evening was theirs – his and Willi's – and no one else's. The performance was thoroughly enjoyable. Afterwards, they stopped for a late supper at a restaurant near the Rialto Bridge. There was candlelight and strolling musicians, the perfect end to a special day.

The night was balmy, perfect for strolling. They wandered the streets, arm in arm for an hour before returning to the hotel.

Willi was in the shower, happily singing her version of "La Traviata." Ross chuckled when she tried for a high note and squeaked – the whole scene was so domestic he suddenly missed his kids. He checked the time. It was only seven thirty in New York – an opportunity to catch Amy at home. The line was busy, of course. Ross waited, then tried again. This time it rang through and Amy was on the line, her voice broken up by static.

"Amy? We've got a lousy connection."

"Dad? Where are you? We've been trying to get hold of you."

"What's wrong? I'm in Venice. Is it Pop?"

Suddenly the line cleared.

"Did you say you were in Venice?" she asked.

"Yes. I came for a few days."

"Cool. Don't worry. Pop's fine. That explains why we couldn't reach you. I called the number you left. The hotel told me you'd checked out. I wanted to check with you before releasing the furniture."

"What was that you said about the furniture, sweetheart?"

"You know. That man at the auction house. Mr. Fredericks. He called first thing this morning. Like seven o'clock. Said that you had agreed to sell. I stayed home so that the transporters could come in and crate the furniture. I tried delaying it 'til I could speak to you, but they were real mean and pushy. They had a check, made out to you."

Ross felt like he'd been gut-punched by Mike Tyson. Willi appeared at the bathroom door, wrapped in a towel.

When she saw the expression on his face, she whispered, "Darling, what's wrong?"

He glared at her and she flinched.

"Dad? You still there?"

"Yeah, sweetheart. Say again. When was this?"

"Today. They were here late this morning. Out by noon. Did I do the right thing? They showed me the agreement. It looked in order – and the check was certified."

"You did fine," he lied, his blood pounding.

What use was there upsetting her? It was too late to do anything about it. By now the furniture was on a cargo plane bound for Vienna,

"The house feels kind of empty . . . but a hundred twenty-five thousand dollars . . . it's a fortune of money."

Hanfnagel was a heavy-weight all right – and a dirty fighter.

"Yeah, it's a lot of money," he said dully.

He couldn't bear to look at Willi.

Ross forced himself to act normal with Amy. "How are the folks? Everything okay there, sweetheart?"

"They're great. I gained two pounds on Grandma's cooking, so I escaped back here to starve myself a little. Pop's leaving for Florida tonight. You're a good influence. He decided to take some time off. Wait'll I tell Grandma you're in Venice. What's it like?"

"I just got here . . . " He gritted his teeth, unable to continue.

"When are you coming home?"

He paused, then replied, "Early next week. There's some unfinished business I have to settle in Vienna."

"Have a great time. Bye, Dad."

He hung up and moved toward Willi. She was frightened by what she saw and backed up. "What is it, liebchen?"

"Don't *liebchen* me, you bitch," he warned. "You set me up. I'm a goddamn sucker."

He turned his back on her and stared blindly out of the window. Then he looked back at her over his shoulder and mimicked, "Let's get out of Vienna. Just the two of us. To hell with the furniture. Sure – what a laugh – only the laugh's on me."

Willi turned pale and clasped her hands together. "What did your daughter tell you? What happened? Tell me, Red."

"Your father stole my furniture. That's what happened."

"He'd never do that," she exclaimed.

"Of course. Not your gentlemanly, cultured, civilized Daddy."

He let her feel the full blast of his outrage. "I told him that I wouldn't sell to him unless Lucy Mosel consented. He wasn't about to let her decision, or mine for that matter, stand in the way of his getting what he wanted. You said that he'd kill for it. He didn't have to. He had you as a weapon . . . "

Ross gave her no quarter, confronting her relentlessly. "Daddy has Fredericks cut a check and order up the transport. Neat! No questions asked. He sends movers to my house. They wave an agreement and a check in my daughter's face – push her around when she balks. She calls, but can't reach me. You've seen to that. Tell me, liebchen. Whose idea was it to get me out of Vienna?"

"My . . . my . . . " she stammered.

"It was his idea, wasn't it?"

Her long-lashed lids flicked rapidly as she struggled with her confusion. "He . . . he saw that I missed you – that I was upset. He wants my happiness."

"He wants my furniture!" Ross exploded. "And he's got it. What a sweet scam. If I try to get it back, he ties me up in court for years. He knows I don't have resources for that route. He figures I'll grumble a little, take the money and say fuck it. He doesn't know me, Willi."

"This must have been Dolph's idea."

"Trust you to try to get your old man off the hook again." She took a step toward him, but he held up his hands to create a barrier. "There's no way I'll live with this. Dolph is his errand boy but you're his tool. And you stuck it to me, but good."

"Believe me when I say I'm as shocked as you are, Red . . . "

"Oh, sure. You're a big believer when it comes to bad news about your father. Like you didn't know about his being a Nazi, right? All these years – playing hostess for him and his Nazi buddies."

He shook an accusatory finger at her. "You saw plenty – heard plenty – but you acted deaf, dumb and blind. You're still doing it. You want to know the score, speak to Annalee . . . "

Ross grabbed his suitcase and started tossing his clothes in. "I'm out of here. I'll find a room for the night and go back to Vienna in the morning. This isn't over. They haven't heard the last from me!"

"What about us?" she asked tearfully.

"Us?" he asked incredulous. "There is no *us*. There's only you and him!"

Ross slammed out of the door and raced down the stairs. In the lobby, he calmed down long enough to ask the night clerk for a second room.

The man looked at him as if he was crazy.

"Put the bag in a room, any room, will you? I need some fresh air. I'll be back."

He'd been fucked into a coma by Willi, while her father was also busying fucking him. Ross gagged on the humiliation. He was on a short fuse. He'd fallen for her – but good – and landed on his head. Broken – but not broke. A hundred twenty-five thousand dollars wasn't chopped liver, he reminded himself. Go home, Cortese. Stop being a dickbrain.

Then he thought about meeting Lucy Mosel. What would he say to her? What could he offer her now? Just sympathy and a share of the money. Some consolation.

His gorge rose. He decided to go back to the hotel.

In the new room, he opened his suitcase and was assaulted by the sight of his crumpled clothes. They looked like the garments of a disinterred corpse. He stepped back, holding his breath, afraid that a putrid odor would confirm his belief that death was in the room. With a muffled cry, he flipped the suitcase upside down, emptying its contents onto the floor. The videotape which Avia had left for him lay amidst the scattered clothes.

At dawn he settled his bill. The deskman told him that Willi had already left. He didn't care. He caught the vaporetto and then a cab to the airport.

Ross purchased a one-way ticket on the morning flight to Vienna. He bought the morning edition of the *Herald Tribune*, made his way through security and sat at the bar, sipping an espresso and reading the newspaper.

Most of it barely registered, until he came to a small item about a brutal murder in Vienna.

"Oh, no," he gasped, reading Avia Hirsch's name. "God, no."

She was just a kid. That hellhole of a city. Those sick, murderous bastards. He'd referred to them as clowns, he remembered with guilt. Some clowns. He'd call Abe when he landed, to offer not only condolences, but whatever help he could.

Boarding was announced and a determined Ross moved quickly onto the plane. He found a bulkhead seat and sat down. In ten minutes they rolled out and were airborne. Ross closed his eyes.

The scent of a familiar perfume seemed to surround him. He heard her voice. "Is it alright if I sit here?" Ross hadn't seen her board. Willi slipped into the aisle seat, allowing the empty middle one to serve as a no-man's land.

"No." He could barely stand to look at her.

"Please. Let me explain. I called Father. Dolph made . . . "

Her lower lip was trembling. He unbuckled and stepped past her into the aisle. He took two steps, then stood motionless, leaden – unable to move further.

A stewardess came up and insisted, "You must take your seat, sir. We've received word from the pilot that we're heading into turbulence."

"You bet your life we are," Ross snapped.

He left her open-mouthed and moved to the rear of the plane. Willi stayed put.

Ten minutes later, the plane dropped suddenly with a loud groan of metal joints. Passengers cried out. The pilot announced that in a few minutes they would be through the worst of it. Not me, buddy, Ross thought. Not me.

CHAPTER THIRTY-ONE

Forty minutes later they landed. Ross disembarked down a flight of steps directly onto the tarmac. Willi had been among the first passengers to leave the plane. He saw her standing near the entrance to the terminal, twenty yards away, waiting for another chance to snare him.

Two armed officers stood at the foot of the steps conversing with the stewardess. She pointed to Ross.

"You are Herr Cortese?" one of the officers asked.

"That's me."

"Step over here," the man demanded stiffly.

Ross followed him. "Your passport, bitte."

Ross handed the passport to him. "What's the problem?"

The officer nodded to his partner. "You will come with us."

"What the hell's going on here?" Ross bristled.

His outburst prompted them to take up positions on either side of him, hands on the butts of their guns.

"It seems that your name, Herr Cortese, appears on a list of undesirables. You are forbidden entry into Austria. You will be taken to a holding station. From there, you will leave Vienna for a destination of your choosing, as long as it is outside of our borders."

They each put an arm on his elbow. He shook them off.

"I must inform you, Herr Cortese, you are in our custody – and we expect your full cooperation until your departure."

"What's the charge? I'm an American citizen with a good passport." The officer shrugged. "I insist on calling the American Embassy."

"You'll be permitted to use the telephone in the holding station. Now, please. Come with us." The man's tone had become strident.

Willi watched the drama unfold. Perplexed, she moved a few steps closer. "What's going on, Red?" she cried out,distraught.

"Ask your father, *liebchen*," he shouted sarcastically.

Ross offered no resistance as they took him into the terminal through a security door. The police led him down a small corridor and into a sparsely furnished room. One officer remained with Ross. The other man stepped out for a few minutes and returned with his suitcase and coffee.

The hospitable Viennese, he muttered to himself. They don't miss a beat.

Ross phoned Thomas at the Embassy and was told by his secretary that he was at the morning staff meeting. He explained the circumstances and she promised to inform her boss as soon as the meeting was over.

"One more thing," he said to her. "Could you look up a number for me."

"Of course," she replied.

"The Center for Holocaust Research. It's on . . . " Shit, what was the street? "Rudolf something . . . "

"I'll look it up . . . Here it is."

He wrote down the number and thanked her.

"Another local call?" he asked the guard politely. The guard shrugged and motioned him to go ahead. Ross hesitated, then dialed. He heard Abe's gruff voice on the other end.

"It's Red Cortese." There was silence. "I read about Avia's death. I'm terribly sorry."

"Thank you," was the curt reply.

"Look. I really planned to come over and talk to you. And to see if there was any way I could help out," Ross whispered. "But I'm in an odd situation. I was in Venice for two days. Now they won't let me back into Austria. I'm in a holding station at the airport. I'm being deported as soon as I choose a flight out."

"What are you talking about?"

"You heard me. I've been declared an undesirable. No explanation. They don't want me in Vienna."

"Who?"

"The Hanfnagels."

"Did you have any further contact with Avia before you left."

"You don't know?"

"To my everlasting regret, I was away from Vienna."

Ross looked over at his guards. They were drinking coffee and apparently paying no attention to his conversation. Nonetheless, he lowered his voice still more.

"She came to me at the hotel. Asked for my help. Showed me the videotape. I said there wasn't anything I could do – but I did give her a name . . . Doschenko."

"Doschenko?" Abe gasped. "I found that name and an address among her papers."

"I gave it to her, God help me. According to Thomas at the Embassy, he's ex-KGB. This Doschenko works for the official I mentioned to you. You know who I mean? The buddy of my so-called host."

"Neurath . . . yes. That could be it," Abe thought aloud. "Avia was getting closer – and became a threat to them."

"I should never have given her that name."

"You blame yourself. I blame myself. It won't bring her back. She fought for her life, you know. They found skin scrapings under her nails. She marked her killer."

"They'll find him . . . "

"Fat chance. They're not even looking."

"How can I help?"

"What can you do? You're about to be deported," he said, his voice soft, but tinged with sarcasm. "Thanks for the call. It may help. I won't let them get away with this, I promise."

"Watch your back, Abe. You could be next on their list."

"Good-bye, Cortese. Good luck to you."

As Ross hung up, a nervous airport official rushed in with a print-out of the day's departing flights. He handed them to Ross.

"What's the story?" Ross probed. "Why kick me out today, when a few days ago I was fine?"

"The computer offers no explanation. You are on a list and Immigration has no choice but to expel you."

It only took two phone calls for the door to be slammed in his face, Ross thought.

Hanfnagel to Neurath. Neurath to Immigration. He was glad that Willi had seen him marched off like a criminal. Even a con artist like Hanfnagel would be hard pressed to find a convincing explanation.

Willi rang the bell and, when there was no response, leaned on it heavily. A shocked Erich Hanfnagel appeared at the door. "What is it, liebchen? I thought you were still in Venice."

She moved inside, but remained in the foyer. "What is going on, Father?" she pleaded. "Red called New York last night and discovered that his furniture was removed by Fredericks' people – without his permission. We argued and separated last night, but came in on the same flight this morning. He was denied entry into Vienna."

"Dolph took matters into his own hands, liebchen. He felt that Cortese reneged on his word and was attempting to squeeze more money out of me – after I had treated him so well. There are limits to dealing with such unscrupulous people. I paid the man well for furniture which was stolen in the first place."

Willi's head was spinning. "Why was he stopped at the airport?" she challenged.

"He assaulted your brother in the bar of the Royale, Willi. I see he made no mention of that to you."

"Red would never do such a thing."

"Really, liebchen? Your brother's arm is in a sling. A hotel employee witnessed the assault. Are you aware of the fact that your Herr Cortese was charged with police brutality in his own city?"

"He was cleared of those charges." Willi answered back. Then she stopped, puzzled. "How do you know about that, Father?" she asked, suspicion in her voice for the first time.

"Why, Victor Neurath made inquiries on my behalf as soon as Fredericks informed me about the furniture. I needed to know with whom I was dealing. Now listen to me, Willi. Isn't it better that Cortese return home rather than face charges in Vienna? If word got back to his department, it would damage an already shaky career." He touched her shoulder lightly. "You must forget him, liebchen. He's not for you."

CHAPTER THIRTY-TWO

There was a loud rap at the door of the airport holding station. The guard jumped up and opened the door.

"Thomas – American Embassy," the man announced, as he ambled in carrying two containers of steaming coffee. "I see they got you some," he said, noticing Ross's empty cup.

He pulled up a chair and slouched into it. "Give us some privacy," he said to the guards. When he saw them hesitate, he snapped, "You heard me! He's not going anywhere."

The two men stepped out of the room, leaving the door slightly ajar.

"What the fuck's going on here?" Ross demanded.

Thomas shrugged. "You forgot to wear a glove when you stuck your finger up Dolph Hanfnagel's ass. He accused you of assault. Some *doings* in the bar of the Royale . . . "

"It's a frame," Ross said. "The Hanfnagels are up to their elbows in shit. They don't want me around to advertise how they stink."

"The bartender backed his story."

"I was in the bar talking to this woman. Dolph shows up uninvited and calls her a Jewish whore."

His sudden pallor scared Thomas.

"You alright, Cortese?"

"No, I'm not. The name Avia Hirsch mean anything to you?"

"Not off hand."

"She was the woman in the bar. She was beaten to death two nights ago. In her apartment."

"Oh, yeah. I read about it. Sorry about that. Robbery and homicide, wasn't it?"

"Was it? She was onto something. You heard about the concentration camp videogames kids play here?"

"Yeah, I've heard rumors . . . "

"They're the lowest form of hate porno. She showed me one.

Avia thought she had a lead to their source. She suspected that the Hanfnagels are involved in the manufacture and distribution of the tapes. What if she got too close?"

"You know something – I pegged you for a six-pack of trouble the minute you showed up at my office."

"I know. All you care about is retirement and your condo. Goddammit, you're still on the government payroll. Do your job!"

"You still don't get it, do you? My job is to keep the lid on things. You, my friend, want to blow it off."

"What if I told you these bastards stole my furniture right out from under me in New York?"

"Neo-Nazis *and* stolen furniture. You're a bad movie," Thomas scoffed.

"Bad movie or not, it's the truth. I refused to sell the furniture to Hanfnagel without first talking to the survivor of the Mosel family, the original owners of the pieces. What follows is this – Neurath tries to fuck me over, claiming my father stole the furniture. When that doesn't put the lid on it, Hanfnagel figures a way to get me out of Vienna. Then while I'm gone, he arranges for a pick-up of the furniture in New York."

"You report the furniture stolen?"

"No. They boxed me in. They left a certified check."

"They paid you?" Thomas asked, incredulous.

"Yeah," Ross said weakly.

"That's the damndest theft I ever heard of."

"Can't we appeal the order to throw me out?"

"What *we*, Lone Ranger? I'm not putting myself on the line to satisfy your conscience. Look, Cortese, I feel for you. But it's not just my ass. Vicky Neurath called me. Said if you give them any more grief, he'll personally inform your superiors at NYPD of the assault charge. Go home, Cortese, before you wind up in a jail cell or maybe even the Danube."

"They don't want me in jail. They want me three thousand miles away."

"Look, pal . . . "

"No, you look," Ross pressured. "I've got lots of reasons to be back here. I'll take my chances that they're bluffing. The last thing they want is me in open court. Just get me past Immigration."

"I wish I could help you, Cortese, I really do. The trouble with being a diplomat is you compromise with scum. You missed the morning flights to New York. You can spend the night on a couch and be escorted to the crapper every time you've got to take a leak –

or go someplace else. Take my advice and get out of here."

They've won, Ross recognized, feeling bitter and helpless.

Thomas stood and reached for Ross's reluctant hand. "You're lucky, you know. You're leaving. Don't quote me, but once you look past the pretty architecture, the place really does stink."

He went to the door. "Fly safe. See you on the golf course."

Ross picked up the airport timetable and studied it. He could fly Air France to Paris, catch an early evening flight to New York and be home by midnight. Just what those cocksuckers wanted him to do. He felt his heels dig in. They were not going to push him around and get away with it.

He reviewed the schedule carefully and spotted just the right entry – a flight to Trieste departing in forty minutes. That was it. He'd be on it. He would drive from Triest to Udine. He notified the guard, who contacted the airline personnel. Thirty minutes later, they escorted him onto the Austrian airline flight. He found his seat, belted up, and in a few minutes, the plane took off. The landing gears lifted with a loud bang.

"Everything is alright, Meinherr," the stewardess reassured.

"Sure. Everything's just fine," he responded with a sarcastic bite.

She backed away, careful to keep her distance for the remainder of the brief flight.

A beaming Erich Hanfnagel ushered both his son and oldest friend into the dining room and proudly pointed to his newly-arrived acquisitions. He opened the bottle of vintage Krug champagne, filled three glasses and lifted his.

"Gentlemen! Permit me to offer a toast to Herr Cortese, who made this day possible but could not be with us. Sadder, wiser – and definitely richer, we wish you a safe landing in New York."

He smiled broadly at them. "Thank you, Dolph. Thank you, Victor, for contributing to this successful outcome."

"I would have paid to see his expression when Immigration took him away," Dolph said, still smarting from their encounter at the Royale.

"Look at the ensemble," Hanfnagel urged. "Isn't it absolutely magnificent?"

The gleam in his eyes was suddenly replaced by a cloud. "Only one thing . . . The Klimt. If that, too, could only be found."

"Who knows, Erich? Perhaps one day," Neurath consoled him. "By the way, where is Otto?"

"Indisposed," Hanfnagel replied.

"So I hear from our Russian friend. Anything serious?"

"He'll live, the dumb ox." Dolph said, "That Jewish bitch dug her claws into him and marked him."

"Has there been much protest from the Jews?" Hanfnagel asked.

"Surprisingly little. Her colleague at the Center raised the question with the investigating officer of possible Bavarian Underground involvement. The officer denied it. This Feder didn't press it. We're keeping an eye on him."

"Are we on schedule?" Hanfnagel asked.

"Yes. Doschenko will do a run-through tomorrow. He is confident that the plan is flawless."

"Be prepared, Father," Dolph declared. "The day is near when the politicians will turn to you as Chancellor – because only you can unite the right and the conservatives in a ruling coalition."

"A man is fortunate to have a son such as Dolph, is he not, Vicky?"

"Indeed, Erich," Neurath agreed. "This apple did not fall far from the tree."

CHAPTER THIRTY-THREE

At the small, modern airport in Trieste, Ross rented a car, obtaining directions and a map from the clerk at Hertz. The highway skirted the industrial port city. Udine lay seventy kilometers to the north, the signs to the town clearly marked. The initial leg of the route extended along the Adriatic coast but he was in no mood to appreciate the views. Switching from the local road to the autostrada, Ross accelerated, then watched in amazement as powerful cars passed him at one hundred ten and twenty miles an hour. Outgunned again, he thought morosely.

He switched on the radio and played rock music loud to blot out the memories of Willi which kept recurring. Approaching the exit to Udine, he felt none of the emotional connection he'd hoped for. He drove past nondescript modern housing and light industry, all of which appeared to date from after the earthquake of 1976.

The old town was another story. It was set back onto a hill, with a castle perched on the summit. Ross drove around the Piazzale 26 Luglio twice, missing the road to the summit on the first roundabout. The via Poscolle led up the slope. On his left were warrens of narrow streets and alleys that did not allow for vehicular traffic. He reached the Piazza della Liberte, one level below the castello and its adjacent thirteenth century church.

Fortunately, someone was just pulling out of a parking space and Ross quickly zipped into it. An elderly gentleman approached, wearing an official cap and waving a book of tickets. "Cento lire, per favore . . . "

He tore off a receipt and gave it to Ross. Less than a dime, the cheapest pay parking he'd found in a long time.

"Dov'e . . . si trova l'hotel," Ross explained.

Delighted to help a stranger, the man broke into a gap-toothed grin. "Ah, parli italiano?"

Embarassed Ross hedged, "Io capisco italiano ma parla pocco."

"Bene," responded the old man. Then with a few words and ample use of hands, he offered directions to several hotels. As soon as the man walked away, Ross regretted not asking him if he'd known a Franco Cortese. He looked about the right age.

When Ross reached the piazza with its large central fountain, he began feeling peculiar, almost dizzy with wonderment and nostalgia. His parents had strolled on these same stones. Diagonally across from where he stood was an outdoor café. It looked as if it had been there forever.

He imagined that Momma and Pop had sat there, sipping espresso. He recalled how pretty Momma had been from the photos of her youth in Udine that she brought to America along with a few other possessions. With a sense of revelation and clarity, he retrieved an early memory of her in New York, her face marred with worry and fatigue.

His recent lessons in the ugly history of those times now led him to appreciate how difficult those first five years in New York must have been – his parents living daily with desperate uncertainty, knowing that their families faced mortal danger – either from the German occupation, or the allied bombings. Their native land had become a battleground.

He chose a table on the edge of the piazza. The waiter, a balding man in his early thirties, sized him up from the bar. Ross waved and the man came over immediately. Speaking to Ross in Italian, a quizzical note entered the man's voice. "I get you something?"

"Uno vino rosso . . . . e biscotti, per favore."

The waiter smiled shrewdly and switched into English. "You from America. I have cousins in New Jersey. Hoboken. You know Hoboken?"

Ross nodded. "You speak a good English."

"I visit a few times. I got an ear. Where you from?"

"New York City."

"A great place. Empire State. Radio City. How you come to speak Italian?"

"I was born here. In Udine."

"Hey. That's a-right. You no make joke?" The guy was genuinely excited.

"No joke."

"Me. I'm Salvatore. Ferruci." He put out his hand.

Ross took it. "Cortese. Ross Cortese."

Salvatore laughed, pointing to Ross's hair. "That's good. Rosso.

Cortese . . . Cortese."

He repeated the name, musing over it, cross-checking it against his memory-bank. Ross hoped that he'd recognize it.

"Do you know any Corteses?" he asked eagerly. "My Pop, Momma and I left a long time ago. Nineteen-forty."

The waiter shook his head. "A long time ago, amici. Before the war. You lucky. Fifty years. You been before to see family?"

"No . . . first time."

"First time? Why you wait so long?"

A good question, thought Ross.

"We celebrate. I bring vino. Good vino rosso. Friuli vino." Salvatore walked off murmuring, "Cortese . . . Cortese."

He returned a few minutes later with a plate of biscotti, a bottle of wine and two glasses. "I tell my padrone I take some time."

He carefully extracted the cork and poured a little into the glass, then swirled it, plunged his nose in, sniffed deeply and tasted. "It's good. I think you gonna like."

Salvatore poured generously, they saluted each other with their glasses and they drank.

"Try the biscotti. You want . . . you dip. S'okay."

"Must be a local custom. Pop does it all the time."

"Your folks. They living?"

"Yeah."

"Cognome di mamma? . . . Noma di famiglia."

Maiden name, Ross realized. "Angelico."

Salvatore frowned, disappointed that he could not make a connection to known inhabitants of Udine. "So who you visit now?"

"The family's gone as far as I know. There may be some distant cousins. I'd like to find someone who knew my family. Can you help me?"

The waiter studied patterns on the surface of the wine as if reading tea leaves. With one eye squinting and the other eyebrow raised, he nodded. "You come to the right place. What business you in, Rosso?"

Ross hesitated before saying, "Police."

Salvatore whistled. "Polizia."

"Strictly vacanza, Salvatore."

While they were chatting, several tables became occupied. The owner called on Salvatore to give him a hand. "I'm not working tonight. What you say I show you around? We eat a pranzo, you and me."

"Only if dinner's on me."

"I meet you at your hotel. Where you staying?"

"I don't know yet."

"You listen to Salvatore. You go to San Giorgio. Piazzale Cella. I call for you." He hustled off and returned in a few minutes."

"You got a room. I come . . . take you up nine o'clock."

"Bene."

"Ciao."

"Wait a minute," Ross called out. "Give me the check."

"On the house, amici. Ciao."

"Grazie. Ciao, Salvatore."

Ross found the Piazzale Cella and a warm welcome at the hotel. The manager offered him a drink and they sat in the small bar for half an hour, comparing family trees. He excused himself after a second drink and went to his room. There, he turned the shower on full force, nearly scalding himself, then stayed under for a long time, trying to wash away the emotional grime of the past few days.

After waking from a long nap, Ross dressed for dinner and waited eagerly in the lobby for his guide to arrive.

When he did, they strolled up into the old town, chatting first about their families, then about Ross's work with NYPD. The last light of day, tinted with purple, was visible in patches through the overhangings of the arcades and balconies that lined the cobbled streets. The glow of old streetlamps added to the atmosphere of strange calm.

Inhabitants of all ages strolled through the alleys and passageways. Though the shops were closed at this hour, the restaurants and tavernas were lively.

"Bene. Adiamo a mangiara!" Salvatore pointed to a small taverna. "My friend Bruno's. You gonna like his place."

Noise, laughter and cigarette smoke floated out of the open door. The bar was packed, the tables fully occupied – almost exclusively by men. The portly proprietor embraced Salvatore. They were welcomed loudly by patrons at the front of the bar. Heads turned.

Salvatore shouted an introduction.

"Mi amici, Rosso Cortese. Americano di New York. Figlio a Franco Cortese, nato su questo vicinato."

That was all they needed to hear. Rosso, revealed as a onc-time homeboy was surrounded by back-slapping, well-wishing locals, vying to buy him a drink. Salvatore left him at the bar and disappeared through the crowd. He returned in a few minutes and beckoned to Ross.

"I make this big surprise for you, mi amici."

He led Ross to a table in the rear where an elderly, white-haired gentleman sat with two younger men – one Ross's age, the other, a boy in his late teens. They all bore a strong family resemblance.

The old man's face was weather-beaten, etched with a grid of fine lines. His hands were sun-spotted and arthritic. He looked like a man who had worked outdoors all his life. Salvatore made the introductions.

"Ross Cortese, Guissepe Barzini. Suo figlio, Paolo e suo nipotino Nuno."

Three generations, Ross thought. He leaned over and shook the hand of the seated patriarch. It was warm, dry and firm. The eyes which studied Ross were a beautiful shade of pale blue, all the more striking contrasted with his dark chestnut complexion.

Guissepe motioned Ross to sit opposite him. The younger Barzini pulled up two chairs. A waiter brought glasses and another bottle of red wine. "Offerta della casa."

Ross was touched by the welcome. He told Guissepe he would always carry a special memory of the warmth and generosity of the people of Udine, his people. Salvatore filled in when translation was needed.

As Ross spoke, Guissepe's eyes searched him with an intensity that made him uncomfortable. The old man raised his glass and downed the wine in one gulp. Then he spoke, in a gravelly baritone, "Franco e Gina . . . come stanno?"

The words were spoken with the warm, easy familiarity of an old friend.

Ross felt the way he had as a kid, riding the Cyclone in Coney Island: mounting excitement, then, as the car trembled on the edge of free fall, a dry-mouthed sense of panic.

The younger Barzinis and Salvatore grinned. It seemed no surprise to them that Guissepe had known this American's parents. For Ross, the revelation presented an opportunity to gaze through this man's eyes as if they were a window looking out upon an unknown past.

"Good . . . they're good. You knew them well?" Ross stuttered.

"Si," the old man replied.

He had last seen Gina and Franco on their visit to Udine many years ago, but had not heard from them since. Guissepe asked Ross to tell him more about the family.

Ross did, relying more and more on Salvatore to translate as the concentration required to conduct the conversation in Italian fatigued him.

They reacted to his mention of Annie's death with genuine, heartfelt sympathy.

Guissepe smiled as he pointed to Ross's head of hair. "I remember this bambino with his red hair."

He sighed, gazing at Ross and seeing his own youth. "Your Poppa and me . . . we was the best of friends . . . from when we was little kids. Together, we went over the mountain, more than one time."

"Over the mountain?" Ross asked.

"Your Poppa? He never tells you?"

Paolo was quick to explain. "It's what every boy does to become a man. He carries something forbidden across the border between Italy and Austria. Here, it's a tradition . . . a rite of passage."

"You mean smuggling . . . "

"Whatever you want to call it," he shrugged. "Sometimes cigarettes . . . sometimes the grappa . . . other times."

No, he never talked to me about it, Ross thought.

Nuno burst in excitedly, "They took people over in the war, Poppa Guissepe tells me."

Guissepe squinted his dark eyes, as if looking far away. "That day is like yesterday . . . " he said, his voice reduced to a whisper, his eyes darkened.

"What day, Poppa," Nuno asked impatiently.

Paolo touched his son's arm lightly, a gesture urging patience.

"It's the day Franco Cortese comes back . . . driving a fine truck . . . and with this . . . this Rosso . . . this bambino, wrapped like baby Moses. Two weeks old. This kid had big lungs, I tell you."

"From where are they coming?" Nuno wanted to know.

"They come back from Vienna," Guissepe replied.

What's he saying – that I wasn't born here? The old man must be crazy – or senile, Ross thought. He has me confused with someone else.

"Hey, Rosso," Salvatore said. "I thought you told me you was born in Udine."

Ross didn't respond. What am I going to say, that Guissepe's nuts? Best thing to do, he decided, is to listen politely, then get the hell out of here. He had hoped to learn something about his father's past, but this was too much.

"Let Guissepe tell the story," he finally said, finessing the question.

The old man continued. "My friend, Franco, he wants to learn better to finish the furniture," Salvatore translated.

"He goes to work for a maestro in Vienna. He's supposed to be there one year. Gina. She loves Franco so, she waits for him to come back . . . to open his business so they can marry."

Ross felt chilled, though the taverna was warm.

"Gina – she's a beautiful woman. All the boys want her. But she waits for Franco. After more than a year, he comes back in this truck." Guissepe paused for effect. "With this bambino." He pointed his thick thumb at Ross.

Ross, caught in a wave of doubt was pulled under. He fought for breath. God help me, he thought. He's telling the truth. I can feel it.

"Gina . . . she's only a young girl," Guissepe went on. "Maybe eighteen. She takes this bambino . . . loves him like he was her own. Am I right, Rosso?"

Ross nodded dumbly, unable to say a word. He felt sick with fury and fear. Guissepe's eyes welled with tears as he looked at Ross. Ross had an urge to throw up.

"Be right back," he mumbled, and hurried into the small W.C. He locked the door behind him, leaned over the bowl and dry heaved. He wanted to pound his fist against the door and scream to high heaven, "Why me?"

He wanted to take his father and squeeze the truth from him.

He forced himself to calm down, splashing cold water on his face. Then he studied himself in the mirror, his eyes blazing with a frightening intensity. Yes, it was his face. There was the razor nick from this morning's shave to prove it. But it had changed. If Guissepe's story was true – and in his bones, he knew that it was – the life he had known for fifty-two years had just been blasted to pieces.

If Gina wasn't his mother, who was? If Pop had fathered him, why wouldn't he have also brought the woman back with him from Vienna? And maybe he wasn't his real father either. Neurath's file, which he had damned as a fabrication, mentioned a truck.

Ross's vehement defense of Pop now rang hollow. Did Pop steal him like the furniture? If there was nothing to hide, why hadn't he been told the story of his birth? Who was he? Did Gina know the whole truth – or had Pop lied to her as well?

Guissepe had unwittingly betrayed Pop's lifetime of deceitfulness. Ross dried his face and hands with the grimy towel and returned to the table.

Guissepe saw his expression. "Ah, Rosso, Rosso. It's a hard way to begin life."

Salvatore put the unspoken question to Guissepe. "What's happened to Ross's real momma – who was she?"

His reply confirmed Ross's worst fears. "Maybe you tell us, Rosso.

Your poppa. He never wants to talk about what happened there. Even to me. His best friend."

What do I tell him? That I don't have a fucking idea? Ross asked himself. That I'm as much in the dark as he is. I don't know if Pop rescued me or stole me?

He filled his glass with grappa. The men watched in amazement as he swigged the smooth but fiery liqueur intended for sipping in one great gulp.

"He never talked to me about it either, Guissepe," Ross said. "Not one fucking word."

They were silent. Ross stared past them. For him, the restaurant had gone silent, as if someone pressed a mute button. He heard only the distant thud of his heart, felt it might burst at any moment. This sensation provoked a terror larger than any he had ever known. He wanted *not* to feel, but pain ripped at his gut. He had to confront his father. Can I believe anything he says to me?

Oh, God, he suddenly despaired, as it occurred to him for the first time that his real parents might still be alive – in that goddawful city.

"You don't look good, Rosso," Salvatore said, bringing him back.

"Franco never told you about your momma?" the old man asked.

"Never," Ross said, in a voice he did not recognize as his own.

"Dio mio," Guissepe whispered, shaking his head.

"I've got to get back there . . . to Vienna," Ross insisted, his desperation evident. "The frontier crossings are closed to me."

He explained that he had been forbidden entry into Austria and then went on to describe Hanfnagel's doubledealing with the furniture.

"That's the furniture your Poppa brings with you in the truck," Guissepe exclaimed indignantly.

Your Poppa, Ross thought. A stranger was more like it.

His meeting with Lucy Mosel took on new meaning now. It was her family's truck that Franco had driven from Austria into Italy. She might know something about – he paused in mid-thought – *his identity*. It was all connected in some way to the furniture.

"I've got questions to answer – scores to settle," he said bluntly.

They were Italian and would understand that. He leaned in toward them. "I need to go over the mountain. It's the only way I can get back in."

They looked at him as if he were crazy, all but Guissepe. Guissepe spoke and Ross needed no translation. "You go over in the morning."

The old man took charge of the planning.

"Tarvisio o Passo di Monte Croce Carnico?" asked Nuno of his grandfather.

"What do you think, Paolo?" Guissepe turned it back on his son.

"Tarvisio is no problem, Poppa. Close to Villach and Klagenfurt. We take two cars."

"Rosso has a rented car," Salvatore interrupted.

"Bene! Nuno and Rosso cross the pass on foot. Takes them three, maybe four hours. We wait at the base of Passo di Wurzen. Two hikers come. Nuno and Rosso. I drive Rosso to Klagenfurt for a train to Vienna. You see a problem, Poppa?"

"It's a good plan, Paolo."

"Why not drive Rosso to Vienna? Maybe he needs us there." Nuno asked.

The kid wanted action, Ross thought.

"You gonna need a gun?" the boy followed up eagerly.

Guissepe tapped the side of his head with his index finger. "Use your head, boy. They find Rosso in Austria, they throw him out again. They find him with a gun, they put him away.

"Paolo! You're the same size as Rosso. Go home, find hiker's clothes and boots for him. In summer, there's lots of Italians hike in Austria. We leave before six A.M. Rosso will be on the other side by mezzogiorno. Salvatore, take Rosso back to the hotel for sleep."

Ross doubted there'd be any sleep for him that night. He said goodnight to Salvatore and wandered Udine's streets for two hours, his mind a maze of questions more tortuous than the twisting streets of the old town. When, finally, he accepted that the answers would be found in Vienna – nowhere else – he returned to the hotel.

Willi got out of bed and went into the bathroom. Her head was pounding and she felt febrile. She found the thermometer and checked her temperature. It was normal. That's about the only thing that is, she thought grimly. She had left her father's apartment confused and troubled by his facile explanation and shaken by Ross's angry accusations.

She had arrived at her office and found a day-old message from Rudy asking that she call when she returned from Venice. She called Freiheit immediately but neither he nor Jacky were there. The cashier believed that they were visiting a friend in hospital. Willi had tried to focus on work, with little success.

Now she took two aspirin, washed them down with water, went into the living room and poured herself a stiff drink. Her conversation with Rudy when he'd finally returned her call replayed itself one more time.

"Annalee was hospitalized night before last," he said.

Why does he sound angry, she'd wondered. "What's wrong?"

"Chest pains. They're still evaluating whether there was damage to the heart."

"My God. Can I see her?"

"Tomorrow. There's something you should know."

"What's that?"

"Her heart seizure followed a visit to her apartment by Father and Vicky Neurath."

"What did *they* want from her?"

"They pressed her for Lucy Mosel's address."

It was as if a dike that she had built over a lifetime suddenly crumbled and sea water came flooding in, sea water carrying a tide of filthy debris. Would her father stop at nothing to have his way? she asked herself, for the very first time.

Willi went back into the bathroom and found an outdated bottle of sleeping pills. She took two, went to bed and felt the painful pounding of head and heart while she waited for the sedatives to take effect.

Ross, exhausted, fell asleep at three, only to be awakened shortly after five by Guissepe's knock at the door. Paolo's clothes, well worn and clean, were a reasonable fit, as were the boots. He checked himself out in the mirror. He looked the part of a Tyrolean hiker. Ross transferred the bulk of his belongings from his suitcase to a commodious backpack Barzini had supplied and went downstairs.

Guissepe was at the wheel, Salvatore in the rear of the rental car, continuing to serve as translator. As they drove north, Guissepe explained that he had arranged to rendezvous with Paolo and Nuno at a truckstop outside of Tarvisio. From there, Rosso and Nuno would be driven up to a pass near the junction of Yugoslavia, Austria and Italy to begin the trek over the mountain. Their route should be clear. The Austrians had concentrated their border patrol along the Yugoslav frontier, seeking to halt the influx of refugees from the Balkans.

The old man squinted at the northeast sky, sniffed the air and shook his head, a little worried. "It's clear now, but there could be a summer storm coming."

This said, he began to reminisce about his boyhood days with Franco. About how the thirties had been terribly hard for the

Barzini and Cortese families.

"A couple times, your poppa, his brothers and me, we go out at night and steal the chickens so our mommas can put food on the table. We tell 'em we work for it, cause if they find out we steal, they break our heads."

Ross listened, but as far as he was concerned Guissepe was talking about a stranger.

Tarvisio was ninety-six kilometers away. For the last thirty, the road snaked between the lower slopes of the Italian Tyrols, thickly studded with pine forests. They reached the rendezvous point in time for breakfast and a pit stop.

As they prepared to leave, the old man inquired of Ross, "You got Austrian money?"

"Not much. A few schillings. Some lire and dollars."

"I make the exchange for you in the bank at the frontier. We see you over there." He pointed beyond the mountains.

Ross and Nuno piled into the car with Paolo. They pulled out onto S13 and climbed two miles on the winding road. Then Paolo took a sharp right onto a dirt road which led them deep into the forest. That road ended without warning in a small clearing.

"This is it," Paolo announced. He wished them godspeed, backed around and drove away.

Nuno gestured to Ross to follow carefully in his footsteps. The last thing they needed was for Ross to sprain an ankle. The grade was deceptive. Ross first realized what he was up against about twenty minutes into the hike. Already his legs ached. He was out of shape. A look down the trail revealed the forty-five degree angle of their ascent.

An hour later, chest heaving with effort, he called out in distress, wrestled out of his pack and flopped against a tree.

Nuno apologized for climbing so quickly. He had forgotten Rosso's age and "inesperto." The youth looked at his watch and broke into a grin, saying something about making good time.

Ross gulped greedily from the canteen. They rested in the shade and Nuno promptly fell asleep.

Ten minutes later, Ross woke him. "Let's go."

As they continued the climb, they heard the rumble of thunder in the distance. Forty-five minutes brought them to the top of the pass. For a moment, Ross enjoyed the striking view of the Austrian prairie below.

Bursts of blue, white, mauve and deep purple wildflowers dominated the landscape, but any satisfaction was quickly mitigated by the threatening storm rapidly moving their way. Slate clouds, bursts of lightning, crackling thunder and sheets of rain filled the sky.

"We go as far as we can before it hits, then find shelter," said Nuno.

The descent was no less demanding than the climb and they had only gone a short way down when the storm struck. Nuno pulled Ross under an overhang of rock, opened his backpack and removed two plastic slickers. They wrapped themselves against the downpour and watched the sky turn dark, as if night had fallen. Between the pelting heavy rain and the black sky, visibility was reduced to a few feet. An occasional huge, jagged bolt of lightning threw the forest into a shadowy bold relief. The display was awesome.

The storm passed as quickly as it had come, the sky restored to a bright blue streaked with magenta. Ross was eager to move out, but Nuno cautioned him, pointing to the muddy soil. It would be slippery going. They made their way carefully, encountering no difficulty until they were nearly half-way down the mountainside.

Nuno, distracted by the scurrying sound of an animal, looked back over his shoulder. He failed to see an exposed root, tripped and started to fall. Ross instinctively leaped to catch him and in so doing, lost his own footing on the slick, muddy surface. He went sliding sideways down the cliff and fell ten feet before grabbing onto a vine. He hung there helplessly, trying to dig his boots into the crumbling dirt of the mountain, not daring to look down. He knew that it was a long drop.

Nuno peered over the edge and called out to him.

"Hold on, Rosso," he pleaded urgently, "I got a rope."

Ross felt the vine slowly tearing away with his weight. Desperately, he looked around for a handhold. The thought that he might die here on this mountain galvanized him. Six feet down, a thick, exposed tree root protruded from the cliffside. This was his only chance if the vine gave way.

Nuno shouted, "Un momento."

He didn't have a minute. Ross felt the vine separating from its berth, and him with it. He took a deep breath, tried to picture the location of the tree root and let go. He dropped, and as his arm banged the root, he seized it in his left hand. His descent slowed, then halted. He felt as if his arm was being pulled from its socket. He was unable to bring the other arm up to gain a hold. Dangling in space, he sought a footing. Nuno's rope dropped into sight.

"Over to the right," Ross shouted.

Nuno responded. Ross grasped the rope with his free hand, then shouted, "Got it!"

Ross knew that he could not hold on this way for long. "Wait," he yelled as Nuno continued to pull, hand-over-hand. The boy paused.

Ross looked down. Was that a crevice in the face of the cliff? He kicked at it twice, enlarging the small opening, sufficient to wedge his foot into it. With the added support, he twisted his body and reached up to gain a solid grip on the rope with both hands.

Now, with Nuno's aid, he worked his way up the cliff. Once over the edge, he remained there on his hands and knees, 'til the heaving in his chest eased. Then Nuno helped him to his feet and together, they staggered to safety.

They sprawled beneath a tree, reliving the close call. Nuno was exhausted, Ross jumpy – high on adrenaline, eager to get going. Fifteen minutes later, they set off again, making it to the base of the mountain nearly on schedule.

Paolo was sitting on the hood of his car, sunning himself – waiting for them as planned. A couple of minutes later, Guissepe and Salvatore drove up. Wasting no time, the old man handed Ross an envelope containing Austrian currency and bestowed farewell kisses on his cheeks. "Buona fortuna, Rosso."

Ross had known these men for less than a day, yet he felt like they were family.

"Avanti, Rosso," said Paolo, motioning to his car.

Once en route, Ross described to Paolo as best he could, how Nuno had saved his life on the mountain. Paolo nodded, solemn and full of pride.

They said little more, stopping at a gas station on the outskirts of Villach where Ross washed up and changed out of his muddy clothes. His hands were cut and bruised, but he considered himself fortunate to have escaped more serious injury.

In less than an hour, they arrived in the bustling town of Klagenfurt. In center city, they spotted signs to the railroad station and followed them without difficulty.

"Molte grazie, Paolo," Ross said, exiting the car.

"Prego, amici," the Italian responded, gripping Ross's hand hard.

He tossed Ross a salute and departed.

Ross flung the backpack over his shoulder and went inside. A train was scheduled to depart for Vienna at twelve-thirty. He'd be on it. As he waited, he heard only German spoken. The mother tongue, he thought bitterly, detesting the sound of it.

When the departure was announced, he followed the crowd and boarded. His ticket was punched by a conductor who, pegging him for Italian, switched to that language and informed Ross that dining car service was offered in two sittings, six and seven-thirty. Ross thanked him, found his seat and let the rocking motion of the train lull him to sleep.

CHAPTER THIRTY-FOUR

Abe put down the telephone and went to the office safe. From it, he removed the loaded automatic, then tested it, chambering a round. Two years ago, he had spoken at a university forum on the threat of renascent Nazism. Afterwards, he'd been attacked by a skinhead with a bat. Badly shaken, he enrolled in a self-defense course which included weapons training, thus qualifying for a permit to carry a gun. The automatic had never been out of the safe from the day the permit arrived. Now Abe hefted the weapon, itching for an opportunity to find and confront Avia's killer. He pocketed an extra clip and locked the safe.

Cortese had pointed him to Doschenko. He had an address, but no face. When he contacted the Israeli Embassy, the officer in charge, with whom he'd worked before, promised an expedited search of Tel Aviv's files. But that would still take time. Cortese had mentioned Thomas at the U.S Embassy. Abe called him next. At first, the security officer had resisted the discussion. Abe reminded him of the brutal murder of an innocent young woman and rubbed in Doschenko's connection to the KGB.

"I hear she fought like hell," Thomas acknowledged. Finally, he said, "I should have my head examined but I'll give you a look at the file. A look . . . that's all. And not here . . . "

Abe suggested a meeting place in two hours time and Thomas agreed. With a face to go along with Doschenko's address, he'd stake out the man's building.

Now he had to shake off the watcher he had spotted this morning. A Mossad agent had once explained to him that surveillance, other than electronic, worked only as long as a subject was unaware of it. There were myriad ways to escape scrutiny.

Abe pulled up the shades, then switched on the radio and the fluorescent lights. He called a supporter of the Center, an elderly man, and asked him to phone the office periodically. Once this was done, he made his way cautiously out of the building via the basement, through an alley and over a wall. He would use the subway and buses and double back on himself. He wanted no one following him to his meeting with Thomas, or to Doschenko's address.

Two policemen had Ross pressed in the corner of a crowded space, their sweating, piggish faces inches from his brow. Hot, rank odors filled his nostrils. As they glared at him, he shut his eyes. Maybe that would make them go away. One spoke to him in German as the other squeezed his arm. He heard screams of pain. They were his.

"Meinherr . . . Meinherr . . . "

Opening his eyes, Ross looked up into the red, angry face of the conductor. The man hastily removed the hand which had been squeezing Ross's shoulder and reminded him that he was ten minutes late for his sitting. He insisted that if Ross wished to eat, he must go to the dining car immediately.

Though he had little appetite, Ross ordered dinner. It was a way of passing the time. While waiting for service, he tried to focus on a course of action. He had been driven this far by rage. But apart from tomorrow's meeting with Lucy, he had no plan. He needed to look up the birth records for February 1938, but was not free to move about Vienna at will. He doubted that Neurath and the Hanfnagels would risk his arrest and attendant publicity. But how far would they go to shut him up?

The private salon of the Royal Hotel, once a nobleman's palace, was a study in elegance. Its ceiling was frescoed, Tiepolo-like, with angels and cupids floating in a powder-blue sky. The walnut panelled walls were inset with mirror so that guests could see themselves reflected as they played the social game. The fashionably dressed guests were enjoying Krug champagne, beluga caviar, hors d'oeuvres and Erich Hanfnagel's renowned urbanity when Willi came in.

"You're late, sister," Dolph criticized. "My wife had to play hostess in your absence."

"She's very capable. You'd find out, if you gave her a chance," Willi rejoined stiffly.

"Ah, yes, you're such a good judge of character," Dolph shot back snidely.

Noting that he wasn't wearing bandages or a sling, Willi retorted, "You heal fast."

"Good news is restorative."

Erich Hanfnagel saw Willi, excused himself and went to greet her. "Liebchen. You're late," he whispered, kissing her hand. "I count on you to be at my side at these events."

She wanted to say, I count on you to be the man I worshipped, but I don't know where that man has gone. She decided this was not the time to confront him. Before doing so, she needed to know from Annalee exactly what transpired during his and Neurath's visit to her apartment. Willi had stopped by the hospital earlier, but the fragile woman was in no condition to discuss the matter.

Hanfnagel studied her. "You look pale. Are you ill?"

"No, Father," she covered quickly. "Just the last minute rush. Something came up at the office."

It was no lie. In fact, something had – and she needed to return to her apartment as quickly as possible. She forced a smile. "Is everything going smoothly?"

"Impeccably. The floral arrangements you selected are exquisite. A new florist?"

She nodded. "And the hors d'oeuvres, Father? Are they satisfactory?"

"Better than ever." He beamed her his most approving smile.

Dolph could not stand to listen to their exchange. He scowled and stalked off.

"I'll take a vodka on ice," she said to the waiter, passing by with a tray of filled champagne flutes. "Make it a double."

"Immediately, madame," he replied.

Hanfnagel, frowning, waited until the waiter was out of earshot. "You are stressed, liebchen. Let me send you to Baden Baden for a few days. The rest will do you good."

"We'll see," she said.

"And Willi . . . consider this," he said with a sigh. "Your brother works hard on behalf of the family's interests. He is a bit prickly at times – but I wish you'd make an effort to get along better with him."

The waiter returned and Willi picked her glass of vodka off the tray. She took a long drink.

Hanfnagel, alarmed that she was acting strangely, said, "Are you sure that you're feeling alright, Willi? You don't seem yourself."

"I'll be fine, Father." She thought of the person she had left behind in her apartment.

The room was filling quickly. They had invited two hundred and almost everyone had accepted.

“I think it’s time for music, don’t you?” she asked.

“Whenever you decide, liebchen.”

Willi moved off to speak to the conductor, while Hanfnagel spotted some late arrivals. They were major Viennese political power brokers. Dolph had suggested the cocktail party a month ago. “Invite the crême de la crême of Vienna,” he had urged. “Industry, science, business and government – whatever their political persuasions. Our public relations people will remind the city that they were brought together under one roof by the only man who could do so – Erich Hanfnagel. It will serve as a convenient reminder in the days of crisis which will follow.”

“Dolph,” Hanfnagel had replied with a smile, “not only is the idea brilliant, but your eloquence is most persuasive.”

Dolph and Victor surveyed the glittering scene from the sidelines, observing as Erich Hanfnagel worked the room. They were congratulating themselves on the success of their scenario when Victor noticed Willi hurry from the room.

The two men went over and drew Hanfnagel to one side. “Is something wrong, Erich?” Neurath asked. “I’ve never known Willi to leave a party until she’s seen your last guest to the door.”

“Maybe her boyfriend’s back in town and she has hot pants,” Dolph joked.

“Crude and unfunny, Dolph,” Hanfnagel said sternly. “But your sister’s behavior is a bit unusual . . . ”

Victor sidled away, left the salon and went into the lobby. He checked Willi’s home number and dialed it. It rang for awhile before an anxious voice came on the line: “Hello? . . . Hello? Who’s calling? Rosso? You there? . . . ”

Neurath listened and then hung up.

CHAPTER THIRTY-FIVE

Ross remained in the dining car 'til nine forty-five, sipping a cognac. As the train entered Central Station in Vienna, the bile rose up in him. He thought bitterly, "Welcome to your place of birth, Ross whoever-you-are . . . "

The terminal was lively. Lots of young people with backpacks. He paused to study the big board with train schedules. There were night trains to Zurich and Venice. His way out – after he accomplished his purpose. He was fifth in an orderly line of arrivals waiting for taxis. Dropped at Am Hof, he headed for Freiheit.

Two policemen were on duty across from the café. Neurath had no reason to expect his return but Ross decided to play it safe and enter through the kitchen. He stepped into the alley and froze in his tracks. Ten yards in, two skinheads were snorting powder. One looked up, saw Ross and shouted a warning to get the fuck out, understandable in any language. Ross backed out, but not before the second skinhead looked up. It was one of the boys who had roughed up the African youth. Ross glanced back. The 'head was staring in his direction. The recognition had been mutual.

"O.D., you miserable shits!" Ross cursed under his breath, as he left the alley.

Changing his tactics, he played the fatigued hiker. With his shoulders slumped and head bowed, he entered Freiheit through the main entrance. Once inside, he chose an inconspicuous table and set his backpack on the floor. Heidi was taking orders two tables away, her back to him. She turned, still writing, and recognized him. She started to greet him but caught the slight shake of his head and stopped.

When she came over, she leaned across the table flirtatiously, signalling left with her eyes to a table in the center of the room. "Polizei," she whispered.

"I spotted them when I came in. They're not looking for me."

"If Jacky comes over, they'll get curious. I'll bring you a beer. Drink some. Then go to the men's room. I'll tell Jacky you're there. He'll join you."

"Rudy's not here?"

"No."

Heidi returned with the mug of beer. "Wait a few minutes – then go."

After a couple of swallows, he eased out of the chair and strolled to the toilet. Jacky came in a minute later and locked the door behind him. "You're crazy," he whispered.

"Crazy isn't the word."

"You should not have come back. It's dangerous."

"You want to debate the subject in the john?"

"What can I do for you?"

"I need a place to stay."

Jacky thought for a moment. "I have just the place. I'll get the keys. Wait a few minutes, then meet me on Am Hof. My car's parked there. A gray Opel. Five minutes. No more."

Ross waited impatiently, then returned to his table, picked up his backpack and left the café unnoticed. Outside, he moved down Naglergasse in the direction of the Am Hof. His neck itched. He looked back. Two skinheads sauntered after him. He recognized the one from the alley; the other looked like an iron-pumping buddy. For the moment, they kept their distance.

The patrolling officers were half a block away, moving in the opposite direction. Ross picked up his pace. That only emboldened the skinheads who assumed that he was running scared. He heard them behind him, getting closer, muttering curses. He knew the signs. They were working themselves up for a fight. Under other circumstances, he would have welcomed it, but he could not afford an incident now. Jacky pulled up, brakes squealing, and Ross hopped in. "Make tracks," he urged.

The skinheads recovered from the unexpected intervention and dashed past the car toward the Am Hof. It wasn't long before Ross heard, through the open window, the sound of motorcycles revving up.

The fuckers are coming after us, he thought, and I got no weapon. "Have you got a loose tire iron in the trunk?" he asked Jacky.

"Yes."

"At the next light, or when traffic slows down, I'm hopping out."

Jacky looked ahead at the cars. "Now's as good a time as any. We're not moving. Something must be blocking traffic."

"Okay, flip the trunk release." Ross ran around back, lifted the trunk lid and grabbed the tire iron. It would have to do.

Back in the car, he watched for the skinheads through the side mirror. They moved up, announcing their presence by loud and repeated revving of their motors.

"Where are we going?" Ross asked.

"Across the canal to Leopoldstadt."

"What's there?"

"You'll see." Jacky maneuvered around a stalled truck and shot ahead. "Why are they following us?" he asked.

Ross jerked his head back toward their pursuers. "One of them wants to pay me back for the other night outside of Freiheit. The other's in love with himself – and wants to prove he's worth it."

Jacky shook his head in disgust. "Have you heard about the girl we met at the Center – Avia Hirsch?"

"Yes, she was murdered," Ross said grimly

"They buried her yesterday. Such a terrible tragedy."

Finally they were able to work their way out of the traffic of the old city. The road ahead was clear. Jacky took a left into Rotenturmstrasse.

Ross heard them before they moved alongside, like an official escort, one on each side, grinning like death's heads. Jacky started to close his window.

"Don't!" warned Ross. "These assholes feed off fear, like vultures on dead flesh."

They crossed the Marien bridge over the Donau Canal. The bank of the canal was lined with tall office buildings. Behind their modernity lay the past, a dense warren of crisscrossing streets. The bikers were tailgating them now and Jacky started to speed up.

"Easy, Jacky. I doubt if they'll make a move. They hunt in packs. Two on two are not their odds . . . "

Jacky nodded and wove the car through the quiet, dark, twisting streets of Leopoldstadt.

"This is the Second District," he told Ross. "Jews settled it in the late seventeenth century. History has left its mark here – both good and bad. We're close to our destination – Schiffamtstrasse. What do I do?"

"Pull in down the block from the building. Don't park in front, even if you see a space."

Jacky veered into the residential street, its silence shattered by the noise of their motors. He found a parking space and backed cautiously into it.

Without waiting for the car to come to a full stop, Ross leaped out like a madman, brandishing the tire iron. He started after the skinheads. They stared in disbelief. Only when his relentless pace convinced them that he was in earnest did they kick into gear and flee around the corner. The sound of their motors cut off suddenly. They were playing possum.

Ross raced back to the car. Jacky locked up and quickly led Ross into a building a few doors up from where he'd parked. On the outside, it looked like any tenement. Inside, the hall showed signs of extensive and attractive renovation.

Jacky explained as he led the way up four flights: "When I put together some money a few years ago, I sought to make an investment. An American friend in real estate said to me, 'Forget stocks and bonds. Buy a building. Bricks don't walk.' I bought this one. It's over two hundred years old."

He unlocked the door to a tidy apartment. The living room was furnished with a sleep sofa, a pair of well-worn leather chairs and a small desk and chair. On a cart were a television set, VCR and cassette player. One entire wall was composed of a built-in bookcase. Framed posters, reminiscent of those at the café, were hung above the couch. A small kitchen off to the right of the foyer, a bath and two small bedrooms completed the space.

"Who lives here?" Ross asked.

"I rent it out to university students during the academic year. It's summer and I'm between tenants. You're welcome to use it, Red."

They jumped at the sharp rap on the door. Ross reached for the tire iron. Jacky checked the peephole.

"It's Rudy. I left word for him where we'd be."

"I hope those fuckers didn't see him."

Rudy entered and hugged Ross. Ross found it painful to look at him. His presence brought Willi closer. "You know the story?" he asked Rudy.

"I know what Willi told me. They claim you hurt Dolph."

"Not enough."

"Why did you come back?"

"Lots of reasons. Lucy Mosel among them. Annalee arranged for me to meet her. Tomorrow."

Rudy looked first at the floor and then at Jacky.

"Come on, Rudy, give it up," he insisted. "You have something to say, just say it."

"Annalee is in the hospital . . . her heart."

"How bad?"

"The doctors tell us that her condition is stable. They anticipate recovery, but they are quick to add that at her age, only God knows."

"When did it happen?"

"Just after you left for Italy . . . "

Ross's eyes never left Rudy's, his gaze steady. Rudy looked away, unable to maintain eye contact.

"You're still holding out on me. Let's have it."

Rudy crumpled like a levee battered by rising tides.

"Father and Victor Neurath . . . " He choked on the names.

"Sit down. You look like hell."

Ross motioned to the easy chair and Rudy dropped into it, dead weight. Ross pulled over the desk chair, reversed and straddled it, leaning forward attentively. Rudy began slowly.

"Willi mentioned to Father that you'd found Lucy Mosel and had arranged to see her when you returned from your weekend. That night, around nine, Father and Victor Neurath, always the gentlemen, paid Annalee a visit, carrying flowers and chocolate."

"The didn't waste any time, did they?"

"They wanted to know what she had told you . . . she insisted that they leave."

"Good for her."

"Not so good. Neurath suggested that failure to cooperate could result in unpleasant consequences. Social security checks lost or delayed . . . claims denied . . . audits . . . services cut off."

"Those ruthless bastards." Just wait 'til I get my hands on them, he thought to himself.

"She told them nothing. Half an hour later, she suffered severe chest pains and called an ambulance."

"I feel responsible," Ross said, anguish in his voice. "I want to see her."

"You'd be arrested," Jacky reminded him.

"As far as they're concerned, I'm in Italy or on my way back home."

"Wouldn't Neurath have her visitors watched?"

"What for? We're yesterday's news. Hanfnagel has what he wants."

"But . . . why not stay here? Let us bring Lucy to you."

"Does Annalee know my situation?"

"I very much doubt it. Visits were strictly limited until yesterday. I've said nothing to her. She was sleeping when Willi went to see her this afternoon."

"Let's assume my meeting with Lucy's on for tomorrow." Ross looked at his watch. "We're scheduled to meet at one o'clock in the lobby of the Royale. Get there early and sit near the concierge desk. She'll ask for me. They'll tell her I've checked out. Don't make your approach in the lobby, wait 'til she's on the street. Then explain the situation and bring her here. Better still, bring her to the hospital. I'll meet you there."

"Are you sure that's wise?" Jacky pressed.

"I'm sure."

"Alright. Agreed," Jacky said. "Right now, try to get some sleep. We'll come back in the morning."

They shook hands soberly. Ross locked the door behind them. He was alone with his thoughts and feelings – and right now, that was a very dark place to be.

Abe was in a foul mood. It was midnight. He had been watching Doschenko's building on Gumpendorferstrasse for seven hours now – ever since making contact with Thomas.

The embassy official had finally said, "In for a penny, in for a pound" and given him a Xerox of the photograph in the file. "If you tell anyone I gave it to you," he warned, "I'll deny it. Good-bye and good luck."

Abe had shown the photograph to a boy of about ten who was rollerskating in front of the building. "That's Mr. Rietsmann. His apartment is up there," the kid said, pointing to the second floor.

It had been difficult to maintain the surveillance without attracting attention from the block's inhabitants. When night fell, Abe took a window table at the "beisl" down the street. From his niche in the cozy room near the coal stove that heated the place in winter, he could observe the building.

He ordered the simple dinner recommended by the proprietor, then stretched the meal of knodel and roast chicken to more than two hours, making small talk with a few locals and sipping large schooners of tap beer. Now it was closing time.

Abe had a face, a location and an alias, but there was no sign of Doschenko. Now he had to leave. He decided to drop the surveillance for the night. Maybe he would have better luck tomorrow.

Abe's gloom was in stark contrast to his adversary's mood. Doschenko had joined his team at the safe house. There, they reviewed assignments, studied photographs of the target and his bodyguard, and checked out weapons and equipment. Finally, they performed a dry run on a street comparable to the site of the planned assault, using a rented rather than a stolen van. It had gone like clockwork. Everything was in order.

Two hours ago, the countdown had begun. First, team A picked up the patsy, neatly securing him in an upstairs room where he was force-fed sufficient drugs to keep him high. Doschenko wanted to ensure that when the man's body was autopsied, the blood levels would scream drug use.

CHAPTER THIRTY-SIX

Ross came out of the shower in Jacky's apartment, wrapped the towel around his waist and went into the kitchen. It was one A.M and he was wired awake, a walking time bomb. He needed to defuse. Looking through the cabinets, he found a bottle of slivovitz, nearly full. He poured a shot and carried the glass into the bedroom.

As he sipped it, the rawness burned his throat, reminding him of grappa and his night in Udine, little more than twenty-four hours earlier. It came back at him with brutal clarity. Ross thought about Franco Cortese. Who was this man he'd loved as a father and what had he done?

Ross had spent time with the victims of muggings and assaults. Now he felt like one of them – the urge to inflict pain upon his victimizer was both powerful and terrifying.

An old rotary phone on the night table loomed large. Is this dinosaur in service, he wondered. He sat on the edge of the bed and had to will his hand to lift the receiver. There was a dial tone. His heart jackhammered. He dialed the international code for the U.S and heard the tone. An operator came on the line and said, "Can I help you?"

He froze and hung up.

He refilled the glass and went into the living room. The only thing that seemed real was the life that he had made with Annie – thank God for that. She was lost to him, but he had his children. He wanted badly to be with them now, to hug them and hold them tight. He needed the comfort of their presence.

Ross returned to the bedroom, picked up the phone and repeated the procedure. This time, he gave the operator his father's number. The phone rang, once, twice, three times. Then it was heart-stopping time. Momma's voice, tremulous with anxiety, came across the wire. "Hello?"

"Momma? . . . It's me . . . Rosso." As if he had to explain who he was.

"Mother of God, we was so worried. Where are you, figlio mio?"

"In Vienna, Momma. Didn't Amy tell you?"

"She tells us you're in Italy. She says you gonna go back to Vienna . . . but we can't find you there."

"I'm here, Momma."

The line crackled with tension.

"Are you with your Poppa?"

"What are you talking about? He's in Florida."

"He told us he was going there. But he goes instead to Vienna."

"Pop's in Vienna?" he asked, incredulous.

"Si. He gets to Vienna yesterday . . . in the morning. The hotel tells him you're gone – not coming back no more. Your Poppa . . . I don't know what to do. He calls me, tells me he's there and I hear no more."

Ross became aware of a pain in his wrist. His knuckles were the color of a blank page. He had been crushing the receiver in his grip.

"Your Poppa says he must go to be with you."

"Why?" he pressed.

"He loves you so much, Rosso."

"Where's he staying, Momma?"

"Dio mio, I don't know. He didn't tell me."

"Don't you worry. I'll find him."

She spoke softly and with tenderness. "Rosso, sweetheart. You know all of us . . . we miss you. Please come home soon, you and Poppa."

She sought to neutralize his pain and create a security zone for his return. He wondered if she could sense what he knew.

"Momma. There's something I need to tell you."

"Si. Si, Rosso. Tell Momma," she beseeched.

He wanted to, but could not say, I've been to Udine. Instead, he whispered, "I love you, Momma . . ." His cheeks were wet. "See you soon."

"Adio, Rosso, figlio mio. Va bene. Adio."

She didn't hang up. He heard her listen for his breathing. It was up to him to break the connection. Ross hung up the receiver and, using the silent, empty apartment as a container for his grief, cried until he was exhausted.

Convinced that it was over, he headed for the bathroom. Like the aftershock of a quake, a final shudder passed through him. He caught himself full face in the mirror and was jolted by the eyes staring back at him.

Ross went to the bedroom window and looked out at the night street. Franco Cortese was somewhere in Vienna. Ross was sure that he had come to protect his secret. Well, he would learn that it was too late for lies. Ross reached for the telephone. He had not forgotten her number. After two rings, she picked up.

"Willi?"

"Red! Thank God you called. You're in New York?"

"Just listen," he demanded. "My father's in Vienna. Have you heard from him?

"Yes. But where are you?"

"Never mind where I am. Where's Pop?" Ross insisted.

"Here with me. Fortunately, he brought the number you left with Amy. He called from the Royale. I explained that you . . . you left Austria – and were on your way home."

"You told him what happened?" Ross asked coldly.

"No." Her voice was so low that he barely heard the reply. "He was quite agitated," she continued. "I assured him that you were alright and convinced him to spend the night here."

"Who else is with you?" Ross asked sharply.

"No one."

"Let me speak to him."

"He's sleeping. He was exhausted by the time that he got here. Where are you? In New York?"

You wish. You and your father, he thought to himself. "How do you expect me to trust you after what's gone down?"

"Gott in Himmel, you're not in Vienna. You wouldn't come back."

She waited for a reply but none was forthcoming. "You're here," she gasped. "*You are here.* I know it."

He imagined he could hear her wheels turning. Was she frightened that he had returned to retaliate against her father?

"Please listen to me, Red. I don't want you to be hurt."

He had to convince Willi that he was no threat.

"The business with the furniture is over," he lied. "I despise the way it was done, but I've been paid. I'm back for one reason and one reason only. I went to Udine – and learned some things about my family while I was there. I'm counting on Lucy Mosel to shed light on them. I can't say more. Don't mention this to my father. Not a word."

"I promise . . . I won't. I want you to know this – no one means more to me than you do." She added emphatically, "*No one.*"

"As much as I'd like to believe that, it's hard."

"You must," she said softly. "Because it's the truth. Tell me where you are. I'll bring your father to you. I want to help. You'll have your meeting with Lucy – then I'll drive you and your father across the border. No one will know you've been here."

His alarm went off. She wanted him out of Vienna real bad. He'd play that card.

"Okay. Bring him here. After I meet Lucy, you can get us out."

"Where are you staying?" she asked, relieved and grateful.

"In a building on Schiffamtgasse. It belongs to Jacky."

"Yes. The one he owns in the Second District. I've been there."

"Fourth floor. I'll be waiting . . . and Willi – if you care at all for me, don't tell a soul."

"Care for you? I love you, Red. Trust me."

Sure, Ross thought cynically. You and me. All the way.

"Red?"

"Yeah?"

"I'll be there soon, liebchen."

He groaned inside. How he despised the hollow ring of that endearment. He heard in it the echo of Erich Hanfnagel's voice, sweet-talking her into his pocket. Standing at the window, he parted the curtains and stared down at the deserted street. It seemed impossible that he had been born in this city. There had to be a mistake.

A concerned Victor Neurath went directly from Erich Hanfnagel's cocktail party to his own office. There, he reviewed his private files. Over the years, he had vetted a number of young, ambitious uniformed members of Vienna's Police Department for their politics, and ultimately, their personal loyalty to him. Those he selected were organized in cells of two. None knew the identity of any but his partner. Each believed in Neurath, supporting the cause and following orders without question. The men had been well-rewarded with promotions and plum assignments.

For tonight's mission, Victor chose a recent recruit, Dietrich Franz, mid-twenties, three years in the department and chomping at the bit for action.

Neurath's phone call interrupted Dietrich in the midst of sex with his wife of three months but that made no difference to the young officer. The idea of secretly serving the Deputy Commissioner was thrilling, and Dietrich, like his father and grandfather before him, believed in the restoration of a greater Austria, under strong leadership. Neurath gave Franz the address of a building on Favoritenstrasse in the Wieden district and asked him to report on the comings and goings of a resident named Willi Hanfnagel and her male companion. The Commissioner demanded a complete description of the woman's companion, should he surface.

Franz arrived at ten thirty and parked opposite the 1950s apartment building, one of the few good ones put up in the early postwar period. His interview with the white-gloved doorman was non-productive. The man knew nothing. He had come on duty at nine. The police officer swore him to silence, then returned to his car and waited.

The lights in the apartment on the seventh floor were turned off at eleven-forty, then came on again at one thirty-two A.M. At one forty-five, a white BMW pulled out of the building's underground garage.

The Commissioner had informed him that the Hanfnagel woman drove such a vehicle and provided the license plate number. The number matched. The BMW sped off down the street. There were two people in the front seat. Dietrich could not be certain if they were a man and a woman. He turned on the ignition and followed without lights.

CHAPTER THIRTY-SEVEN

Ross heard the footsteps and opened the door. He feared this moment more than the barrel of a loaded gun pointed at him. Pop's eyes were downcast as he climbed the last step and reached the landing. When he looked up and found Ross framed in the doorway, he was shocked by what he saw. His son stared at him, his eyes pitiless and his hands clenched into fists, as if ready to fight.

Franco's chest heaved, but it was not from the exertion of climbing the steps. Willi, behind Mr. Cortese, believed that Ross's hostile expression was directed at her and felt frightened.

Without a word of greeting, Ross led them inside and double-locked the door. When Pop tried to embrace him, Ross stiffened. The old man drew back, his face flushed, his eyes showing the hurt he was feeling.

"Pop . . . " was all that Ross squeezed out.

Willi stood apart, watching apprehensively.

"What's happened, Rosso? You in some kind of trouble? Willi here . . . she says you gonna explain why you're in this place."

Ross looked at Willi, then went to the window and scanned the street. It appeared empty and silent. He turned and saw Willi staring at him in dismay. She knew that he mistrusted her.

"What are you doing in Vienna?" Ross challenged, his manner clearly accusatory.

Pop was shocked. "I don't understand . . . what's the problem, figlio mio. When I call home to tell your momma you're not here, she tells me you got a good price on the furniture. Now, you're all upset . . . "

"Get him a drink," Ross snapped at Willi. "There's slivovitz in the kitchen."

Frightened by his tone, Willi silently followed his command.

"I asked you what you're doing here," Ross repeated.

Franco nodded. "After you left New York, Rosso . . . every time I closed my eyes, I kept seeing you in this place. My heart ached. There's so much you don't know."

"I've been finding out."

"I came because I want to be the one to tell you."

"You're a little late. I've been to Udine. To Bruno's. I met an old friend of yours, Guissepe Barzini. His grandson got me back over the mountain – the way you took me out."

Pop staggered. Before Ross got to him, Willi, standing in the doorway, rushed over and placed a protective arm around him. She led him to a chair and offered him a drink.

He looked up at her, then at Ross through clouded eyes and began to speak: "I should have told you a long time ago – but when? How do you tell a child such a story? You wait. Then the child becomes a boy and you say, let the past be past. It will bring only pain and confusion. By the time he is a man, the lies have been lived so long, the love alone becomes the truth."

Ross did not dare move closer to the old man. He feared that if he did, he would explode. His questions bore the charge, bursting rapid-fire, his voice metallic, matching the taste of blood in his mouth.

"Who were they? What did you do, Pop? How could you take me away from them?"

"You think I could've done that?"

Willi looked like a bystander to a bombing. Franco was crying now. She reached out to take the old man's hand.

"What am I supposed to think after a lifetime of lies? I know what I feel – alone!," Ross screamed.

"You've never been alone, figlio mio."

"Don't call me that! I'm not your son."

"You are my son," Franco cried out. "I'm sorry, Rosso. I loved her with all my heart. I never stopped loving her. I never forgot her."

"Who? For Christ's sake, who are you talking about?" Ross pleaded.

"Ariella . . . Ariella Mosel."

Ross heard Willi's sharp intake of breath and saw her, frozen in place, eyes startled wide, a deer caught in the headbeams of an oncoming car. He held his breath. He was seeing himself, not Willi.

He shook his head, as if, having demanded the truth, he now had to deny it. "Ariella Mosel. How could that be?" he gasped. "How could it be?" he repeated.

He recalled now the curious way the old lady looked at him from that first encounter in the lobby of Hanfnagel's building. Had she known? Ariella Mosel – *my mother*? It was impossible. He recalled the picture on Annalee's piano. She was just a girl. He fought disbelief.

"Forgive me, Rosso," the old man said. "I couldn't save her. *Dio mio*, I tried . . . but I was too late."

Ross murmured her name, over and over again, and with each repetition, he felt that he was thrusting a sharp-nosed shovel into frozen earth, exhuming her corpse.

He heard Willi mumble something. She turned back toward the kitchen but stopped short. Ross sat down opposite Pop.

All of the ambient light seemed concentrated on the anguished face of Franco Cortese. His eyes were deep pools, filled with suffering. "Ariella." he intoned mournfully. "She was your momma."

"And my father?" Ross asked, nearly choking on the words.

Pop's head snapped back, as if caught by a vicious uppercut; his eyes lost focus and rolled up. Ross worried that he was suffering a stroke. Then Pop shook his head and drew himself up with dignity, an aged fighter coming off the floor with the eight count.

He spoke quietly and proudly, seeking to assure that there would never again be doubt. "Me, Rosso. *I'm* your father."

Ross buried his head in his hands. Pop and Ariella. It was unbelievable. He was a penniless Italian working man; she, a beautiful, educated girl from a wealthy family. A Jewish family at that.

If it's true, Ross thought incredulously, I'm half-Jewish.

"It's hard for me to believe," he said. "If it's true, why didn't you tell me before? I feel like I've been cheated. I want to know it all. Right now!"

"I'll tell you. In time, I'll tell you everything," Franco promised, at last relieved of the burden of silence.

For Pop the worst is over, Ross thought. For me, it's just beginning.

Willi sat down next to him on the small sofa. He felt the heat coming off her body and found himself longing for her comfort.

Pop began again. Ross had to strain to hear him. "I told you my boss sends me here. Mr. Mosel is retired, but comes into the shop every day. His son, Joshua, runs the business. He's a good businessman, but Kirmen, Mr. Mosel, he's the artist. Rosso, they were such fine people. They treated me good . . . they found me a room not far from the shop."

It was pouring out of him now, having been held back so long.

"One day . . ." Pop let out a sigh. "One day, into the shop comes Ariella. Her beauty makes my breath stop. Such a face. Such beautiful red hair."

Ross self-consciously raised his hand to his hair.

Franco paused, his expression a weave of love and sorrow.

"I am in love with her that minute. I pray to God that I will see her again. After one week, we meet on the street. We stop and talk. I know only a little German. She knows more Italian. We have coffee. We talk. I find her soul more beautiful than her face.

"Rosso, such gentleness, such love for life. She makes me see things in a new way. Very soon, the love is on both sides. You are its fruit. When we find that Ariella is pregnant, we go to her family. Joshua . . . Fanny . . . Kirmen. They are very angry at the beginning. It is a deep hurt for them. Ariella . . . she is fire and pride. She makes them understand . . . to see how much we love. After a time, they say yes, we can marry . . . "

Pop went dumb. Drained. There was a slight tremor in his jaw and he was breathing hard.

"Don't quit on me now," Ross insisted.

Pop forced himself to continue. "They say we can marry. They ask one thing . . . " His pause filled the air. "They ask that we bring you up in the Jewish faith. They explain to me that in their faith, the religion passes from the mother. I say we will raise you with love and with the teachings of your mother's people . . . "

He sobbed, covering his eyes with his hands. "But I didn't keep that promise."

I'm a Jew, Ross thought. His father's tears made it undeniable. Ross turned to Willi, defiance in his gaze. His eyes spoke for him and she knew what he was saying. She responded by gently taking his hand in hers. He looked at her gratefully, then moved to his father and knelt beside him. They held one another.

Ross pressed his head against his father's chest so that he could hear the beating of the old man's heart while Pop stroked his hair. Father and son cried together, joined in sorrow as they had been once before when they shoveled earth onto Annie's coffin.

Ross looked at his father. Pop was running on fumes. "Why didn't Ariella come out with us?" he implored.

Franco felt the urgency of Ross's need and forced himself to resume the story.

"When we married, Ariella was five months pregnant. She gave birth to you in a special maternity place outside of the city. February fifteenth, nineteen and thirty-eight. You came out a fine bambino. We were so happy. Kirmen had the papers for America. The fifth of March . . . Ariella is home in Vienna . . . she has this hemorrhage. We're very scared. The doctor says it's not serious. She's going to be fine. She needs to rest. He says not to move her. The city is crazy . . . in an uproar.

"Ariella . . . Joshua . . . Kirmen . . . your grandma, Fanny . . . all of them say to me, you leave now. Take the baby and go across the border into Italy. We will join you soon . . . when Ariella can travel. I say no. They say '*You must go.*' I was a kid. What did I know? I listened."

If you didn't, Ross thought grimly, I'd be dead, too. Another Jew, on the pile of corpses.

"I load the truck with furniture Kirmen made for Ariella . . . your furniture Rosso . . . "

You don't know yet, Pop, Ross thought. That was taken from me, too.

"Kirmen gives me a few more pieces to sell in Italy for money for America. Kirmen and me, we hide you in the truck. I drive through the night, stopping only to feed you and change you. In Udine, I wait . . . I wait. I telephone. Ariella is asking about you. She feels stronger each day. Soon, she says, we will all be together." He heaved a terrible sigh that shook his whole body. "It never happens . . . " he cried.

"You should have told me. You should have found a way."

The old man's eyes acknowledged him.

"Did you know that Lucy survived?"

"Not 'til Willi told me."

"I'm meeting her – in twelve hours."

"I'm glad you found her."

"Are you okay?" he asked his father, in a softened tone, concerned for his health. Franco nodded wearily.

"And you?" he said, suddenly confronting Willi. "Now that you've heard it all . . . where are you going to be in this?"

"With you!" she cried, throwing herself across the space that separated them, into his arms. "With you, with you. I'm sorry, so sorry."

Her head burrowed into his shoulder and her arms clutched him tightly. The touch of her body tore at him as Hanfnagel's words came back: "My interest is in the furniture, not the family." Of course, he wasn't interested in the family. They were Jews. Now, as then, a young Jewish woman had lost her life – murdered. If Avia was right, the Hanfnagels were purveyors of old poison in new bottles – monsters. Ross determined there and then to bring them down.

Lost in these thoughts, Ross had shut out the world. But he could not remain deaf to the growing roar of engines. Rushing to the window, he parted the curtains and saw a dozen or more motorcycles crowding the street in front of Jacky's building.

He switched off the lights. Pop started for the window. Ross warned, "Don't go near there."

"What's happening?" Willi asked fearfully.

"History repeating itself."

"What are you saying, Rosso?" Pop demanded.

"Skinheads. A dozen of them. I'm sure they're looking for me."

"Call the police," Willi blurted out, then realized that there was more threat than security for Ross in that solution.

"Don't worry. Someone will," Ross shakily reassured them.

On the street, the skinheads began shouting threats to burn out the "Jew-building". Three of them ran inside.

The sound of the biker's jackboots echoed loudly throughout the building. A woman's terrified scream rang out. The yelling and cursing came closer. Before Pop or Willi could say a word, Ross herded them into the small bedroom, then closed and locked the door. It was pitch black.

He held Willi close and knew from her ragged breathing that she was panicking.

"The police will be here any minute . . . isn't that so, Red?" she gasped.

"Sure," he soothed. "We'll be fine. Breathe through your nose – slow, steady and deep. They'll call it quits soon . . . " Unless they firebomb the place, he thought.

"This can't be happening," she insisted.

"Why not?" Pop demanded. "It happened before."

The thugs were pounding on doors, shouting and laughing. "Araus. Araus Juden schweinhund."

Ross felt that Willi was verging on a scream. Suddenly, they heard a series of loud whistles. The pounding ceased as the skinheads responded to the signal and retreated down the stairs.

Willi pushed to get out of their dark prison but Ross restrained her. The silence felt ominous. Ross waited a long moment, then cautiously opened the bedroom door.

"I think they're gone," he said. He went to the window and studied the situation on the street. The bikers were mounting up, revving their engines. One of them reached into his sidesaddle and pulled out what Ross feared was a Molotov cocktail. It was. The skinhead lit the wick and tossed the gasoline-filled bottle at a window on a lower floor. It missed, striking the brick wall and exploding. A brief, intense gust of flame flared, then died quickly and harmlessly with nothing to feed it.

The wail of sirens cut through the night.

"The police," Willi said, forcing a smile. "See. They did come."

She joined Ross and Pop at the window. The bikers pulled out in formation and were gone. Several police cars entered the street.

Exhausted by the ordeal, Willi sought shelter in Ross's arms. There was blood on her lip where she had bitten it. He took her into the kitchen and pressed a cold wet towel against the wound to stop the bleeding. She pushed his hand away and said, "They must be stopped – and prosecuted," she said indignantly.

"We'll see, but I wouldn't lay odds," Ross responded cynically. "But you can be damn sure of one thing . . . "

"What's that Rosso?" Pop interrupted.

"The cops already have a good idea of who these bums are." Ross checked out the street again. "The police are coming into the building," he announced.

"They'll want to know if anyone was injured. You'll have to handle this, Willi." She nodded dutifully.

A firm knock at the door was accompanied by a loud shout: "Polizei!"

Ross and Pop retreated into the bedroom.

There was a second knock and Ross heard Willi greeting the officer. The policeman questioned her briefly. Ross heard him say, "Guten nacht, fraulein."

Willi shouted something at him as his heels click-clacked down the steps. Ross came out of the bedroom and switched on the lights. She turned to him, her face tight, her feelings masked. "The officer said they got away. I said, did you pursue them? He didn't answer me . . . "

The facial muscles around her mouth twitched. Ross knew the sign. She was holding back a howl of pain and rage.

"He didn't answer me . . . " she repeated.

"So? What are you going to do?" he needled.

"I'll report it to the Commissioner. He'll hear from me." There was a note of hysteria in her voice.

"You still don't get it, do you?" he persisted. "Still the good little Austrian girl. Bow down to those above. You're going to report it to Neurath. What a joke! When are you going to stop kidding yourself? You heard Pop's story. The same scum has come up from the sewers where we thought we flushed them . . . Ah, what's the use?

"We can't stay here," he stated firmly. "The word is out that I'm in Vienna. Sooner or later, it'll get back to Neurath or Doschenko."

"We can go to my apartment," Willi said. "We'll be safe there."

What choice do I have? Ross agreed. Hopefully, it was the last place they'd look.

They shut the lights and locked the door behind them. He helped Pop down the stairs, holding his arm, for fear that he might take a tumble on the steep steps.

When they reached the downstairs foyer, Ross directed Willi to walk to her car alone.

"Pull up in front of the house. Release the lock on the back door. While Pop gets in front, I'll slip into the back and stay down on the floor."

Dietrich Franz had re-positioned his car a block away to avoid involvement with the skinheads and his fellow officers. From this vantage point, he observed the woman and an elderly man in the white BMW as it pulled away. He followed the car back to Willi's garage. Noting the time in his diary, he settled back in his seat. It was an exciting night. He hoped that the Commissioner would be pleased with his report.

Victor Neurath enjoyed a second cup of breakfast coffee with his wife's delicious streusel. Franz had reported in. It appeared that Willi Hanfnagel, accompanied by an elderly man, had paid a middle of the night visit to a building on Shiffamtgasse. The building was later raided by skinheads. Neurath rubbed his chin. The old man must be Cortese senior, in Vienna and looking for his son. Had Cortese managed to slip back into Austria? It seemed unlikely, but what else would account for such a strange visit?

He decided to check on the ownership of the building and its rent rolls when he arrived at the office, as well as obtaining police reports on the disturbance. What had prompted the raid? He needed to know. If Cortese was in Vienna, they'd find him. If he expected his day in court, he'd be sadly – and terminally – disappointed. On this day, of all days, the last thing he needed was an outsider's meddling.

CHAPTER THIRTY-EIGHT

Ross awoke with a start, unsure for a moment where he was. Then it all came back in a rush. He was in Willi's apartment. Willi's head was nestled in his arm. He looked at her sleeping form. The woman in my arms, he thought, was born and lived in the apartment in which my mother grew up. It was the Mosel legacy that brought her to his door. And despite her protestations of love, it could very well tear them apart before another day was done. "Wake up, Willi," he said softly.

"Liebchen," she greeted him sleepily.

"Do me a favor and quit calling me that, okay?"

Willi nodded guiltily. "I'll go and get breakfast," she said.

She dressed hastily and left the apartment without a word. Ross showered, dressed and then woke Pop. He went into the living room of the sparsely furnished apartment. At least here, Ross noted with satisfaction, she had separated from her father. The furniture was tasteful, clearly expensive, but contemporary. The sofa was covered in an inviting off-white nubby fabric in a diagonal pattern. Plump throw pillows picked up the bright colors of a beautiful tribal rug. A glass top table sat on a bronze, sculptured base while the photographs and prints on the wall were modern.

Willi returned from shopping with eggs, fruit, rolls and pastries. Little was said as they only picked at the omelets she prepared. They were on their second cup of coffee when the doorbell rang. Willi ushered in Jacky and Rudy. She had phoned them just before falling asleep and filled them in on the reason for the sudden move, asking that they come by first thing in the morning.

"Pop, this is Willi's brother, Rudy, and his partner, Jacky Gold. Rudy, Jacky – my father, Franco Cortese."

Pop shook their hands in turn.

"Are you safe here?" Rudy turned to Ross and asked.

"As long as we're the only ones who know that I'm here, yes."

"I'll drive them across the border into Italy after their meeting with Lucy Mosel," Willi added.

"Good," said Jacky. "Each hour that passes increases the danger. Vienna is unfortunately a small town."

"Where have I heard that before?" Ross asked wryly. "Well, whatever comes of the meeting with Lucy, there's something else I've got to do while I'm here."

He didn't need to look at Willi to feel her fear.

"What?" Rudy asked.

"Have any of you heard of a videogame called Konzentrationlager?" He looked from Rudy to Jacky to Willi. He could tell by their expressions that they knew *something*.

"There was a story or two in the press some months ago," Jacky replied.

"Have you ever seen one?"

"Of course not." Jacky was repelled by the idea.

"How about you, Willi – you know about them?"

"Only what I've read in the paper. They're frightful and perverse."

"Then have a look. It's something you should see." He retrieved the tape from the backpack and slid it into the VCR. He watched them as they viewed it. Pop spoke first. "This is garbage, Rosso. Turn it off."

"The games are out there, Pop. They're selling them to kids." Ross clicked the remote and the screen went blank. "Make no mistake about this – the people who are producing this filth must be stopped."

Willi regarded him as if he had lost his marbles. "That's a problem for the authorities."

"Yeah, well, what did your goddamn authorities do for you last night?" he snapped.

She looked shamefaced.

"Avia Hirsch brought this tape to me at the Royale. She was following a lead. I think that's what got her killed. Don't believe the story in the paper about a bungled burglary."

Ross suddenly decided to take the plunge. He peered into the dark, cold water, took a deep breath and dove right in. "She had reason to believe that this sick shit is being manufactured and distributed by the Hanfnagels."

Willi let out a loud, chilling cry. Pop and Rudy moved to help her.

"No," she insisted. "I'm alright." She looked at Ross and with an eery calm said, "Go on."

"Avia told me that the Prosecutor needed more evidence in

order to act. Apparently, they were close to moving against the production facility a couple of months ago – but there must have been a leak. The operation was suddenly shut down and presumably moved before the prosecutor could launch a raid. Someone had to have warned them."

"It's truly awful, but it doesn't concern you," Rudy offered.

"Oh, but it does. I feel responsible for what happened to Avia . . . " Ross paused. "Dolph saw her speaking to me in the bar of the Royale – not long before she was killed."

"Are you saying that you believe he was involved in her murder?" Jacky asked, appalled.

Ross looked at Willi. "It's a possibility."

He saw her tremble.

"But what can you do?" Rudy asked.

"Use myself as bait – try to spook them into a move. Your father and brother are arrogant s.o.b's. They act as if they own this town. Maybe they do. We'll see. I want to let them know that I'm onto them. To shake them up."

"If what you say is true, they might have you killed, too," Jacky cautioned. "You met the Storm troopers last night. They're for cheap hire. I'm sure that *you* they'd kill for nothing."

"I'm aware of that."

If I'm a Jew, he thought, here's a Jew who won't go down without taking some of them with me.

They were aghast.

"Rosso," Pop begged. "Stay out of it. Your family needs you."

"I've got to do this, Pop – for my family."

Willi spoke. Her face was tight, her voice strained. "Dolph came to me several months ago and asked if I would lease space to him – for his video manufacturing and distributing operation."

"He wanted to use your factory as a cover," Ross interrupted.

"You don't know that for sure."

"So, what did you say?"

"I agreed. I had a great deal of unused space . . . I didn't think anything about sharing some of it. Dolph moved in – overnight, in fact – and he began immediately to separate his quarters from the main area. He soundproofed, air-conditioned and brought in electronic equipment."

"I've got to get access," Ross demanded.

"I don't know how you'd do it. He keeps his area tightly restricted. My employees are forbidden entry. He has his own cleaning crew. Reinhold, you know, Dolph's son – you met him at the Opera – has been working there since his school year ended."

Willi paused and made a direct appeal to him. "I'll help you in any way I can. I ask one thing in exchange. Don't judge my father without proof. Whatever he may have done in the past doesn't prove that he's part of this. I have no trouble believing that Dolph is capable of such a crime. He's a vicious man. But not Father.

"Dolph manages Father's business interests. That includes the video company. Father is totally preoccupied with his charities and public service. You witnessed his reaction to Dolph's filthy mouth at dinner. Remember?"

"You've made a steady stream of excuses for your father," Ross reminded.

"Not true. I accept now that he connived to get the furniture from you. And rest assured, I won't readily forgive what he did to Annalee. But this . . . "

He pitied her desperation. "Come on, Willi. Knowing your father, do you think he'd let Dolph run a shoe-shine stand without somehow having a hand in it?"

That stopped her for a moment, but she quickly returned to her initial position. "I won't believe this of him without proof."

"Fine! Neither will the Prosecutor."

The phone rang before she could reply.

Willi picked it up immediately and asked the identity of the caller. She turned to Ross. "It's for you. He won't give his name."

"It's got to be Abe. I left this number at the Center."

He took the receiver from her. "Abe? Listen carefully . . . Never mind how I got back . . . I've got a lead on the production facility for the videogames . . . Yes . . . Don't leave your office . . . Keep the line open . . . I'll call as soon as I know for sure. You've got to be ready to move fast. "

Ross turned back to Willi. "If your factory is the site for production and distribution of this poison, we've got Dolph," he declared emphatically. And Erich Hanfnagel as well, he added silently.

"What's next?" Rudy asked.

"You get going. We'll meet at the hospital – as planned."

"Be careful, for God's sake," Jacky cautioned as he and Rudy headed off to Café Freiheit.

CHAPTER THIRTY-NINE

Victor Neurath set his elbows on the desk in his office and read the report a second time. The building on Schiffamtgasse belonged to one Jacob Gold. Business address: Café Freiheit. He was Rudy Hanfnagel's partner and lover, Victor knew. A Jew. Why would Willi Hanfnagel go to this address in the middle of the night? If Cortese was in Vienna, and Neurath's instinct screamed that possibility, was Willi involving herself with him and the Jews? It seemed unlikely, for she was a girl who had never opposed her father. But the idea troubled him nonetheless.

He knew that Dolph would dismiss his concerns as paranoid, but it was a policeman's paranoia that had served him well over the years. He dialed Dolph's number.

"The big day, eh, Victor?" a jocular Dolph responded to Neurath's greeting.

"I don't want to put a damper on your enthusiasm, but something's come up that requires our immediate attention," Victor said, succinctly detailing the circumstances.

As predicted, Dolph minimized the problem. That was a serious flaw in a leader, Neurath recognized.

"Humor me, Dolph. Contact your men and find out what led to the attack on Schiffamtgasse."

"When you put it that way, how can I deny you?"

"Get back to me as soon as you hear, alright?"

"Yes, yes, Victor," Dolph soothed. "I'll meet you shortly before four at father's. I've got new Cubans. Champagne, cigars and news bulletins."

All well and good, thought Victor. In the meantime, better safe than sorry. He phoned the patrol division.

After Rudy and Jacky left her apartment, Willi turned to Ross. "I better call my secretary and tell her that I won't be in today."

Ross nodded. She went into the bedroom to use the telephone.

Ross seized the private moment to ask Pop a difficult question, but one that concerned him greatly. "What does Momma know . . . about what happened in Vienna?"

"Gina knows everything. I wrote to her from Vienna and I explain that I met Ariella and that I would marry her. I wish for Gina that she find someone who will make her happy.

"The day I returned to Udine – with you, Rosso – our friends tell her. She comes to my house. She still has feelings for me. Such a woman. She helps to take care of you when I go back to look for Ariella. When I found out . . . Ariella . . . that she's dead . . . Gina is there to comfort me – and care for you. That woman loves you with all her heart . . . and what a momma she's been to you."

"I love her too, Pop . . . I always will."

Ross felt tears well up in his eyes. He knew Momma's love down to his marrow, but right now it only added to his torment. He had never had a chance to love – or be loved by the woman who gave birth to him.

"Dio mio, I forgot," Pop said. "I brought this here for you . . . "

He took out his old, worn wallet and slipped a small tattered photo from a compartment. He offered it hesitantly, as if each step into that reality so long postponed required an additional effort of will. Ross reached for it, held it, and finally gazed down at the fading snapshot. He was at once moved by her slender, lustrous beauty and her youth.

"When was this picture taken?" Ross asked.

"She's carrying you in this picture. She's not yet showing. The third month. You see how happy she is?"

When Willi returned to the living room, he offered her the picture. She studied it for a minute, and seemed captivated by Ariella's youthful beauty that was apparent even in the faded photo. Then she looked at Ross tenderly, choking with emotion, and said, "You resemble her, you know. You have her smile."

Ross took back the picture and carefully placed it in his wallet. Willi put her arms around him and wept for his loss. When she wiped away her tears and composed herself, he said firmly, "Willi, listen to me. I have to get a look at your factory."

She nodded and hugged him tighter before heading toward her bedroom.

"Call your foreman now," Ross said, "and ask if Dolph or Reinhold are around. Make it seem casual. If he says no, find out if he knows their work schedule. Repeat his replies out loud. We'll take it from there."

Willi felt as if her whole life were being called into question. She dialed the phone wondering what the answers would mean for her future. "Gerhard. How are things?" she asked her foreman. Following Ross's instructions, she spoke so that he would be able to follow the conversation.

"Good, fraulein Willi. We're caught up on shipping."

"That's good news. Have you seen Dolph or Reinhold?"

"Your nephew's here now. Shall I call him?"

"No, don't call Reinhold, that won't be necessary," she demurred. "Just tell me – when's the best time to reach him?"

"I'd say morning is the best time. He plays soccer from noon to two."

"Reinhold leaves at twelve, you say?"

Ross came close and whispered, "Congratulate him on his productivity. Tell him the men are doing a fine job and deserve the afternoon off. Tell him to shut down the warehouse at noon."

Willi completed the call as instructed.

"That's that," said Ross. "Let's go . . . First stop . . . a hardware store. Pop, you come along. We can use a good lookout."

Willi drove to a hardware store not far from the factory. Ross sent her in to purchase a set of locksmith picks. The owner looked at her with a raised eyebrow, but wrapped the tools. When she returned to the car, Ross said, "Drive to the warehouse, but park where we can observe the entrance without being seen."

They drove into an industrial area. Loft buildings from earlier in the century stood beside small, modern factories and warehouses. Willi turned the corner, then braked suddenly.

"What the hell?" Ross said.

"There," she pointed. "The two-story gray building is mine."

He saw what had jolted her. A police car was parked twenty yards down from the entrance.

"They could be cooping," Ross suggested.

"What is *cooping*?" she asked.

"Cops find a quiet, out-of-the-way place to park and take a snooze. Have cop cars parked here before?"

"I come so rarely . . . I'm not sure."

"Is there another entrance?"

"You see the wide alley?" she pointed. "The delivery entrance is in there."

"Alright. It's nearly noon now . . . "

"Look!" Pop interrupted.

A dozen or so men exited the warehouse.

"Is that all of them?" Ross asked.

"I don't see Gerhard – or, for that matter, Reinhold."

It was ten past the hour when Reinhold hurried out, carrying a large gym bag. He took off down the street.

"Looks like he's racing to his soccer game," Ross observed.

A minute later, another man came out. "That's Gerhard," Willi announced.

The foreman locked up and went off.

"Okay, Willi. Go over to the main entrance. Start to unlock the door, then act as if you suddenly noticed the police presence. Then walk over and introduce yourself as the owner of the warehouse. Ask if there's a problem in the area. If they're sleeping, just go inside and let me in through the delivery entrance."

He watched as she crossed to the factory. "Two blasts on the horn, Pop, if trouble comes our way."

"Be careful, figlio mio."

"No sweat."

Willi approached the police car and spoke to its occupants.

So they are on duty, he thought grimly. Ross waited a few minutes, then made his move into the alley. He heard the release of the inside bolts and Willi opened the door.

One light was on at the far end of the warehouse, but even with her face in shadow, he could see the tension in her eyes.

"What did the cops say?"

"They flirted . . . said they were there to keep an eye on me."

"Maybe that's more truth than poetry. Let's get cracking. Turn on the lights and show me Dolph's workspace."

She led him to the rear of the warehouse and pointed to the new wall and a metal door with double locks.

"It may be alarmed," he said as he opened the package and removed the picks. He went to work on the first cylinder.

"What will you do if you can't open it?"

"Don't worry." He probed, working to catch the tumblers.

"Are all police taught breaking and entering?" Willi asked nervously.

"Only New York's finest." He heard a click. "That's one. If an alarm goes off, shut the lights off, exit the front door and act scared. Keep the cops occupied for a minute. Tell them you came to check on some papers, next thing you knew the alarm went off. I'll duck out the alley-way."

The second cylinder yielded. “There.” He pushed the door and held his breath. No alarm.

Ross took a deep breath and stepped inside. Using a pencil beam flash, he found the light switch.

The fluorescents cast a green glow in the windowless space. The orderly room was cool and there was the tell-tale hum of an air conditioner. To their left, a large area was occupied by shiny new electronic equipment. Ross guessed that it was video-editing and copying apparatus. A state-of-the-art VCR was on the same metal table. The far end of the room contained heavy-duty shelving, piled high with hundreds of sealed cartons stamped with coded letters and numbers. A desk, two chairs, a double-sized filing cabinet, a large safe and a copying machine comprised the remainder of the room’s contents.

Ross selected a carton from the shelf and opened it. He removed a videotape and slid it into the player. Fast forwarding through the usual warnings, he pressed Play. It was a porno film. The family enterprise, he thought sardonically.

Two cartons later, he hit the jackpot. Not videotapes, but videogames, their title clearly and boldly imprinted. KONZENTRATIONLAGER. Checking for matching serial numbers, he found several dozen cartons containing the videogame. Willi was standing near the door, a study in shame.

He walked briskly across the room to the filing cabinet and with little effort, sprung the lock. “I need your help with this,” he called to her, loud enough to break the trance she seemed to be in.

Moving stiffly, she came and sat at the desk, examining the files as he handed them to her.

“What have you got?” he asked.

“They’re invoices. Lists of subscription clients and retail outlets.”

“Do they name the products?”

She nodded curtly. “With typical efficiency. Here. Konzentrationlager. One hundred twenty-five copies to Bluevideo, Frankfurt. Two hundred and forty copies to Video-energie, a fine shop in downtown Vienna. Here’s another. Good God,” she hesitated, stricken. “The owner is a close friend of my father.” Willi felt ill.

“Make copies,” Ross said, “while I clean up. But first . . . ” He picked up the telephone and dialed the Center. “Abe?”

“Yes.”

“It’s Cortese. I found what you’re looking for – all you’ll need to bring those fuckers down. The videogames, equipment, invoices.”

Ross gave him the address of the warehouse. “Willi Hanfnagel knew nothing about what her brother was doing here. I'm sure of that. You've got to make that clear to the government's prosecutor!"

"They'll need a search warrant. This will take some time," Abe countered.

"You don't *have* time. If the authorities hesitate, threaten them with the media. But shake a leg. We've got to go."

Ross did his best to return the room to normal, resealing the cartons and placing those he had tampered with beneath untouched boxes. Willi finished her Xeroxing, placed the copies in her bag and returned the originals to the cabinet.

She regarded him sorrowfully. "Reinhold is Father's pride and joy. He's just a boy. How could Dolph involve him?"

"Your brother isn't in it for the money alone. I've seen the man in action. That sicko believes what he says."

He hesitated before adding, "Reinhold grew up with hate in his oatmeal. What do you expect?"

Ross wondered what shit Erich Hanfnagel had served up to Dolph. The dirt would come out in the wash and it satisfied Ross to be the active ingredient in the detergent.

"I wish I could make it easier on you," he said sternly. "But you asked for proof . . . and now you've got it."

She looked down at the floor. "I won't believe it of Father until I hear his admission."

"If that's what you're waiting for, don't hold your breath. He'll have some soothing story to lubricate your doubts and get himself off the hook. The man's a master."

"Can we leave now?" she asked, tears in her eyes. "I feel . . . I feel as if I betrayed my family."

"What?" he exclaimed, disbelieving. "You see this crap and can say that? Who betrayed who, Willi?"

She looked as if he had slapped her.

"I'm sorry," he said, softening his tone. "I wish I could make it easier on you. Come here"

He held her for a moment, then said, "Go outside and wait with Pop. I'll lock up and leave by the alley door."

Ross took a few minutes to work the cylinder of the first lock back into place. As he started to tackle the second, he heard two honks on a car horn.

Willi came running back. "I saw from the window. It's Dolph! He's here . . ."

"We're getting out – right now."

"No, I'm staying," she said. "If he comes . . . "

"No way."

Ross grabbed her hand and pulled her toward the side door. They worked their way down the alley. At the juncture of the alley and street, Ross pressed tight against the wall and cautiously peered around the corner.

There was a Mercedes parked behind the squad car. No one was in it. Risking a second look, he saw Dolph striding toward the front entrance. "Once he's inside, we make a run for it. Don't look back."

"If I stayed, I could delay him," she explained.

"If you think I'd leave you with that animal, you're crazy. I'll drive. You direct."

He looked again. "He's inside. Okay, let's go." He took her hand and they dashed across the street.

Dolph closed the door to the factory behind him. He had received word that last night's storm troopers attack was directed against an American seen leaving Café Freiheit with the owner. The description fit Cortese. He had called Victor immediately with the news, to find that patrol officers staking-out the factory had just radioed in that a woman, identifying herself as Willi Hanfnagel, had entered the premises alone at twelve-fifteen.

"We are in the final countdown," Neurath had said, as if Dolph needed a reminder. "We can't afford trouble now. Go to the factory and empty it of anything that might be incriminating – tapes, masters, files. I mean *anything*."

"That will take hours."

"Then get started at once."

The lights were on, but not a soul was in sight. Where the hell was the work crew? Dolph wondered. He drew his Mauser and felt reassured. Deep down he hoped that he would find Cortese here. He was ready for him.

Dolph quietly prowled the front of the factory. He reached the door to his space, listened carefully, but heard nothing. He unlocked it and went in. It appeared undisturbed. Disappointed, he lit a cigarette and sat behind his desk. There was no sign of Willi. She must have come and gone – the purpose of her visit and the whereabouts of her employees, a mystery. Ah, well, he thought, there are a few phone calls to place until Otto's arrival and Reinhold's return.

"Who was that went in?" Pop asked Ross as they drove away from the factory.

"Dolph Hanfnagel."

Pop's face darkened. He turned to look at the back seat, where Willi was huddled, her face ashen. "You okay, sweetheart?" he asked softly, as if speaking to a hurt child. Her response was to break into tears. He wished he could reached back and pat her hand, but the headrest was in the way.

Ross checked the rear view mirror. A cop car was two hundred feet behind them and closing.

"We may have been spotted when we left the factory. I'm not taking any chances. Put on your seat belts."

And with that warning, he stepped on the accelerator, skidded around the corner, then made a quick left turn. He had to lose them.

CHAPTER FORTY

Abe tried reaching Prosecutor Alma Zeiss. He finally got through to a Herr Afsig, her deputy, only to be told that she was in conference. Emphasizing the urgency of the situation, Abe explained the circumstances to Afsig, who promised to inform Zeiss as soon as her meeting ended. Abe gave him the address of Hanfnagel's facility.

He paced his small office for ten minutes, then tried again. This time, neither the Prosecutor nor her deputy were available. Outraged, Abe left a second message with the secretary, threatening to contact the media if they did not act at once. He decided right then and there that he'd have to go himself. He could not wait. Too much was at stake.

Abe made his way to the location Ross had given him. There, he saw Dolph Hanfagnel and a big man loading cartons into a van. They were clearing out – warned yet again by friends in high places, he angrily assumed. This time they would not get away.

Weapon drawn, Abe slipped into the warehouse through the delivery entrance. He heard voices and tracked them to Dolph's office. Taking up a position outside the door, he didn't have long to wait before Hanfnagel and the other man stepped into the corridor, arms loaded with cartons. "Back inside," Abe ordered sharply. "I won't hesitate to use this."

He hoped to hell the Prosecutor or the police arrived soon.

"Who are you?" Dolph snarled.

"Avia Hirsch's colleague. Does her name mean anything to you?"

Hanfnagel's associate, a big brute of a man, instantly turned his face away from Abe. Abe caught the move, shifted his own position, then gasped. The man had tried to hide the lacerations on his left cheek. There was no doubt in Abe's mind – Avia had torn that cheek with her nails, marking him as her killer. He felt the tension increase in his finger on the trigger. He ached for an excuse to gun the man down.

Dolph saw the fire burning in the Jew's eyes. The man's a fanatic, he thought. There'd be no bargaining with him. He meant what he said. He would shoot them down, if he had to. Why didn't he? Who was he waiting for? Cortese? The authorities? How had he discovered the location of Dolph's operation?

Abe could see Dolph's hesitancy and he let him know it. "You have good reason to be afraid, Hanfnagel. It's no longer only the hate games, but murder."

Dolph responded with a huge sneer. Before Abe could say another word, he suffered a painful blow to his skull, which knocked him to his knees. Quickly, Dolph relieved a semi-conscious Abe of his weapon, then said proudly, "Well done, Reinhold."

His son's return from soccer practice at this moment was most fortuitous – a sign that nothing could interfere with this day's outcome.

"Truss the pig, Otto. Then the two of you must hurry to empty the workspace of all cartons and papers. Do it now! Understood?"

"Yes, Father."

"Leave the Jew to me," Otto growled.

Abe awoke to find himself tied and bound to a chair, his head throbbing from the blow. I should have killed them when I had the chance, he thought, cursing himself for a fool.

Dolph came up to the chair, tapping Abe's gun against his palm. "You're awake, Herr Jew. I've been waiting. How did you find us? Was it Cortese?"

"What difference does it make. You're through."

Dolph punched him in the gut. Abe gagged, then vomited on himself.

Reinhold, carrying out a load of cartons, laughed. "Now he smells like a Jew."

Dolph worked Abe over for fifteen minutes but Abe said nothing. "We've wasted enough time. Finish loading the van," Dolph ordered. "This dead Jew will be your last load. Now mach schnell!"

It took a half an hour, but finally Ross lost the police. He drove into the northern part of Vienna by a circuitous route and parked on Ruthgasse, near Wertheimsteinpark. They were fifteen minutes away from the hospital.

"I hope Lucy waits," Ross said. "Let's leave the car and take a taxi, in case they've put your license plate number out on the squawk box."

"No," Willi said firmly. "I'll take the car and put it in my garage."

"You're not coming with us?" Pop asked, his disappointment plain.

"I can't . . . I need some time alone." She sounded oddly detached to Ross. Like she was slipping away.

"Alone? Or with your father?" Ross challenged.

"I said alone," she said wearily. "I can't handle it now. Please try to understand."

He nodded reluctantly. If he didn't show trust now, there could never be anything between them. He remembered her words at Jacky's apartment. "I'm with you . . . with *you*."

He got out and Pop followed suit. Ross opened the rear door for Willi and helped her from the car. He tilted her chin and kissed her softly. Her lips, once warm for him, were ice cold. Then Willi got behind the wheel and turned the window down.

"What will you do now?" he asked.

"Honestly, Red, I don't know . . . " She stared at him. "Good luck with your meeting," she added, her voice breaking.

"Come on, Pop," Ross called, moving away from her. "There's a taxi stand down the block."

CHAPTER FORTY-ONE

Pop studied the pained expression on Ross's face as his son stared out of the taxi window.

"Talk to me, Rosso."

"I don't know whether or not to trust her, Pop."

"She's a good woman," Franco said. "She loves you."

"If only it were that simple," Ross said with a sigh.

It was nearly two when they arrived at the renowned Allgemeine Krankenhaus where the greats of Viennese medicine, from Semmelweiss to Freud, had studied and practiced. The huge medical complex was spread out over acres of park-like lawn. Buildings dating from the eighteenth and nineteenth century stood alongside contemporary boxes.

After checking for police presence and finding none, the two men went inside.

"Here." Ross handed his father the slip of paper Rudy had given to him. Written on it was Annalee's name and room number. "Show this to the clerk and ask for two passes. I'll wait here."

"Ja?" Ross heard the clerk snap as Pop stepped to the counter.

"Zvei, bitte," Pop said politely, handing her the paper. She eyed Franco, then examined the paper. Flipping her Rolodex, she found Annalee's card. Ross picked up the word "verboten."

Ross moved up behind him and whispered, "What's up?"

"The lady says we have to wait."

"Bullshit. We need to go up now."

Before Pop could say a word, the clerk declared, "*Nein! Der reglen. Das is gegn die bestimmung.*"

Ross came up with his badge case. He held the gold detective's badge up close to her face. "Polizei!" he avowed coldly.

The woman's face became flaccid with fear. "Now!" he reiterated.

"Jawohl, Meinherr." She reached under the counter and with a trembling hand turned over two passes. Ross closed the leather case and replaced it in his pocket, then fixed her with a hard look.

When they stepped off the elevator, they found Jacky pacing in the corridor. "We were worried about you. You're alright?"

Ross nodded. "How's Annalee?"

"Her condition is improved, thank God."

"Is Lucy here?" Ross asked.

Jacky nodded soberly.

The door was slightly ajar. "Wait here, will you?" Ross said to them. "I'll call you in."

His father nodded.

Rudy was standing by the window.

A silver-haired woman sat beside the bed, holding Annalee's hand and speaking to her. Ross recognized her profile from a photograph that graced Annalee's piano top; one which had captured her in lively interaction with Ariella.

Lucy sensed his presence and turned full face to him. Her eyes widened in startled of recognition. Then her lips parted, as if she was about to speak, but there were no words. She stood, her eyes filled with tears, and reached out to him. He moved hesitantly and entered her embrace. She held him as if he were a child.

Ross looked with amazement into the face of his mother's sister as she in turn gazed joyfully at the image of her sister's son. Their eyes asked a thousand questions, yet their lips were silent. Lucy smiled – a wide, beautiful, welcoming smile.

Annalee, watching them closely from the bed, smiled too. Ross said softly, "My father's outside. I know how much he wants to see you."

Somehow, he assumed that she would understand English and she did.

He went to the doorway and called out to Pop. It was Franco's turn to come into the room. Recognizing Lucy, he nearly collapsed. He was transported back in time and Ariella's absence was made all the more terrible.

Ross took his father's elbow and supported him as he went to Lucy. It was their turn to hold one another. They swayed back and forth, orphans in a storm of sorrow and lost love.

Ross left his father and aunt murmuring together and walked to the window. Rudy took his hand and held it tightly. "I have no words for what I learned here today. Only deep sorrow for you and your father."

Ross nodded. He was right. There were no words to encompass this truth. "Where's Willi?" Rudy asked with a frown. "I thought she was coming with you."

"She said she was going home."

"Did you find what you were looking for?" Jacky asked, as he moved into the room.

"Yes. It was all there. Videogames, tapes. I'm afraid Willi couldn't deal with it. Some of it may incriminate your father, Rudy."

Ross groaned inwardly as he suddenly flashed on Willi putting the invoices in her purse.

Before Rudy could absorb the news, Annalee signaled them to her bedside. Pop and Lucy were seated now, across the room, deep in conversation.

"You understand, don't you?" Annalee said to Ross, her voice weak. "I could not be the one to tell you."

"You knew from the moment you saw me, didn't you?"

She nodded sadly. "I saw Ariella in you at once. The resemblance is unmistakable."

She paused to take a few deep breaths. "There's something I must tell you. I dare not wait. I've lived in fear of this knowledge for more than fifty years. At first, I feared for myself and my husband. Then, for Rudy and Willi whom I love as if they were my own."

She looked over at Lucy and Franco and captured their attention, then went on, raising her voice just above a whisper. "Only Lucy and I know the full story of what happened on that day. Until today, it has never been told."

Annalee's eyes rolled back and she closed her eyelids, as if recoiling from what she had witnessed. Ross took her hand. It was ice cold. He held it firmly in his. She found her voice, clearer and stronger than it had any right to be, given her condition.

"On that terrible March day, Erich Hanfnagel, arrogant in his gauleiter's uniform, stood on the street outside of our building. He pointed up at the windows of the Mosel apartment and gave orders to his Storm Troopers to remove the Mosel family. He followed them upstairs and into the apartment. I witnessed this from my window. A few minutes later, I heard their screams. I still hear them."

Ross could hear them, too. He wanted to blanket the sound by screaming Hanfnagel's name. He looked at Pop and Lucy. They reached out for one another's hands, both pale as they awaited Annalee's next words.

Exhausted, the old woman rested for a moment, then with a major effort of will, continued. "I saw Lucy, huddled in a doorway across the street. When I reached her, she was unable to speak. Neighbors were shouting that two women had jumped from their window. I saw a crowd gathered around the bodies of Fanny and Ariella. I took Lucy by the hand and fled. By that night, she was safe with my relatives in the country. Weeks later, when I was able to visit her – she told me what she'd witnessed."

Annalee sank back in her pillow, looking to Lucy.

Lucy nodded, understanding that she must continue the narrative. She stood, straight-backed and wraithlike, still holding Franco's hand. "As God is my witness, I saw my mother and sister thrown from the window by Storm Troopers. Like broken birds without wings, they smashed into the sidewalk not twenty feet from where I stood."

Pop gasped convulsively. His chest heaved with the effort to hold back wrenching sobs. Lucy leaned down and comforted him. Ross was now beyond shock, beyond emotion, as if nothing more he could hear would surprise him. Hanfnagel was personally responsible for the wanton destruction of his family. He summoned up a picture of himself throwing Hanfnagel from that same window. It did nothing to ease the painful emptiness he felt.

He listened as Lucy took a deep breath and continued: "Hanfnagel came to our apartment the day before the Anschluss. Mother was there with Ariella. Ariella, still recovering from childbirth, was napping in her room. Father and Grandpa Kirmen were in the shop.

"Hanfnagel informed my mother that we would be moved to the ghetto with the other Juden when Anschluss came. Mother told him that our family had lived in Austria for nearly one hundred years – that grandfather Kirmen had been honored by Emperor Franz Joseph for his contribution to the Empire.

"That night, Mother repeated to us what Hanfnagel said in reply – 'That is of no consequence. You are Jews. You don't belong here. You never belonged here. This apartment is no longer yours. I claim it – and all that is in it.' Mother tried to reassure Ariella and me, but we were so frightened." Lucy sipped water from the glass Rudy handed to her and went on with her story.

"It will be alright, Mother soothed. Soon Ariella will be able to travel. We will go to Italy to join Franco and the baby, then to America.

"The grownups sat down and made plans to leave. Later that night, without telling anyone, Mother slipped out and went down to the river. She could not bear the thought of Grandma Rosa's silver falling into the Nazi's hands. She threw the wrapped bundle into the

Danube. It was only a token, but it was her outcry, her defiance. To this day, no doubt, it lies buried in the river mud."

Lucy reached for Annalee's hand and they exchanged sad smiles.

"Mother gave a few small objects to Annalee. She would have given more away but feared that she would create trouble for her neighbors. After the war, Annalee returned them to me. It's all that I have left of our family – until now. Now we have you," she said to Ross.

"You're so like your mother. It's as if she has returned to me."

She smiled at Ross, that wide warm smile. He came around the bed and embraced her. She gently stroked his red hair.

"There is one more thing," Annalee added, "so hidden it is nearly forgotten."

They turned to her, questions on all of their faces. "The Klimt portrait of Rosa," she said with emphasis.

Lucy smiled wistfully. "Yes. Annalee is right. When Mother told us in the morning what she had done with the silver, Grandpa stared at the Klimt painting which we all so adored. A few hours later it was gone. I assumed that he had sold it for our passage. I did not know until recently that Annalee had the painting in her possession all these years, too frightened of Hanfnagel to reveal it."

"Kirmen came to me," Annalee said, apologetically. "He said, 'The swine shall not have this.' He gave me the wrapped painting. 'Hide it', he said, 'until this madness is over.' "

She shook her head. "The madness never ended. I knew from Rudy's mother how Hanfnagel coveted the painting. I was terrified – convinced that if he found out, he would retaliate against us all. It has remained in my cabinet from that morning – until now . . . "

Lucy picked up the thread of the story. "Klimt came to Kirmen for a bedroom set. They arranged an exchange. Klimt paid for the furniture by painting a portrait of my grandmother, Rosa, then still a young woman."

The Klimt painting – in the building all this time, yet out of the reach of that greedy bastard, Ross thought with a trace of satisfaction. The day of reckoning has come, Hanfnagel, Ross thought darkly. This time you won't escape justice. One way or another, you'll pay for your crimes. I'll see to that.

"Rudy, come close," Annalee said. "My heart aches for you and your sister."

"Sshh, liebe Annale. We'll be alright. You must rest."

"I pray that you and Willi will find it in your hearts to forgive me."

"Forgive you? What is there to forgive? You've been a blessing to us since our mother died. Without your love, God knows what our life would be."

"You don't know what I did, Rudy. Some years after Lucy's return . . . in an effort to help her, I injured your mother."

"That's impossible."

"Please. You must hear me out."

"Of course I will . . . but first I must call Willi . . . to see how she is."

Rudy picked up the phone and dialed Willi's number. The phone rang eight times, then the answering machine picked up.

"Willi," he said, "when you get this message come at once to the hospital."

She went home alright, Ross thought, home to Daddy. To warn him. He was about to say something, when they heard loud, angry voices in the corridor. Jacky went immediately to investigate the source.

"I've got to get out of here," Ross said.

"Where are you going?" Pop asked. "I go with you."

"No! You stay with Lucy and Annalee, Pop."

In the corridor, he found Jacky blocking a hospital security officer. Behind him stood the reception clerk, a smug look on her face.

"That's the man!" she exclaimed, pointing at Ross.

"I've been told that there is a security matter in this room. Your papers." He stuck out a thick-wristed hand. Ross resisted the urge to chop it.

"He's with me, officer. Visiting a friend," Jacky explained, his tone conciliatory.

"I must see his papers," the guard insisted. The clerk beamed.

"He'll see my backside," was Ross's reply, as he pushed past the guard. "Come on, Jacky. We're out of here."

"I'm taking you into custody. You'll come with me to Security – now!" the guard shouted.

"If I refuse, what will you do? Kill me?" Ross spat out his words in disgust. He and Jacky moved into the stairwell and ran down the steps. The guard continued to shout, but he did not give chase.

On the street in front of the hospital, Ross asked Jacky if he had come by car. "Yes. I'm parked across the street."

"Let's go."

Seated alongside Jacky in the Audi, Ross said, "Take me to Himmelpfortgasse."

"Don't go there. Please, Red. Let the law deal with him."

"Austrian law? I wouldn't expect to hear that from you. He's got it in his pocket."

"You've lived your life defending the law. Don't stop now. If you have proof of Hanfnagel's involvement, use it to bring him down."

"Proof? Willi took it with her. If she went to her father, by now there may be no proof. The invoices destroyed, the warehouse cleaned out . . . and the Prosecutor's left to suck dust."

"There's an intersection ahead," Jacky pointed. "You must choose your direction."

Ross wanted to confront Hanfnagel now, tear down his wall of lies, force him to relive his crimes. Ross knew how to do that. It was his business. He was a cop – and a damn good one. But Jacky was right. He would serve the Mosel family, Avia Hirsch and nameless others best by publicly exposing the Hanfnagel family's sordid affairs, their web of coverup and willingness to murder to protect their interests.

His face-to-face with Hanfnagel would have to wait.

"Willi's factory . . . "

The tires shrieked as Jacky made a quick U-turn.

Willi came out of the building and walked to her car. She resisted an impulse to look back. She felt beset by guilt, as if her family's crimes were her own. She thought of Ariella Mosel and experienced sudden despair. Her privileged life had come tumbling down about her. Meeting Ross Cortese was the best thing that had happened to her in years. Such a man did not come along very often – strong in character, warm and tender – a passionate lover. Willi had never known anyone like him. She was in love with him – of that, she was certain. But at the end of the day, she was still a Hanfnagel. Could he ever forgive her that?

She was prepared to leave Vienna, move to New York – and live with Red, but would he have her? Could they leave the past behind? More than anything, she wanted to try.

Willi checked her answering machine from the car phone and found a message from Rudy, asking her to come to the hospital. She would go there now. Erich Hanfnagel's daughter would face Lucy Mosel and tell Ross what she had just done.

CHAPTER FORTY-TWO

Jacky and Ross cruised the vicinity of the factory in the Audi. There were no signs of the authorities or police. Had Hanfnagel and Neurath succeeded in co-opting them? Jacky parked around the corner from the entrance to the building.

"If I'm not back in fifteen minutes," Ross explained, "raise the roof – call the cops – find a fire alarm – but don't come in. No foolish heroics."

"Look who's talking," said Jacky.

"It's my business. Flip the trunk, will you?"

The tire iron had been left in Jacky's apartment, Ross suddenly remembered as he lifted the trunk lid. He separated the vertical cast iron bar from the jack. That would have to do.

He paused at the street corner and observed the activity around the van. Otto came and went, carrying stacks of cartons, which Reinhold loaded into the gray vehicle. There was no sign of Dolph, but that didn't mean he wasn't around. They were clearing out, as Ross had feared. Was Willi responsible for the warning? It broke his heart to think so.

He steeled his resolve, tapping the tool on his palm. He waited 'til Otto dropped one load, then headed back down the alley. Reinhold, taking a break, lit a cigarette. He was facing the opposite direction, so Ross sprinted down the block and came up behind him. He used the bar to throw a potentially lethal chokehold on the boy. "Who's inside?" Ross demanded. "Now . . . or you're dead meat." He smelled Reinhold's fear and tightened the grip.

The kid wasn't prepared for any of this. "Don't hurt me," he wheezed. "My father – he's got the Jew from the Center."

Abe had come on his own, brave but dumb.

"Who else?" Ross demanded.

"Otto . . . Otto. No one else. I swear."

Otto would be back in a minute. "Unpleasant dreams," Ross said, striking Reinhold with the tire iron, hard enough to put him out, but not do permanent damage.

He lifted the limp body into the van, leaving the door ajar, then ran down the alley, hoping to surprise Otto as he emerged from the factory interior. Instead, he ran into him. Otto dropped the cartons and went for his gun. Ross stepped back and swung the iron at Otto's arm, throwing all his weight behind it. He heard the crack and the scream of pain. The Browning clattered to the ground as Otto was reduced to a one-armed cripple. He stood there, stunned, holding the injured arm. Ross noticed the deep crimson gouges on Otto's pale face. He made the instant connection.

"You killed her," he shouted.

Otto saw the blood in Ross's eyes. In a desperate attempt, he dived for the weapon. Ross, in a cold fury, used the tire iron again. He smashed it against the man's forearm. A large jagged end of broken bone protruded at a sharp angle through the skin. In shock, Otto crumpled to the ground, barely conscious. Ross picked up the 9 mm and checked the clip. There was a round in the chamber. Seven remaining.

He left the collapsed hulk lying in the alley and went into the factory.

He knew the way. The door to Dolph's workspace stood ajar. Ross held his weapon in firing position, took a deep breath and burst in. Mistake, he thought, as the frantic movement in Abe's eyes warned him that Dolph was behind the door. Before Ross could turn, he felt the cold steel of Dolph's weapon press into his back.

"I hoped you'd show up, Cortese. Where are Otto and Reinhold?" Dolph punctuated the question with a hard poke in the spine.

"We've got them outside."

"You're lying. There is no *we*."

"I didn't come alone. I'm not that dumb. I came with friends of Abe here. They've got your boy. And Otto."

"I don't believe it." He prodded Ross. "Place your weapon on the desk."

Dolph recognized Otto's old Browning. "If you came with others, you came empty-handed."

"It didn't stop me from getting this far."

"You've gotten very far, haven't you?" Dolph taunted. "Consider your enviable position."

Despite the show of bravado, Dolph's initial flood of confidence was slowly ebbing. There was no sign of either Reinhold or Otto.

"We informed the authorities," he declared. "They're on their way."

"You're lying."

Abe joined in. "Deputy prosecutor Afsig. The Prosecutor's Task Force will be here any minute."

Dolph laughed. So that's who these fools were counting on. He knew Afsig by reputation. The man was lily-livered; so constipated, it took him a week to take a shit. By the time he acted, *if* he acted, they'd be long gone – as would Cortese and the Jew.

"You're out of your league, Cortese. You don't know who you're dealing with."

"He boasted to me of a plot to kill a Cabinet official," Abe called out anxiously.

"It's proceeding even as we speak," Dolph said, glaring at them. "When we come to power – and the moment is near – we'll deal with garbage like you."

"You'll never come to power, you tinpot Hitler," said Abe.

"You think not? This government will be brought down in a matter of days. My father will be Austria's next Chancellor."

"Your father? You're insane," said Ross.

"Your father has as much chance of becoming Chancellor as I do," Abe taunted. "And we know where I'm going to end up, don't we?"

"Don't think it for a minute, Abe," Ross called out to him." He's not going to do to us what his father did to my family, Ross thought, seeking a move.

"Within the hour, the Minister of Justice will die at the hands of a trio of drug-crazed immigrants," Dolph gloated. "A thoroughly orchestrated hue and cry will force the resignation of the coalition government. There are important politicians prepared to call my father out of his long retirement from politics – as a man known for his love of Austria and affiliated with no party."

"And his son's affiliation?" he challenged.

"The fact that I'm sympathetic to the right will help, not hurt. Besides which, no one can hold the father responsible for his son's political activities. That would be unfair and undemocratic." He laughed cynically, as he added, "A Jew should know that."

"Are you finished boasting, you dumb shit?" Ross challenged, trying to shake him up. "I still don't see your boys. Did they go for a beer?"

Dolph was sweating. His eyes narrowed. If Reinhold and Otto didn't show up in a minute, he would have to act. He'd shoot Cortese.

But if there were others outside, he would need help. He put the phone on speaker and punched in Victor's private number, keeping a sharp eye on Cortese as he did. There was no answer.

He heard footsteps in the hallway. Panicked, Dolph turned sideways, the gun wavering between Cortese and the doorway. It was the opportunity Ross had waited for.

Otto stumbled across the threshold, one broken arm slack at his side, the other grotesquely angled. Dolph stared at him. Ross made his move, seizing Dolph's gun hand. "Help me, Otto," Dolph cried.

Otto stood there, mouth agape, swaying helplessly. Ross found the pressure point on Dolph's wrist and squeezed for all he was worth. Dolph's hand went numb and the gun fell to the floor. Ross pounded a short, vicious left cross to his cheek. The bone cracked and Dolph howled as Ross shoved him into a chair.

Ross lifted the Browning from the desk and placed it in his belt. Then he picked up Dolph's Mauser and pointed it at him. "Hands flat on the desk – in full view at all times," he warned.

Ross walked over to where Otto stood, gray-faced and clammy. He held the gun to his forehead. "I should kill you for what you did to Avia. I still might."

He kicked Otto's legs out from under him and watched him topple over. The big man landed on the arm with the compound fracture and the lancing pain put him out again. Dolph watched, horrified as Ross untied Abe.

"You look like hell," Ross said.

"Yeah, but I'm alive," Abe responded.

"Make him tell you where the assassination is to take place," Abe urged.

"That's exactly what I'm going to do."

"Nothing to tell." Dolph found it painful to speak. The motion of his jaw caused agony. "I lied . . . "

"You're lying now. You tell me everything or I tattoo your cheek with the butt of this gun."

He brought his thumb up against the discolored, swollen flesh on Dolph's cheek and Dolph screamed. Ross hefted the weapon by the barrel, as if it was a hammer. "Who, when and where?"

Dolph thought quickly. He would force himself to endure the pain. His freedom, if not his life depended on the successful execution of the mission. The hit team had to escape, ensuring that no one could connect him to Doschenko and the Bavarian Underground. All that he would be accountable for were the videogames – and no Viennese jury would take that charge very seriously. There was the Jewish bitch, Hirsch, but Otto, loyal trooper, would take the fall for that.

"I'm out of patience – and you're out of time," Ross said ominously.

"Take the gun away. I'll tell you what I know."

Ross removed the gun butt, but maintained it an inch away from Dolph's face.

"Tonight – at six o'clock," Dolph dissembled. "The Justice Minister visits a nursing home."

"The address!" Ross shouted.

"Only Neurath and Doschenko know," Dolph yelled back.

Ross was sure that he was lying. "How many on the hit team?" he demanded.

Dolph hesitated. There was no harm in providing the details as long as Cortese bought the big lie and was delayed. Dolph looked at his watch surreptitiously. Soon, the event would be history.

"Look at me when you speak," Ross warned. "I'll know if it's the truth. No second chances."

"Three men."

"Backup?"

Dolph was silent.

"That's it," said Ross, prepared to strike.

"An off-duty officer . . . to shoot the assassin."

"Give me the address."

"I don't know it." Dolph steeled himself for the blow.

"He's given us a combination of truth, half-truth and lies. I've got an idea."

Ross bent over Otto and shook him. "Get some water, Abe. Let's rouse the murdering cocksucker."

CHAPTER FORTY-THREE

Grenentorgasse was clear of pedestrians and traffic. At three thirty-five, the two men drove up and parked the stolen van a few doors down from the tailor shop. They pulled on their stocking masks and forced one over the head of their drugged captive. Havel offered little resistance as they half-carried him into the tailor shop. The old man was at his sewing machine. His wife heard the door slam and came out from the back room where she was fitting a middle-aged woman. She let out a shriek. Uri slapped her across the face to quiet her.

The heavy-set customer, still in her slip, peeked out, opened her mouth as if to say something, and slumped to the floor in a faint. Uri put the Closed sign in the window of the door. The tailor volunteered the money from the register, pleading with them not to hurt the women. Uri and Vlad herded them into the back of the shop, where they could not be seen from the street.

Laughing hysterically, they referred to Havel by name. "Got any drugs?" Vlad demanded of the owner in a broken, heavily accented German, identifying himself purposely as a foreigner.

"No," the terror-stricken man replied.

They bound and gagged the women so they could not scream, then severely pistol-whipped the man. "Injure him," Doschenko had instructed, "but do not kill him."

Uri threw the drugged Havel onto the woman who had fainted, urging him to fuck her. They shoved his hand up between her legs. He lay there on her, in a near-stupor. She moaned through the gag, her eyes coming open wide with horror. The storeowner's wife wept while the men ransacked the store. Vlad nonchalantly pissed on the floor.

Doschenko had set up an observation post close by, in

Grenentorgassen, 46. The building provided egress to the side street, an extra precaution. He had a perfect overview of the killing field. It was three minutes to four. By now, his team had completed the first phase of the operation, the store secured, the old man beaten.

"A coma would be perfect," Neurath had suggested clinically.

"Picture the gnadige frau on the nightly news – reminding Austrians that drug-ridden foreigners had done this to her husband – and that two killers were still at large." One picture would be worth ten thousand shock troops.

CHAPTER FORTY-FOUR

The second pail of water accomplished the goal. "Uhhh," Otto groaned, opening his eyes.

Ross turned to Abe. "He doesn't speak English. Tell him that the police have samples of his skin from under Avia's nails. His only hope of a plea-bargain is to cooperate with us now."

Abe choked on the words. How could he bargain with Avia's murderer? But he knew that Cortese was right to play this card. When Abe finished translating, Otto nodded. He would tell them what he knew.

Dolph saw what was happening and shouted, "Otto, zei stimm!"

Otto looked at Dolph with contempt. Two minutes later, they had it all. "It's four o'clock. Not six."

"Where?"

"Grenentorgasse, fifty-six. Not far from here."

"You know how to use a gun?"

"Yes," Abe said, wincing from pain in his rib cage as he bent to retrieve his Walther from Dolph's drawer. He found an extra clip for the Mauser and tossed it to Ross.

Ross went to a shelf in the far corner of the room and removed a spool of heavy rope and a knife. He tied Dolph's wrists and ankles to the chair and as he did, asked him, "Where's Willi in all this?"

"Where she always was," he flaunted defiantly. "A Hanfnagel, first, last and always."

"Right," Ross responded glumly, pulling the rope extra tight as he put in the final knot. Playing it extra-safe, he did the same to Otto's ankles, though the hulk wasn't going anywhere in his condition.

"My hands are numb. You've cut off circulation," Dolph protested.

"That's not all we'll cut off by the time we're through with you," Ross promised. He turned to Abe. "Let's get the hell out of here."

Ross led the way, pausing to check on Reinhold. The boy was alive, beginning to stir. The keys to the van were in his pocket. Ross locked him in the rear, then raced around the corner to Jacky.

"I was getting ready to raise the alarm." Jacky said.

Ross spoke rapid-fire. "Listen carefully, Jacky. There's a plot to kill the Minister of Justice. It goes down at four o'clock. Grenentorgasse, fifty-six. Go into the factory. Get on the phone and reach someone in authority. There's no time to lose. Demand that they send the anti-terrorist squad. Hanfnagel and his henchman are tied up in his office. Reinhold's locked in the van.

"Here's a weapon," he said, handing the Browning over to Jacky. "You won't need it, but just in case. Here's the safety. Release it, point and pull the trigger."

Jacky was aghast at the prospect.

"Car keys?" Ross held out his hand.

"In the ignition."

Abe came limping around the corner, hiding his pain.

"You sure you're up for this?" Ross asked.

"I wouldn't miss it," Abe replied.

"Can you drive?" Ross asked him.

"I'll manage."

They got in. Abe turned the motor on, released the hand brake and took off, wheels smoking.

"We've got fourteen minutes," Ross said. "Can we make it?"

"It will be close," Abe said, his expression a study in determination as he accelerated around a slow moving truck. They heard sirens in the distance as they raced against the clock.

CHAPTER FORTY-FIVE

Doschenko scanned the street. At four o'clock, he spotted the Minister's Mercedes 420E pull up into the no-parking zone in front of the entrance to the nursing home. The driver went around to the side to open the Minister's door. As the Minister was about to exit, the car phone rang. He looked annoyed at this delay, but he picked up the receiver.

Like clockwork, Doschenko's team burst out of the tailor shop. Vlad propped Havel in front of him like a shield and fired wildly in every direction, to distract any passerbys. Uri, simultaneously, aimed at the Mercedes from the doorway and fired. The Minister's driver drew his automatic to return the fire, but was struck by a round in the upper chest and slumped to the sidewalk.

The Minister dropped the phone receiver and ducked into the well of the back seat. He knew it was a matter of seconds before they came for him. Keeping low, he pushed open the door, prepared to make a run for the nursing home entrance.

Doschenko's planning had assumed that the Minister would be out of the car and cut down by now in a hail of bullets. It was a minor wrinkle, he reassured himself as he watched Uri start across the street to finish off the Minister. Vlad continued firing. Then, suddenly, a blue Audi tore around the corner and came bearing down on Uri.

Uri turned to fire at them but was too late. Before Ross could say a word, Abe floored the accelerator, aiming for the gunman in the street. The car barreled into him and sent him flying. His body landed thirty feet away, a heap of broken bones.

Immediately on contact, Abe hit the brake, skidding to a halt beyond the Mercedes and the remaining shooter.

"Back up," said Ross. "We need to give the Mercedes cover."

Abe threw the car into reverse as Ross fired at Vlad through the open window.

"Abort!" Doschenko screamed into the radio, communicating into earpieces worn by his men. "Get out."

Vlad, recovering from his initial shock, opened up on the Audi. By that time, Abe had positioned the car to block the Mercedes and he and Ross were out the door. Doschenko recognized the American. Vlad was pinned down, but Doschenko could not risk his men being taken alive. He reached out to Neurath's man with the pre-arranged code. "Clean-up immediately."

The Minister remained crouched behind the Mercedes, next to where his driver had fallen. The man's breathing was labored. "My driver's seriously hurt. We need help," he cried.

Ross shouted back, "Keep your head down." He had to take the shooter out.

It took less than a minute for Brent, the off-duty policeman, acting as Doschenko's mop-up man, to drive his Opel around the corner and down the one-way street. He pulled up facing the Audi and fired from the driver's window, putting three rounds into the man in the doorway. Vlad fell, dead on the spot. Brent leaped from his car, identifying himself to the men behind the Audi. "Polizei. The situation's under control. Stay where you are while I check."

Ross got the message and was at once suspicious. "Like hell," he thought.

He lifted his head carefully and watched the cop examine the shooter's body in the doorway, then move after Havel who was crawling away from the carnage. As Brent prepared to shoot the unarmed man, Ross shouted, "Drop it," and fired a warning shot. This is Neurath's man, he felt certain, here to make sure there are no loose ends. Brent wheeled, pointing his weapon at Ross. Without hesitation, Ross fired at him and the man fell to the ground, wounded. As Ross retrieved the shooter's weapon, the minister said, "What have you done?" That man identified himself as an officer."

"He's part of the conspiracy," Ross explained.

"I have to believe what you say. The Prosecutor called to warn me of the attempt. That call, along with your intervention, saved my life." The man was beginning to shake badly.

Sirens blaring, a cavalcade of official cars and ambulances entered the street from each end. Staatspolizei and Prosecutor Alma Zeiss, rushed up. "Are you alright, Minister?" she asked.

"My driver is badly wounded. He needs help."

"While you're at it, get someone in the tailor shop," Ross reminded her. "The people inside may need medical attention."

"At once," she replied and swiftly gave orders. She turned to Ross. "We arrived at the warehouse as you were leaving. Mr. Gold sent us after you, but it appears that you managed the situation quite well," she said with a smile.

"Thanks to Abe Feder." They both looked over to the Audi. Abe was sitting in the car, taking deep breaths.

Ross pointed to Brent, lying wounded on the street. "That man is a rogue cop. Take good care of him. He'll lead you straight to Victor Neurath."

"What are you saying? That Commissioner Neurath is involved in this?" the Minister demanded. "It's impossible."

"You've got a lot to learn, sir," Ross insisted.

Alma Zeiss began explaining the situation. The Minister looked stunned, shaking his head as if to deny the truth.

"One last thing," Ross interrupted. "There's a man named Doschenko. Former KGB. He organized the attempt on your life. He's gone by now, probably on his way out of Austria. Security at the American Embassy has a file on him – you surely have one, too, if Neurath didn't dispose of it. I'd put out an all-points alert at airports, train stations and border crossings. Contact Interpol. Probably won't help, but it's worth the try."

Zeiss turned to her Chief and said, "What are you waiting for?" He ran to his car to call in the command.

"You got Dolph Hanfnagel and his crew?" Ross asked.

"They're in custody." She offered Ross her hand. "We're grateful, Cortese."

The Minister suddenly remembered his mother in the home. She had heard the gunshots. What must she be thinking?

"I must see to my mother, Alma," he said.

"Of course, Minister," she replied sympathetically as he hurried off.

I must see to my mother, too, Ross thought bitterly. "I'll be in later for a statement. I have something to take care of first."

He went over to the Audi. "That was some piece of driving."

Abe nodded wearily. "I hope I never have to do it again."

"Take care of yourself," Ross urged. "Let a medic look you over."

"Where are you going?" Abe called after him.

Ross did not reply. He went around the police barriers. Television crews had already arrived and were setting up. Reporters hurled questions at him. Tightlipped, Ross forced his way through the crowd that had gathered. He walked a few blocks before finding a taxi. He gave the driver the address and settled back in stony silence.

The driver observed him nervously with repeated glances through the rearview mirror. He must see the look on my face and it scares him to death, Ross thought. His adrenaline was still pumping and he knew that his heart was racing. He read the name on the hack license – Milosz Vassilief. Eastern European, he guessed. Immigrants drive cabs, just like New York. Hard-working people trying to earn a living for their families. These were the "vermin" that the Hanfnagels wanted to "sanitize." Dolph Hanfnagel would never acknowledge, even when they locked him away, that *he* was the sick rat, carrying the plague. If anyone needed sanitizing it was the true believers who did not hesitate to do violence for their goal of purity.

Why won't you let yourself see it, Willi, he wanted to cry out to her. Tear the scales from your eyes. Bleed, if you have to, but goddamnit, free yourself!

The cab entered the old city and it dawned on Ross that he had purposely kept his thoughts away from Erich Hanfnagel, afraid of what he'd find. Reflexively, he touched the weapon in his belt, reassured by the cold steel.

CHAPTER FORTY-SIX

"Himmelpfortgasse," the driver announced, as they pulled onto the street.

"Let me out here," Ross said, pointing to Hanfnagel's building.

Inside the entrance he pressed all of the bells except for Hanfnagel's. Several occupants responded on the intercom.

"Bundespolizei," Ross snapped.

He was buzzed in immediately.

As the elevator passed the second floor landing, a door opened and a middle-aged couple peered out at him. He motioned them back inside.

Where is Dolph, Hanfnagel wondered. He was to be here at four. It's not like him to be so late.

The apartment bell rang at last. "Ein moment, Dolph," he called out and headed for the vestibule. Opening the door, he found himself face to face with Ross Cortese.

"You," he gasped. His expression rapidly changed from welcome to incredulity to fear.

"I don't know what you're doing here, but you better leave at once," Hanfnagel said stiffly. "I say this for my daughter's sake. She still shows some concern for you."

"Concern, my ass. You just don't want blood on your fancy carpets."

"No one talks to me with such disrespect."

"Get used to it," Ross responded. He looked past Hanfnagel. "Where's the rat with rank?"

Hanfnagel was taken aback. The man's impudence was astounding. "Herr Neurath is visiting – if that's who you're referring to – and he's armed, if you have any thought of harming me. My son is due any minute."

"Don't hold your breath . . . Move inside," Ross said, pushing

Hanfnagel ahead of him with Dolph's Mauser.

Victor Neurath stood up from beside the sofa, reaching into his jacket. "Forget it, Neurath!" Ross warned.

The Commissioner froze at the sight of Dolph's Mauser. "You better figure if *I'm* here, you guys are in deep shit."

The implication sank in and Neurath's jaw quivered. His eyes moved back and forth between Ross and Hanfnagel.

"Arrest him," Hanfnagel demanded.

"Yeah. Arrest me, Victor. But first let me have your gun. Ease it out slowly and hand it to me butt first."

Ross released the safety on his weapon. Neurath complied.

"You guys really believe you can hide your shit-stained underwear behind the guise of respectability forever, don't you?"

"You," he barked to a shaken Hanfnagel, "with your checks to the opera and gifts to museums. Smell the smoke. There's a firestorm headed this way – and it's going to burn down the House of Hanfnagel."

Ross's fury had found a vehicle and was building speed.

"You want to know what I'm doing here? I wanted to be the first to tell you. You're through. I dropped a bomb on your operation."

"What does he mean, Victor?" Hanfnagel asked anxiously.

Neurath's temper flared. "It means that you were a fool not to listen to me. I warned you to keep a distance from the videogames – to arrange for a third party to produce them. Cortese must have learned that Dolph was using Willi's warehouse – with your daughter's help, of course."

A look of utter disbelief appeared on Hanfnagel's face.

"Willi would never . . . " Ross could see he had second thoughts. "And if she foolishly did, so what? An embarrassment is all."

But his mind raced – if this is true, it could ruin all my plans.

Ross carefully backed up to the entrance to the dining room, careful not to turn his back. "I see the furniture's arrived. You were right, Hanfnagel. The pieces do belong together . . . "

"I paid you well for the furniture, Cortese. Why would you want to harm me and my family?"

"Your family? You miserable excuse for a human being. You *killed* a family for this apartment and you whine about what I'm doing to you and *your* family?

"I know what happened here. I know that you and your Storm Troopers killed four innocent people. Beat the men to death and threw the women out of the window like so much garbage. You've lived in this apartment – filled with their belongings – *their home,* since that day. Did you ever hear their dying screams in your sleep?"

"You're out of your mind," Hanfnagel shouted. "I had nothing to do with that. The records make it clear."

"Neurath's phony records, Hanfnagel. But I have eyewitnesses who will name you."

"Is that what this is about, Cortese?" Neurath asked.

"It's about four dead Jews – and the greedy fuck who murdered them. I'm going to take it all away from you, Hanfnagel, like you took it away from them. The apartment, the furniture, the paintings . . . everything." Ross pointed the gun at Hanfnagel.

"Never! It is rightfully mine. My forefathers fought beside the Habsburgs against the invaders. We gave our blood for Austria. The Jews came from the East and exploited our people. What right did the Mosels have to live here? They were not Austrian."

"They worked for it. It belonged to them . . . you self-centered son of a bitch!" Ross declared.

Hanfnagel refused to hear him.

"Believe me when I say that I respected Mosel's achievements. I was a student of architecture. He lectured to our class on Design. One day, he invited us to study this building – to take tea in his home. I could not believe my eyes. Hoffman, Koloman Moser, Klimt . . . " he closed his eyes remembering that first moment he stepped into the apartment.

"This apartment was a veritable museum of the Secession. He was living like a king, while my family, having fallen, lived in near poverty. I determined to one day own such a home. A month later, my brother came down with tuberculosis. I was forced to leave school and support the family. There were no jobs, except manual labor. It was the Depression."

He rubbed his eyes, as if to wipe away the humiliation of the experience. "The following year, I joined the National Socialist Party . . . "

"Nazis . . . a bunch of fucking murderers . . . " Ross yelled at him.

"Nein. A political party dedicated to improving the lot of the German people," Hanfnagel insisted. "They promised change. By nineteen-thirty-eight, I had risen to the rank of gauleiter. Anschluss was inevitable."

Hanfnagel looked through Ross, reliving those days, defending his life.

"When Anschluss took place, it was a certainty that Jews would be relocated and their property and possessions expropriated. The Mosel apartment and its contents still burned in my mind. It was only right that as gauleiter, I should have it. I meant the Mosels no harm. I came here and ordered the woman of the house to prepare to move. I catalogued the contents. When I returned the next day – furniture, paintings, silver . . . things were missing." An ugly expression crossed his face.

"Mosel stood defiant, with a smug look on his face. I told the troopers to teach him a lesson. But things got out of hand. I never meant for them to die."

"They resisted," Ross said sarcastically.

"Yes. Exactly," Hanfnagel seized on the words. "You must understand. The Jews seek to fill you with their lies."

Ross stared at him coldly. "*I am a Jew*, Hanfnagel. A Mosel."

He stopped to let the truth register. From their expressions, he could see that neither Hanfnagel nor Neurath believed him.

"Yes. I am Ariella Mosel's son. That truck you said my father stole, Neurath? I was hidden in it. He brought me to Italy to wait for my family. But they never came. You two saw to that."

Ross levelled the gun in a line with Hanfnagel's chest. Only now did Hanfnagel fear for his life. His lip quivered as he pleaded, "Don't be foolish, Cortese. You can kill me, but what will you gain? This apartment will still be mine. And after I'm gone it will belong to Dolph and Willi. Put the gun away. I'm a wealthy man. I'll . . . "

"You're a thief and a murderer," Ross cried. "You're wealthy alright . . . and this time, you can't cry poverty to explain away your crimes. Dolph and Reinhold were picked up at the factory by the Bundespolizei."

"Embarrassing, but hardly fatal," Neurath asserted. "No Viennese court will convict a Hanfnagel on such charges. At most there will be some fines."

"It's not just hate games," said Ross, shaking his head. "The two of you face charges of conspiracy and murder."

Neurath tried to laugh that off. "He can't be prosecuted for what took place in 1938. It's beyond the statutes."

"You're both guilty. I can execute the sentence here and now," Ross reminded him.

"You're not a killer," Neurath said.

"I can use Hanfnagel's excuse. You resisted. By the way, where's Otto? Butler's day off?"

Hanfnagel darted a worried glance at Neurath.

"You should be worried," Ross said sarcastically. "We've got Otto. Avia Hirsch was investigating your activities. She paid for that with her life – but she brought you both down."

"I know nothing about this Avia Hirsch's death. And Otto will never implicate me," Hanfnagel insisted.

"That's what you think. He already has. He vomited you up like a bad meal."

"The man's a criminal sociopath. Erich was trying to rehabilitate him. Whatever he says will be judged a lie," Neurath avowed.

Ross moved to him and stuck the gun barrel under his chin.

"You've got an answer for everything, don't you? Otto told us about Grenentorgasse. I suppose that's a lie, too?"

Sweat poured from the Commissioner's forehead. He looked as if he was having a heart attack.

"The hit team's dead or in custody. The Minister of Justice is alive – and mad as hell. His driver took a slug. The Prosecutor is on her way to take you in. Doschenko will knock the last nail in your coffin," Ross threatened. "You are going down. You *will* do time."

Neurath collapsed onto the sofa. Ross turned back to a cowering Hanfnagel whose last shred of composure was gone. "As for you . . . "

Hanfnagel backed away. The window beckoned to Ross and he had a momentary flash of his mother standing there beside her mother.

Hanfnagel froze in fear as Ross moved toward him. "Please," he pleaded, "it was an accident."

"Don't give me that crap. Not any more!" Ross seized Hanfnagel's arm and dragged him to the window. Opening it wide, he forced him to lean out over the ledge. "This is how they died – by your hand."

"I didn't do it – it was the troopers. I couldn't control them."

Ross pushed him further out, shifting his grip to Hanfnagel's belt. Ross held him there, dangling like a sack of potatoes. "You gave the orders."

"Don't, Cortese. For God's sake . . . "

"What do you know about God?"

The door slammed. Ross looked over his shoulder and saw Willi rush in, followed by Pop.

"No, Red. Please . . . "

"You don't have to beg for his worthless life. I have no intention of killing him. I want him alive – for the world to see what a piece of shit he is."

He pulled him back inside and Hanfnagel slumped to the floor. Neurath made a move for the door, taking advantage of the sudden intrusion.

Franco blocked him and shoved him back into the room.

"I knew we'd find you here," Willi said. "I was afraid of what you'd do."

"I'm sure you were. Dolph said you were a Hanfnagel, first, last and always."

Willi recoiled as if he had slapped her.

"Is Dolph alright, Willi? Where is he?" Hanfnagel managed to ask.

"Dolph is where he belongs! In prison."

"Don't say that, liebchen. He's your brother."

"He's a brute – and a criminal. You're responsible. For years, you looked the other way and never stopped him. He followed your orders."

"Untrue. I insist that you apologize for saying that to me."

"Never!" she shot back.

Ross listened in amazement.

"You don't mean this. You're under the influence of this man. Where is Reinhold?"

"In jail . . . along with his father – and your assassins."

"I had nothing to do with any of this," Hanfnagel maintained. "Ask Victor. He'll tell you," he whispered. "They lie. They want to stop me from becoming Chancellor."

"You, Chancellor? Never! I know the ugly truth about you. Soon everyone will," she said brutally. "I see you now, Father. I'm no longer blinded to your cruelty.

"It was *I*. . . I myself who brought the invoices for Konzentrationlager from Dolph's office to the Prosecutor. *I* who demanded that action be taken without delay. By tonight the name of Hanfnagel will be synonymous with shame in Vienna," she shouted in his face. Her whole body shook as she said, "That you could live in this home after destroying its occupants, after destroying your own family . . . that is a measure of . . . " She bowed her head and shook it in despair.

"No, Willi," he whispered.

But she was not finished – there was more to get out: "I shall never forget my mother's pain, those months before she took her life. I thought that I was to blame for her death. Only your approval allowed me to live with myself. I needed it desperately. I sought it endlessly. Poor Rudy never had it. A lifetime of blame and self-hate . . . 'til he was fortunate to find real love with Jacky" – she leveled her gaze at him – "which made you despise him all the more.

"Today, Annalee told us everything. How she came to Mother with the story, years after Lucy's claim had been refused. Mother pleaded with you to right the wrong – to return the Mosel legacy to Lucy. You treated her with contempt, called her a Jew-lover."

Hanfnagel withered under the assault.

"Day by day, we watched her spirits fade, her despair deepen – until she could no longer see us. And you denied her help."

She forced herself to continue through her tears. "I never wanted to know the truth, but now, God help me, I do.

"You . . . " She raised an accusing finger. "*You're* what killed my mother!"

A strangled cry escaped from Hanfagel's throat.

She turned to Ross. "Please, Ross. Take me away from here."

He put his arm around her and began to lead her away. She stopped in the doorway of the salon and turned to her father one last time. "Oh, yes."

Hanfnagel flinched, sensing that another blow was coming.

"The Klimt portrait you coveted? It never left this building."

He gasped. "What? Where is it?"

"What does it matter? You'll never see it. But you should know that the woman in the portrait was not Wilhelmina van Brugen. She was Rosa Mosel."

She laughed sardonically. "Imagine. All those years – your perfect woman – and she was a Jew."

Her laughter turned to sobs.

Ross tightened his grip on her. Pop followed them out to the vestibule. They heard Hanfnagel call out to her, "Come back, liebchen . . . "

The elevator was there on the landing. Ross held Willi close as they descended. Outside the building, he asked her, "Where do you want to go?"

Before she could reply, Hanfnagel shouted her name. "Willi!"

His high-pitched scream jerked their heads upward. They stared at him as he leaned out of the window. "I insist that you return at once."

The words demanded, the tone pleaded. Willi looked up, as if a stranger was calling out to her.

"Please, liebchen, come back. I need you. I am your father," he declared.

Faces of neighbors appeared at windows on both sides of the street.

"You're nothing to me!," she yelled back, then did a sharp about-face and ran.

"Willi!" Ross called.

Pop started after her, but Ross held him back. "Let her go. We'll catch up to her later."

He could not take his eyes off Hanfnagel. The look on his face, even at this distance, was chilling – pure malice.

Hanfnagel became aware that his neighbors were observing him and retreated inside. He brushed past a defeated Neurath and hurried to the small study that had once been Kirmen Mosel's. The room was furnished exactly as it had been the day that Hanfnagel moved in. The huge desk taking up most of the study was Mosel's masterpiece – and he, Eric Hanfnagel, had possessed it for fifty-two years. Yet, the sense of power he had always experienced at the sight of it failed to occur. He stared at it, feeling dazed and weak. Like an old man, he thought with disgust. He ran his hands over the warm veneered surface one more time.

Then he unlocked the side drawer and reached inside.

Ross continued staring up at the window, even after Hanfnagel had disappeared from view. Franco touched him lightly on the arm, breaking the spell. "Okay, Pop . . . "

Then the two men turned and walked toward Karntnerstrasse. A moment later, they heard a loud gunshot.

Ross was frantic. "He cheated me, Pop. The bastard cheated me again."

Franco stopped him from going back. "It's over, *figlio mio,*" he said and Franco led him away. Perhaps now, his son could begin to grieve.

CHAPTER FORTY-SEVEN

The Austrian public was reeling from a media blitz, Ross learned over breakfast. Newspapers, television and radio reported radical right-wing claims that the assassination attempt was a plot by State officials to discredit them. The left demanded an immediate crackdown on the neo-Nazi movement and its supporters. For its part, the coalition government made appropriately high-minded speeches, while treading cautiously through the political minefield, awaiting the first opinion polls.

Ross's role in saving the life of the Minister featured prominently in the news. Abe, recovering from the injuries inflicted by Dolph Hanfnagel during his brutal interrogation, had asked Ross to tell his story. "Remind Austrians," Abe urged, "of that dark, ugly chapter in a book that is still open to the same page." For the past thirty-six hours, Ross had honored Abe's request – with a vengeance.

Hanfnagel's funeral was scheduled for noon, two days after his suicide, at Karlskirche. Ross reached Karlsplatz at eleven forty-five. As he crossed the busy square, he recognized the Secessionist style of the marble and gold leaf pavilion which served as an entrance to the subway station. The name on the commemorative plaque read Otto Wagner – 1901. One of the decorative motifs reminded him of Kirmen Mosel's work. It struck Ross then that his greatgrandfather and Otto Wagner probably knew each other and might even have been friends. Shouts from the south end of the square intruded on his reverie. He hurried in that direction, past a memorial to the great composer, Brahms.

Large crowds were gathered outside the church. Security was tight. Two groups of demonstrators were separated by cordons of police in riot gear. On one side of the plaza were hundreds of neo-Nazis, many of them skinheads. They've been drawn to this event like leeches, Ross thought, swelling themselves with pride on the blood of their dead hero. They shouted curses at their opposite number, a smaller group who stood silent, their placards held high. Each sign was inscribed with one word in large, bold letters – SCHANDE!

Ross asked a well-dressed passerby if he spoke English.

"Yes," the man replied.

Pointing to the placards, Ross asked, "What does that word mean?"

Embarrassed, the man muttered, "Shame," and hurried away.

Ross crossed the street and pushed through the crowd. He took up a position enabling him to observe the entrance to the church. Only a handful of people entered to attend the service. It appeared that the elite of Vienna were putting a distance between themselves and the Hanfnagels. Not surprising, since a half-dozen prominent citizens had been picked up and held for questioning as possible co-conspirators.

At ten before noon, Reinhold Hanfnagel and his mother arrived. Unlike Dolph, who remained in jail under constant observation, Reinhold had been released on bail. The pair started up the church steps, on a wave of cheers. Torn between the gravity of the moment and a wish to acknowledge his family's supporters, Reinhold turned and looked their way. They responded by raising their arms in the fascist salute and shouting "Heil!!" Reinhold nodded, then turned and took his mother's arm and entered the church.

As the clock chimed twelve, a second limousine pulled up in front of the church. Ross watched as Rudy helped Willi from the vehicle. She was dressed in black and heavily veiled. It was the first time he had seen her since her disappearance two days earlier. Jacky stepped out of the car. The skinheads surged against the police line, shouting death threats. The two men circled protectively and helped her into the church.

Ross cold see that her knees buckled for an instant on the threshold. He started toward her, then stopped. There was no way he could join her – not feeling as he did. He wished only for Hanfnagel's eternal damnation.

A few minutes later, Ross left the scene and began the long walk back to the building on Himmelpfortgasse. Annalee, discharged from the hospital, had asked him to come to her home. Lucy and her family would be there. En route, he could not shake loose the insistent, painful images of Willi kneeling and praying in the church; he could hear the intonations of the priest in the Latin of his childhood. He remembered himself at Annie's funeral. Everything mixed together in his mind and he felt sad, embittered and lonely.

Walking through the streets of the old city, Ross tried, without success, to rid himself of his dark mood. He came upon an old synagogue and paused, gazing at the Hebrew inscriptions on the stonework, indecipherable to him. He suddenly wondered if the Mosel family had come here to worship and tears welled up in his eyes. It occurred to Ross to go inside, but he decided that he was not ready. He promised himself that one day he would be – and continued on his way.

CHAPTER FORTY-EIGHT

Ross's gloom melted like ice on a summer day in the warmth of Lucy's embrace. His new-found family gathered around, eager to meet him. Abe was there, too, the ache from his broken ribs and bruises nothing compared to the pain of Avia's loss. But he found a smile as he witnessed the joyful reunion.

Lucy called Ross's attention to the Klimt portrait, taken out of hiding at last and hung over the mantle.

"That's your great-grandmother, Rosa. You were named after her."

Ross held back tears, but it was apparent to all of them that he was overwhelmed.

"Will he be alright, Franco?" Annalee asked.

"You and me," Pop said, "we know that burying a momma takes an hour. But you keep her with you for a lifetime. My boy, after a lifetime – he's found his momma, but she's gone. Gina and Rosso talked for a long time yesterday. She told him, he's got to find a way he can keep Ariella." Pop's hand gestured around the room. "This is the start. He needs help. Like me, he don't know how to ask."

Ross brought Lucy's daughter over to Pop. "Did you know that Elena's an attorney?" he asked him. "Her firm will handle our claims against Hanfnagel's estate."

Wrapped in the caul of his thoughts, Ross hadn't heard the door. The look on Annalee's face caused him to turn in that direction. Rudy and Jacky were standing there.

"As far as I'm concerned," Rudy declared, "the apartment and all of the Mosel furnishings belong to you and to Lucy."

Ross went over and squeezed his arm appreciatively.

"Don't get too excited," Jacky cautioned. "Rudy was disinherited long ago.

"It's not what's in his hand to give, but what he gives from his heart," Pop said.

"Erich Hanfnagel's last will and testament," Rudy said, "names my sister executor. His holdings are huge. Willi has decided she'll share her portion of the estate with me. We propose to buy out Dolph's half of the apartment and its furnishings. He'll need every penny to pay for lawyers – not that they'll do him much good."

"This is Vienna," a cynical Ross reminded him. "You never know."

"You've earned your mistrust the hard way, Red," Jacky acknowledged, but then tried to lift Ross's spirits, reminding him that the police had Otto, the surviving member of the hit team and the rogue cop, Brent, in custody. "And your testimony, of course."

"We'll see, Jacky. We'll wait and see," Ross responded, keeping to himself his fear that those men might not live to go to trial or might be subjected to pressure to renege on their testimony. The authorities needed Doschenko to cement the case for the prosecution and guarantee long prison terms for Dolph and Neurath. The Russian had disappeared, without a sighting. Ross knew that a man with Doschenko's training and skill, a major-league survivor, had stashed money, passports and I.D., as well as several escape routes out of Austria. In all likelihood, they would not find him until he surfaced again to serve another master.

Rudy took Lucy's hand. "We want to make restitution to you and your family."

"I thank you, Rudy, for all of us," she said softly.

Ross went to the table and poured the schnapps. When each of them held a glass, he lifted his and toasted to a better future. Godfrey, Lucy's husband, added the proverbial "L'chaim."

Ross overheard Annalee asking Rudy about the funeral service.

"Thankfully brief," he answered. "Dolph had the certificate for the funeral plot and made all the arrangements from jail. I could not face going to the cemetery to witness Erich Hanfnagel buried next to my mother, may her sweet soul rest in peace. Willi went there without me."

"How is she holding up?" Ross inquired.

"Willi is a strong woman," he replied.

The bell rang. Ross knew before Lucy opened the door who would be there.

Willi stood framed in the doorway, ill at ease, her face chalk-white against the black dress. Lucy kissed her and drew her inside.

Franco patted Ross's arm. "I learned from your greatgrandfather Kirmen that you give a special gift to your children when you accept the love they choose. I tried to follow that advice with you and your sisters."

"You did, Pop," Ross acknowledged gratefully.

Lucy brought Willi to them, then moved away. Pop took her hands in his. They were ice cold. He held them, rubbing to warm them, then kissed her on the cheek and left. Ross and Willi stood inches apart, facing each other, alone in the center of a room resounding with the innocent laughter of two of Lucy's grandchildren.

"How are you?" he asked awkwardly.

"Not well."

"I wanted to be there for you, but I couldn't. Not the way I felt. I used you, Willi – to get at him. And that pushed him over the edge . . . "

"No, Red. My father took his life not because of anything I said or did. But for one reason – and one reason only. His facade was stripped away. He couldn't bear to live with the prospect of a trial – and the humiliation – all of which he brought upon himself. I know that now with certainty."

"I hope you do. As for me, I'm heading back to New York. Back to my kids, my family – and to work. I'll return to Vienna to testify at the trial." He forced the next words out, against great resistance. "I care for you, Willi. A great deal. I just don't see how we can get past who we are."

"I already have," she said decisively. "I want you to try." She reached up, touched his cheek, and pulled him toward her for a kiss. He found himself responding.

Suddenly, the hellish cacophony of roaring motorcycles invaded the room. The family converged at the open window. A biker gang of neo-Nazis, some in brown shirts, wearing swastika armbands, blocked the street in front of the building. They looked up and chanted, "Juden araus . . . " and "Heil Hitler . . ." then cheered as one of them pulled cans of spray paint from his saddlebag. Franco and Abe leaned out and yelled down at them. A bottle was thrown. It bounced off the brick ledge, barely missing them. Ross rushed out the door and raced down the stairs. He reached the street in time to witness the gang's departure. The acrid exhaust of their motorcycles choked him. Thick plumes of black smoke drifted slowly skyward, soon to become part of the dark cloud formation hovering over the city. Ross turned to the facade of the building. Crudely painted on it in bright yellow was a large Star of David.

Willi ran to him. She followed his gaze and saw the desecration. Ross looked up at the frightened faces in the windows. He turned to Willi and made the merest gesture. She came into his arms and they held each other. Then they walked back into the building.

Together, they would wash the wall clean.

EPILOGUE

Tel Aviv, November 22, 1990 – Yad Vashem, the Memorial to the Holocaust announced today that a major painting by Gustav Klimt, hidden for years to protect it from Nazi theft, has been donated by two Viennese women, Annalee Speitz and Lucy Mosel Frankel. Mrs. Speitz, a Gentile, saved the life of Mrs. Frankel, a Jew. Mrs. Speitz's name has been added to the rolls of 'The Just'.

The subject of the Klimt portrait is Rosa Mosel, wife of the internationally-renowned designer and cabinetmaker, Kirmen Mosel. Mr. Mosel, his son, Joshua, daughter-in-law Fanny and granddaughter Ariella were killed in Vienna during the Holocaust.

Mrs. Frankel is the surviving granddaughter of Rosa and Kirmen Mosel. She resides with her family in Vienna.

New York Times, March 15, 1994 – The United States Holocaust Memorial Museum in Washington announced today a special exhibition of early twentieth- century Viennese furniture designed and crafted by the Secession master, Kirmen Mosel for his own home.

Mosel and three members of his family were murdered in March 1938 in Vienna, early victims of Nazi persecution. The exhibition is scheduled to open in December, 1994, on the eve of Chanukah, a holiday commemorating Jewish resistance to Roman persecution.

The exhibit is made possible through a generous loan from Lucy Mosel Frankel and Ross Cortese, surviving members of the family.

David Peretz is a psychiatrist, psychoanalyst, writer and editor. **THE MOSEL LEGACY** is his first novel. It was inspired by events in Europe during the past decade which suggested that history could, indeed, repeat itself.

Dr. Peretz has co-edited fifteen books on the subject of death, dying and bereavement. He serves on the faculty of the Department of Psychiatry at Columbia University College of Physicians and Surgeons, and is Chairperson of the Advisory Board of the American Institute of Life-Threatening Illness and Loss.

He and his wife, Eileen, an award-winning interior designer, live in New York and spend part of the year in Paris. They are proud, happy parents and grandparents to Deborah, Ray, Adam, Heather, Hillary and Isaac.